High Praise for
EVERYTHING IS JAKE
by Jethro K. Lieberman

EVERYTHING IS JAKE gives us a new sleuth to follow: T.R. Softly, whose latest assignment takes him into a world of political intrigue that requires all his considerable talents to unwind. Smoothly written, with humor and insight, this smart book holds your attention to the very end.

ANNETTE GORDON-REED, Author, *On Juneteenth*; Carl M. Loeb University Professor, Harvard University

EVERYTHING IS JAKE brilliantly immerses the reader in a suspenseful ride from beginning to end. It is a smart and entertaining read, and the perfect novel for our times, pointing to even more difficult civil liberties issues than we've yet experienced, in a future just being born. This is exactly the novel I would expect of Jethro K. Lieberman—an exceptional legal scholar and a masterful writer.

DEBORAH ARCHER, President, American Civil Liberties Union, and Professor of Clinical Law, New York University School of Law

EVERYTHING IS JAKE is everything a great thriller is supposed to be: complex, ambitious, and chock full of surprises. Jethro K. Lieberman has fashioned a truly terrifying tale that picks up where the January 6 attack on the Capitol Building leaves off. His quirky hero, T. R. Softly (who is anything but soft), is a rare and refreshing new voice in the genre, as driven as he is determined.

JON LAND, *USA Today* Bestselling Author, *Murder on the Metro*

JETHRO K. LIEBERMAN guides us expertly through his narrative in prose that rings clear and true. Driving his creation is pop neurology propelled by suspense, the whole cruising at elite altitude. This whodunit of a palimpsest will overwrite your brain leaving a remnant buzz of pleasure and delight.

STEPHEN SPOTTE, Marine Biologist; Author, *Animal Wrongs*

THIS IS A BOOK for the multitudes. Dickens lovers will cherish this story—the crazy names, the jaundiced view of lawyers, the cases that go off the tracks. And so will readers of Mario Puzo—the dark plots, the psychotic families, the parricide in *Jake* that resonates with the fratricide of *The Godfather*. There is even food for fans of the bumbling detective Jacques Clouseau. An hilarious romp through a justice system gone haywire. It would be criminal not to read it.

JAMES D. ZIRIN, Former Southern District of New York Prosecutor, Author, and Legal Analyst

WHAT FUN! *Everything is Jake* is built around an ingenious conceit that keeps readers on their toes with a genre-hopping style that goes from legal drama to juvenile detective to adult detective to political thriller to romantic comedy while lacing the whole thing with doses of political satire. . . . Satisfying and sweetly amusing.

RICHARD PATTERSON, Director, *The Gentleman Tramp*

JETHRO K. LIEBERMAN'S debut novel—a notable departure from his previous books on the American legal system—is an original, highly entertaining take on detective fiction and political intrigue, starring, among many memorable characters, the brilliant sleuth T. R. Softly. Written with flair, it will test the most ardent mystery buffs.

ROBERT KIMBALL, Musical Theater Historian; Author, *Crisis and Compromise: The Rescue of the 1964 Civil Rights Act*

AN EXUBERANT TALE, wrapped in good-natured humor, and has something for almost any taste: missing persons, courtroom drama, coming of age, unbalanced politicians, romantic edges, even a dose of neuroscience, with a theatrical explosion in the White House that may seem wholly fanciful and yet eerily familiar, all in pursuit of secret agents working—literally—in the "deep state." The writing is smooth and assured, the story perky and quirky, the denouement a surprise, though maybe it's just what you'll be hoping for. One thing's certain: it's a novel take on the mayhem around us.

SANDOR FRANKEL, Author, *The Accidental Philanthropist*

FANTASTIC. . . . There were times that I found myself doubting everything could be pulled together . . . but Lieberman masterfully ties up all loose ends creating a remarkably woven tale – perhaps the best new book I've read in . . . a decade? Longer? Highly recommend.

ANDREW JASON COHEN, Professor of Philosophy and Founding Director, Program in Philosophy, Politics, and Economics, Georgia State University

A WHIMSICAL TALE of a secret plot to make seriously bad guys incriminate themselves. . . A broad, sweetly fantastical satire just perfect for readers in the mood.

KIRKUS REVIEWS

Everything Is Jake

Everything Is Jake

a T.R. Softly Detective Novel

Jethro K. Lieberman

THREE ROOMS PRESS
New York, NY

Everything Is Jake
BY Jethro K. Lieberman

© 2021 by Jethro K. Lieberman

ISBN 978-1-953103-11-6 (trade paperback original)
ISBN 978-1-953103-12-3 (Epub)
Library of Congress Control Number: 2021935398

TRP-093

First edition
Publication Date: October 12, 2021

BISAC category code
FIC022090 Fiction / Mystery & Detective / Private Investigators
FIC030000 Fiction / Thrillers / Suspense
FIC037000 Fiction / Political
FIC050000 Fiction / Crime

COVER & BOOK DESIGN:
KG Design International: www.katgeorges.com

DISTRIBUTED BY:
PGW/Ingram: www.pgw.com

Three Rooms Press
New York, NY
www.threeroomspress.com
info@threeroomspress.com

For Jo

who wondered one day
why I hadn't written a book
something like this one

"We're all of us sentenced to solitary confinement
inside our own skins, for life."

Tennessee Williams, *Orpheus Descending*, Act II, Scene 1 (1955)

"The first such problem—later identified as philosophical—
that I remember worrying about was when a grown-up
used the words 'If I were you,' and I wondered how we
would notice the difference if she were me!"

Philippa Foot, *Natural Goodness* (2001)

"Commit nothing to paper, and certainly not
to a computer or a cell phone. Keep it in your head.
It's the only private place we have left."

Frederick Forsyth, *The Cobra* (2010)

———

Ode to My Brain

I know a veiled place behind the eyes
That sees the truth but utters lies.
I sense a muffled place behind the ears
That hears alarms and mutters fears.
A shuttered place behind the nose
Sniffs out friends and calls them foes.
And churning high above the chin
Is weary darkness waging sin.
What cheeky thing must that place be?
That dark conspirator is me.

Poster hanging on Zesto Moffin's office wall

A Zesto Moffin Guarantee of Authenticity

By the time you finish reading this book,
the story could well be true—
or might have been
or may yet be.

CONTENTS

PROLOGUE . . . . *i*

DRY RUN 1

Chapter 1: *Repent* 2
Chapter 2: *Review* 25

Interlude 1:
Presidential Treat: My Friend Romo
(Statement on a Federal Plea) 33

Chapter 3: *Replay* 34
Chapter 4: *Recant* 53
Chapter 5: *Rebuke* 60

Interlude 2:
Presidential Treat: No Friend of Mine
(Statement on a Federal Sentencing) 65

THE MAKING OF A DETECTIVE 67

Chapter 6: *Softly Awakening* 68

Interlude 3:
Presidential Treat: Close Those Borders
(Statement on Immigration) 88

Chapter 7: *Softly Assembling* 90

Interlude 4:
Presidential Treat: States' Rites
(Statement on Reinvigorating America) 100

Chapter 8: *Softly Ascending* 102

Interlude 5:
Presidential Treat: A Most Honest Fellow
(Statement on Ethics) 114

Chapter 9: *Softly Connecting* 116

Interlude 6:
Presidential Treat: Pull the Trigger
(Statement on the Second Amendment) 131

ON THE SPOOR 133

Chapter 10: *Curious Incident* 134
Chapter 11: *More Curious Incidents* 160
Chapter 12: *Fingered* 175

Interlude 7:
Presidential Treat: Enuff Already
(Statement on Spelling) 189

Chapter 13: *Softly Seeking* 191
Chapter 14: *Softly Descending* 209

Contents
(continued)

Subsection-S 221

    Chapter 15: *Geeks Bearing Grifts* 222

    Interlude 8:
    Presidential Treat: Wither Weather?
    (Statement on Climate Change) 240

    Chapter 16: *Cognitive Dissidents* 242
    Chapter 17: *The Scenario Master* 258
    Chapter 18: *Why Am I Here?* 270

    Interlude 9:
    Presidential Treat:
    (Statement on Major Governmental Reorganization) 284

Bold New Age 287

    Chapter 19: *The Mejacian* 288
    Chapter 20: *Something Sort of Oddish* 315
    Chapter 21: *The Setup* 329
    Chapter 22: *Technical Correction* 337
    Chapter 23: *The Tale According to Softly* 354

    Interlude 10:
    Presidential Treat: The Gig Was Rigged:
    Everything Is Fake 367

Hearts and Minds 369

    Chapter 24: *Uppen Atom* 370
    Chapter 25: *A Workaround* 388

    Interlude 11:
    A Treat from Your President:
    The Greatest Crime of All Time 394

    Chapter 26: *The Cause of It All* 396

Author's Disclaimer 409

Acknowledgments 411

About the Author 415

Everything
Is Jake

PROLOGUE

EXACTLY WHAT BEFELL THE PRESIDENT OF the United States has never been fully understood. His last misadventure in office—an occasion his unshaken supporters were certain could not arise—was explained as an illness or a tragic mistake or a failure of handlers. Not even the First Lady accepted his oft-proclaimed view that he'd been defrauded. Now, some years after he departed down a trail of denial and recrimination, the prurient details have faded. Most Americans have let their recall crumble and have moved on, preferring to repress the episode as they have forgotten the man. But the truth always remains, even if buried or rejected. The truth, or some part of it, clings to memories or hibernates in closets until someone comes poking.

So held T. R. Softly, consulting detective, whose motto, *Felix vir qui potest rerum omnium cognoscere causas*, he took loosely from Virgil: "Happy is the man who understands the causes of all things." It was a maxim that up to now had carried him far.

But in an era of complexity, confusions, and Rumsfeldian unknowns—that is, some short time after the evolution of sea slugs—even the most accomplished investigator cannot grasp all things, like which dark corners require light. Or as Reggie, Softly's man at the newsstand, unflaggingly proclaimed when countering doubts about who did what in the neighborhood: "'Cuz you ain't found it in the papers don't mean it didn't happen."

What Reggie meant, properly considered, is that no event, no matter how spectacular, has but a single root. "Defeat is an orphan," the saying goes, but of course defeat has as many forebears as victory—indeed, more; they're just in hiding. So it was that the river of the White House scandal was fed by multiple streams, most of them far below ground and therefore uncharted, and the primal one, perhaps, too narrow to navigate.

The current that Softly cruised began in an odd courtroom proceeding that had, as far as he knew when he took on the quest, nothing to do with him or the president. Only later did he begin to suspect he was not the author of his story but a character in it, not a member of the audience but a puppet without strings confronting a body he could never have been expected to encounter on a stage without clues. Still he pressed on, buoyed by a cheery optimism that he would soon get to the bottom of it. This is the record of his journey and of the cause of it all.

Dry Run

Most crimes occur in the shadows.
This one plays out in court in plain view
of an observing world.

CHAPTER 1

REPENT

SOME YEARS AGO, ON A SUNNY Friday in early May, still vivid to crime buffs, a bold new age commenced, or the visible part of it anyway, when Romo Malbonum, the Deckled Don, talked himself into a life sentence to be served in a maximum-security federal prison.

No one had ever heard a story to rival it, not even jaded crime-beat reporters with decades on the job. It was the Mother, the Fairy Godmother, the Emperor, the Deity of all Confessions. The screeching headlines—"DON'S DEBUT: I DID IT ALL," "BIG SHOT: SHOT BIG"—beckoned readers to the tale Malbonum cobbled over-night and recounted, unvarnished, to a courtroom crammed with lawyers, prosecutors, police, judicial clerks, and a senior politician or two. It was the longest, juiciest blockbuster of an open confession ever heard at the Thurgood Marshall United States Courthouse in lower Manhattan.

The crime lord's tale of deceit, larceny, mayhem, flaying, and murder—a spree lasting the better part of four decades—took six hours and forty-seven minutes. The nasally narrated monologue was all the more remarkable because its disclosures were unforced and until then unknown.

At 9:30, a serene Malbonum strode into the courtroom accompanied by his grim minder, an FBI agent silent and scowling. Anyone looking would first have seen the prisoner, if that's what he was, standing at the security gate, being searched the third time that morning for weapons and phones. Malbonum wore his charcoal worsted Jermyn Street suit as lightly as his age. Barely past sixty-two, he could have passed for fifty, his wattle-free neck encased in a straight-collared starched white shirt. His full head of gray hair was six feet two inches above his highly polished Oxford brogues. He stood erect as the Marine infantry lieutenant he had been in Vietnam, a survivor of too many battles to recall.

No one noticed him at first, no one who counted. Interest picked up when he took his seat at the defense table with Jedidiah Cardsworth Tillinghast, Esq., paragon of the New York bar, an equally bespoke man who could have been his older brother, but was, more understandably, his counsel. Soon, word began to circulate that the Deckled Don himself was up to something on the third floor. It was Malbonum's first appearance in any court.

The grapevine disgorged its succulent secret, and by 9:50 the room was nearly full. Young court clerks, straightening their ties or plumping their hair, squirmed into their jackets as they hurried through the large arched doorway to find empty seats behind the lawyers' tables. They nodded silently to several senior federal prosecutors and sat cheek by jowl with seasoned law enforcement officials and others who were determined to claim ringside seats to an event with likely attendance bragging rights: three plainclothes United States marshals, more than a handful of prosecutors from the Manhattan district attorney's office down the block, six judicial secretaries, a New York City deputy mayor, the police commissioner, several court officers, four police detectives and at least one captain, and others whose names and positions have been lost to the record.

At precisely the hour, a door on the side opened between two flags, and the judge, black-robed and somber, wearing rimless eyeglasses and carrying a thick binder under his arm, walked toward his accustomed seat, a high-backed, heavily padded black armchair centered on the bench. It was not an honor for him to be there; as in all cases, his name had been selected at random to preside over the hearing.

Conversation ceased. Only the faint scream of a passing ambulance below pierced the courtroom silence.

To the distaste of judicial purists, the bailiff modified his usual opening cry with a courtroom rap: "Oyez, oyez, oyez. Your backbench chatter subsiding, the Honorable Judge Horton Pickscreed presiding, the United States District Court for the Southern District of New York is now in session, waiting to hear a most damnable confession. All persons having business before the Court draw near, give your attention and you shall be heard. God save these United States and this honorable court."

Unspeaking, the judge settled into his chair and looked about the room, his face impassive.

"Mr. Tillinghast," he finally said, enunciating each syllable as he fixed on the defense counsel table.

Tillinghast stood. "Your Honor."

"I'm delighted to welcome you though it is a surprise to find you here," the judge said, smiling faintly. "It's been quite a while since you've been in these criminal parts."

"I like to keep my hand in the game now and then, Your Honor."

The judge turned to the prosecutors' table. "Mr. Carverman, does the government have any objection? You know that Mr. Tillinghast was my college roommate. You're not here to seek my recusal?"

"No, indeed not, Your Honor," said Glanville L. Carverman, the United States Attorney himself, a short dapper survivor of political wars who wore a perpetual air of astonishment and satisfaction that such a clever fellow as he had survived for so long in the highest echelons of the legal system. His dark brown wool windowpane suit fit impeccably on his five-foot, six-inch frame. He was doing his best to appear somber and imposing.

"I understand we're here to entertain a plea by your client." Judge Pickscreed said, turning away from the strangely over-eager Carverman and back to the always reserved Tillinghast. He looked down at a paper in front of him. "Romo no middle initial Malbonum is your client?"

"Yes, Your Honor."

"Very well." The judge leaned back. "Mr. Carverman."

"Your Honor, as you can see from the summary on page one of the prepared materials, Mr. Malbonum has been charged in a criminal information with 279 counts of violating more than fifty provisions of the United States criminal code. Since the charges speak for themselves, and Mr. Malbonum is here to plead, I shall refrain from any further statement, except to move, as I believe my colleague here, Ms. Greenstock, informed your clerks we would, that these proceedings be video recorded." Carverman pointed to a younger woman sitting next to him, assistant U.S. Attorney Mallory Greenstock.

"Not because the defendant would like a copy of his maiden performance?" The judged raised his eyebrows in mock surprise, his glasses slipping partway down his nose.

"No, sir. In these perversely parlous times, we think it imperative an audiovisual record be maintained."

"You mean in these times when everything is a conspiracy?" the judge said, pushing his glasses back in place.

"You have read my mind, Your Honor."

"Mr. Tillinghast, objections?"

"None, Your Honor."

"I assume from your request, Mr. Carverman, that you came prepared."

Carverman looked to Greenstock. "We did, Your Honor," she said, pointing to the bailiff, who raised a thumb and nodded to the judge, presiding from the bench.

"Very well," Judge Pickscreed said, with a flip of his hand, "despite the decided irregularity of this request, I will grant it.

See to the equipment and we will resume when the recording has begun."

Two technicians, Farrell and Moti, set up digital recorders on spindly-legged tripods at either end of the judge's bench and focused the lenses on the lectern at the defense table, as a court aide placed a glass of water on its top ledge. The crew stepped back from the cameras when red lights appeared. The bailiff stuck up his thumb again.

"They are recording?" A nod from Farrell to the bench.

"Well, then, Mr. Tillinghast."

"Your Honor," Tillinghast said, standing alongside the table, "I represent Romo Malbonum, who appears today voluntarily and at his own request, to plead to many and various charges enumerated in the information filed three days ago and now before the court. And, I might add, against my advice."

"You advised that I not be presented with the charges?" Deadpan. It was an old game.

"No, Your Honor, I advised my client not to confess to the charges. But he has determined to proceed."

"Then let's get on with it."

Judge Pickscreed riffled through the thick binder. He settled on one page and said, "Mr. Malbonum, please stand." As the chair scuffed back and the defendant rose alongside his counsel, the judge continued. "I assume, Mr. Malbonum, that you have a copy of all these charges, conferred with your counsel about each of them, and are prepared now to plead to each. Am I correct in that understanding?"

"Yes, Your Honor," Malbonum said resolutely, without waver or tremor.

"Are you willing to waive the reading of each charge?"

"We are, Your Honor," Tillinghast answered.

"Good," the judge responded, "because otherwise we might be here for days." He sought Malbonum's eye.

"Playing this by the book," the judge continued, "I am required to advise you that under Rule Eleven of the Federal Rules of Criminal Procedure you have the right to a jury trial, to be represented by counsel, and to confront adverse witnesses. You have other like rights, which you may waive, including the right to be informed of the nature of each charge and the possible penalties on conviction. Do you affirm that you understand these rights and that you are waiving each?"

"Your Honor, I have discussed these matters extensively with Mr. Tillinghast, I am aware of my rights, and I affirm my desire to waive them."

"One more thing, Mr. Malbonum. I am required to determine that your plea is voluntary and does not result from force, threats, or promises, and further, I must determine that there is a factual basis for each plea. These latter two requirements may not be waived."

Tillinghast responded. "Your Honor, I speak on behalf of Mr. Malbonum, and I believe the Government concurs, in suggesting that he be allowed to plead and then to make a statement, a typescript of which is in your binder. It provides factual context for each charge. Although it may be unusual, Mr. Malbonum also seeks the opportunity to explain himself in the account that he presents today."

The judge looked across at Carverman, who nodded.

"Again, this is all extraordinary, gentlemen, but I gather, Mr. Tillinghast, that you and the government have negotiated at length and jointly agree that this course of proceeding will obviate any grounds of appeal. We would not want to go through all this today only to repeat it at greater length on a future occasion."

"Yes sir, and no sir. That is correct, Your Honor."

"Very well, then, Mr. Malbonum, we shall proceed accordingly. Do you affirm that your plea is voluntary, not influenced by force, threats, or promises?"

"I do, Your Honor."

"And how do you plead?"

"Guilty, Your Honor."

"To each of the counts?"

"Yes, Your Honor."

"Very well, you may now proceed, Mr. Malbonum, bearing in mind that before I can accept your pleas you must persuade the Court through sufficient detail that you are actually guilty of each charge."

Tillinghast handed his client a fat binder of his own and sat. Malbonum stepped to the lectern and put the binder on it. He opened the pages but did not look down. He paused for a moment, then sought the cameras.

"My name is Romo Malbonum. I am the grandson of Enrico Malbonum, who came to this country from Sicily in 1895 at the age of five, and who died in 1980. His son, my father, was Stewart Malbonum, who was born in 1918 and disappeared in the 1960s."

"Mr. Malbonum, please tell me you are not mounting an orphan defense."

Malbonum shook his head. "No, Your Honor, I am not, nor would I. I offer it strictly as personal background."

"All right, get on with it then."

"I shall not dwell on my ancestors' lives or accomplishments, except as necessary to help explain my own motivations and life choices. My grandfather arrived in America penniless. He lived with a second cousin of his mother in Brooklyn and was put out to labor on the day he turned ten. He had had no schooling in the United States. But he worked hard and in his early twenties became a master stonemason. By the time he was twenty-seven, he had several craftsman working for him, and when he turned thirty-five he ceased working with his hands and founded the Malbonum Construction Company, which I have had the good fortune to serve as chairman to this day. My grandfather lived with his mother's cousin until he married my grandmother when he was twenty-two. At that time he rented a floor of a home two blocks away. Later he bought the whole house and stayed there the rest of his days. In time he enlarged it and bought land all around it. I was born and raised in my grandfather's house and eventually inherited it and have lived there ever since."

As Malbonum warmed to his theme, he stretched to his full height, once or twice smoothing down his hair, as if to signal that no wind in his face would deter him from his fateful plea. He stood rigid, eyes on the judge.

"I adored my grandfather, perhaps because I was his first grandchild and he was my champion. From an early age I remember taking walks around the neighborhood with him and learning the names of trees and stones and why this or that building looked the way it did. My father, on the other hand, was another story. He was a sad sack, and therefore, I think—I mean, I've read Freud but I'm no shrink—he was a brute. He was supposed to have been named 'Steward.' My grandfather thought the name could describe his role in life, to take care of the family business, but somebody made a mistake at the hospital, and his birth certificate said 'Stewart.' In a family full of Tonys and Luigis and Salvatores, the teasing he got led to a massive sense of inferiority. He could never please Grandpa. In turn that led him, I'm sure of it, to lash out whenever he got frustrated, which was pretty much every day. I don't know if he beat me when I was tiny, but I remember from at least when I was five being spanked and reprimanded for every little infraction of whatever code he imagined he oversaw that day. My father worked for my grandfather, and that made it all the worse.

"My grandfather knew what was going on. He didn't interfere with his son's family relations, but he was worried about how my father treated me. Grandpa told me years later that's why I was sent to boarding school when I was nine or ten, and after, to Andover. I was sad to be apart from my grandfather. He came solely for my graduations, but I saw him when I was home during school breaks and summers. When I was twelve or thirteen, he would talk to me about what I wanted to do with my life. I would tell him I wanted to work for him. He would pat me on the head and say 'No, you don't; it's enough that your father does.' I had no real idea what his business was. All I knew was he often had closed-door meetings in a wing of the house off limits to everyone not directly involved. As I got older, my grandfather would frequently talk to me about different careers and job choices and traditions, but never his. He was stern only when I would tell him I saw no good reason to continue my schooling. 'You will go to college,' he said, 'and get the education I never had.'

"I was lucky. I got into Princeton and majored in philosophy. I think Grandpa suggested it. 'It's good to know how to tell when you're thinking whether you're thinking straight or crooked,' he'd say, and then he'd repeat a line that became a refrain: 'because you are going to need to know how to do both.'

"But it was no better with my father when I was home on holiday. It was worse. He landed some punches, and sometimes the bruises showed. I tried to defend myself for the first time, not very effectively, when I was fifteen. Grandpa gave me boxing lessons to occupy me that summer, and for a time my father lightened up. Then one day in the summer before my junior year at Princeton, he hauled off and slugged me over some trivial offense; I think he thought I had come home too late one night when I was out with his car. I told him that was the last time. He snickered. 'What are you going to do? Shoot me? In your grandfather's house?'

"Well, it gave me the idea. A couple of days later I ran into one of my grandfather's assistants, a young fellow named Eddie, though everyone called him Saddles because he wore those shoes. '*That's* a shiner,' he said. I told him I tripped on a rug. 'No you didn't, kid,' he said. That surprised me. I didn't know anyone could tell. 'We know what's going on. You know, we all feel sorry for you but your grandpa, he tells us not to interfere. But you ask me, you're old enough now and big enough, you should take care of it. Someone did that to me, I'd shoot him.' For some reason, I blurted out, 'I don't have a gun.' Saddles laughed. 'That's a good one. You don't have a gun. And if you did?' I think I glared at him. He just waved and winked.

"A week later I found a small package under my pillow. There was something hard inside. I ripped it open and a gun fell out. A Walther PPK; you know, James Bond's gun. Six inches long. Weighs a little over a pound. There was no note. I couldn't imagine how or why it got there. Then I remembered the conversation with Saddles. He never said a word about it, but late that afternoon I saw him leaving the house. He walked over to me and asked, but it was more like a command, if I could clear my calendar for Saturday.

"He was waiting for me in his car Saturday morning. We drove to a rifle and pistol range on Staten Island. 'No one gets a gun without a lesson,' he said. 'I'm probably not up to your Princeton standards, but what I teach is practical.' I hadn't brought the Walther; I didn't know we were going to use it. 'Didn't expect you to,' he said. He produced an identical Walther from his trunk. With a straight face, he said, 'I hope you've got yours tucked away safe. These things are dangerous.' We spent the day there; he even bought me lunch. For a neophyte instructor, he had a flair for explaining. No theory, no fancy words. I guess you could call it a practicum in the mechanics of shooting, the ergonomics of melding body to pistol. He demonstrated how to grip, how to stand, how to sight and aim, how to stow the gun in my clothing. How to strip it down, put it back together. How to load, chamber a round, put it into single-action mode, and—but you don't need details. Then for hours, until it got dark, I learned to fire it. Learned about pressure on the trigger, adjusted to the recoil, got comfortable loading, aiming, cooling it down. I wasn't proficient when it was time to leave, but I could pull it out of my jacket and hit a target on the range. 'Feel better?' he asked on the way home. I thought about that, longer than he liked. 'Sure you do,' he said.

"That might have been that. I suppose things could have worked out differently. I put the gun away. I mean I hid it, as much from myself as from anyone else. I did not want Liliana, our housekeeper, to find it or—God forbid—my mother. Most especially my father. So I stowed it where I thought no one would search, taped in a holster against the underside of my desk drawer about six inches off the floor, and pretended I forgot it. Then came the holidays. December 22, I was in my room that night, reading. It struck me immediately afterward that my father socked me with his fist but fate socked my future. Anyway, I'm sorry, Your Honor, I don't mean to prolong the story, which I'm only at the start of."

Malbonum paused to take a sip of water from the glass on the lectern. The judge signaled him to move on.

"The point is, I was sitting in my room in my desk chair reading, and suddenly the door opens, no knock, and it's my father, spluttering, raging. He's yelling at me for going through his things, spying on him, invading his sanctuary, all sorts of nonsense. I had no idea what he was talking about. Apparently Liliana had moved some stuff around on his desk in his office; I never did find out. Of course, I told him it wasn't me, whatever he was accusing me of. I hadn't been near his stuff. But he wasn't listening and came right up to me where I was sitting and socked me on the jaw. Knocked me down. My arm was flung under the desk and brushed against something. It was the gun. Without thinking, I slipped it out and pointed it up at the ceiling.

"'Whoa!' he whistled, like he was actually impressed. He put up both his hands, as if to surrender. But he was only feinting. It could have ended if he'd backed up. But he was drunk. He mumbled 'Hah,' as if to say, who are you kidding, his fist cocked. I thought the sound of a shot at the ceiling would scare him, but he lunged at me, and he was moving too fast. The bullet went straight through his forehead. A single crashing bark of the PPK. He dropped as if his legs had disappeared. Landed a foot from me. I backed up into the chair, my heart pounding, feeling flushed and dizzy. I don't know how long I sat, a couple of minutes probably, and there was Grandpa standing in the doorway. He took one look, stepped in, and closed the door behind him. Very quietly.

"I was petrified. I had just shot my father. There was his father, my grandfather. I had killed his son. I can still see Grandpa staring at me, expressionless. Then he said, 'I suppose it could not be helped.'

"'I warned him,' was all I managed to say.

"'I'm sorry for you, Romo,' my grandfather said. 'It's not the life I would have chosen for you. The life you'll now have. I had been hoping for so much more. But things are what they are, and I suppose I felt in my bones this day would come. Everything is going to be different now. You'll come to work for me—you'll learn the business, the real business. Oh, I don't mean immediately. After you finish college. You must get your Princeton degree. We're all proud of you, our Ivy League boy. You keep studying, get good grades. You can still build your book collection.' I must have had an astonished expression on my face, which he took to mean about the books, but it was astonishment at everything he was saying. 'Of course I know about your book collecting,' he said. 'I envy it. The carpenters will come tomorrow and enlarge the downstairs library. It will be for you. A man must follow his passion, and you're lucky to have found yours so young. But now, tonight, we must make your father disappear.'"

Reviewing the video when it was later made available to lawyers working on the case, many were struck by Malbonum's self-possession. Throughout he was composed, calm, confident. After a lifetime of reticence, his preternatural presentation shone an intense spotlight on his subterranean existence that revealed a coldness at the center of his heart. He was imperturbable, his steady stare frequently causing Judge Pickscreed to look away. He stood straight, nearly still, occasionally raising his arm in a gesture of defiance or perhaps of triumph.

"And that," Malbonum said, "is when and how it all started. Somehow Grandpa kept everything quiet, that night and for the rest of his life. We moved my father's body outside, a couple of hundred feet behind the gazebo fronting the garden—space enough when your house sits next to surrounding lots that Grandpa bought over the years and tore down the houses on. I spent two hours digging a hole under Grandpa's watchful eye. When he declared it big and deep enough, we rolled the body to the edge. Grandpa stared down and spoke to his son. I remember pretty much all of what he said.

"'Stewart, I'm sorry it's come to this, you miserable wretch. I suppose it's somewhat my fault. Not enough of this, too much of that. But mostly it's your fault. You were a man—or you could have been. You had a family. Children to watch out for. Instead you chose to beat your own son. You were smart enough at business, and you never cheated me, as far as I know. But that's not enough to make a life. At that you failed. And now you are to disappear. *La morte viene quando meno s'aspetta.* (*Death comes when you least expect it.*) Your wife and family will wonder where you went, how you could have vanished completely. Some will suspect foul play, and in time all may mourn you, maybe even your son, but no one will ever know the truth. Who knows if that would comfort you. But the sorrow, my son, is that you had no chance to open your heart to the errors of your years and repent. If you cannot acknowledge evil, you are not a man. Without repentance, a man is nothing. And now be gone. *Oggi in figura, domani in sepoltura.* (*Today in person, tomorrow in a grave.*)'

"That was my grandfather's eulogy for my father. I don't know what else to call it. We pushed the body into the waiting hole. I spent another hour or more covering it up. A week later, our gardeners strayed wide of their ordinary precincts and planted a redoubt of small trees around that unhallowed ground, while my mother raged inside, wondering where her faithless, wandering husband was. For years she stood in front of windows, staring out. In time her anger faded as she abandoned her initial belief that he had run away. She eventually accepted that he had met a tragic end. As indeed he had.

"For nearly two years after that until the day I graduated, my grandfather reflected not once about the split second that changed my life, other than to help ease my mother over her rage and then her doubt, worry, and fear. He and I talked about many things when I was home, but never that. On graduation day in early June, immediately after the commencement ceremony in front of Nassau Hall, with my family gathered round to take pictures of me and my friends in cap and gown, Grandpa pulled me aside and said quietly, in a voice portending nothing out of the ordinary, 'meet me tonight in my office at eleven, after family dinner.' I had plans to celebrate with my pals in the drinking emporiums of New York City, but I understood that my new life had begun and was taking me elsewhere.

"That, Your Honor, is how my life led to the one I am here to answer for today. I apologize for taking the court's time in telling the story of my innocent life. I know that it does not justify all that follows but hope that it helps explain. I will refrain from describing what my grandfather imparted to me the evening of my departure from the Ivy League. I learned I was joining what one of my grandfather's deputies, known as Big Knife Jackson because of his fondness for stilettos, called the Knivey League. I spent a year and a half at my grandfather's side daily or traveling with Saddles, Big Knife, and their associates, learning the business. I was away but once, my time in the Marine Corps, a couple of years after school. Grandpa offered to fix it but I didn't want him to. I said it would give me a better profile if I served. He agreed. 'Might even learn something,' and afterward I understand he meant about leadership, loyalty—and treachery."

Before Malbonum could continue, Tillinghast walked to the lectern and whispered in his ear. Malbonum shrugged, stepped back, yielding to his lawyer.

"Your Honor," Tillinghast said, "Mr. Malbonum now intends to discuss directly the matters with which he is charged. He is prepared to talk without break but will of course defer to your sense of timing."

"How long?" Jude Pickscreed inquired.

"Perhaps six more hours."

The judge peered at his watch. "In view of the desirability of pressing on, we will skip the lunch break," he announced to a roomful of dismayed onlookers. "But I capitulate to the necessities of our aging population, mainly, your presiding judge. We will reconvene in ten minutes. Do what you have to."

The back row was moving toward the doorway even as the gavel came down. The proceedings resumed ten minutes later because judicial chambers have private bathrooms. The public doors were shut, but remained unlocked; stragglers and those who had to wait in line for public bathrooms trickled in for many minutes more.

Eschewing preface, Malbonum delved into his complex tale of securities, mail and wire fraud, interstate gambling, loansharking, drug trafficking, grand larceny, robbery, tax evasion, racketeering, blackmail, money laundering, kidnapping, aircraft piracy, cybertheft, extortion, bribery, jury and witness tampering, arson, obstruction of justice, solicitation to commit crimes of violence, subornation of perjury, conspiracy—a chronicle of crime and depravity methodically recounted, implicating scores of his associates and providing vivid details of their involvement. It was not limited to family lowlifes like Saddles and Big Knife but included lawyers, accountants, bankers, prosecutors, building inspectors, guards, truck drivers, programmers and software engineers, and all the other functionaries and hangers-on through whom criminal enterprise is carried out daily and massively, usually unchecked, throughout the United States. On and on he talked, calmly, deliberately, unruffled, seeming to relish his role in the complex tale, until at last, shortly after six o'clock, he turned to

Tillinghast, nodded imperceptibly, then faced front and said, "That concludes my statement, Your Honor."

A collective sigh rippled through the room. The spectators were suddenly more animated, sitting up straighter if they had been slouching or unwinding if they had been pressing straight against their chair backs. They coughed and muttered to themselves or their neighbors and fidgeted with papers and pressed hands into pockets, until a weary Judge Pickscreed, who thrust himself up from the slump into which he had fallen for the past hour, gaveled them to order, awakening more than a few who had been dozing to avert stupefaction from the sonorously delivered roll call of remembered crimes and the long, unspooled blueprint that explained them.

"That is quite the statement, Mr. Malbonum."

"Thank you, Your Honor—I think."

"Very well. Speaking judicially, I find no reason to doubt that you have provided the factual predicate for the government's charges. Therefore, I accept your plea of guilty to each."

The judge removed his glasses and pinched his nose near his eyes. "Mr. Tillinghast."

"Your Honor."

"Anything more?"

"No, Your Honor, except to say that I am gratified by the court's reaction to Mr. Malbonum's presentation here this afternoon."

"And this morning!" the judge exclaimed. "But let's see if we can hurry this along now, before it's incontestably night. Mr. Carverman, more from you?"

"For the record, Your Honor, and in the hopes of being expeditious, I move that you direct the defendant to ratify the government's actions in bringing the case to this point and to waive any remaining constitutional or statutory rights he may have in contesting the charges to which you have just accepted guilty pleas."

"Do you want to be a bit more specific, Mr. Carverman?"

"Our objective is to avoid reopening these proceedings in any manner. We ask, therefore, that Mr. Malbonum expressly represent to the court that he does not contest the government's lawful authority to search his home and offices and the curtilage thereto, to tap and record his phone and other devices wherever located and whenever these searches occurred, nor to contest any seizures that resulted or the validity of forensic tests, and to waive all rights in connection with any of these events, including rights against self-incrimination—"

Judge Pickscreed turned to Malbonum.

"Your Honor, if I may, there's more."

The judge turned back and squinted at Carverman, then nodded. "Continue."

"I further move that the court direct the defendant to declare his consent to future searches, whether physical or electronic, and his willingness to cooperate fully as the government continues to investigate any and all crimes that may have been committed by his associates, known and unknown. And that he pledge to accept the outcome of, and to waive any appeal from, these proceedings."

"May I now ask the defendant's response to these extraordinary requests, Mr. Carverman?"

"Certainly, Your Honor."

"I was being snide, Mr. Carverman."

The U.S. Attorney knew when to be silent.

"Mr. Malbonum," the judge said, continuing when the Don stood, "you have heard these requests. I am not going to direct you how to answer. But I am going to ask you to answer."

"Your Honor, my counsel has advised that these requests would be made. I accept them. I mean, I do ratify the government's actions and waive any rights I might have to contest them. I agree to any future government action concerning the matters I have spoken of, and I affirm my willingness to cooperate further and fully."

Malbonum sat down.

"Satisfied, Mr. Carverman?"

"Almost, Your Honor. As has been discussed with and agreed to by the defendant, I also ask that he be fingerprinted and a DNA sample be taken in this courtroom at this moment to assure for the record we are in fact speaking to and hearing from Romo Malbonum, and further that he be directed, in the presence of witnesses, to give a blood sample to show he is not under the influence of or injected with a truth serum or other mind-altering drug or chemical."

"Mr. Carverman," the judge exploded. "I have sat on this bench for more than twenty-seven years, and I have never entertained any possibility that a defendant named X who appeared before me was anyone other than X. Do you mean to say there might be a shred of doubt about who stands here, after what we've heard?"

"No, Your Honor," Carverman said without flinching, "absolutely none at all. But who knows, others may claim it. We do not want to battle denialists beyond these walls. Especially Mr. Malbonum, in future days."

"Why would he do that? Would you do that?" The judged waved his hand at Malbonum to stay seated.

"No, Your Honor," Malbonum said in a hoarse voice. "But I consent to the request."

"But here? In the courtroom? Now? When we adjourn, Mr. Carverman, you can see to whatever tests you wish when the defendant is remanded."

Carverman, startled at the force of the judge's resistance, nodded to his colleague Greenstock, who had put him in this quandary.

She rose. "Your Honor, if I may."

"Speak."

"We think it essential to run these tests in public and to record the scene in public, with Your Honor and all others in this room, including the video, as witnesses. To run the tests behind closed doors might well defeat their very purpose, since the secrecy of the testing might tempt the defendant or others to deny their bona fides. We do not wish to hear him later say 'you faked the blood test; that was not me in the courtroom.'"

Not one to linger in the spotlight, Greenstock sat down abruptly. The judge shook his head and sighed. "Do we have the technicians?"

Carverman answered. "They are waiting outside, Your Honor."

"Very well, bring them in."

A man and a woman entered, carrying small cases, which they opened for the bailiff's inspection. The woman's case contained simple swabs for cheek DNA and equipment for drawing blood; the man's, a small inkpad and cards to take fingerprints. The man pressed Malbonum's inky fingers against the cards, then wiped them clean. The woman instructed Malbonum to remove his jacket and raise his sleeve. As she drew blood and swabbed his cheek, she whispered, "Not a lot of time to watch tennis, I suppose."

"I only watch if Roger's playing Rafa," he responded in a matching whisper intended solely for her ears.

Six minutes after they entered the courtroom, the technicians departed with blood, swab, and cards packed in properly labeled, sealed containers.

Judge Pickscreed turned to the government table.

"Mr. Carverman, anything more?"

"No, Your Honor."

"Mr. Tillinghast?"

"Your Honor, if I may indulge the court, I ask that Mr. Malbonum be permitted a concluding statement—"

"I thought we had already concluded."

"Well, an addendum, then."

"Quitting while we're ahead would be in order, Mr. Tillinghast. It's been a long day."

"Yes, Your Honor, but in view of the gravity and novelty of these proceedings, I pray a bit more time."

Judge Pickscreed blinked, took a breath as if he were about to speak, then simply said, "Proceed."

Malbonum stood and returned to the lectern. Gripping the sides with each hand, he paused for a few seconds, collecting his thoughts. Then he began, slowly and deliberately. "Thank you, Your Honor. You now have my story. It is my full statement. But since some may doubt my motives in making my story public, I hope I may be permitted to address a question that I suspect may be on your mind and many others': Why? I don't mean why I did what I did. I have endeavored to answer that question these past many hours. I mean why have I chosen to come forward and confess?

"I need not have, after all. Had I not stepped forward, there would have been no compelling me, as I understand from Mr. Tillinghast. But something astonishing happened, Your Honor, this very week. It happened not to the world, but to me. My wife, children, and grandchildren have been out of town, and still are. And late one evening last week, after my last meeting of the day, after a light dinner, after everyone had left—well, except my associates who dabble as bodyguards—"

A few snickers greeting this remark skittered across the rows of observers, interrupting Malbonum and prompting a glare from the judge.

Malbonum pressed on. "I went into my library. I so rarely go there anymore. And I suppose I shall never go there again. I have been amassing my collection since my days at Princeton, and there are some rather nice volumes on the shelves. I was idly browsing and one jacket caught my eye. It was called *The Common Good*. It was a slim volume, as you'd expect, I mean, if you're not a liberal." (A single guffaw that collapsed into indistinct coughing sounded behind him.) "I didn't recognize it. I don't remember acquiring it. But there it was, and for some reason, perhaps because I was curious what I'd been thinking when I purchased it, I pulled it off the shelf and sat down and started to read it. What it said froze me. Its essence was this: What does it profit a man who has lived on this earth to have provided only for himself, even for his family, if that is all, if he has not left a deposit behind of something beyond himself, and not merely the dollars he managed to suck in during his lifetime? When it's time to go, can anyone tell from what you did whether there was any reason for your ever being here? I realized my obituary would read, 'Deckled Don Dies.' Deckled Don. That's what they call me. Funny name. Because I buy well-made books, you know. Rough on the edges, smooth inside.

"Your Honor, what could I do to make this right? I can't uncommand my orders. I cannot resurrect my father, I cannot undo the fear nor restore the funds now spent. In short, I cannot undo my sins.

"But I can atone for them, and do so publicly, and suffer for them, and live a new life of bravery. More, I can call on my colleagues across the nation, my brothers, the others who are in this business of ours, who have done equal or similar deeds, to likewise confess error, to quit their careers, to reject our solipsistic ways"— the word prompted more than one expression of puzzlement throughout the room, but Malbonum was heedless and kept on talking—"to put others ahead of ourselves, and to heed the call of our Savior, as He said, *Matthew*: 9:13: 'I am not come to call the righteous, but sinners to repentance.'

"But what good is repentance on a deathbed? That is no repentance, or it is not repentance that aids any but the sinner. That is selfish repentance if it's even real repentance. More likely fake repentance. Repentance is important. It was to my grandfather. It is to me. On my passing, let it be written: 'Deckled Don Dies, Repented When It Meant Something.'" (This last remark has entered *Bartlett's* in a slightly altered fashion, via newspaper accounts that improved on the self-proclaimed epitaph: "Repented when he meant it.")

Before the onlookers were aware that the sermon had ended, Malbonum sat down. For sixty seconds, by the judge's watch, it was unclear whether the stillness in the courtroom was from lack of sound or motion.

Finally, the judge shook himself and rasped, "Mr. Malbonum, anything more?"

Malbonum looked squarely at the judge and said, "No, Your Honor, I have made a clean breast of it. There is nothing more to tell."

He accompanied this statement with a noticeable, toothy grin. Most spectators thought this a clear sign the Don was under some influence or had gone insane. Court personnel supposed that this preposterously rushed proceeding, from first filing to a plea in three days, would be rewound and replayed at a more comfortable lawyer speed. But that would be for a later day if ever. It remained for the prosecutors to seek one more adjustment to bring the flickering proceeding to its weary end.

"Your Honor—"

"Mr. Carverman, my patience is shot."

"Understandably, Your Honor. I rise purely on the question of remand."

"You have a motion?"

"We do. On behalf of the government, I move that Mr. Malbonum be directed to surrender to federal authorities on Monday at 10 a.m. to await sentence."

"And for what purpose should he have a two-day reprieve, instead of, say, being remanded now to the other side of that door? I'm sure we have a marshal or two ready to take the defendant into custody right now."

"It will be extremely useful to the government to continue our interviews and to benefit from the defendant's guidance while searching for materials necessary in our ongoing investigation."

"Mr. Tillinghast?"

"No objection. Mr. Malbonum is agreeable to continued cooperation with Mr. Carverman's office and to surrendering Monday."

"So ordered," said the judge, bringing down the gavel at long last, releasing the onlookers, imprisoned for hours by their morbid desire to see the spectacle whole and to its utter end. No longer quiet or polite, they hurried down the corridor to the restrooms.

All except for Glanville L. Carverman and Jedidiah C. Tillinghast, whom Judge Pickscreed summoned with a waggling index finger to follow him to chambers. Time for them to come clean.

CHAPTER 2

REVIEW

"SHIT, GLAN. 'CURTILAGE THERETO'? What the hell?"

This from Judge Pickscreed.

"You liked that?" Carverman was pleased with himself.

"And Jesus, Jed, 'solipsistic ways'?" The judge wasn't above skewering his former roommate.

Jedidiah Tillinghast rubbed his chin. "That wasn't my statement," he said. "Malbonum said it all by his lonesome. I didn't write his remarks; I only vetted them. He's a Princeton man, don't you know."

They were sprawled out in chambers, the judge having waved them onto the sofa fronting his massive oak desk with drawers on either side that opened with brass pulls. The walls behind the desk and to the sides sported scores of uniformly framed photos of the celebrities with whom the judge had managed to shake hands within his sainted halls of justice. (Judge Pickscreed was loyal to his celebrities, whatever their later fate: a disgraced former chief judge of the state Court of Appeals still beamed from his autographed frame.)

Tillinghast had his feet up on the glass table, privilege of an ex-roommate. The judge was bent over in front of his desk, looking for the bottles he eventually pulled from a lower drawer.

"Jim Beam?" he announced, "Or I got Grey Goose." He fished for three glasses.

"You know me, Judge," Tillinghast said, speaking formally because Carverman was in the room.

"Glan?"

"Whatever you two are drinking."

"Honk, honk, honk, three Grey Geese, coming up."

He poured and carried the glasses precariously pressed against each other, managing to set them down with a clank, unspilled, on the table. He slouched into the club chair next to his guests. Hoisting his drink, he toasted, "All right, boys, *salute!* as our newly convicted Saint Romo Malbonum might say. Plus, what the fuck is going on? Practically nothing in that courtroom today made any sense."

Tillinghast shrugged.

Carverman said, "Honestly, Judge, you probably know as much as I do."

"I know nothing. You've got to know more than that. You're the goddamn United States Attorney. You know everything. I'm just a poor judge who got randomly selected for, well, as I say, I don't know what."

"Really, I swear. I never heard boo about any of this until Tuesday night, when Mallory Greenstock called me direct."

"Oh, yeah, Mallory. Good kid. Would that everyone you had were that bright—and feisty."

"Not so much a kid anymore," Carverman ventured.

"No?"

"Only reason I know, she had a birthday cake last week; green frosting. She's forty-two."

"She put this together?" Tillinghast asked.

"Yep, chief of unit now, organized crime," Carverman continued. "I got a call, middle of the evening. She tells me she's just had an unexpected meeting with the FBI that leads to a more than unexpected outcome. Romo Malbonum is in our sights. She gives me the short version. Do I want her to follow through? Damn straight. Next two days, it's continuous triple overtime. I only got the final briefing last night, an hour before I called you. Most of what I know I heard with you today for the first time."

"You guys aren't shilling for someone? Jed?"

"Swear, Judge. Like Glan says. I got a call Tuesday night. From Malbonum himself. Says he needs an attorney in a hurry. I'm pretty surprised, you know, and I ask him what's the matter with his regular lawyers; they actually know him. He says, 'I don't need shifty-shitty lawyers; I need a real one. Kind who talks to judges.' I tell him I'm hanging up if he thinks he can use me to fix a case. He says no, I misunderstand him; he doesn't want anything fixed. He's done with fixing. He says he's surrendering, talking. Wants it all proper. I tell him for that I charge more. He laughs, says he's sending a car for me. I tell him I'll take my own car."

"This is crazy," the judge said.

"Well, it's unusual, yeah, definitely unusual," Tillinghast said, seeking precision.

"Come off it, Jed. You've never heard of anything like this, ever."

"Okay, yeah, never. But that's me. I'm not a regular; I don't do folks like Malbonum for a living. What do I know? You think something's wrong? You heard the guy. Too detailed to be false. And it's definitely him, isn't it, Glan? I mean, he entertained me at his house, for God's sake. That guy in court."

"Oh, it's him all right. No way these tests are wrong."

"Good, 'cause he signed the check himself."

"Tilt," Carverman said. "You know we're going to forfeit all the assets."

"Not my fee, you're not. Money's from his wife's jewelry sales. Inherited from her mother. Not the proceeds of a crime."

The judge lifted an eyebrow.

"For the record, he told me I could tell you." Tillinghast chuckled mirthlessly.

"Something is very greatly wrong," the judge persisted. "As I keep saying."

"What's eating you?"

"It ain't kosher. It ain't halal. And I include the Pope and the Buddha. Think about it. Don't you see?"

"See what?" Carverman was actually curious.

"Well, top of the head, I can think of eight things."

"Namely?"

"First thing, come on, mother-in-law's inherited jewelry fund? Crap. Someone strained to think up something that stupid. If it wasn't you two, who?

"Second thing, look, his eminence says he's repenting, yeah? He's sorry for all he's done. His decision, all on his own."

Carverman nodded. Tillinghast said nothing.

"Doesn't that strike you as so much hooey? John Gotti never walked in off the street and said, 'Take me, I'm yours.' Malbonum is supposed to be every bit as tough, isn't he? These guys don't do that. No mobster has ever said, 'Gee, I got that old time religion.' So why did he do it?"

"Those other guys didn't go to Princeton," Carverman joked.

The judge frowned. "I'm serious, Glan. Third thing, he read a book? And converted to sainthood? His grandfather said he should? Did his grandpa repent? Nah. And then the fourth thing, the goddamn hours it took to tell his tale. Who can remember all that stuff? And all in three days? Which pushes right against the fifth thing, the speed of this case. Or whatever it is. I get notice on Wednesday my name popped out of the wheel; I'm on for a Friday plea. In two days? From filing to plea, for an information this loaded with charges? I'm told it's urgent. You said when you called last night it was 'essential' we proceed forthwith. Your word. What was so essential? I can't say I learned anything about how essential it was from what happened today."

"Your Honor," Carverman said, putting his drink down on the table and clutching his knees, "I can only repeat what I said when we last talked. The Attorney General himself called. Those were his instructions to me."

The judge shook his head. "Well, I suppose at this moment we can't expect clarity on a matter that's one of the many inexplicable features of this plea. But it leads to the sixth thing that stinks."

"Which is?"

"How exactly did this whole thing start? He didn't come to your office, Mr. United States Attorney. Did he invite the FBI to stop by his house? Did they pick him up on an outstanding warrant? Based on what? Did he walk into FBI headquarters with outstretched hands? I don't think anyone in the courtroom is any the wiser."

"My understanding is that he called the FBI in," Carveman said. "Greenstock told me the deal was to go to his home with her team Wednesday morning. The FBI was already there."

The judge looked at Tillinghast.

"They were there Tuesday night," the lawyer said. "I'm not going to say what we talked about. You know that. But I can tell you in general terms that the subject didn't come up. He began our whole discussion with the blanket declaration that he was set on confessing and cooperating. We went on from there."

"Okay," the judge said, "then there's number seven. The procedures you had me agreeing to in court today. Recording? Why? We only ever make transcripts. We never use video. And then blood, DNA tests in open court? While video recording? You're afraid of something."

"I said in court," Carverman responded, "and I believe it, we don't want some bogus claim that we got the wrong guy."

"Why would anyone ever think so?" the judge demanded. "Who thought up this bright idea?"

"Greenstock is in charge of details," Carverman said. "I'm not sure, but I think she got it from the FBI."

"Exactly," said Judge Pickscreed. "That's the point, and that's the seventh thing that doesn't add up. We got, one, the highly contrived payment. Two, the improbability of the confession. Three, the even more bizarre claim that it stemmed from reading a book happened on in a big-boy library. Four, the length of that speech, like some orator trying to win a prize. Five, today's expedited proceeding. Six, the murkiness of the starting point. Seven, the out-of-line procedures. And eight. You want to hear eight?"

"Come on, Judge."

"You asked him to ratify, Glan. Ratify what? You never spelled it out, and you, Jed, never pushed to ask. He waives his rights to object to anything and everything the government did, whatever the government was up to before he calls them in, without even knowing what? That's some bootstrap, fellows."

"That's not entirely correct," Tillinghast said.

"No?"

"Malbonum and I discussed it. I can tell you the first thing he told me, point blank, he didn't care what the FBI did; he'd go along. Even if they bugged his house illegally? He said yes, whatever."

"You're revealing that part of your conversation?"

Tillinghast shrugged. "He authorized it. Said feel free to tell anyone who asks about his intention to testify."

"I can see why you don't do defense work," the judge said sharply to his friend. "That's—"

"That's what he told me, *Your Honor*. The client has peculiar notions, but I'm representing him faithfully."

"Sorry, Jed," the judge said, "I didn't mean to suggest—"

"Please," Carverman said. "I don't think asking him to ratify implies any bad faith or corrupt dealing. Because that's what you're really suggesting."

"Sure as shit what it sounds like," the judge said. "End runs are for football, not the Constitution."

"Not so sure," Carverman said, looking slowly about the room. "I mean, we're trying to avoid any tie-ups and slowdowns around you fellows here if someone screws up some procedural nicety."

"No," the judge said, "It's more than that. You said something like, 'whenever the searches occurred.' A defendant doesn't need to 'ratify' something you're *going* to do. He can just consent to it. You guys are letting yourself off the hook for who knows what? How long has the FBI been on this?"

"On him?" Carverman asked. "Malbonum? Well, practically forever. But not illegally. They aren't doing that now, haven't been. Not since the old days. Everything is by the book."

"Says you."

"Well . . . " Carverman began but could not conjure a convincing retort, so the judge continued.

"Something happened we don't know about. You said phone taps. Investigators don't announce phone taps, and yet you did it, right in open court. Anyway, what will a tap yield now? None of his people will be talking to him anymore. They're going to want to stuff him way down into that big hole with his father. Your birthday gal must be covering for some prior phone taps, prior searches, off the books stuff—whatever."

Carverman took an audible breath. "Not Mallory. Straight arrow. She's as clean as anyone in the whole federal system. Anyway, what does it matter? Guy's hosed himself. He may have shit for brains though that's not the way I hear it, but whatever he is or isn't, he's walked himself into an impervious, self-sealing airtight box. No one could slip through or out of it. Regardless of what the FBI or anyone did. It can't be appealed. How can it be appealed? He's agreed to it all. I don't think we should obsess."

"Me? Obsess?" Pickscreed looked at Carverman with distaste. "I'm a judge. That's what we do."

"Flamsteen never did."

"Old school."

"Or Overton, Nance, or half the judges in this courthouse."

"Yeah, well," Pickscreed grimaced. "Mostly old school. Anyway, I suppose you're right. Not sure what it means—less sure what anyone can do about it. You better hope it isn't a shitstorm aiming for you."

"Me, why me?" Carverman scowled.

"Because I do what they put in front of me. But you—you're the one putting it."

"We better hope we haven't all walked into it," Tillinghast murmured, drumming his fingers on the table. "Whatever it is."

The White House
Washington, DC 20500

May 3, 2:00 p.m.

A Treat from Your President

My Friend Romo
(Statement on a Federal Plea)

What is this world coming to? is the question on the minds of many mindful people after yesterday's inexplicative plea of Romo Malbonum in federal court in New York. Mr. Malbonum is well known to many people in the worlds of transportation, trucking, philanthropy, and finance, fiancé, finance.

I have known Romo Malbonum, a distinguished American, for many years and am pleased to have called him My Friend in our joint battle against people who would tear down our country. Low life scum. He was instrumental in our great election victory, not just a major donor. He is a fighter for all things American. America on the move. Here and there. Hither and yon, we literary types would call it. Why would federal prosecutors so shamefully besmirch the reputation of an upstanding American, who deserves a little privacy, after all, like the rest of us. Privacy, a guaranteed American value. Hooray for privacy. How many of you know it stems from private? Which makes you wonder about Army ranks.

Action taken: I'll spend the next hour getting to the bottom of this.

Technical Correction to Presidential Treat, today's date: The first sentence of the second paragraph in the presidential treat on Romo Malbonum's federal plea should have read " . . . for many years and was pleased to have called him an ally . . . " An errant White House spellchecker was solely responsible for these word substitutions and also for the inadvertent use of "inexplicative" to mean "inexplicable," misspelling "finance" and repeating it, for improperly substituting the words "instrumental in" in place of "incidental to," and for failing to delete the word "just" in the phrase "not just a major donor." The spell checker has been upgraded as of 1:30 p.m., as if it nattered.

CHAPTER 3

REPLAY

WHATEVER IT WAS HAD BEGUN THREE days earlier. Ordinarily, an extravaganza like Friday's court proceedings would have required extensive federal legwork and paperwork lasting months (or occasionally years). Had Malbonum been a typical client, he would have engaged a former federal prosecutor to meet for a drink with an old colleague, now a senior prosecutor, who toward the end of the first Chardonnay would wonder almost as an afterthought how she "might react" if someone on the government's radar was willing to negotiate a plea, say to end an ongoing investigation. Her client would confess to various misdeeds but only under certain conditions: a lighter sentence or a shorter charge sheet. If the government agreed, names would be named.

But in this case whatever it was unfolded *backwards*. At eight o'clock the preceding Tuesday evening, when Mallory Greenstock was sitting in the Undersludge, a nondescript, dimly lit restaurant with a dark bar in a basement not far from the U.S. Attorney's offices behind Foley Square. Most nights, prosecutors, federal agents, defense lawyers, and the occasional city police officer claimed most of the tables. Awaiting a friend for dinner, she was scribbling the next day's to-do list on a small pad when she became aware of someone standing at her side. She looked up and saw a man of medium height wearing a rumpled tan suit and a quizzical expression. He was holding a badge from the FBI.

"Do you have a moment?" he asked.

"And you are?"

"Special Agent Dewey Sisal," he said as he pulled out the chair opposite her and lowered himself into it.

"Do I know you?" she asked when he offered his hand. "You look faintly familiar."

"We may have met a few years back at an assistant U.S. attorneys conference. I was on a panel. But not really. Met, I mean. Congratulations on your promotion, by the way."

Greenstock shrugged. "Hang in long enough."

"Yeah."

"You?"

"Fourteen years last month."

"That's something. So, anyway, what's this? You just happened to be passing by? Or have my plans for the evening changed?"

Sisal laughed, an easy, unforced sound of pleasure that she had gone straight to the point. "I was up in your office looking for you. One of your colleagues told me he thought you'd be here."

"Usually people call me first," she said, "before dropping in at dinner. Especially at eight o'clock."

"Sorry," he said. "One of those things. Came up suddenly. Or into focus."

"What did?"

"Listen, it's too significant and sensitive to talk about except in person. Give me five minutes. I promise it'll be worth it. We could go back to your office."

She leaned back. "I'm listening."

Sisal came right to the point as well. What would she say, he mused, to handling a major case, hundreds of charges, but no real work, everything pleaded to by one of New York's—hell, the country's—most notorious and ruthless gangsters, no deal necessary.

"Come again?"

"A guy clearly on your scope. We think we got him. All the stuff, big time: bank and stock fraud, money laundering, yadda yadda yadda. He'll go down without further investigating; no need to start low and go up the chain. Save us years. Bring it all to us. Plus he names names, lots, with evidence to put them away, probably forever."

She waited while a waitress put down a glass of water and asked if Sisal wanted something from the bar. He shook his head. Greenstock picked up a few cashews but left them in her hand. "What's the catch?"

"Not much of one. It has to be a greased-lightning response. You'll have at most two days to get it down on paper signed."

"What's he want, this gangster?"

"Nothing."

She popped the nuts into her mouth. Chewed. "That doesn't make any sense."

He smiled affably. "Probably not. And yet."

"He's going to plead and take down his crew and squat in lockup doing a forever stretch without anything in return?"

"Far as I understand it. Possibly ease up on the wife and kids. Don't know."

"Who's in charge of this?"

"I am."

"You're in charge, and it's only 'far as you understand it?'"

"Yep."

"Explain this to me again."

"There's a guy, big name. You know the name. Never been caught. Never been in court. He wants to come in. Wants to confess. To all his sins or, anyway, enough of them that no one would ever look for more or even care if there were."

"Real crimes?"

"Like I said. Several that amount to murder, except those may not be charged, but all the rest, big time financial crime, probably anything else you can think of, in an organized way. He'll never see daylight again."

"But we have to hurry?"

"Yes, it's got to be done snippety-snap, zippety-zap. As in, he has to plead in court this Friday, latest."

"Is he represented?"

"Will be."

"The usual family lawyers?"

"No, that's the odd thing. Not any of them. He's calling in someone special, a well-known counselor, uptown. Doesn't normally handle these guys. Someone clean."

"Can you tell me who your target is?"

"Only if you're ready to go."

"Starting when?"

"Eight tomorrow morning. That's the deal. We'll pick you up, right in front of your office. Drive you to the guy's house. You'll hear whatever we've learned in the meantime on the way there."

"Can you tell me where?"

Sisal gave his "you better be on the level, sister" stare, held her glance. "Brooklyn."

"Big place."

"Not that big."

"Then what?"

"Then it's all yours. You'll have him for the next two days. You get him on record—names, dates, stories, locations, evidence, the works, everything. That's your business. Only thing we ask is he has to be in court pleading to everything on Friday. You'll need to set it up."

"Why?"

"Why what?"

"Why Friday?"

"Beyond me. I'm not the strategist; I'm just the tactician. I do as I'm told."

"You'll be with me tomorrow?"

"No. You and your team'll go with a couple of my colleagues. The agent in charge on scene, Chuck Vlastic, you'll meet when you get there. I'm leading the task force to round up the co-conspirators. As they get named, one of your people lets us know, we get warrants, we go pick 'em off. Take people you can trust. It's all happening in a hurry; tell them chop chop. And record it all—everything."

"This is for real? Not some stupid joke that the usual pranksters are playing on me?" She brushed aside a strand of flaxen hair to ensure the fisheye would not be wasted on him.

He was undeterred. "Mallory, if I may, I don't come to places like this for laughs. This is as real as it will ever get. Could be the biggest case of your career. Decide. You in?"

She looked at the nuts, the bartender, the door, then back at Sisal. She held her wine glass at eye level, considered what little was left in the glass, then nodded once. "Far as I'm concerned, let's do it."

"Good." He hoisted the glass of water, took a sip, and thumped it on the pitted table. He took a deep breath, watched her put her glass down, and said, "Who else is concerned?"

"My boss, the U.S. Attorney. A case like the one you're describing? Straight to the top. Along with details."

"How long will that take?"

"You tell me who you've got in your sights, answer a question; I'll call right now."

"What question?" Sisal frowned.

"Who else knows about this matter?"

"No one. Well, not counting the big boss in Washington," he said. "Big, big boss?"

"My big big, not yours."

"And that's it?" Greenstock said, hoping it was.

"My small team," Sisal replied. "I don't know what the guy's lawyer knows. And I guess a few others know bits and pieces. You now know more than most of the small group who know something."

Sisal watched her down the remaining wine. A student of facial features, he admired her earlobes and the understated jade earrings that matched her eyes, after admiring the short straight nose, smooth cheeks, generous mouth, and firm chin and neck. He also noticed the absence of a wedding ring.

"You going to tell me who?" she demanded.

His mouth opened into a wide smile. "Ever hear of a guy called Romo Malbonum?"

She put a hand to her lips to stifle her surprise. "Holy Christ."

"Even if he isn't holy."

Greenstock stared at him for a long moment, then put one hand to her heart and looked heavenward.

"What's that for?" Sisal asked.

"Joy," she said. "If what you say is true, you have brought me joy, Special Agent Sisal."

"Why would I lie to you?"

"I don't know," she said, "but most people do."

"And what would two hands to your heart mean?"

"Rapture," she said, "but I doubt your investigation could bring me that."

She fished for the phone in her purse and tapped the speed dial for the U.S. Attorney's mobile phone. "Listen," she said, when he picked up on the second ring, "I've got something." She summarized the facts so succinctly that Carverman had only one question, which he asked not to elicit information but to sputter his surprise at the demand.

"By Friday?" he said.

"That's what he says."

"In court on Friday," Sisal said loudly.

"Who was that?" Carverman asked.

"The agent, Sisal. He's underscoring his demand. Plea on Friday."

"Can you do it?"

"Of course," she said.

39

"That's my—" Carverman was about to say "girl" but caught himself and shifted smoothly to "unit chief."

"We're on," she said, hanging up.

"I suggest you get going, assemble your people, get your ducks in line, full court press."

She sat upright, twirling a gold bracelet. She reached for her purse.

"Go," he said, "I got this, courtesy of the Bureau."

She got up as he fished for his wallet.

"Tomorrow," he repeated. "Eight o'clock."

She took a step away from the table, then remembered why she was at the restaurant, and as she walked briskly toward the door phoned her friend to postpone the dinner. Then she called the senior member of her team, with instructions to verify Sisal's bona fides and set up the play.

When she stepped outside, Sisal picked up his phone and punched in a number on his speed dial. It was answered on the first ring. "She bought it," he said, and hung up.

Most of what Sisal had said was true. He merely omitted that he knew more than he claimed. She might learn he went to Brooklyn after their restaurant rendezvous, but probably wouldn't, and it would make no difference if she did. After she walked out, he threw down a twenty-dollar bill and went to retrieve his car, a seven-year-old Honda. He looped onto the Brooklyn Bridge, taking the route she would be following in the morning.

Nearing Malbonum's home, he pressed another number, also picked up on the first ring.

"It's me. I'm seven or eight minutes out. At nine-thirty on the dot, do it."

Which they did, four minutes later. A muffled boom reverberated through the foliage surrounding the house, and the five agents outside waited until the incandescent flash faded. Then they burst in through three doors and raced to their positions assigned when the assault was planned the previous day. Months of observation, phone taps, and bugs in the house and cars gave the planners confidence that Malbonum's family would be out of town and that his three close "associates" would be at their usual Tuesday night dinner in one of the restaurants on Third Avenue in Bay Ridge. Sisal pulled into the eighty-foot driveway that arced around the back. He walked through an open door past an agent stationed inside.

"The others?" Sisal asked.

"Searching the house."

"The big guy?"

"Chuck's got him. Downstairs, like you thought."

Sisal pressed a button. "Good work, fellas." His hollow voice came out in harsh static on the agents' walkie-talkies. "Chuck, I'm heading to you. Bert, call the van on Third Avenue and have 'em round up the boys."

At that moment, a dark-haired woman in a black pant suit and deep blue running shoes strode in carrying a satchel. She was followed by a man who, along with her, would show up in court three days later to take DNA, blood samples, and fingerprints. The man was rolling a hand dolly to which was strapped a green trunk.

"Hustle," Sisal said. "Downstairs, to the office."

They walked briskly to the main staircase that split the house in two, and three of them took the stairs two at a time. The fourth man bounced the dolly down each step.

They could hear the protest as they walked along the corridor leading to Malbonum's study and library. It sounded like "whadauck," but was a hoarse rendition of "what the fuck!" pitched at the top of his lungs. Malbonum was standing near one side of an enormous room, in front of a sofa on the edge of a thirty-foot rug that was centered on rows of gloomy bookcases, lights out, that ran nearly fifty feet down from the desk. He was dressed in gray slacks, a blue shirt, and a seersucker jacket. Nothing looked out of place, except for the cuffs pinning his arms behind his back and the large, red-checked bandana wrapped around his face, tied tightly behind his head and covering his eyes. Vlastic had seen no reason to gag him, leaving his mouth free to vent obscenities, some learned in the Marine Corps, some older choice expressions gleaned at Princeton.

"Pipe down, Romo," Vlastic said. "Your fate is sealed. I'm reading from a script here; that's what it says. Sealed. Hollering will not avail, as my saintly mother used to say. No one's around to hear you."

In a more moderated tone, Malbonum demanded to know, "To what do I owe the pleasure of your company? I'd say you are too professional to be robbers, and too stupid. No one would come into my house to steal. So I'm guessing you're cops. Really, really dumb fucking cops. Your badges are no longer worth shit."

"Actually, we're feds," Vlastic said.

"What'd I do?" Malbonum managed to put surprise into his voice.

"What didn't you do, Romo?" Vlastic said. "Anyway, it doesn't matter who we are. What matters is what you're going to do. You're going to walk with me into your special little room, where we'll tarry awhile." The dark-haired woman choked off a chuckle. Vlastic steered Malbonum by the elbow past several tiers of bookcases. In the middle of the library he pushed him to the left, down an aisle lit by ceiling track lights and through a door that opened into a 300-square-foot panic room, equipped with club chair, sofa, bed, refrigerator, desk, swivel chair, and toilet, sink, and shower cubicle. Malbonum could not see Sisal leaning on a wall, poker-faced and silent.

"Have a seat." Vlastic pushed Malbonum abruptly down into the desk chair. "You won't feel this."

The dark-haired woman raised the bandana over the bridge of his nose, clapped a damp white handkerchief to his face, said, "Truth serum time for you," and pressed firmly against his nose and mouth.

"Hey," Malbonum sighed, and then his head lolled forward.

"Okay." Sisal spoke aloud for the first time in the downstairs arena. "You all know what to do. From here on, the clock is running, so follow the script. No one comes in here without Chuck's okay. Let's do this."

Ten minutes later, Malbonum woke up. He was sitting uncuffed in the chair, his arms in his lap, the bandanna removed. As he regained his sight, he looked around the room and nodded once.

"Okay," he said calmly, "you got me. Tell me how you want to play this. What do you want me to do? Do you mind if we do whatever it is in the library? Much more comfortable."

"Sure," Vlastic agreed. He stepped up to Malbonum, holding the Don's left forearm to steady him as he rose. The two of them came out, trailed by the dark-haired woman. The others stayed behind. Vlastic closed the door behind them. Malbonum was led to the sofa and gently helped down. "Still woozy?"

"Yeah, a little."

"It'll pass. Take it slow. First order of business, out of curiosity: Mr. Malbonum, you watch tennis?"

"Not a lot. Only when Roger plays Rafa."

"Okay, not on tonight. You call your main man instead."

"My main man? Oh, you mean my major domo."

Vlastic tittered. "Yeah, the Romo domo."

Malbonum smiled briefly for the first time that evening. "Okay, that'd be Saddles. Hand me the phone over there. What am I saying?"

"You tell him to round everyone up. All your guys. Everyone. Even your lawyers. They're to hightail it to the West Virginia hideout, right away. Everyone. No excuses. Tell him to stay put and you'll be there Friday night. Big pow-wow, involving the future of the enterprise. You got that? And remember, we're monitoring this call."

"How do you know about West Virginia?"

"We know about everything," Vlastic said, lips pursed. "We have been listening to all your calls, watching all your cars, listening to what's gone on inside your houses and your hideaways for the past nine months. That's why we're moving now. Time for this baby to be born. Call your guy. And remember, we're listening."

Malbonum did as instructed, sounding firm when Saddles demurred, loud enough for Vlastic and the woman to hear him.

"I hear you, Saddles," Malbonum responded, "but I got my usual guys here. Nothing to worry about. Yeah. Throw a feast for the boys. They'll appreciate it—and stay put. Call me when you're all there." He hung up.

"How was that?"

"Real good, Mr. M, real good. You sound exactly like the boss."

"Don't you forget it."

Vlastic registered a flash of alarm, then relaxed. "I won't."

"Okay, what do you want from me?"

"You're finished here. You need to understand that. You're going down. Your boys are going down, and a lot of others too. You want to get ahead of it. You cooperate, we cooperate. You talk, you plead, we deal."

"Why should I? If we're all going down—"

"Your family, Romo. We're going to take care of your family."

"You're just like we are."

"We're nothing like you are."

Malbonum smirked. "Whatever you say. Okay, I'll play along."

"Good. My associate here is going to set up some recording devices for our long night of talk."

"And you are?" Malbonum asked, turning to the short, dark-haired woman standing alongside.

"You can call me Helene," she said evenly. She pulled five small black circular objects, each with a tiny silver antenna on an edge, and distributed them a few feet from where Malbonum sat. He watched her curiously. It was a matter of a minute.

"How do you know I don't record what goes on here?"

Helene shrugged. "I don't." She nodded at Vlastic that the devices were recording.

"Good," he said. "Now, then, Mr. Malbonum. Let's start. You're going to need a lawyer. We've got one in mind. A good one."

"Who?"

"Don't worry. He's not one of ours. He's independent, a pillar of the bar. Few can afford him. But you can. Here's his name and phone number. Put it on speaker and call him now. Don't let him say no. Tell him it's a short consultation. Three days at the outside. It'll be wrapped up Friday. But it starts tonight. You're sending a car, already in front of his door. Preliminary conversation. He'll be back before anyone knows he's gone."

Jedidiah Tillinghast took the call at home, more surprised that Malbonum had his private number than that it was Malbonum on the phone. In a career of nearly fifty years in conference and counseling, he had long since come to expect late night calls from people whose names he knew only from the newspapers or from muted conversations with colleagues over drinks at their clubs.

"You must understand that I am not primarily a criminal trial lawyer," Tillinghast told his caller.

"And I would argue, contrary to your implication, that I am not a criminal," Malbonum retorted.

"My blushes," Tillinghast said. "Still, I must point out that I rarely do trial work of any sort. And if I may be bold, I would suppose you have a stable of lawyers in your line of work."

"My line of work?"

"The construction business. And all that goes with it."

"I take your point, Mr. Tillinghast. But I don't need a trial lawyer, nor, if you will pardon the expression, any of their sort."

"Their sort?"

"Shifty-shitty shysters. I don't need them. I like the kind who talk to judges."

"Then you've got the wrong man, Mr. Malbonum. I won't continue a conversation with someone asking me to fix cases."

"No, no, you misunderstand me, sir. I should have said, the sort of lawyer who is respected by judges. I don't need a fix. Done with all that. I confess that I've surrendered and am pleading guilty. I suppose that will make me a criminal, at least technically. I am calling in full confidence that you possess most precisely the wisdom and experience of which I am most in need. I need someone to shape a statement I intend to make. I need the best, and I'm told you're it. Can you possibly clear your desk?"

"How long do you need me?"

"Three days tops. Hearing is Friday—I'm told."

Tillinghast was silent, mulling it over. It made no sense, no matter that he knew nothing about it. This isn't how the big defendants get rolled. Way too fast. Way too ambiguous. Still, he was intrigued.

"For this kind of service, you know, I'm likely to charge more."

"I'll take out a loan."

"When and where do we meet?" the lawyer asked.

"I've sent a car; it's waiting down at the curb." Malbonum followed the script.

"Thanks, Mr. Malbonum, but I've got my own car. You need to level with me. I don't do half-assed."

"You'll get the whole ass, which is me, that I can assure you." He recited his address and clicked off.

For the next several hours, Malbonum talked, mostly with Vlastic. They were sidetracked for an hour when Tillinghast arrived, clearing the room to let lawyer and client confer. Once, when Malbonum wasn't able to make himself clear enough for the needs of the FBI, Helene went into the panic room to visit Sisal and the others. She stayed less than ten minutes, and when she came back she rephrased the previous question, opening up a new line of inquiry that eventually resolved the matter to Vlastic's satisfaction. At 5 a.m., Vlastic wrapped it up. "I'm told you need little sleep. I'm afraid we're going to put you to the test. Get some shuteye. Then up around nine. Shower. We'll have breakfast, and when we're done a new team will arrive. You need to be sharp. They will be with you all day and probably into the night. And more the next day. We want to know every last detail. If you don't know, forget something even a little, tell us. We'll take a break, help you remember. We want it wrapped up at this end in two days. Thursday night, latest."

Malbonum stood, stretched, and announced he was going to sleep in his bedroom. Vlastic said he'd be right along. Outside the door. In case Malbonum needed anything.

"Don't you sleep, Chuck?" Malbonum asked.

"Why?"

"I'm curious."

"Night shift," Vlastic said.

"While we sleep, you just sit there?"

Vlastic regarded his charge for a long moment. Malbonum was impassive, his face composed, emotionless.

"I read poetry," Vlastic said at last.

"Poetry? What good is that?"

"It tutors the art of recollection."

"Do you recall much?"

"I remember it all."

"I must take lessons. Sounds an essential skill where I am going," the Don said in a voice tinged with regret.

When Malbonum left the room, Vlastic turned to Helene. "You figure he's bugged his own house?"

Helene nodded. "Let's assume so. We play it straight until we find the equipment."

Greenstock arrived shortly after nine Wednesday morning. She and her team entered the dining room, where the FBI was catering a full breakfast. Malbonum, refreshed, sat at the head of the table, wearing white linen slacks and a blue-and-white striped shirt. He rose when Greenstock walked in. Vlastic was standing near the doorway. "Special Agent Chuck Vlastic," he said, extending his hand as Greenstock approached. He pivoted smoothly to Malbonum and introduced her. "This is Assistant United States Attorney Mallory Greenstock, head of the organized crime unit, and her associates."

Malbonum thrust out his arm, and Greenstock obliged. He had a firm, dry handshake.

"Ms. Greenstock. My executioner."

She stiffened, then caught herself and offered her own brief smile. "As I understand it, we don't do death penalty for your crimes."

Malbonum recoiled. "I wasn't being literal, Ms. Greenstock. How about some breakfast?"

He held a chair out for her next to him. They sat and ate, joined a few minutes later by Helene, who nibbled hurriedly, then rose to heap food on two more plates, which she carried out of the room. "The guards," she said, but she took the food back unseen to the panic room and locked the door.

Tillinghast arrived fifteen minutes later. He declined breakfast. "Up early. Just coffee."

At ten they retired to the library. Tillinghast reminded Malbonum that he wasn't under obligation to talk. Ever cautious, Greenstock read him his Miranda rights for the third time since he began talking twelve hours earlier. Malbonum dismissed the formalities. "Let's get on with it."

They worked in non-stop relays for the next thirty-eight hours. Malbonum held forth, his words recorded. The recordings were transmitted in real time to the office in Manhattan where a master document was being shaped for court. Twice on Wednesday Vlastic stopped the proceedings and wandered down the aisles, turned left, and made for the panic room door. Neither Greenstock nor Tillinghast had been offered a tour, and they did not ask but gratefully accepted the respite. The first pause allowed Greenstock to call her office to discover that Judge Pickscreed had been selected to hear the plea. She phoned his chambers and briefed one of his clerks on the urgency of the case. She told him it would take many hours. Was the judge free, or could he clear his calendar, to hear a plea on Friday? The clerk promised to call back within two hours. As Mallory's team broke for a late lunch, the clerk called to say the judge had scheduled all of Friday for the plea though he expected to hear from someone no later than Thursday that the matter was on.

At four o'clock the first day, Tillinghast asked for a recess. "Need some alone time with my client," he offered to Vlastic's raised eyebrows. "Confession may be good for the soul of the client," he said, "but not necessarily for the sole defense counsel. I'm advising my client to shut up about a matter that has now arisen until he and I can talk. Give us thirty."

The others got up, grabbed notepads and laptops, and ascended the stairs to the main level.

"What's wrong?" Malbonum asked.

"Aside from whatever it is you're doing?" said Tillinghast.

"I know it seems strange."

"That's an understatement. It makes no sense whatsoever. I thought you were a tough guy. You seem to have folded, for no discernible reason."

"Nevertheless, don't let's keep picking at that scab. That decision is made. The train has left the station."

"Yeah, I'd say it's already arrived at the other end."

"Then?"

"I can't do much for a client who wishes to confess to every federal white-collar crime I've ever heard of and some I haven't. And I don't usually muck about with more earthy crimes, like homicide."

Malbonum was impassive. "But?"

"But I don't think you need murder raps hanging over you despite whatever this is. I want you to let me suggest an alternative approach to that line of inquiry. I'm not advocating you lie about it. Lord knows, I don't commit perjury or suborn it, and I'm not trying to put words in your mouth. So I aim to discuss those charges with Greenstock. You weren't there; that's what I heard you say. You didn't know what your guys were planning. You didn't give any such orders. Do I have that right?"

Malbonum hesitated, considered, conceded. "Right."

"Then you give me carte blanche to fix this up with Greenstock."

"Only that."

Tillinghast regarded him. "I almost think you're doing this for the glory."

"Go Tigers," Malbonum said.

The interrogation resumed at a placid pace. A continuous video played at high speed would have shown people sitting, standing, walking; a dog wandering in and out; a cat curled asleep on a sofa or now and then standing to the side of a table, staring up into a bowl of drifting goldfish; an occasional tray of drinks and cookies appearing in the scene and then winking out. For a few intermittent moments, the camera would have recorded Greenstock and her colleagues clustered in a corner talking, every so many hours marveling at the improbability of their mission. What could possibly account for a mobster like Malbonum openly confessing a lifetime of crimes, and in such a carefree manner, when if he had but kept his mouth shut the authorities would never have come close?

By Thursday night, the thick manual that Carverman and Tillinghast would cart into court was complete. Greenstock was satisfied. Malbonum had consented. Tillinghast too. Greenstock called to alert Carverman that things were wrapping up and she was relinquishing active management of the case. Tillinghast rode home in silence to get a night's sleep.

Sisal, presumably, was still in his command bunker overseeing the rounding up of Malbonum's minions though no one outside the panic room had seen him. On Friday evening, immediately after Malbonum's confession had ripened into conviction, Greenstock alerted Vlastic. Calls went out. More agents arrived to reinforce the FBI's skeleton crew monitoring movements at the safe house in West Virginia where Malbonum had sent his associates two nights earlier, ostensibly to avoid capture. The order was to move before the news spread that the boss of these underworld burghers had been taken captive and was "going down the river" for good. As were all his confederates, idly playing pool and awaiting his promised Friday night call. Malbonum wasn't allowed the privilege. In West Virginia, the FBI, in the words of the special agent in charge, subdued the household in "one swell swoop" without incident.

Over the weekend, Malbonum returned to his home to continue singing. Agents wandered in and out, but Malbonum didn't appear to care. He was quiet, passive but cooperative, pressing his thumb against keypads that opened drawers and safes, signing whatever was shoved into his hands, answering all questions put to him. A grounds crew was dispatched to a thickly wooded area behind the house with orders to dig until they found human remains. Carverman returned the case to Greenstock, now that his picture on the front page of most U.S. dailies was consigned to the trash. For Greenstock, the past days were prologue: she had acquired sixty-three additional cases to bring to plea or trial—the largest haul of mobsters bagged in a single net in memory.

By late Sunday afternoon, technicians stowed the recording devices the FBI had set up and confirmed that their electronic sweeps of the house showed Malbonum had none of his own. Most of the agents had withdrawn from Brooklyn, leaving only Helene, Vlastic, and the invisible crew in the panic room. Helene allowed herself a rare moment of introspection when she said, "Everything looks copacetic." Malbonum toasted them with his last cold beer.

The next morning, a squad of federal marshals arrived to take their prisoner into custody. The door opened almost instantly. A scowling Vlastic stood slightly behind his cuffed companion, a sneering, ranting, roaring bear of a man in a track suit and sneakers, spewing abuse at his captor, demanding to know "what the fuck is going on?"

Romo Malbonum had inexplicably had a change of heart. The Deckled Don was bellowing, "Get me my fucking lawyers."

"I'm not your servant, Mr. Malbonum," Vlastic said quietly. "No one's in the house. And you're a convicted federal felon, down for the long count. These marshals are here to escort you to federal incarceration, pursuant to your conviction and while you're awaiting sentencing. I don't know what your game is, but I'd chill out if I were you."

"Prison? Conviction? I have no fucking idea what you're talking about. I'm not going anywhere."

"Yes, you are," said the chief marshal. "You're coming with us right now."

Malbonum was shackled around the ankles and frog-marched to the waiting car.

"I have rights!" Malbonum screamed.

"Not many anymore," Vlastic said and slammed the door on the vacated mansion.

"Case closed?" one of the marshals asked him.

Vlastic looked around the estate as Helene and the other agents scrambled into the one remaining car.

"It is for me," he said. "Until fifteen minutes ago, I'd have thought it was for him too. Now he's having second thoughts, but I guess from here on in it's your problem."

Ten minutes after the marshals and the agents had departed in their separate cars, a back door of the mansion opened and Dewey Sisal emerged alone. He squinted at the sky, looked back down across the yard, climbed into the Honda Civic that had been unobtrusively parked by the side of the garage, and drove in the opposite direction.

CHAPTER 4

RECANT

MALLORY GREENSTOCK COULDN'T REACH DEWEY SISAL. Minutes after hearing of Malbonum's change of heart that morning, she made two calls to the FBI switchboard in Manhattan and four to Sisal's private number. The switchboard promised to relay her messages. For a time Sisal's mobile delivered the same excuse: "I can't take your call right now. I may be in seclusion. If you think you need to hear from me by the day after tomorrow, leave a message." After a time, the mailbox pronounced itself full. Chuck Vlastic's phone had similarly retired.

Greenstock was panicked, then angry and annoyed, and finally exhausted and baffled. Despite every assurance, every promise, Malbonum no longer welcomed his fate. Worse, to anyone who asked he denied complicity in summoning it. He disclaimed acquaintance with the players in his downfall and disavowed awareness of having voiced it. Denounced the miscreants who led the world to believe his confession was truthful, rather than an obvious pack of lies. Derided the book-length list of charges. Declined the guilt that only days before he had embraced as a noble calling. Disparaged the mob howling him on to permanent prison, heedless that he had been defanged, denatured, dismantled.

He was, in short, insanely recanting the unrecantable. Hadn't they recorded it lock, stock, and Farrell—invoking the technician's name was Greenstock's small, unsuccessful attempt to restore herself with humor. Didn't they have Malbonum's affirmative DNA, his negative drug tests, his fingerprints, his ratifications, his waivers, his continuously expressed consent, the voice analysis? Greenstock found herself repeating this speech, telling it to anyone who asked, especially Tillinghast, and her boss, repeatedly to her boss, Glanville L. Carverman. This done deal was a deal done. Malbonum was being lawfully held honestly, honorably, professionally, defensibly, and after sentence doubtless permanently. No review possible.

Except that no matter the earlier pledges, any court in the land would hear a motion to withdraw a plea.

Greenstock importuned Malbonum. "I'll get you Tillinghast. He'll call to explain it."

Malbonum declined, snarling that he'd never heard of this shyster who apparently railroaded him into this "cluster pickle." He refused to believe that straight from West Virginia his own lawyers were unavoidably being detained in a long-term holding cell. Mallory showed him the unedited courtroom video. He watched it twice and returned it two days later proclaiming the lookalike "an obvious actor."

She ordered psychiatrists, more drug tests, forensic teams, sparing no expense. They took ten days and came back concurring: it was the real Malbonum at home, the real Malbonum in court pleading guilty and confessing all, the real Malbonum who assisted the FBI and Greenstock herself before the marshals took him away. And this was the real Malbonum now. He was not on drugs then; his system is clear now; there were no signs he had ever ingested any unlawful substance. He was angry but not crazy. The news media reported the test findings. The Internet demonstrated its carrying capacity. The conspiracy blogs crackled.

Since he could be called as a witness, Tillinghast refused to assist Malbonum further. But he offered free advice in a brief phone call. "They won't withdraw a plea just because you say it wasn't you who pleaded guilty. Anyway, everyone saw you. I'm not sure I'm sorry to say you're stuck. It's what you wanted."

Two days later, a new lawyer in tow, Malbonum was back in court. Greenstock opposed his motion to vacate his plea. The lawyer, out of his depth, put his convicted client on the stand. Malbonum's testimony was extravagant. It ran roughly that his house had been broken into by "thugs who posed as federal agents." He had been cuffed and forced into a chair. He recalled being covered with a red bandanna. "Truth serum time for you," they said. Then he must have been knocked out, because the next thing he knew it was five days later and he was being manhandled by U.S. marshals. He had no memory of entertaining Greenstock and her associates. He did not know Tillinghast. He did not remember eating. He could not explain the videos that showed him doing those things, much less the courtroom oratory. All he could recall, he insisted heatedly, was a "fuzzy sense of being asked some questions by a male voice in a dark room while lying on a bed."

"What did the voice sound like?" Judge Pickscreed asked, puzzled at the flimsy testimony.

"Like a guy's voice."

"But any distinguishing characteristics? High or low, raspy, smooth, steady, uncertain, resolute, sincere, sympathetic, barbaric, overheated. You know, like that."

"Normal guy's voice."

"And you don't know what he asked you."

"Not really. Something about my papers, maybe."

"Maybe?"

"And then my life story, all of it. I never told anyone before then, ever, about my father's disappearance."

"In other words, the same sorts of things they asked you about that we all saw on the home video."

"I suppose. But not my father's story; they didn't ask me that on the videos."

"But you're not denying it."

"I'm not admitting anything."

"And is that all?"

"No, there's more."

"Tell me."

"There's a clincher."

"What's a clincher?"

"Thing proves it wasn't me."

With a fountain pen his clerks had given him on his birthday some months earlier, the judge checked off items on an imposing personal to-do list he had slipped inside the Malbonum case folder. He noticed he had forgotten to call his wife. After a minute he realized the room had fallen quiet because it was his turn to speak. Scowling, he looked around and said, "Okay, let's have it, this clincher."

"There is no copy of *The Common Good* in my library."

Judge Pickscreed pulled his head back, puzzled. "I don't follow."

Malbonum sounded excited. "Don't you see? On the recording of 'my' testimony, at the end, explaining why 'I' had confessed. The guy on that tape said he read a book called *The Common Good* that 'I' found in my library. Well, it isn't there. I don't own it, never even heard of it. Anyway, I wouldn't read it."

"Why not?"

"Don't believe in it. There's your good and my good, and the two aren't common."

"No doubt," the judge said. "Counselor"—he pointed to Malbonum's new lawyer—"did you actually advise your client on this point?"

The lawyer reddened. "We discussed it, Your Honor."

"Not extensively, I hope. Well, this one time, Counselor, I won't hold it against you. Candidly, Mr. Malbonum, I have to say that is the sorriest clunker of a 'clincher' I have ever heard."

"But Your Honor—"

"You do not come into this courtroom and think that you can avoid legal consequences by complaining about a book title you yourself mentioned in court. You'll have plenty of time where you're going to read up on the concept of self-serving testimony. Is there anything else?"

"Your Honor," Malbonum protested unavailingly.

Mallory Greenstock, who had taken her boss's place in the courtroom to oppose the motion, was brief. She offered the experts' considered opinions on Malbonum's identity and presented a forensic pharmacologist who testified that even if some chemical substances could induce a subject to talk against his will, there is no known drug that reliably and consistently leads to truth telling, especially over an extended period of time, such as the six hours and forty-seven minutes Malbonum spent in the courtroom nearly two weeks earlier. In short, Greenstock said, "He can't recant what everyone saw."

Judge Pickscreed took no time to consider. "Motion denied. Off with you, Mr. Malbonum. You might consider reading such a book when you find your new library in whatever common-good facility you might be settling into in a few weeks."

Several days later, it was reported that four other high-profile "perps," until then untouched, had unbidden and cheerfully surrendered themselves "in solidarity with our brother Romo." One was the reputed Los Angeles head of the second largest drug cartel in South America, having no known connection with New York construction companies or their friends; two others were bosses of criminal syndicates in Chicago and Tulsa; the fourth was the Sour Kraut, Genzman Kreutscher, aka the "Alibi King," in San Francisco. For ten million dollars, Kreutscher would provide an airtight alibi for any billionaire charged with underage sex offenses. Somewhat lesser fees applied to alibis for murder and less heinous crimes. Kreutscher was the first of those four to confess in open court to a long list of charges; the other three pleaded guilty twenty-four hours later.

They did not, however, claim to have been sequestered in dark rooms or tell their life stories in court. Their on-camera performances were limited to confessing and narrating lengthy tales of crimes committed over many years. When the U.S. marshals arrived two days after each guilty plea, the now convicted felons squawked as loudly as Malbonum had, repudiating their confessions and avowing absolute incomprehension at their present circumstances. The presiding judges were equally unmoved. The newly unrepentant penitents were whisked away to await sentencing.

Rash columnists, impetuous bloggers, and foolhardy television commentators ventured several incompatible theories. One had it that these arch fiends, collectively known as the Recanters, confessed because the idiots had drunk fouled water—so those with secrets to withhold should drink from sealed bottles. Or the defendants were the victims of some malign force that suspended their will to resist an underground government—so a word to the wise if you've ever sinned: flee to the woods. Or, more wobbly still, these unrepentant sinners were like the villains in popular action novels about a secret agent who takes over other people's bodies just by blinking—so cover your head and face in aluminum foil. Or, it was the Russians or the Chinese or the Iranians, because they can do anything—in which case we're all doomed. One breathless up-and-comer speculated that the mobsters were cloned and tricked into testifying, and it all worked out until the Originals found out. Others had opinions too. Even the president of the United States chimed in, hectoring the crime bosses to "man up."

To all of which sophisticated editorialists sensibly pointed out that however malefic our foreign enemies, they must still obey the laws of physics and biology—they can't body swap or zap people with invisible rays that purge the soul of unholy secrets. After all, Malbonum and his ilk went out of their way to cooperate in demonstrating they really are who they say they are; what more, the sober columnists wondered, needs explaining? Ought we ask the exasperated reader to believe someone with a Star Trek teleporter duplicated the defendants down to their DNA? Likewise, the nitwit who cried cloning is as scientifically uninformed as he is pea-brained—as if a clone would emerge from a vat fully formed, the same apparent age as the Original. And are we to assume that without any signs of surgery someone implanted brain transmitters invisible to body scans, which can be switched on for days at a time? Were the confessions prompted by some form of telepathy, or, holy smokes, an unrevealed law of nature that miraculously struck five prominent crime lords and only them? As for the Russians or the Chinese or the Iranians: really? So the battle wore itself out, from heated brawl to sputtering squabble that eventually departed inside pages and exited the nightly news, until the Recanters were finally banished to the wasteland of late-late cable gabble and Internet loons.

CHAPTER 5

REBUKE

Six weeks had passed since the confession, and still no sign of the FBI agent who had started it all, when Romo Malbonum again stood in Judge Pickscreed's courtroom, this time for sentencing. Malbonum wore exasperation and anger plainly on his face.

Sitting alongside her boss, Mallory Greenstock scanned the courtroom audience. No Sisal. A stir at the front and the bailiff's opening "Oyez" returned her attention to the bench. Judge Pickscreed was making his entrance and went directly to his seat. After hearing from Carverman and the new defense counsel, he turned to the defendant. "Mr. Malbonum, this is your opportunity to say what you will before I pronounce sentence."

"I have nothing to say, Your Honor, except that this whole proceeding has been a sham."

"You did much better your first time in here, Mr. Malbonum. As you know, I have already heard your life story, and I am prepared to accept your earlier testimony as explanation and remorse for your conduct."

"Do what you want," Malbonum said sullenly. "But that was not me in the courtroom."

Judge Pickscreed raised his glasses to his forehead. He fished a tissue from his pocket and dabbed at an eye faintly twitching. He said loudly, "Mr. Carverman, I thought I heard the day of the plea that all that unorthodox testing in the courtroom would keep this man from saying 'that was not me in the courtroom.'"

"I cannot explain it," the U.S. Attorney said. "But we did it to keep him from getting away with it."

"Indeed," the judge said, "and he will not."

He turned to Malbonum. "Your disdain and impertinence cannot help your case."

"It's not my case. It's not any kind of case. I've been framed. Someone's out to get me. It's all a lie."

"I had supposed you would offer me a reason to temper justice with mercy, Mr. Malbonum, in view of the remarkable testimony you offered six weeks ago—that and your evident earnest contrition. But something none of us understands has obviously altered your view."

Judge Pickscreed stared at Malbonum, who was standing at attention alongside his attorney behind the defense table. The judge spoke to him directly.

"This has been the most profoundly astonishing and perplexing proceeding in which I have ever been involved. You voluntarily pleaded guilty to 279 separate felonies. You cooperated unbegrudgingly, at least for a time. You did not resist what I would consider, were I in your shoes, outrageous requests by the government. You expressed remorse—again, for a time. You pledged to help unravel what could be unraveled, and the record indicates you cooperated for two days after your plea. You may remain a valuable asset to the government for years to come. Your childhood recollection had its affecting moments. You have made major charitable donations far and wide over the years. But I have no rake that will sift through the rubble of your story and pile the evil over here so we can measure it against the good in a separate heap over there. How could anyone assess a fair sentence under these circumstances? For once I rejoice that the law has an answer from which there is no escape. The law sentences you; I do not have to."

The judge looked down at notes on his legal pad and indulged in a long sad sigh. When he looked up again, he spoke more resolutely, grateful that this occasion on the bench would be brief.

"As I reckon it," he said, "aided by a lengthy set of computations prepared by Mr. Carverman's able assistants, the minimum sentence—and that means I have no choice in the matter—is 5,022 years, taken in all. To hand you the maximum seems superfluous, and some term below it would be equally bootless and would require a method of balancing that I have already said does not exist. I sentence you, therefore, to the mandatory minimum term of years set forth in the federal statutes for each count, to be served consecutively. As an aside, I observe that since prisoners may be released after serving eighty-five percent of their sentences, you will be eligible for parole sometime around the year 6280 *anno domini*, give or take a decade or two. I further order that you undertake restitution to all your victims to the full extent of your assets, regardless of time limit, under the Mandatory Restitution Act. Do you understand what I have said?"

"Yes, Your Honor," said the haggard man, standing in a shriveled suit that struck Greenstock as more cage than armor. He looked three inches shorter than when he had stood confidently in the same courtroom six weeks earlier to accept responsibility for his life's misdeeds.

Gratifying as the sentence was, Greenstock heard it as background noise against the insistent clamor for understanding. This was not a case but a circus, the courtroom proceedings not the main event but a sideshow. To what, though, she could not imagine. Wearily, she walked the short blocks back to her office, pushed open her door, dropped her purse on the ground, and sank into her desk chair, where she sat dejectedly, her head buzzing. The phone rang.

"Hi," said a voice she remembered, "sorry for taking so long to get back to you."

"Sisal." She sat up straight, reached for a pencil, and held it over the blank page of a legal pad next to her phone.

"Yes. You called?"

"Some weeks ago. I think that emergency has passed. Where have you been?" She didn't expect an answer.

"Busy, as you can imagine," he said.

"Thought I might see you this morning, have a little chat."

"Sorry."

"Too busy to get to court today?"

"Much."

"What I've been reading about?"

"Probably."

She sighed, waiting. The pencil was motionless.

"Everything is jake, then, as our president might say?" He sounded sincere.

"Yes, just peachy. I suppose you can't tell me anything about it."

"I truly cannot. I'm sorry. 'Need to know' and all."

"Nothing you want to let me in on?" she said, her voice dripping in honey-coated venom.

"No."

"How about you have Chuck Vlastic call?"

"Chuck who?"

Greenstock composed herself for several seconds. "You know I can't drop it."

"I think you should, but I'm guessing you'll do what you have to."

"Count on it. I always do."

"I expect nothing less. In the meantime, let me say you were fantastic. It was a pleasure working with you. Doubt the opportunity will present itself again, but if it does, I'll look forward to it."

"Goodbye, Mr. Sisal."

"You have a nice day, counselor."

She kept her hand on the phone for some moments after returning it to its cradle, her eyes trying to resolve the dust in the air in front of her, not seeing the building next door from the window behind her desk. Then with a snap of her head to clear her vision, she reached out a well-manicured finger and buzzed her secretary.

"Lydia, get me Softly."

The White House
Washington, DC 20500

June 12, 3:00 p.m.

A Treat from Your President

No Friend of Mine
(Statement on a Federal Sentencing)

Never has a president, and being one, take it from Me, suffered more than I have, awash like I've had it up to here in unfounded claims and statements about My supposed close personal friendship with a federal prisoner sentenced today. I can scarcely bring myself to name him, Romo Malbonum. Romo Malbonum. Romo Malbonum. All anyone's talking about. Several Press fiends have distorted My earlier Treat on the subject, claiming I referred to this self-confessed crime wave as My friend. Well he's no friend of Americans of that we can be sure. Look what he confessed to. Of course, prosecutors are liars, but assuming some of what they made him say is true, look what that leaves. I barely know the man, if I ever knew him at all. Never met the loser, in fact. Who's to say? It is an utter and despicable fabrication to claim he played a role in Our campaign. It was a spellchecker gone bezonkers in the White House that confused this criminal with My good friend Shlomo Hal Fortnum, who did play an outstanding role in leading our campaign finance team, as everyone knows. I trust that now that the facts are at hand, My lowlife critics will stop making things up and start reporting the Truth. And I say this as a very steady unruffled person.

Action taken: The rogue spellchecker is being wiped clean and then replaced.

Bottom line: America is in real trouble if the leaders of major enterprises can't take a position and stick by it. Never deny what you say by the grace of your free speech. Say something, stand by something. If you say it, man up. Only a wuss recants.

Technical Correction to Presidential Treat, Today's Date: Shlomo Hal Fortnum is the cover name of an agent of the CIA. He is being recalled immediately. The proper rendition of "fiends" is "friends." A new version of White House speller technology will be enhanced with the latest Name Block feature.

The Making of a Detective

*T. R. Softly travels by rail from Washington
to answer Mallory Greenstock's summons.
The monotonous rhythm of movement sinks him
into a revery in which he relives events that have
led to his present pass, beginning with the instigating
moment three decades earlier.*

CHAPTER 6

SOFTLY AWAKENING

WHEN HE WAS NINE YEARS OLD and newly in the fourth grade, T. R. Softly was clocked by a repulsive sixth grader who had just ventured on a career in bullying. It was early in the fall and TR, as everyone called him, was heading home across the field behind the school when without forewarning he was felled by a blow to his jaw and found himself pinned to the ground.

"You got coins?" a surly voice asked from a large, shadowed face that loomed over him, dimming the sunlight. The face looked odd, fringed by a garland of unfocused green leaves, brought inward from the tree branches when his scrambled brain temporarily suspended the third dimension.

TR couldn't make out who it was because he was dizzy and his eyes were teary. If he could have seen his assailant clearly, he still would not have known the face, because the bully—really a bully-in-training who only three weeks earlier had apprenticed himself to a marginally more advanced gang of junior ruffians—spent his school day in a room two floors above TR's fourth-grade class. Too stunned to speak, TR lay mute, suddenly conscious of a throbbing at the back of his head.

"I'm talking to you," the older boy said, pressing against TR's shoulders.

Someone from behind suddenly shouted, "Hey! What's going on?"

As if he had been blown back by a heavy wind, the sixth grader released his prisoner, bounded to his feet, and streaked away across the field. A moment later another indistinct face peered at TR and asked if he was hurt. TR, still flat on the grass, thought he should say no but the word emerged as a sob.

"Whoa, let me help you," said the interloper, a teacher assigned to patrol the field. She offered her hand and hoisted him up. Back on his feet, TR declined an invitation to be escorted to the nurse's station, insisting that he wanted to go home.

"Can you walk?"

"It's only four blocks," TR managed.

"Who was that next to you?" the teacher inquired. She seemed to be stalling him.

"I don't know."

"Did he attack you?"

"He—" TR was not yet adept at the quick comeback.

"Because it looked to me like he was holding you down."

"I tripped," TR offered.

"Is that so?"

"Yes."

"Tripped backwards?"

"I fell," he amended.

She smiled at him. "Well, I see you don't want to say. Maybe it was a simple misunderstanding?"

"Yes."

"Okay, then, but before you go, tell me your name so I can check on you tomorrow."

"T. R. Softly."

"T. R. That's interesting. What do your initials stand for?"

"Nothing."

"Nothing? But they must stand for some name. Your parents gave you letters?"

"Yes."

"Just letters?"

"People call me TR."

"Well, then, TR, you go straight home. Clean up. Rest up. I'll ask for you tomorrow."

He looked at her with uncertainty until she nodded. Then he turned and headed to his house, three and a half blocks away along the well-trod path through the trees on the north side of the school yard. It would not do to have been brought home in a car. Then his mother would know. She would tell his father, and that most particularly would not do. How could he admit to his father he was beaten up, even if a teacher's chance arrival spared him the pulping he would have suffered had he chosen to defend his pocket change?

Intent on regaining the safety of his home, he did not see that a girl, a classmate of the bully's, was following him a discreet distance behind.

He neglected to find a mirror before his mother saw him. From her horrified expression he knew he had miscalculated and now was sunk. She took in the red welt on his cheek, the swelling lump on his head, and the matted grass on the back of his shirt and in her voice of practiced hysteria demanded to know what happened.

"Teddy slipped at school," she told TR's father when he came home from his mail route an hour later. TR's mother was the only one who called her son Teddy, a tribute to the twenty-sixth president. Family legend put TR's great-grandfather in the White House serving the first President Roosevelt. More likely their son was rendered "T. R." to highlight the Softly family surname.

TR's father, a realist and a cynic, wasn't buying TR's story.

"Slipped? No, he didn't," he said, not for the first time calling his son on a bald-faced whopper. "The boy is lying."

Though TR had changed his shirt and combed his hair, his welt had spread and the color deepened.

"But he told me—" his mother began.

"Looks to me he got walloped," his father said, cutting her off brusquely. "What have I told you, TR? Tell it like it happened."

TR backed down immediately, nodding his head in sorrow.

"You did? You got hit?"

"Oh, Teddy," his mother cried.

"Who?" His father was now on the scent.

The story tumbled out.

"And you have no idea who it was?" his father demanded.

"No, I didn't recognize him. He's not in my grade."

"An older boy?" Mr. Softly was outraged. Older boys hitting younger ones was improper, a major breach of the elder Softly's Code of Good Manners & Breeding, a mentally well-thumbed code, often expounded but never committed to paper, among them: *you don't hit girls, you look out for your juniors, and you do not strike without provocation.*

"What are you going to do about it?" his father asked. They were seated in their modest living room, father right next to mother on the pale green sofa. TR perched on a white armchair. The furniture styles did not match, each piece cast off years before by the two sets of grandparents. A side table and a hideous oversized bronze lamp came from a maternal great-aunt. As TR feared, this sit-down was not going to continue as the "what happened at school today?" talk that normally took two minutes at dinner. No, this parley threatened to become a soul-searing search of events from tick to tock with mandatory responses. The threat turned real when TR's initial gambit, an expressive shrug, backfired spectacularly: his father raised his brow, stared TR in the eye, and said, "Don't pretend this will go away."

TR trembled. He had no idea what he was supposed to do. He scratched the back of his head, the sure signal he was feeling frustrated or distressed.

"We could kill him. After you find out who he is," his father essayed.

"Martin Softly!" his mother said in feigned shock, "you know that violates rule number eleven." She winked at TR. "Punishments must be proportionate."

The elder Softly grumbled. "Wanted to make sure everyone is paying attention."

"I could hit him back," TR said, putting his toe into the murky waters of propriety and protocol.

"You could if you knew who he was. And if you could beat him. Do you think you can beat him?"

"Not sure," TR said, trying to suppress the giggles that came on when he didn't know the plan.

"Good. That's an honest answer. And likely not, if he's an older one. He's already clobbered you once."

The father looked the child up and down, as he did every day, waiting for his short, skinny, tousled son to bulk out to fighting height and weight.

"Then—what?" he prodded.

TR sighed. It was clear that his father was returning to his glory days as an army training instructor, embarked now on another of his tutorials for the practical edification of his only offspring. To be expected: it happened at every decent opportunity, at least two nights a week.

"Find out who he is?" TR said hesitantly.

"Excellent first step," his father said, expressionless.

TR could not tell if he was being sarcastic so waited for more.

His father drilled down. "Yes, start there. But how will you do that?"

"Look for him around school."

"But what if he spots you first? What stops him from belting you again?"

"It's recess. There are teachers," TR said, trying to sell his unformed plan.

"Lots of ways to hit someone no matter who is looking," his father said, refusing to buy. "Look, you could wait for him when school's done. How many ways are there out of school?"

"Three that kids can get through."

Mr. Softly beamed. "That's a nice distinction. Good. Okay, well, you take three days, at most. Each day you stand near one of them, hidden. Don't let him see you. You spot him at one of those exits."

"Yeah," TR said, concentrating. His father was laying plans. This could be a good one. But he wasn't going to make it easy. Not his style.

"And if you do spot him, then what? How do you identify him?" The elder Softly stared at his son, willing him to understand the problem.

"I—"

"You follow him."

"Or have friends do that for you. That way he won't know he's being followed," his mother said, surprising him. Ordinarily she discouraged her husband's war plans.

His father indulged her. "That's a good idea, if you've got trustworthy friends up for a little adventure."

TR nodded his head slowly. "Maybe, yeah."

"Where will you follow him?"

"Wherever he's going?"

His father snorted. He looked at TR's mother. "You can't fool our boy," he said with a wink, but then turned back to TR and frowned. "Where do you want him to go? Remind me why you're following him?"

"To find out who he is."

"Yes, that's right. But how will following him help?"

TR kept silent. He was frustrated. Maybe being in the army was harder than he thought.

"Think, boy. Where do *you* go after school?"

"Home."

"Bingo."

TR suddenly understood. "I want to follow him and see where he lives."

"Because if you see where he lives, then you—"

"Have an address."

His father hit his knee with the flat of his hand, in exuberant delight. "And how does an address help you?"

The fog dispersed.

"I tell you!" TR exclaimed.

"Exactly."

"Because you know who everyone is."

"That's what a mailman is for." His father grinned broadly and announced he would wash up for dinner.

The subject was not broached at the table. TR was quiet, silently reviewing the earlier conversation, convincing himself he could carry out the plan. When his father finally pushed his plate to the side, TR's mother backed up, scraping her chair against the bare oak floor.

"Now that we've got everything settled," she smiled, "how about some apple pie?"

She reached for their plates, and in a burst of euphoria TR stood up, without prompting, to help her clear. Sometimes life could be satisfying, even thrilling. TR did not resist lights out. He was eager for the new day.

He rose an hour early, well before his father threw open the door to awaken his son with a hearty "uppen atom," the standard daily greeting. It was clear to TR what the words meant: "The world awaits; there's energy to burn; let's burn it." (TR supposed an "uppen" atom was an energy-bestowing vitamin found in cereal. It was not until the eighth grade, when he came across "at 'em" in Rudyard Kipling or someone that TR realized his mistake, but by then it was much too late to alter his understanding of the phrase. Uppen atom remained a steadfast call to a resolute future each morning of his life.)

That morning he dressed carefully, made his bed, loaded his backpack, and read the rest of *Boys' Life*, which his father had delivered two days earlier. TR took as auspicious that it carried an article about tracking animals in the woods.

In the kitchen, wearing her "world's best mom" apron, his mother said, "You're in a cheery mood." TR nodded, hoping she wouldn't jinx the operation by talking about it. But his mother remembered the rules and set out his usual bowl of cereal without further comment. He ate quickly and was soon out the door, closing it with the usual thud. The brass knocker clanked its daily farewell.

Morning traffic was light. TR was conscious of his footfalls along the sidewalk, and then, half a minute later, of someone talking in a musical voice he did not recognize.

"Why did he hit you?"

The question came from somewhere behind him, perhaps from across the street. TR looked around. Pivoting, he saw an older girl about two steps to his rear, standing in the crook of a mulberry bush on the grassy median dividing the suburban street, which curved to the left three houses down. He turned to her and paused, unsure what she was doing there. Only years later would he come to know that at this moment the trajectory of his life had fundamentally swerved. Now, he merely felt confused.

"Didn't you hear me?"

He remained mute, the puzzlement plain on his face.

"I'm walking to school, same as you," she said. "Come over and let's walk together."

As he crossed the single lane to the median, staring down at the pockmarked speed bump with a painted white X a few feet ahead, she nodded at him and said, "Looks like Junior beat you up bad."

"Who?"

"Junior, the guy who shoved you down on the field yesterday. I can't believe you don't remember?" Like most of her proclamations, the rising inflection was neither fully a question nor a demand for explanation.

TR was unsettled, his brimming confidence and resolve evaporating as he contemplated another stranger invading what had been, until the afternoon before, a relatively carefree existence. He opened his mouth to say something but closed it when he found nothing in his mind worth voicing.

"You must be TR Softly," she said breathlessly. "I saw you come out of the Softlys' house. You wouldn't be there if you aren't TR Softly, would you? I mean, not at this hour, with a backpack."

"I'm—" He finished the thought by nodding. "But—"

He stepped onto the median and looked up. She was a head taller. Her eyes, a piercing green, surrounded by a slight crinkling at the edges, struck TR as inquisitive and amused.

"I'm Khaki," she said, extending her hand. "You can shake it, since this is the first time we're meeting. I don't have girl cooties, or whatever."

Her hand was cool, her shake firm but brief, as if she feared *he* might be a cootie-bearer, though she said nothing to indicate such a belief and did not wipe her hand on her pale red gingham dress. Her hair was auburn, a shade of the dress, and it fell in ringlets to her neck. Taking time to look at her freckled face, it registered on TR as cute although he might have said that about any girl under the circumstances. She happened to be the first one he ever examined up close.

"What are you looking at?" she demanded. "I wiped my face after breakfast."

"When you say you're khaki, I mean, you don't look—"

"That's not my color, dummy; that's my name. Khaki. Khaki Blumenthrace."

"Khaki?"

"Girls in my family have color names. My mother is Violet. Luckily, Amber and Jade were taken. Cousins."

"You go to Archwold Public?"

She opened her mouth in surprise. "Are you really that dumb, chum? I told you. That's why we're walking there, isn't it? I'm in the sixth grade. I have Mrs. Givens. You're in the fourth grade; you have Ms. Drayer."

"How do you know all that about me? How do you know anything about me?"

"I've been investigating," she said, motioning him to keep up as she resumed her tramp down the median. She kept her eyes on the ground to avoid the minor sinkholes that were likely entrances to labyrinths maintained by neighborhood voles and pocket gophers.

"Investigating what?" he demanded.

"Junior. I've been following him since last Friday."

"But he beat me up only yesterday. Why would you follow him last week? And if you followed *me* yesterday, you *couldn't* have followed him."

She snickered. "It doesn't all revolve around you, TR Softly. Listen, my friend, there's a scientific rule against thinking you're at the center of the universe."

"What rule?"

"It's called the Copernicans Rule."

"What's Copernicans?"

"Copernicus. Don't you know anything? He's the scientist who figured out the sun doesn't circle the earth. It's the other way around."

"What's the earth *and* sun got to do with the guy who hit me?"

"Willikers, TR." Her face flushed nearly the color of her hair. "Don't you get it? This isn't about *you*. Well, until yesterday, and anyway, you're only a small part of it. I've been investigating a long time now—more than a week. You're what they call a by-product." She tilted her head to study her new companion. "Boy, we've got a lot of work to do—to get you up to speed, I mean. But forget all that for now. I'll work on that later, once we get this case solved." Why she felt emboldened to declare TR her future mission she could not have said, nor could she explain when TR asked years later. Already at eleven she was self-assured, straightforward, unafraid, and unpretentious though exuding a faint air of superiority, as if to announce, "I'm grand, but I recognize that's not your fault, so I won't lord it over you."

TR shook his head and stamped his foot in frustration. "What case? I don't understand what you're saying."

"I'm sorry," she said. "My dad says I talk too much sometimes and don't explain myself very well. I'll try to be clear. I'm a detective." She paused for a moment. "But keep that to yourself."

"But you're just—"

"What, a girl?" Her eyes narrowed.

"A sixth-grader," he responded.

"So what? I've read all of Nancy Drew. I've been working on cases since I was your age, or younger."

"And you've been following somebody named Junior—"

"The guy who socked you yesterday after school. I saw him do that. I saw Mrs. Givens get you up."

"That was your teacher?"

"Sure. And when you left, I followed you home. How else do you think I found you this morning?"

"But *why?*"

They had now walked down the median to its ending in a T on Middlefield Road, which fronted the school. The large archway entrance recessed thirty feet from the sidewalk. The path to the five wide stone steps leading up to the main dark oak doors was crowded with elementary schoolers scurrying to beat the bell.

"I'll tell you later. Meet me here when school lets out. Okay?"

"I suppose, sure," he said, realizing he no longer had any reason to follow the bully to his lair. Khaki Blumenthrace already knew who he was.

"Fine stuff," she said brightly, and hurried ahead of him without a backward glance.

TR's gloom gradually dissipated. By lunch time he was filling with optimism. By early afternoon a sense of euphoria overpowered him, deafening him to his classmates' jeers when he failed to respond to Ms. Drayer's repeated directives to solve a math problem on the blackboard. He scooted out the door when the bell rang, arriving at the three o'clock rendezvous ten minutes early. He leaned against a stone pillar that edged the front steps. It was topped by a bronze eagle that the friskier, older students swaddled in shoestrings, threadbare scarves, and oddments of yarn. He felt his head pounding as he awaited the revelations Khaki had promised.

He saw the red dress before he saw her stepping from the dark interior of the school lobby onto the brilliant sun-drenched stairs. A taller figure stood beside her, whom he made out as Mrs. Givens only when they came much nearer. It appeared that Khaki was holding her hand and practically pulling her toward TR.

"This is my friend TR," Khaki said when they stood next to him. "He's my neighbor."

"My goodness," Mrs. Givens said, suppressing a smile as she turned into a small patch of shade and removed her sunglasses, letting them dangle from a light blue chain around her neck, "is there anyone you don't know?"

"Not many," Khaki replied without irony or amusement. Facts Are Facts was a maxim she lived by.

With a start, TR now noticed that Khaki wore transparent braces on her teeth, but she was smiling openly, not at all self-conscious.

"This is Mrs. Givens," Khaki said, looking him in the eyes. "You met her yesterday."

"Yes, we did," the teacher said. "And I told you I wanted to check up on how you are."

"I'm okay," TR said, reddening. He felt the flush and would have blamed it on the bright sun had anyone been cruel enough to mention it.

"You do look better," Mrs. Givens said, her gaze lingering on the welt still visible on his face. "And I'd ask you more about what happened, but Khaki assures me she's got the situation in hand and will make sure it doesn't happen again. Is that right? Are you comfortable with that?"

"That's—yes," he said.

"All right," the teacher said, "but if it does happen again, I want your word that I will hear about it because I won't have a thing like that in my school."

"Yes, ma'am," TR said, as if responding to a drill sergeant.

"You certainly are a lucky boy to have such a friend," Mrs. Givens added. She nodded at each of her young charges and walked back into the building.

"Isn't she neat?" Khaki said with an exuberant whoop. "I just love her."

"You promised to tell me," he said, impatient to avoid wasted time and sentiments.

"I did, and I will. Let's go get ice cream. Follow me."

Giving TR no chance to protest, she marched two streets over to Town Center, a grid of blocks surrounding a park with benches. The park encircled a municipal hall, the mayor's office, and the police station. On the blocks facing the park sat the public library, a recreation center, and a raft of stores, including a pizzeria, laundromat, nail salon, sports emporium, consignment shop, bank, the Center Luncheonette, and Jolly's, the stationery and notions boutique. Some storefronts stood empty, victims of a recession now happily receding. A recently opened bookstore was shuttered. You had to go many blocks over, behind the older mall with the supermarket, hardware store, diner, and Chinese restaurant, to find the aging Cropcross Book Annex, with a gloom from the 1930s that shrouded its twisty aisles in darkness and which would be a source of delight and mystery for TR when later, in high school, he engaged the proprietor in long conversations about the book business. At the far end of Town Center stood the Cone and Scoop, an ice cream parlor catering to school children with pocket change.

Khaki paid for TR's ice cream, after hearing his confession of indigence, "but no more than two scoops—and in a dish." (Cones were fifteen cents extra.)

Seated, she now told him the story. It had started twelve days earlier when the girl who sat behind her reported that she had been accosted by their mutual classmate, Junior Skootums, until recently the class clown, who had become dark and hostile. During recess he had demanded that the girl pay him fifty cents a week or she'd be sorry. Khaki said she'd get right on it.

She began watching Junior's movements, noting his habits and his "points of contact." One day she followed him home. She saw the others whose gang he appeared to want to join and the kids he appeared to be menacing. She also learned where the gang members lived. She had seen that TR was one of their targets. She decided to approach him because he was Junior's sole non-sixth grade prey and might not as clearly understand his peril. She tore a page from a spiral bound notepad, printed four names and addresses with a purple pen, and told him to tuck the piece of paper in his pocket.

By the time TR burst through the front door his father had already changed and was waiting for him with his mother at the white Formica kitchen table, nibbling from a bowl of peanuts.

"You look happy," his mother said.

"I know who they are," TR hooted, letting his backpack thump against the wall behind his chair.

"Already?" his father asked with a look of some surprise. "You got it all?"

"The guy who hit me, his name's Junior, he's in the sixth grade. He lives at 3215 Dumont Street—"

"That's the Skootums," his father said.

"Yep."

"It's the corner clapboard house with the half porch, three blocks over from the Shell station along Belroona. Did you see him go in?"

"Well, no."

"Then how do you know—"

TR interrupted with a breathless account of the day. When he concluded, he could tell from the puzzlement on their faces that his presentation had been less than orderly. He'd have to work on that. He pulled out the scrap of paper that Khaki gave him and showed it to his father.

"These are them?"

"The other three guys, they're older."

"I thought they were all older."

"I mean older than Khaki."

Martin Softly regarded his son for a long moment. "This new friend of yours, Khaki, what's her last name?"

"Oh, it's like Blumen-something, Blumenthrock, Blumen—"

"Blumenthrace?"

TR nodded.

"On 38 Nebbles Street," his father said. "A couple of blocks over. Blumenthrace. He was in the army too. Or has something to do with it. He gets stuff from them now and then. They get both papers."

Former Staff Sgt. Martin Softly was discomfited by the people in town, including some of his friends, who subscribed to *The Daily Ledger Herald*, the more liberal afternoon paper. He swore by *The Excelsior Union Gazette*, the right-of-center morning paper that he read at four-thirty before dinner. But he usually found a way to be pleasant to those who took both.

"This Khaki Blumenthrace," Martin asked, "how long did you say you've known her?"

"Since this morning."

TR's father let loose with one of his patented belly laughs. His mother grinned broadly.

"That long, huh? Do you trust her?"

"Why shouldn't I? She's nice."

"She did buy him ice cream, Martin," his mother pointed out.

"That clinches it," his father said, still laughing. "Well, all right, what's your next step?"

TR was silent.

"What your next step should be," his mother intervened, "is that you should write it down."

"You mean this?" TR asked, picking up Khaki's note and waving it. "It's already down."

"Not good enough, Teddy." She was now talking in her librarian's voice.

She got up from the table, opened a kitchen drawer, and took out several three-by-five note cards.

"Here's what I think," she said. "You take one of these cards for every person in this story. You write down their names, last name first, up here, see, in the upper left corner, and you date the card. And then put down what you know about them."

"Like what?" TR asked.

"Well, you know where they live; write down their addresses. You know they know each other; write that down too, like, say, 'acquainted with' or 'connected to.' And whatever else you know. Like this bounder, put down he hit you yesterday and that he's in Khaki's class. You get the idea, you know, like every library book has a card. Every person should have one too."

"What's a bounder?"

"A rotten fellow," said his father. "That's a good idea, what your mother suggests. Why don't you go do that, before dinner, so you don't forget."

His mother had her head inside a lower cabinet, looking for something. She pushed aside a pile of shopping bags and eventually extracted a metal box with a silver oval handle on the top. Etched on the front were the words "S & H Green Stamps." She handed it to her son.

"Put your cards in there. It'll fit them fine."

She stood up and fished in her purse for her wallet. She handed TR two crisp one-dollar bills. "Buy a whole pack of cards tomorrow down at Jolly's." Then she smiled more broadly and brought forth two more bills. "And keep this for emergencies. You never know when you might need to buy a lady some ice cream. Now scat you two, I'm cooking dinner."

TR went to his room to inscribe his notes. "SKOOTUMS, Junior," he wrote on the top left, followed by the date. Had he been asked, he would have confidently asserted he had been restored, after an aberrant twenty-six hours, to his quiet fourth-grade life. But in that subconscious belief he was entirely mistaken. The poke of fate that morning was a diffuse nudge away from suburban mediocrity though to no defined shoreline. By late afternoon it had become a robustly focused force propelling him toward a future with more precise features and from which he would be powerless to escape, even had he wanted to. Though he would eventually make landfall far from his hometown, he began his life's journey in his room then and there, having been irresistibly drawn into the orbit of the town's most eccentric creation.

For her part, had she been pressed to explain her actions, Khaki might have said that TR was her Pygmalion. Though she had consigned her dolls to the attic when she was seven (after spending two years naming, tagging, cataloguing, and assigning them to an elaborate genealogy), she viewed her new acquaintance as the next step up, a pliable child whom she could fashion as she wished, without having to feed and clothe him or remind him to brush his teeth. TR was to be her first sustained experiment in psychology.

She was waiting for him by his front door the next morning at eight, a practice that became settled for the next seven years—all the rest of their school days together. In her breathless style she said she had solved "the Junior problem." She plucked a note from her backpack and thrust it at him. With widening eyes, he read the block lettering. Her spelling and rhetorical flow were not yet informed by the maturity of her later reading:

> *I talked to my uncle. He's an army ranger sniper. He knows how to*
> *shoot people and wound them without killing them. He says he will*

shoot Jr's parents in their knee if Jr. doesn't back off and quit his gang
&or hits anyone ever again. He can exspect it to happen at any time.

The rest of the plan was simple. She would pass the note to TR when Junior was watching. Because he was that kind of nasty boy, Junior would yank it away before TR could see it and run away to read it and be scared and that would be that.

TR demurred. "That's a bad plan," he said.

Khaki glowered. She did not like being contradicted by her juniors. "Why?"

"Because it isn't true, is it? You could get in trouble if Junior shows the note to anybody, like Mrs. Givens. If Junior doesn't believe it, he'll get mad at us, and we'll never get rid of him."

"I do have an uncle," she insisted. "And he is in the army."

"But you wouldn't ask him to shoot someone, would you? And anyway, he wouldn't ever do it, would he? Plus you spelled 'expect' wrong."

Khaki considered his objections, concurring reluctantly. "Then what do you think we should do?"

"My father will take care of it," TR said brashly, because his father could take care of anything.

TR relied heavily on that knowledge when he presented the unassailable logic of his own plan that evening at dinner, after telling his parents about Khaki's idea and his rejection of it. His father harrumphed. But his mother spoke up and said what TR suggested made sense.

"You could go talk to this Junior, in that special way of yours," she said sweetly, arching a single eyebrow, a gesture that invariably prompted in her husband a wave of affection and desire for his helpmeet. Martin affected to think it over, but the instant she spoke he was persuaded.

"Tell you what," he said. "Think you can get this Junior to meet you with his pals tomorrow night at the corner of the schoolyard? About, let's say, eight o'clock?"

TR nodded.

"How will you arrange that?"

"I'll ask him."

"That's one way to do it," his father said. He rose from the table. "I'll get the coffee, Luana."

His mother blushed. Becoming the waiter meant he was pleased as punch at his wife's daring stratagem.

TR told Khaki of the plan the next morning and she volunteered to carry the invitation to Junior and demand he accept it. Which he did. That evening, at two minutes before the hour, Martin walked calmly and slowly to the appointed place with TR.

"We won't show ourselves until they're all there," he said.

As father and son approached, TR whispered to his father that the four louts were assembled.

"Good. You go over there and talk to them."

"You're not coming? What will I say?" TR was suddenly anxious.

"I'll be coming from the other direction, don't you worry."

Thus emboldened, TR walked straight across the street and onto the school grounds. Junior and his three overseers watched him coming.

"What you got for us?" one of the older ones said when he got close.

"Nothing," said TR.

The four boys turned to face the oncoming fourth grader, disbelieving his denial.

"What? But Khaki said—," Junior began.

At which point Martin, who had circled the massive trunk of an old sycamore on the edge of the schoolyard, came around noiselessly, behind TR's interlocutors. He grabbed Junior and one of the other boys by their upper arms. A paralyzing fear gripped their vocal cords, stifling screams. The other two boys scattered but not before one snarled, a bit tremulously, "You'll never catch me, sucker."

Junior and his caught companion were shaking.

TR was about to speak when his father barked, "No names. Say nothing."

TR froze. This had not been part of the plan.

"You," said Martin to his son, "I want you away from here. Go home. Wherever that is."

"Please!" Junior whimpered.

Unable to contain himself entirely, TR smirked at his tormentors, and then walked briskly away. Five minutes later, he was home. Ten minutes after that, his father opened the door.

"What happened?" TR, on tenterhooks, asked.

"They won't bother you or your friends again," his father said unemotionally.

"But what did you—"

"Let's just say I taught them the wisdom of forbearance. I'll explain when you get taller." The subject was now closed.

The White House
Washington, DC 20500

June 12, 4:15 p.m.

A Treat from Your President

Close Those Borders
(Statement on Immigration Reform)

A Presidential Treat earlier this morning indicated that under the terms of a Major Immigration Reform proposed by the White House at 8 a.m. this date, all persons with invalid visas, technically defaulted green cards, or without other valid documentation ("undocumented non-citizen border crashers") will be deported within 48 hours of Notice of Non-Documentational Status to one of several dozen lands now denominated as Colonies of Major Countries of the World and which the United States would undertake to acquire such as the Bahamas, Greenland, and the Falkland Islands, either by purchase or under power of Eminent Co-Jefe.

It has come to My attention that among the named territories on the extensive list attached to the draft proposal were Canada and Virginia. After extensive study, the Secretary of Commerce has determined that Canada and Virginia are no longer colonies of any World Power. Department policy planners consulted an outdated register of colonial dependencies improperly classified as current in the Department's Registry of Colonies. American people #BeAssured no one currently working in this Administration was responsible for this trifling error (or any error), nor will such be tolerated in any future moment ahead. Only Top-Notch People.

Action taken: The Registry has been corrected. All outdated lists have been returned to deep archives, access restricted. The nitwit responsible for consulting the bad register is Margaret Tangiers, a low-level clerk in the Department's Office of Colony Registration. Effective now, Margaret Tangiers, you're fired.

Technical Correction to Earlier Post of Correction of a Presidential Treat: Margaret Tangiers' official title was Director, Office of Colony Registration, U.S. Department of Commerce. Unknown at this time is whether she is the Margaret Tangiers who is niece of the President's sister-in-law. An errant White House spellchecker was responsible for rendering "Domain" as "Co-Jefe" in the corrected Treat. The spellchecker has been replaced.

CHAPTER 7

SOFTLY ASSEMBLING

FOR SEVERAL WEEKS AFTER THE BULLY'S threat had been, in Khaki's word, "neutered," TR could be forgiven for thinking his life had changed only in acquiring Khaki as a new friend. That the two walked together to and from school most days thereafter was to him no oddity though his parents would have been perplexed, for the first few months at least, had they been fully aware of this daily routine. They did note that their son had become more resolute, concentrating more assiduously on his tasks, including those he assigned himself.

Every afternoon before dinner, while his father read the paper, TR inscribed data on his growing collection of note cards and fought off the family cat, Qwerty Uiop, who thought she had prior claim to the interior of the card box and would pounce from a higher vantage whenever TR opened the lid. (TR's mother claimed, in the usual version of the story, that the cat had named herself when one day as a kitten she walked along the top row of Mrs. Softly's Smith Corona portable electric typewriter.) By Thanksgiving, the card collection had outgrown the tin box, prompting TR to ask for a paid job around the house so he could buy a bigger one.

On most of their school walks, Khaki prattled about detective work. Much of what she expounded was her version of Nancy Drew plots. The enthusiasm in her voice warmed him to their telling, and before long he relished his growing skill at solving the mysteries before her tales ended. But Khaki talked of other things too, invoking split infinitives and electromagnetism, notions that baffled him.

"I can't talk to you if you don't know things," she said. "We've got to move you along. I will teach you everything you'll need to know to jump ahead."

In mid-October, Khaki offered him a lesson in "tailing a suspect." The following Saturday morning they met in Town Center in front of Merton's Sports Emporium. Khaki was waiting for him. She signaled silence with a finger to her lips and withdrew into the recessed entrance to the Center Luncheonette next door, where she whispered, "I saw this guy go in Merton's. We're going to tail him."

"Why?"

She frowned at him, as if to say, wasn't that why they had gathered there?

"I mean, why him?" he asked.

"He looks worth trying to follow. Not a pushover."

They waited in silence. The man emerged a few minutes later carrying a shopping bag. He was tall, six feet at least, clean-shaven, trim, with a square jaw, a long thin nose, and close-cut light brown hair. He wore a leather bomber jacket, tan slacks, rubber soled boat shoes, and a pair of dark blue wraparound sunglasses. He walked briskly, away from his aspiring trackers, as if overdue for an important appointment. When he was three doors down, Khaki whispered, "Come on," and they fast walked to catch up. When the man paused at the corner light, Khaki spun around to peer into an adjacent store window.

"Don't let him see you looking at him," she hissed.

TR turned on his heel to follow her gaze away from the corner. The light changed and their quarry strode into the crosswalk. Khaki scurried into the intersection, some twenty steps behind. TR followed close, swerving to avoid other, more leisurely, pedestrians. But the man was already across the street and suddenly he disappeared behind a row of luxuriant yellowing aspens that ran the length of the block. They paused on the far curb, squinting into the blinding sunlight, straining to spot him. People milled about on the sidewalk, but none resembled their target. TR turned full circle, thinking the man might have crossed to the far side of the street. But he saw nothing. They had lost him.

Khaki shrugged disconsolately. "Willikers," she said, walking slowly and aimlessly a few feet down the block, then pausing opposite a long, backless stone bench by a sheltered bus stop. TR stopped next to her. "He beat us," she told him.

From three feet away they heard a sudden hiss. "Are you kids following me?" the man said. He was sitting on the bench, his back to the street, staring at them. His bag was open, revealing two yellow and red bungee cords ending in black hooks. They looked to TR like deadly whips. He froze in fear.

"Oh, Daddy, you're scaring him!" Khaki said almost imperiously, and then fell into a fit of giggling.

TR noticeably sighed as Mr. Blumenthrace stuffed the bungee cords back in the Merton's shopping bag.

"This is TR," she told her father.

"Well, my goodness, the famous TR Softly," her father said without a trace of condescension. He stood up straight, extending his arm. "Angus Blumenthrace. I am indeed pleased to meet you."

Unaccustomed to the ritual but minding his manners, TR shook his hand.

"Come, let's talk," Mr. Blumenthrace continued. "I simply must learn all about this marvelous young man Khaki appears to dote on. Have you eaten? Let's get something. Follow me."

He marched them at a fast clip back across the street. Khaki scrambled in the intersection to clutch his hand. TR jogged behind, not closing the distance until Mr. Blumenthrace held the door for him at the luncheonette where they had tried to be inconspicuous some minutes earlier. Khaki's father took them to a booth in the back, told them to order liberally from the menu, and then peppered TR with questions as if they were the oldest friends catching up after a long separation. Mr. Blumenthrace learned all about mother Luana the librarian, Martin the mailman father who knew everyone's address, and TR's hobby, people cataloguing.

"And what are you interested in?" he asked, as TR licked his fork clean of the apple pie sinfully eaten before lunch. "You know, after the fourth grade. What do you plan to do with your life?"

"Khaki is teaching me how to be a detective," he answered openly.

"Is she now? How marvelous!" Khaki's father said, as if no one would wonder at TR's sincere proclamation that a fourth grader would soon become proficient in an art that often deflates even its most seasoned practitioners. Especially Mr. Blumenthrace, who, it developed, was himself a detective first grade with the municipal police department although TR did not discover this astonishing detail until Thanksgiving, when the two families officially met over a turkey dinner at the Blumenthrace home. At that same dinner, the two fathers seeded a friendship, nurtured by shared memories of their military service in Vietnam. Martin had been a supply sergeant, Angus a major in military intelligence. But that day at the luncheonette, thrusting money on the table and rising at last, Khaki's father said he was overdue at home, where he had to employ the bungee cords on a tipsy pair of boxes in the garage and then escort Khaki's mother to a long-awaited garden party.

"All in a day's work," he said with a parting wink.

On the last day of school before the winter holidays, Khaki handed TR a festive green and red envelope with his name in white marker in her inimitable block script across most of the front.

"Put this under your tree," she commanded him, and "don't open it until Christmas."

Khaki and her family would be visiting her mother's family, an overnight car trip away. TR's aunt and uncle, his father's brother and wife, and his loathsome older cousin Sterling would be celebrating Christmas at his house. In past years, TR would have moped, but this year he saw the advantage of ten days' freedom from school: he could bring his name catalogue up to date.

The first weeks after the day he enrolled Junior Skootums's name on Card Number One, TR diligently conscripted a new card for each new person he encountered. His entire fourth grade class was now in the box. School staff (principal, janitor, teachers he knew), some of Khaki's friends, and his mother's co-workers were gradually settling onto their own cards. But the more he thought about it, the more his project threatened to overwhelm him. He was reduced to scribbling into a notebook from which he would transcribe onto cards on the weekends. In recent days, not only schoolmates shared space in the catalogue but also waitresses at the luncheonette, the salesclerks at Jolly's, and many others TR encountered. He made a point of learning at least one new thing about anyone he met. If he talked to a bus driver, he would record the exchange: "Pete, how long you been riding these buses?" The answer, "thirty-two years," would be inscribed on Pete's card. By Christmas, TR's catalogue housed three hundred people. On many cards he noted connections: "knows mom" (on later cards rendered "LS"); "friend of Khaki's" (who became KB; and the notation, "FoKB"). He finished his labors two hours before his unloved relations arrived the afternoon of Christmas Eve, their false enthusiasm grating him as it did at each of their holiday reunions.

The next morning all six gathered around the tree. The two children strained to reach for gaily wrapped presents on the outer edges of the fir's lower needles. TR had long since mastered the

Protocol of Presents, as Martin Softly labeled it the year TR discovered the trick. He memorized the location of the largest of each present for the adults, and as the parents reclined in their elegant holiday bathrobes (worn exclusively when entertaining—or being—guests) and sipped from their mugs, he handed the largest wrapped gift to each.

"Why, that's so sweet of you," Aunt Doxie gushed, putting down her mug to receive the box.

As she tore at the wrapping, TR distributed the other three, which allowed him to herd his own presents outside the tree's skirt. He regarded the four boxes of varying dimensions, and also a letter that days earlier he himself had placed on the largest box, sitting against the side wall. Ignoring cousin Sterling altogether, TR pushed aside Qwerty Uiop the cat, who had been perched atop his boxes, surveying the room for a hint of food. Sterling uttered a shriek when Qwerty landed on his lap. The cat leaped down and walked away, tail high. TR shook his head in disgust at Sterling, took the envelope, and leaning back in a chair next to the boxes carefully opened the flap.

"That's the best one?" Uncle Evan said, surprised that TR had left the more solid offerings for later.

"It must be," TR's mother said, "it's the one from Khaki."

"It looks like a letter," Evan said, his puzzlement continuing.

"Khaki is his friend, not a store," Luana explained.

TR held the card inside the envelope in both hands and stared at it. The adults ceased tearing at their packages. The sudden quiet made TR's "Hey" all the louder when Sterling snatched the card and smiling odiously read it aloud:

This card can be exchanged for lessons bringing you up to speed, guaranteed to save you one complete year of school. Signed: Your friend Khaki (Blumenthrace). P.S. This is serious. P.P.S. I mean it. P.P.P.S. If you accept, you have to do it. P.P.P.P.S. There's a quiz at the end.

Cousin Sterling's high-pitched guffaws ended abruptly when he realized that the rest of the room had fallen silent.

"What does that mean?" Aunt Doxie asked.

"Why that's—" Martin sputtered. "What *does* that mean, TR?"

"She's going to give him the answers to the fifth-grade quizzes next year?" Luana suggested.

TR shook his head and studied the note intently for a few seconds. Then his face lit up in embarrassment.

"She's going to get me skipped a grade."

"No kidding?" his father said, slapping his thigh. "Can she do that?"

"The better question is can Teddy do that," his mother said, her eyes glistening. "And I'm sure he can."

"Well, isn't that nice," Aunt Doxie said. The room resumed its ritual unwrapping and the conversation drifted on with requisite oohs for revealed but unwanted gewgaws. No further comment was addressed to parsing Khaki's note though TR's relatives did look askance at the shiny black 1,000-card box with the pull-out drawer that he eventually liberated from a box along the wall. (TR thought the drawer might last him all the way through high school. He was overly optimistic: it topped out fifteen months later.)

Khaki showed up three days before New Year's to begin her tutoring. She gave TR one month to polish off the rest of fourth grade—the easy part, she said—and the next four months to learn all of the fifth. Khaki was not an intuitive teacher, so TR became an intuitive student. He learned to explain just what it was he was not understanding, and she would come back the next day with an improved lesson plan. She plied him with books and quizzed him on their content. He read about Copernicus. He wondered why Nancy Drew's adventures were integral to the fourth-grade curriculum but never complained to Khaki about it; he simply dug in. By March, he had plunged into Edgar Allan Poe and Arthur Conan Doyle at her father's suggestion, after TR explained to him one

Saturday at the luncheonette that the world's greatest detective was Nancy Drew. (His views altered in the years ahead.)

As Khaki sped him through the fourth grade, TR learned to rely on a dictionary, mastered the multiplication tables, undertook fractions, saw patterns that emerged from the equations in his math book. He learned there were more important leaders than Cub Scout den mothers and mayors and absorbed the fourth-grade account of governors, legislators, judges, and presidents, which the textbooks simplified to the point of fiction. Fifth-grade social studies took him into maps, a bird's eye history of the U.S., and its system of checks and balances. Mastering the fifth-grade "hard" vocabulary took a week. Fifth-grade science lightly surveyed elementary biology (including a murky process called evolution), atomic structure (electrons whizzing around nuclei), and meteorology (cloud names and a loose version of the atmospheric carbon cycle). Some sciences he found more entertaining than others; some more practical; and some, like geology, seemed useless, until he read that the great Sherlock Holmes knew all about soil samples. Sometimes TR flagged. For a time he regretted the loss of his nightly television programs until he concluded they were boring and that it was much more gratifying to prove to Khaki she was succeeding as a teacher. He felt that she had become his treasured older sister and he could not let her down. She wanted him to skip a grade, so he would learn what he needed to do to justify her effort and her faith.

During spring break, Khaki decreed a pause in the formal course work. This week, she announced, would be devoted to pleasant diversion. TR would develop a sense of humor, which she would deliver first through the art of punning (and when he mastered the form, he could move on to witty epigrams and majestic aphorisms). For elementary school, though, puns would do. TR reacted to her sober announcement as he always did, demanding to know what she meant and why it was necessary, and then, regardless of her answer, acquiescing. She regaled him with puns that would excite fifth graders who might understand them and seventh graders who were not yet fully acculturated to penning the panning of punning. Q: "How can you tell Santa is in the room?" A: "You can feel his presents." Khaki thought that a pretty good one, and it neatly illustrated the architecture of the genre. She made it clear that adults would groan at all the punning riddles she urged on him. Most adults, having squandered their cleverness by attending stupid schools and closing their minds to everything not on the reading list, couldn't own up to verbal elegance; they sneered to cover their insecurity. Khaki told TR to stow his anxiety if he couldn't deliver choice puns immediately. They would ripen with his vocabulary. The week passed by uneventfully though she was much amused by her own dandy witticism when Spot, a neighborhood dog, did its business one morning on the painted speed bump near TR's home.

"Look," she said, pointing an outstretched finger at the dog, "Spot marks the X."

One Saturday in May, short on index cards, he said he'd race her to Jolly's. He beat her by fifteen seconds. She bent over and held her knees, gulping for air. Talking over her wheezing, he asked her a question.

"What does the inside of a clothing store share with an outside run to it?"

Still catching her breath, she shook her head.

"Khaki pants," he said.

Puzzled, she stood up straight, then understood and hugged him. She was bewitched and wanted to show him off. He was her handiwork, and she now knew they would not dare reject his bid to skip the fifth grade though she wasn't clear why she couldn't negotiate the deal directly with Mrs. Givens. Khaki broached her scheme at the end of the month, and all Mrs. Givens would say was, "My goodness, Khaki, what a plan."

When Khaki raised the issue more formally in early June, Mrs. Givens explained that these sorts of decisions must be worked out between parents and the principal and that she had already broached the idea with the elder Softlys. That satisfied Khaki, since the matter was, after all, being attended to by the top bananas, as her father called anyone in charge. TR's parents were not at all surprised when the principal called them in to talk it over. Mrs. Givens was in the room, and because they were all in accord, TR had his papers stamped that day.

Khaki enrolled in an arts and crafts summer camp. She assumed TR would join her in the eight-week session at the local Y; they could walk together. But TR had other plans, which he announced to his parents at dinner after the last day of school: karate lessons at a dojo in the mall near the Cropcross Book Annex. The senseis accepted students who were at least ten, an age that had been ripening on TR for three months. Martin Softly was delighted and Luana accepted her husband's solemn declaration that no one ever got hurt learning martial arts. At least, he told himself silently, not much at the age of ten.

The White House
Washington, DC 20500

June 13, 6:00 a.m.

A Treat from Your President

States' Rites
(Statement on a Plan to Reinvigorate America)

A lot of blather blah, blah, blah about getting things moving again after skittish markets insanely tanked and I'm just the person to do it because America moves with Me and My trucking company. And has been for practically forever. America moves on trucks. Always moving. But do it right. The opposition notice I'm not saying "loyal" wants to give your money to the government to spend. But government always spends wrong. My plan is at very top genius level because I'm reversing money flow. Always about flow. Ask anyone. Person standing next to you. You have to turn, open mouth, talk. Try it. Like flowing waters and streams. And think of when a dam breaks. Water crashing through. Powerful. Here's plan language from lawyers. So simple. "All bona fide companies incorporated in America may bid at public auction for the exclusive right to substitute their names for home state names on all official documents." Campbell Soup, headquartered in Camden, could stake out New Jersey. Two proud new words for the Garden State: Camden, CS. Of course no shooting old-timers for still calling it Jersey. But you could fine them. Huge incentive for entrepreneurs. It's the free market rite of branding. States, why shouldn't you be able to cash in? It's your name. Sell it.

Action taken: Submitted to Congress. Pass in a week.

Bottom line: The dumb knuckle economists will shut up once our little recession is nipped in the bud.

Technical Correction to the Presidential Treat, Today's Date: Federal legislation affecting names of states is unconstitutional and was not intended to be and is not being forwarded to Congress. A superannuated spellchecker mistook the word "plates" for "states" and omitted "except the military" from "government always spends wrong." As the president said at his morning press conference, "Idea is to auction rights to state license plates. It's recession poof! Selling spell checker too if anyone wants it. Check eBay listings. Will autograph. Ha ha!"

CHAPTER 8

SOFTLY ASCENDING

THE EDUCATION OF T. R. SOFTLY proceeded apace. Khaki bided her time, hoarding her surprises, telling him in the second week of his studies in the sixth grade that he would soon be back in training to skip the seventh grade as well, so that the following year they could at last take classes together. Reviewing seventh-grade lessons while taking sixth-grade courses proved far less troublesome than what TR had to endure the year before. Learning had now become a skill and a habit.

His new classmates knew they had a star in their midst and did not press their advantage in weight or height except for one burly boy two rows over who decided to take TR down after school one day in early November but found to his dismay that the "skinny little short kid" he detested for being smarter was also a darn sight faster or slipperier or luckier. The onlookers applauded in astonished admiration when the burly boy found himself on the ground with a bruised shin, scraped elbows, and, judging from his throaty groans, other minor injuries. The challenger did not press his claims again, and TR was secretly regarded as awesome by several of the girls. TR paid them no attention—in his world girls were, at most, simply friends.

In March, turning eleven, he bought his next thousand-card pull-out card drawer. He finally grasped that the task he had set for himself, to catalogue everyone he met or who was known to someone he knew and to set out the particulars of the connection, lay in a complex dimension he was only beginning to perceive. It was not just that the people eligible for inclusion multiplied at ever increasing rates, requiring new cards weekly. It also was becoming clear that a card was always incomplete. As new information became available, TR was frequently forced to return to cards already settled in the boxes. At the age of eleven he did not lose sleep over these difficulties, because his thoughts did not venture far into the future. Echoing his father, he regularly said to himself, and occasionally out loud to others when presented with problems he was able to forestall, "I'll tackle that when I'm taller."

The solution to his record-keeping problems presented itself fortuitously a year later in the spring of the eighth grade, into which he had been duly deposited as Khaki had schemed. The evening news had broadcast a story about a postal truck hijacking in which the thieves made off with more than $80,000 in cash being transported from the main post office to its bank. A witness to the heist said that one of the two masked bandits shouted out the window "You'll never catch me, sucker" at a cursing postal driver who had been pushed to the ground. TR knew that phrase. It was buried in his people catalogue—he had stumbled upon it a few days earlier when filing new cards. Two hours of searching uncovered its utterer: Billy Philton, now a high school senior, one of the gang to which Junior Skootums had apprenticed. Billy hollered those words before racing away from Martin Softly that night near the trees.

TR bounded down the stairs to tell of his discovery. His father was in the living room watching M*A*S*H but turned it off when he heard what his son was reporting.

"I know that family," he said, staring at the ceiling. "Father's name is Eustace. Eustace and Marjory Philton. Thirteen Pine Street.

You think the son got that expression from his old man, and the old man's the robber?"

"Maybe. It could be a clue, anyway," TR said.

"Yes, it could be. Tell you what. Let's call Khaki's father."

Det. Blumenthrace came to TR's home with Khaki fifteen minutes later to hear the story for himself, deciding after a few minutes to go directly to his office.

"Khaki's welcome to stay here," Martin Softly said.

"Kind of you," Khaki's father responded, adding after a moment's thought, "but why don't Khaki and TR come down to the station with me."

"Yea!" Khaki shouted, grabbing TR's hand and practically yanking him out the door to their car.

At the precinct, the detective quickly found a record of Eustace Philton's arrest for armed robbery five years earlier. But charges had been dismissed for lack of evidence. Khaki's father said it was thin, but it was something, and he'd see about a warrant in the morning.

As was her way, Khaki set things astir when school ended the next day. She dragged TR along on a walk to the Philton house, marched boldly up the short path, and taped a note to the front door.

"Come on," she said as she skipped back across the street where TR was waiting. "Let's go stand under that tree on the corner and watch."

Twenty long minutes later, Billy Philton arrived home, tore off the note, and went inside. A 1970 turquoise Camaro soon careened around the corner and lurched to a stop in the driveway. A man in his late thirties jumped out and banged at the door. Eustace Philton opened it promptly, looked out at the street, but paid no mind to two school kids talking under a tree on the corner. He yanked the man in and slammed the door.

"Let's find a pay phone and call my Dad," Khaki said.

They walked down the street and found a phone booth two blocks away from their target. Det. Blumenthrace picked up on the first ring, and in her usual animated jumble Khaki burst out with the story.

"What did the note say?" her father asked.

"It said, 'I know that your father took the postal money. We're coming for you.'"

"I thought it would be something like that," he said in a tone of exasperation. "Okay, now this time, stay put. We're coming."

Khaki hung up and without a word of explanation to TR raced back toward the Philton house, TR alongside. They arrived in time to see two men jump into the Camaro with two large sacks. The car backed out with a squeal and roared off. In less than a minute, a police car pulled alongside Khaki, who pointed down the road, shouting "Camaro" and the license plate number. It was over in minutes, the two men in custody and the postal bags with nearly all the cash in the back of the police car.

TR figured his reward was the unusual pizza night out, courtesy of the beaming Det. Blumenthrace, who took both families to an Italian restaurant to celebrate. News of the capture made the afternoon edition of the *Ledger Herald*, and even Martin Softly bought a copy. The story was short on details; it took another day before TR and Khaki were lauded under the headline "Who's the Sucker Now?" for cracking the case.

The more important news came a few days later. The post office had offered a reward of five percent of any money recovered to anyone whose information led to the thieves' capture. The bags held $79,629.19, yielding a reward of $3,981.46. Payable to TR, Det. Blumenthrace decreed. Although Khaki had proved an equal in the investigation, he thought it unseemly for a reward to go to his own daughter, much to her chagrin. TR resolved the dilemma. He proposed the money be earmarked for the Public Service Detective Agency.

"What's that?" Martin Softly and Angus Blumenthrace asked simultaneously.

"It's our new detective company, the one Khaki keeps yakking about starting."

"Yeah, when you get taller," Khaki said, sticking her tongue out.

"Well, I'm taller today," TR said, jumping up into the air. "Can't we use the money for the business?"

"What business?" TR's father demanded.

"My card collection," TR said without pause.

"And detective lessons," Khaki said coolly.

"And secretary services?" TR ventured.

"Secretarial," Khaki corrected him.

"You need a secretary?" his father asked him.

"I'm tired of writing out all those cards," TR said plaintively, as if years of wrenching labor entitled him to assistance in his older age.

Martin Softly and Angus Blumenthrace looked at each other and then burst out laughing. "If your mothers okay it," Angus said. "I guess I don't see why we can't set you up a company and a bank account—"

"And a secretary!" Khaki said with a whoop.

And so, after many evenings of discussion over popcorn and ice cream, Pro Bono Detection Services (PBDS) was born, the more dignified name being the suggestion of Luana Softly. Co-owners of record were the four parents, in trust for their children until they each turned eighteen. Co-chief executive officers were TR and Khaki. They hired a community college student with good references at $2.50 an hour to maintain and refresh the people cards collection, and to help TR with keywords—a new category. The postal heist had taught him the importance of indexing not merely names but data that might prove useful in identifying people and their activities. Not solely "Skootums" at the head of cards, but also "Bullying," "Archwold Public School," "Wound Types," and "Taunts." Not just "lives at 61 Woodley" but also "Room 36 Quiet

Pines Motel every Tuesday at 4 PM." At their first board meeting, which they resolved to hold once a year unless "urgently necessary otherwise," Khaki's motion to hire one or more school chums at fifty cents an hour to develop "people connections" won unanimous approval. Now they could add "Room 36 paid for by Pastor Glewton." Several months later, in the ninth grade, they hired their first out-of-town "People Coordinator," a cousin of Khaki's across the state. Over the summer, TR continued with martial arts; Khaki spent July and August taking lessons in detection from a retired police captain who had served with her father.

In high school, TR no longer had to spend his spare time skimming Khaki's reading assignments to skip a grade, so he found ample time to explore what mattered, like coding and programming. Without yet knowing how, he sensed that the future of his connections project would depend on computer capacity, not the number of card drawers he could store in his bedroom. He also took up track. By the spring of his junior year he was running a six-and-a-half-minute mile. Not elite, but respectable. He thought he might shave some seconds when he was taller, but he was quickly running out of height. By his senior year he reached his adult growth of five feet, eleven and a half inches and was rueful about not attaining a full six feet. Once he asked his doctor if he'd be willing to fudge the chart. The doctor asked why it mattered, and who would know the difference anyway if TR lied. But TR never did.

The summer before they graduated, Khaki talked TR into more lessons in the detective arts. Through weeks of bungled surveillance attempts, he would learn to probe for clarity, ambiguity, and precision. What TR thought definitive turned out to be mostly relative. Looking right or left depends on the side of the street you're on and the direction you're walking. "Down" and "up" are indistinct. Overly detailed directions can't be memorized or read while in motion. Height is a drawback as much as a boon; ditto open space, familiarity, anonymity. You need context and history; bare knowledge of the here and now can lead to errors.

"That's true even for the simplest things," Angus said one evening when TR told him what he was learning. "The captain sends us out to find *the* cause of a crime but they don't come in solitary packets. Think of it this way. You're on the bank of a river. The edge gives way and you fall into the water. What caused you to get wet? The water? That won't satisfy your captain or a court. Why did you slip? Maybe the soil collapsed. What caused that? Someone digging or fire that burned away the vegetation? Why was he digging? Who started the fire? Why? Maybe a careless smoker dropped a match. Who taught him to smoke? Who gave him the match? Maybe a landscaper failed to replant because he was drunk and didn't go to work. Where'd he get the alcohol? What is the real story? Who is the who of our Whodunit? How much time have you got to go how far back?"

TR scratched his neck. "But aren't people responsible for what they do?"

"Sometimes. The law gives us investigators some protection there. It often tells us when to stop asking what caused the cause. But not invariably."

"But usually? Like the law says you're not allowed to shoot someone. Or you can't use drugs. I mean, wouldn't you have arrested Sherlock Holmes if you had the chance?"

Detective Blumenthrace stroked his chin and regarded the boy with some care. "Why in the name of all that is holy would I do that?"

"Because he was a criminal," TR said emphatically.

"Really? I thought Holmes unfailingly cooperated with Scotland Yard."

"He used cocaine." TR was agitated at admitting his idol's weakness. "That's against the law."

"Not back then it wasn't," Det. Blumenthrace said. "My job is to enforce the laws, not to get people to behave. An act can be legal one day and illegal the next, or the other way around, and that doesn't mean it's any better or worse, more right or wrong, to do those things one day and not the next. *That* doesn't change; only the law does. If I thought Mr. Holmes was sitting in his day room, injecting the stuff this very day, I wouldn't go out of my way to bring him in. Not everyone who's committed a crime deserves to do the time. We couldn't afford it. Put everyone away? Behind bars? The taxpayers would go nuts."

TR understood that, ultimately, cause can be hard to pin down, but the idea of balancing the cost of crime against the price of its enforcement was a revelation that would trouble him for years; the proposition upset his sense of fitness and order, as did much else of what he was learning outside the classroom. Only in his officially sanctioned school reading (and teachers' lectures) was the world presented as orderly and meaningful. So TR came to realize a real truth: much of what we're told, and some of what we know, is untrue. He added these thoughts to a commonplace book he called "For My Taller Years" that he expected would help lead him, eventually, to the bottom of things.

Mostly, TR thought, his life was nearly normal. Normal because outwardly he did what his classmates did—homework, sports, hobbies. Nearly, because he studied far more intensely and deeply than did his acquaintances now that he had a purpose for his learning. As well, his hobby was a business, nascent though it was. During their high school years, the officers of PBDS held three "urgently necessary" meetings, outside their annual New Year's Day gathering, to decide whether to accept paying cases. Two of these cases offered rewards, the other came from a would-be paying client. They accepted each, solved each (two with the aid of their names catalogue), and altogether pocketed $7,862.13. They authorized a raise of fifty cents an hour for their part-time assistant, who had graduated from college when they were high school juniors and was now a stay-at-home mom, and gave her a title, Master of the Catalogue. By then it contained 3,116 cards, almost 2,200 of them names; the rest were cross-references. They also agreed to commit twenty percent additional funds to what they once called People Coordinators. Awhile earlier, Luana Softly asked off-handedly about their genealogist because she thought Khaki's cousin across the state was tracking family connections. TR was amused at her misunderstanding, and the widening band of connection sleuths were ever after known as "Genies."

One balmy Saturday evening in the spring of their junior year, TR and Khaki walked to Town Center to see *The Godfather* for the fifth time. Khaki brought a small notebook; she was writing an English term paper on "The Psychology of Crime Dramas." After the movie they stopped for ice cream and walked back to Khaki's house. At the door, Khaki noticed that TR's normally smooth forehead was perspiring.

"TR, what's wrong?" she said anxiously. "Are you sick?"

In response, he inclined his head toward hers, awkwardly fumbled for her hand, and attempted a kiss on her lips. She drew back stiffly. "TR!" she said in a tone of reproach he had never heard from her. "We are better friends than that. We are friends forever." She withdrew her hand and bolted inside. TR shook all the way home.

The following Monday morning, Khaki met TR as usual at his front door for their walk to school. He began an apology he had rehearsed for hours on Sunday, but she cut him off and offered her own.

"It's all my fault," she said. "I guess I haven't gotten around to this part of things. I know how you feel. I love you too. But it's not like that, I mean, like we're boyfriend and girlfriend. I mean, we are, but it's, well, we're too young for all that stuff and anyway, I think of you as my dearest brother and I'm your big sister. We can't be—you know what I mean, don't you?" She stopped walking, put her hand onto his shoulders and sought his soul with her eyes. "You're not mad at me, are you? I'm sorry. I don't want you to—"

His heart lifted. She wasn't angry with him.

TR smiled shyly. "Of course not. We *are* friends forever, aren't we?" "Forever," she echoed, squeezing her right pinky around his. Then she dropped her hand and they resumed their tramp to school.

As seniors, TR and Khaki mastered calculus, took their fourth year of Latin, read five Shakespeare plays, began but did not finish *Don Quixote*, and applied to college. The question was not which colleges would accept them—bumptiously they took for granted they would be readily admitted to any campus to which they applied—but whether they should go together. You go to college to get an education, Khaki avowed, and if you don't get away from the Old Familiar, it will tie you down and a good part of your education will fly right over your head, lost for all time. This conversation, solely between the two, consumed most of their fall semester and was resolved late in December. Reluctantly but firmly, they agreed to part. On Christmas Day, TR produced a quarter and flipped it into the air. Khaki called heads for Harvard and won the toss.

In early May, Khaki casually asked TR whether he would be attending senior prom. He thought not. After all, Khaki had omitted tutoring in dance; his rapier qualities were in his wit, not his footwork. Khaki ventured inside knowledge that her friend Savannah's boyfriend would be away and Savannah would doubtless attend if TR asked. "She desperately wants to go," Khaki goaded.

TR looked dubious but agreed, to forestall Savannah's melancholy. "If you want me to, okay."

Khaki reared back. She scanned his face, seeking to interpret his blank expression.

"You will?"

"Sure. Don't I always try to help out?"

"But TR, why would you invite *her*? You scarcely know her. Why not *me*?" *Her* mood soured.

"Khaki! You just *asked* me to ask her."

"But wouldn't you rather go with me? Everyone assumes you will. They know we belong together. There'd be a lot of talking if you show up with Savannah and not me."

"I don't—"

"Sometimes I wish I could get inside your head and see what makes you tick. Think about it, TR. It's the senior prom. How could we *not* go together? It's our last big event before graduation. The last pinnacle of our high school education. The event that even *parents* talk about. The pictures. You have to get a corsage for your date, you do know that, don't you?"

That, and much more from Khaki. When he gave her his I-everlastingly-indulge-you smile and said of course he would take her, she resumed a gaiety that had been missing for weeks. On prom night, their parents beamed and between them consumed four rolls of Ektachrome color film.

TR's feet, fleet enough on the outdoor track, were curiously clumsy on the indoor dance floor, to the point that Khaki, who for years had secretly gorged on *American Bandstand* in the privacy of her bedroom, took the lead. "Do what I do," she commanded, but she meant do the opposite, and they spent much of the evening colliding. None of their friends paid attention, engrossed as they were in depleting their energy on rousing moves to the beat of "Funkytown" and the new sensation, Madonna, singing "Holiday" or in clinging tightly when the band occasionally played Lionel Richie singing "Stuck on You" and other dreamy ballads. TR managed to tap his feet for "Karma Chameleon" and held Khaki chastely when the music slowed. If TR had a musical idiom, it was Count Basie, Artie Shaw, Benny Goodman, Cab Calloway, and their swing band cousins, because that's what Martin and Luana played for him when he was young. Khaki, aware of his tastes, suggested he ask the band to play "one of those swing numbers," but he demurred. No one cut in on them, and TR was not tempted to interrupt the fevered gyrations of their friends. Savannah was nowhere to be seen. TR smiled gamely throughout; this was, after all, an All-American thing they were doing.

"Friends forever, right?" Khaki said when the evening drew to a close and TR pulled up behind the Blumenthrace's Buick in the driveway.

"Forever and a day," he replied, walking her to the door.

"You won't ever leave me. And if I go missing, you'll come and find me."

"Leave, never; find, always." He turned to depart.

"If you want," Khaki said, betraying a hint of heightened color, "you can give me a kiss, you know, for a big sister." She turned her cheek to face him, and allowed him a quick peck.

TR spent most of the summer reading, indulging his newfound interest in true crime. In July he encountered Enrico Malbonum in an aging chronicle of New York crime families. The name amused the diligent student of Latin, delighting him with its opposing prefix and suffix. Then he put it out of mind.

In September, TR was at the station when Khaki left for college. As she boarded the train for Cambridge, she called out with a wink and a wave, "Behave yourself, TR. But show 'em who's boss."

The White House
Washington, DC 20500

June 13, 8:49 p.m.

A Treat from Your President

A Most Honest Fellow
(Statement on Ethics)

Hooey to skinflints and blue noses, and all other crabby do-gooders. They assault Me yelling You broke ethics rules. Why do we even have these rules? But I can take it and dish it right back. The First Lady says My thick skull can withstand all blows, and she's never wrong you better believe Me. This time they're crying fake tears about My trucking company. Who cares if it has My name on it. It ought to I built it. Out of nothing. Growed it, as my daddy used to like to say. You have to forgive him. He was Irish. His native language was German. And the idea came to me: trucking! America needs to move. I leased my first truck right out of college, where I met the First Lady, she was homecoming queen, and put my name on her. And it began to roll, one town to the next. Carrying things. What trucks are for. Let's go trucking! I've had my company for more than an entire quarter of one century. I know America. Because I've ridden those trucks. Town to town. And now the fleet is more than one thousand trucks. All types. So what if they carry military goods and stuff? That's what they're for. My profits are no one's business, and anyway, they're under audit. And it works because I'm a very organized hard driving executive you elected for that reason. I'm also a high-born hell of a hunk. Ask the First Lady, she'll tell you straight off. A most honest fellow (proof: see this Treat).

Action taken: None needed. Ethics reports will be filed if time available. A very working guy president.

Bottom line: It's written down: Everyone knows I'm the most honest fellow to ever hold this office.

Technical Correction to the Presidential Treat, Today's Date: The company was established by the President's father, who when he passed on left it to his son the future President when he was twenty-six, with a capitalized value then of less than one hundred million dollars. Current value is disclosed in a pending filing with the Office of Government Ethics, where it will be embargoed for privacy concerns. A malfunctioning White House spellchecker substituted the word "German" for "Irish" and "her" for "it." A service call has been initiated.

CHAPTER 9

SOFTLY CONNECTING

SOFTLY AWOKE WITH A START AS the train lurched out of Philadelphia's Thirtieth Street Station on its journey to New York from Washington. 9:31: it was running on time.

Malbonum. Softly looked down at the name in bold letters on the front page of the morning paper, which had fallen to the floor when he began reflecting on his first encounter with the name. Must be why Mallory Greenstock insisted on his presence in New York, posthaste, hell-for-leather, Now! He supposed she would not complain about an eighteen-hour delay. He couldn't have reached the city earlier than six o'clock the previous evening if he had left when she called, and he preferred to use the time on other pressing matters.

He picked up the paper, flattening the front page. Malbonum. TR retreated to the story on Malbonum's sentencing and lasted two full paragraphs until his eyes fluttered closed and he wandered back to the first time he had seen Khaki on a train. Rail travel habitually sent him to daydreaming. Ever since his own first train ride a week after Khaki went off to Cambridge.

His train had taken him to New Haven, where he settled in with his Yale roommates and learned the execrable Cole Porter football song, "Bulldog." He behaved himself his first semester, adopting a pacific attitude toward the administrators responsible for his courses and schedule. He took what was required except for talking his way into a programming course in lieu of calculus, arguing that he should not have to repeat what he had already mastered. He aced a challenge test to prove it. He spent his winter break and much of February sorting out his ideal curriculum, especially after absorbing lectures from Khaki about the American psychologist Stanley Milgram, whose "small world" experiment helped demonstrate that every human being is separated from every other person by no more than six degrees. Send a package to someone you know with the aim of getting it to a named stranger a continent away and in fewer than six more hops, it will land on the stranger's doorstep. More than a decade later, the idea found widespread popularity in the game "Six Degrees of Kevin Bacon." The degree of separation was the "Bacon number.") TR wondered whether the connections between any two people could be reduced to five or, better, four hops. He sought courses that might help him find the way.

In the spring, he went to the highest administrative authority he could find to plead relief from the normal course rules. He wanted accord on the next three years. He objected to declaring a major because majors were for people who would specialize in an academic discipline, narrowing the student's focus as the years wore on. When he was turned away with "rules are rules," he then found himself sitting in a comfortable leather chair in a clubby office of the dean of Yale College, explaining what was wrong with a foundational principle of one of the world's unquestionably great universities.

"You need a taste of academic rigor," the dean said. "You need to dig down deeper than the content of any one introductory course."

"Why?" TR asked. He was now a solid seventeen-year-old, exhibiting the same fourth-grade innocence with which he had begun his journey though armed with the wiles and a stubbornness he had never experienced and could not even have imagined seven years earlier. He smiled inwardly at Khaki's admonition: "Show 'em who's boss."

"To make you think hard," the dean said, bemused at having such a conversation with a freshman, especially one resisting the most obvious, even banal, points.

"I can think hard in any course if it's a good one. In fact, isn't it harder to have to think about new subjects and new approaches than to think with more sophistication about the same topic, over and over?"

"Is that all you suppose you'd be doing?"

"Look," said TR, imagining himself wrestling the dean to the floor but knowing he could not exhibit his impatience, "take economics. If I wanted to be an economist, I'd understand taking courses in microeconomics, international trade, banking, and all the rest. But I want to learn economics without becoming an economist. I want to study basic principles and problems it deals with. The same for every other subject. I want to learn principles of chemistry without mastering lab techniques. I'd like to know what DNA is, without having to learn all its wrinkles or how to run it down. Other people can do that. Specialists."

"Are you saying you could learn to sing without ever opening your mouth just by reading about it?" the dean sallied, watching for TR's reaction.

"If I took singing, of course I'd sing. But I won't be taking it because I can't sing. I'd rather take a history of music and performing arts—if they're offered. I want breadth, not depth. Well, sort of," TR conceded.

"You don't have the time to do that for everything we teach. I'm sure you know that. And what do you mean, 'sort of'?" The dean's own exasperation was beginning to show, even as he enjoyed the verbal fencing.

"I mean, I don't plan on being a specialist. I've got different plans."

"Everyone is a specialist," the dean stressed. "At least everyone who graduates from Yale. You learn history or literature or math. You prepare to study physics or linguistics or psychology. You can even, God forbid, go over to York Street and write for the college paper, learn to become a journalist though, mind you, it's not officially sanctioned. But everyone learns to do something."

"Well, if Yale creates that many specialists, how can you object if one guy chooses not to be one?"

The dean, who earlier had been and someday would again be a professor of rhetoric, smiled a bit sheepishly. "What is it that you choose to be then?"

"Well, I'm unsure there's a name for it. I intend to be a problem solver. Not a specialist in any one thing. More like, I suppose you could call it, a generalist, open to dealing with human difficulties, whatever they are." TR felt this would be right up the dean's alley. Better than admitting he planned to become a detective.

"That's pretty breathtaking, especially for a freshman."

"I think it was you, sir, who welcomed us last fall by 'exhorting' us—that was your word—to take advantage of all that Mother Yale has to offer. That's always been Yale's promise to her students, hasn't it?"

The dean sighed. "Tell me what you're thinking."

TR pulled a sheaf of papers from a file folder, each page describing a particular course. "Here's what I think makes sense for me," he said, handing a summary sheet to the dean. The course names were listed line by line: American studies, psychology, graph theory, public speaking, computer programming, network theory, art history, daily themes, statistics, Shakespeare, sociology, criminology, chemistry, history of military intelligence. The list went on, including a political science course that caught the dean's eye, political corruption. TR thought it prudent to omit his senior-year ambitions to audit evidence at the law school, forensics at the medical school, and marketing at the School of Management.

"Oh," he added, "and I'm going out for varsity track."

The dean scowled. "For heaven's sake, that's an awfully big commitment. On the other hand, if you took them all, you'd probably have satisfied at least a couple of majors. Why don't we put you down as a computer science major? We can rethink it next year."

"Does that mean I can take all these courses?" TR persisted.

"We need to see how things go," the dean said, lighting a pipe that he had been packing with tobacco for most of the conversation. He puffed once or twice, remaining silent, the smoke curling in narrow bands to the coffered ceiling.

"Tell you what," TR said, playing his ace. "How about we make a deal?"

"A deal? What sort of deal?"

"I understand there are a bunch of nineteenth-century first edition American novels that have gone missing from the library."

The dean choked on the smoke and dropped his pipe on the desk. "How do you know about that?"

"I talk to people," TR said mildly.

"This is supposed to be a highly contained matter," the dean said, his face red. "The police are working on it. What's this about?"

"I know about it because a few weeks ago I asked one of the library staff for some of those books, and that's what he told me. I pressed him a bit since those books are rare and are supposed to be on a restricted shelf."

"I see."

"How about this: if I get the books back, can I get your assurance that I can take my courses?"

"What makes you think you can—"

"I have a bit of experience in detective work. When I was somewhat younger, I helped my local police recover some money—"

The dean snapped his fingers, softening his scowl. "Oh! You're the truck-heist kid."

The dean had read TR's file. Now he brooded on their odd conversation or negotiation or whatever it was they were having or doing, but relaxed somewhat at the revelation of TR's probable bona fides. Finally he slapped the desk, pushed his chair back, and rose. "Tell you what. You go do that. Come back in a week, and if you've solved our little problem, I'd say the sky has no limit."

The dean heard the news three days later. Somehow the brash freshman did do it. The dean didn't know the whole story, and if he had known it he might have been only half impressed. TR phoned the manager of the Cropcross Book Annex back home and explained the problem. If someone were secreting rare books out of Yale's Sterling Library system, where would they be fenced? Presumably somewhere nearby to avoid jeopardizing such merchandise on a long trip. The manager thought he knew who it might be, a slimy fellow who'd been suspected of selling black-market books from a small rare books shop in nearby West Orange. TR persuaded a senior librarian to lend him a similar book so he could be believable to the fellow.

Posing as an agent for the seller, TR showed up the next day and talked his way into Slimy's confidence. Once they were nose-to-nose, he taped the whole conversation. The police arrived three hours later; Slimy, already facing two other inquiries, quickly confessed and gave up his supplier, a graduate student in Yale's English Department who thought it more profitable to sell the books than to read them. A search of the student's off-campus room that evening turned up the missing volumes. The dean got the news the next day and after temporizing for an hour decided that good cheer was the proper response. He phoned TR and invited him to stop by. They sat down again later that afternoon, and after an hour's amiable conversation, the dean signed off on a new major, "Network Studies," giving TR the pick of the curriculum and promising him a tuition-free extra year to pursue a master's degree in the new specialty in case he couldn't fit all the courses into his undergraduate years. The errant graduate student, the cooperative student librarian, the fence, and the dean were all imprinted on new cards in TR's catalogue.

The remaining years glided by. TR took his courses and made two important discoveries: first, that most of what he learned would be useless in the time called later life. The second discovery was contrary to Sherlock Holmes's brave Victorian precept that by eliminating the impossible what is left, however improbable, must be the truth. As he sardonically characterized his realization: *every problem has a solution if you don't exclude the wrong ones.* Not every problem, in other words, has a solution. Too few people learn this truth because too many fashionable thinkers, on both the right and the left, believe they know what is impossible and therefore can intuit what remains and dare to call that the truth. But it is almost certainly the case, TR came to believe, that sophisticated thinkers, unable to contemplate problems without solutions, hold to the cult beliefs in which they were raised, wed to answers that are almost certainly unsound, all because they cannot accept that there may be no answers at all or at least not full and satisfactory solutions to the problems posed. When a detective gets to that point, TR hypothesized, planning to test his supposition in the world he was about to enter, the only way to attack the problem is to restate it.

Oddly comforted by these revelations (themselves untrue?), TR skipped competitions at pool tables, Saturday football games (except The Game, the season's last, which he would spend with Khaki right before Thanksgiving in either New Haven or Cambridge), and other calls on his time. He did, however, lavish a few hours each week in one of the college basements, captivated by and learning the rudiments of letterpress printing, a venerated Yale tradition that would in time become his off-hours obsession. Occasionally, he would spend an evening in the company of a female classmate, or other women whose names his friends would throw his way, mainly to report to Khaki the unsatisfactory nature of their company. Although sometimes possessing her intensity, they had none of Khaki's enthusiasm or vivacity and talked incessantly about their life's ambition to help indigenous peoples by landing jobs as investment bankers at First Boston or as McKinsey consultants. Though he accepted occasional invitations to spend the night, the experience rarely led to second dates.

TR's one concession to collegiality was membership in the Paternoster Society, a group of eight friends devoted to drinking and discourse. The "Paternosterians" would cheerfully allow anyone to infer that they were a dignified order of ardent devouts. In fact they gloried in spending endless Thursday nights guzzling beer and in inebriated, rambling conversation long past the hour when campus bells sounded the new day. The Society's name derived from its rarely understood alternative meaning: a continuously moving elevator in which the platform holding a doorless compartment continuously loops, allowing passengers to enter or depart as it slowly moves to each floor. The paternoster was the Society's metaphor for life itself, like entering a theater in the middle of a movie and leaving when the film cycled to where the viewer had entered. Otherwise, TR preferred to wrestle with transforming data from paper to magnetic storage so he could shrink the Milgram radius from six hops to four or fewer.

Inevitably, the radius got the better of him, and his work would remain unfinished. Time and tide wait for no man, quoth Chaucer, or as the Rolling Stones had been singing it since TR's childhood, for no one. In late May, TR and his classmates stood together for the last time on the Old Campus under a bright sun, smoking the traditional clay pipes and stomping them underfoot. Hometown newspapers ran gushing stories. Inordinately proud of his now grown, bulked out, taller but still tousled son, Martin Softly framed the *Ledger Herald*'s story of TR's graduation and hung it on the wall opposite the front door; thereafter, every guest would talk of Martin's magnanimous spirit in displaying a story from *that* newspaper.

As a present for Khaki, who graduated summa cum laude in psychology and was heading to Harvard Medical School, TR brought a large box to the celebratory dinner with their parents at Durgin-Park in Boston. He handed it to Khaki, who giggled with delight.

"Open it," TR commanded.

"Willikers, TR. Now?"

"Of course now," he said.

She stripped off the wrapping and used a table knife to slit the tape holding the flaps. She struggled to extract the trademarked light blue Tiffany box snugly encased in the shipping carton.

"Oh my," said Luana Softly when it emerged.

Violet Blumenthrace beamed. The fathers looked at TR with respect: their boy had grown up and outclassed them. Khaki opened the Tiffany box and fished out an elegant foot-high black and silver art deco ice bucket. Inside were a pair of ice tongs, silver but kitschy, with protruding campy grotesqueries—bas relief figures of Wonder Woman, Superman, TR, and Khaki—painted in garish colors along the outside of the blades. A third piece, wrapped in tissue paper, was evidently the lid.

"Don't unwrap the lid until you tell me what this is," TR said.

"It's an ice bucket with funny ice handles," Violet blurted.

"It's more than that," TR said.

"I'm not sure," Khaki said after a moment's reflection.

"Okay, well, let's order, and you think about it," TR said.

He set the bucket next to Khaki on the banquette. They ate a convivial meal, and before the coffee arrived TR returned the bucket to the center of the table.

"Well?" he said.

Khaki shook her head in defeat. The parents turned expectantly to TR, who arched his eyebrows and imagined himself looking mysterious.

"Well, goddammit, tell us, boy. Your mother can't stand the suspense, even if Khaki can," said Martin Softly to the newly minted Yale graduate.

TR turned to look at each of them for a second or two, his smile broadening in anticipation.

"Yes? Come on, come on," Khaki begged.

With a flourish, he waved the ice bucket lid in front of them, tore off the tissue paper, and held it high.

"It's *tong in chic*," he said resonantly, triumphantly. The same words were engraved with the graduation date on the lid, followed by "To Khaki, forever yours, TR."

Khaki teared up. "My hero," she sobbed, adding quietly, "fine stuff, oh, the finest stuff ever."

"I think they'll explain it later," Angus whispered to his wife as he gave his daughter a comforting hug.

Leaving the restaurant and revived by the cool, late spring breeze, Khaki dabbed at her eyes and said, "It's the best evening ever."

TR put off his fifth year at Yale. At the instigation of a computer science professor with whom he took two courses and who had connections to the intelligence and defense communities, TR accepted a direct commission as an ensign in the U.S. Naval Reserve and reported to Newport, Rhode Island, for training. He spent the first tour of his obligatory three-year hitch as an information technology specialist aboard the Navy's newest aircraft carrier, where he thwarted a computer virus planted by an information systems technician who was angry at the executive officer. TR's reward was promotion to Lieutenant (junior grade). A 4–0 fitness report earned him a second promotion, to Lieutenant, and in recognition of his extraordinary capabilities, a second tour—this one in Washington. Reporting to the Naval Computer and Telecommunications Command, TR built and strengthened classified naval computer systems. He lived in a rented townhouse in Georgetown and on weekends walked the streets of the city, with Khaki as company the one weekend every other month when she visited him. (On the off month, he was in Boston.) If he had walked on a Saturday, he would spend Sunday redesigning the architecture of his Connections Catalogue database to run on desktop computers, which TR understood would soon displace the mainframes on which he had been trained. He sought out, modified, and created his own algorithms to search hundreds of thousands of records and to cross-reference, quicker than a blink, data arrays of hundreds of variables. The software, which he dubbed "Findem," was several years ahead of commercial database programs just coming onto the market.

TR was still working on Findem when he was released from active duty. He gave himself two weeks' leisure, and then, living on savings from his frugal military existence, borrowed desk space and advanced computer equipment from a friend who was a partner at a fledgling IT firm two blocks from Dupont Circle. In a few months, his prototype had become Findem 1.5, supple software suitable for sales. Navy acquaintances sent him to federal agencies willing to test it. Word spread. He soon negotiated licenses to a university alumni office, two executive recruiting firms, and a federal intelligence unit that together paid enough to cover his living expenses and to bring on a full-time employee to install and troubleshoot. With that assurance, he sublet the townhouse and returned to New Haven in the fall to take up his promised fifth year at Yale. Khaki, now *Dr.* Blumenthrace, a neurologist, was in her second year of a neuroscience Ph.D. program at M.I.T.

Because he sought no degree, TR audited his courses. He read assignments and attended classes but saw no need to cram or sit for exams. Much of his time he spent one-on-one, sometimes over sherry, with eminent professors whose subjects he found interesting or of potential use to a detective in training.

The rest of his time he devoted to upgrading his Connections Catalogue and embedding it in his proprietary software. Mostly from reports by 112 Genies in sixty-two cities, the Catalogue by then had more than thirty-five thousand connections and tens of thousands of keywords. Any one record would be unlikely to aid in cases, but aggregated they could yield solid investigative secrets.

TR's system was still being managed by the Catalogue Master, who now acquired a companion title: Executive Director of the

Connections Project. It was a full-time job. With a growing revenue stream, she hired two assistant directors. They and their Genies were no longer Baker Street Irregulars; they now constituted an "operation," with a mandate to reach out to a wide range of "connection professionals" across the country (executive recruiters, human resource departments, reunion planners, postal carriers) and scoop up whatever "secondary connections data" could be located, including employment rosters, government staff directories, and college student listings.

TR aspired to do for connections what Google would much later do for search. Milgram could predict the number of interconnections but could not specify their identities—TR's holy grail. He wanted not only to scale back the dimensionality of the global human network (in some areas of the "sociosphere" he hoped to get it down to a maximum of three), but also to pinpoint specific nodes (Mr. X, to get to Ms. Y, will go through Mrs. Z). In years to come, as information multiplied across the Web, the Project would chase connections online: people in neighborhoods, owners of contiguous seats in sports stadiums, co-workers in office buildings, wait staffs in restaurants, members of local athletic leagues, subscribers to the opera, classical concert halls, and music festivals in every venue in the country—and scores of activities that joined people, even if just for an afternoon. Daily, the project's reach widened.

In his last semester at Yale, TR took his ease, enrolling in a single and final formal class, the law school's evidence course. On his first day in late January, assigned to an aisle seat in the fifth row, he turned to the person on his left. "I'm TR Softly," he said, offering his hand. He was shy of twenty-five; she, perhaps two or three years older.

The woman offered him a friendly smile, shook his hand firmly, and said, "M Greenstock." Then she wrinkled her nose and said, "Actually, it's Mallory. What's your real name?"

Dazzled by her unaffected warmth and merry disposition, he explained, as he routinely did, the peculiarity of his parents' naming convention. In the months that followed, their thrice weekly conversation fused into fast friendship. Their discussions began with TR's discovery that in class actual evidence was never evident: students were not asked to grapple with the world's pap and pith (tire tracks, business records, witness reports). The professor cared only about the rules for keeping a fact from jurors or exposing them to it over the objections of lawyers shouting "hearsay." TR would meet Mallory for lunch after class, sometimes at Mory's, sometimes at the Yorkside (invariably as TR's treat), to discuss these conundrums. Soon, their conversations broadened. More than once she spoke of her ambition to become a federal prosecutor. "You have an urge to purge the earth of scourge," he would sum up, and she'd nod happily every time.

People differed on whether Mallory was beautiful, but all found her earthy radiance irresistible. Tall, slender, joyful, and energetic, she had a bountiful smile that heralded puckish good cheer and exuberant optimism. She could be forward and forthright and projected a buoyant, common touch that soothed all those who came up against her steely determination. TR thought of her (always to himself) as Three-G Greenstock: Grounded, Gregarious, and Gorgeous. And though he had pluck enough to take on the whole world, his self-possession shriveled in her company whenever the subject of their relationship arose. Resisting falling head over heels for her, he rationalized it would be unfair to Khaki.

Khaki herself was intrigued when during one of her weekend visits from Cambridge she finally met Mallory, whom TR had mentioned more than once. "She is one neat lady," Khaki gushed in a phone call with TR days later. "You should take her to the prom."

"They don't have a prom," TR said, before the implication of the comment struck him full on.

"Otherwise you'd be taking me?" Khaki laughed.

TR froze. What exactly was Khaki saying? He couldn't work up the nerve to ask his big sister what she meant. Was she no longer his big sister? Her few words threw TR into deep confusion. To whom must he be loyal? And what was disloyalty?

One day in May on their way to Mory's, Mallory had a question, "Where are we going?"

"To lunch," he responded.

She answered with a lazy laugh, low and lingering, the kind that would sometimes dissolve into a fit of skittering giggles. "I meant after lunch, after many lunches, my fine young friend. This isn't a classroom fling, is it? Pick up the older lady for her steel-trap mind? Dump her when the semester is a memory? When the hourglass has run its sand? This gal doesn't want you to be like that. Are you?"

He tried to answer but found himself stammering, just as he did the day Junior Skootums put him on the ground.

"I may get a sunburn from your face. Am I too much for you? Do I revolt you?"

"What? Mallory, how could you think—"

"Usually when a fellow buys this many meals for a non-revolting female, he claims a kiss or two. Well, you don't revolt *me*. Nothing says I can't claim one." Mallory bent toward him and found his lips.

She was so like and unlike Khaki.

"Poor baby," she said. "It's okay. As long as we're friends forever."

"Forever," he murmured and kissed her back. But that's as far as it ever went, that semester in New Haven.

Those days were now blear with age, as brittle as the image of the trees that appeared like snapshots out the window as the train rolled to New York. TR recalled the summer months following, how after settling on Washington as home and becoming a heavily mortgaged owner of a townhouse on Dumbarton Street in Georgetown, he finally began investigative work ("chief resident agent" for the Pro Bono Detection Services agency, as his business card then identified him). A year later Khaki snagged a university faculty position in the District and moved to a Connecticut Avenue apartment north of the zoo. They saw each other weekly. The months became years and after Mallory moved to New York, every time he traveled to Manhattan he would call; they would dine. He would even kiss her goodnight at her door. He had imaginative excuses for declining her invitations to follow her in. Whenever she otherwise came to mind, he had a recurring vision of working on a case at the edge of a pool with Mallory swimming toward him below the surface, while Khaki came through a door with drinks for two. He would tell himself it was safer to remain uncommitted, that he owed fidelity, bugles blaring, not to particularized flesh and blood but to the majestic sweep of the Categorical Imperative, which enjoined him to treat every woman equally.

As the track plunged below ground, he was jolted awake once again. He called Khaki's number, hoping for a signal. On the first ring it went straight to voice mail, as it had every day for the past six weeks; he scarcely had time to say he was in New York to see Mallory, before the call went dead. When he felt the train come to a stop in Penn Station, he slipped the phone back into his pocket and stood.

Time to answer Mallory Greenstock's summons of the day before.

The White House
Washington, DC 20500

June 14, 3:18 a.m.

A Treat from Your President

Pull the Trigger
(Statement on the Second Amendment)

There's crazy people out there shooting up playgrounds and schools and bars and stuff. Other bad people are running around saying do something do something but what they want is to take away your guns squash your Second Amendment rights to weaponize. Terrible. Worse than the problem. So pathetic. But there's an easy answer, so easy. A bill guaranteeing every person over thirteen, except undocumented non-citizens, the unmolested right to carry weapons for protection or pleasure. My bill also requires certain people to bear arms. All elementary and secondary school teachers, priests and rabbis (but not imams you can't be too careful), bartenders and hospitality workers, airline stewards, waiters, playground and parking lot attendants, postal clerks, and medical personnel. No it won't create trigger happiness as the irresponsibles claim. Because of a slick kicker, which says "any owner of a gun or other weapon present during an unprovoked shootout who fails to use his weapon to take down shooters shall serve at least two years in a federal medium-security prison for every person killed or maimed." That's called "victim equity" though I'd call it obvious. The Attorney General approves, and he's a very fair person. All agree it will work. Note to Congress: pull the trigger on this bill.

Action taken: Going up to Capitol Hill and personally threatening to put a round through the torso of any pusilmanormouse member of Congress who refuses to vote aye by next Tuesday. Just kidding, sort of.

Bottom line: It's written down: Safer Americans, safer America. In less than six months, probably less, actually a lot less, no more crime. Wiped. Out. Believe Me, you better believe it. I'm commander in chief.

Technical Correction to the Presidential Treat, Today's Date: To date, the Justice Department has found no one who concurs that the bill will achieve its objective. Because of a White House spellchecker glitch, the word incorrectly rendered above as "pusilmanormouse" should have been spelled "pusillhandtomouth." The spellchecker is under warranty and the manufacturer has been contacted.

On the Spoor

*The world's lone pro bono detective
accepts an invitation to find a missing federal agent
and unravel the mystery of the unwilling Recanters.
He demonstrates anew the remarkable conclusions you
can draw from the tiniest of evidentiary crumbs.*

CHAPTER 10

CURIOUS INCIDENTS

"Mr. Chief Resident Agent," Mallory Greenstock greeted TR as he walked into her office.

"That's the old title," he said.

"Holy Moley, TR, you've promoted yourself." Mallory squinted at the business card she picked up from her polished desktop the moment TR placed it there. It contained a single word— "Services"—above a ten-digit phone number and the email 1@pbdsagency.com, both superimposed over the letters PBDS in a faded blue watermark that TR's designer described as "some shifting shallow shadings shy of cobalt." A tiny line of Latin, Softly's motto, hugged the bottom of the card: *Felix vir potest rerum omnium cognoscere causas.* Happy is the man who understands the causes of all things.

Then she raised her head and smiled broadly. "My God, the eminent Mr. Softly, looking not a day younger than thirty-something."

"Vast emphasis on 'something,'" TR responded with outstretched arms.

Mallory folded into the hug.

"Here we are in the twenty-first century," she said.

"You said that the last forty times we've gotten together."

"Still true."

"You're looking happy."

"Happy to see you," she said. "You do look handsome in that thirty-something way. Must be the standard gray on that exciting dull gray suit. At least the tie has color."

He looked around her office, absorbing the wide Venetian blinds, the bookcases, the caramel-colored club chair, and the large photograph on the back wall, centered over a hand-me-down leather sofa, of an immense bouquet of blue, gold, and green flowers in a large butterscotch vase with a Chinese motif.

"Elegant," he murmured, pointing to the vase and flowers. "From one of your many suitors?"

"You tell me," she deadpanned. "You sent it."

"I did? That photograph?"

"The flowers, dummy. *I* took the picture. Flowers lasted barely a week, you cheap bastard. The picture keeps on going."

"I sent you flowers?"

"Or your identity was hacked."

"Why did I send them?"

The lawyer in her looked askance, unsure how to read his blank expression. "Because I was promoted too?"

"Chief of Unit," he said, amusement playing across his face.

Her look of disapproval melted. "Oh, you do remember."

"Nothing about you I don't remember." He wanted to say, "like how gorgeous you are," but clung to his customary silence. He handed her a small squishy package.

"For me?"

"I couldn't find one for Lydia."

She tore away the wrapping. It was a white T-shirt with the word "Boss" imprinted across the front in red.

"Keep it in mind," she said in a peremptory tone. She crinkled the shirt in her right hand and dropped it on the desk.

"Speaking of which," he began, but she cut him off.

"Not here. Let's go to lunch."

They rode the elevator in silence and walked west at a leisurely pace to Lafayette Street. TR took in on his right the imposing Corinthian columns of the iconic U.S. Courthouse and the New York County Supreme Court Building. From an inside suit pocket he extracted a pair of gray-tinted aviator sunglasses, a gift from a friend whose time as a pilot overlapped TR's carrier service. He didn't mind occasionally receiving mock salutes from random naval officers who recognized the genuine article though he was careful not to imply otherwise that he had ever flown a plane.

"Super cool," Mallory said.

"Always protect the eyes," he said, and then blandly asked, "Where're we going?"

"Little diner a few blocks over," Mallory said. "Out of the way for the courthouse crowd. A twelve-to-fifteen-minute walk is beyond their comfort zone."

"Hush hush, then," he observed.

"But you knew that."

"Otherwise you'd've told me on the phone yesterday."

They turned north, past the Court of International Trade, and then walked west again along Worth Street.

"This is about the Malbonum thing," TR said.

She nodded. "And the others."

"What's the problem?"

"Everything," she said quietly, the breeze muffling her words. "The whole thing stinks. It doesn't make sense. Nobody does what he did, what all those guys did."

"But he did do it, Malbonum, all that stuff? Isn't it solid?"

"Yeah, he did *that,* all those things. He's paying the price. He truly is guilty of the things he confessed to; I'm sure of it. And he really is in prison; no doubt. But that's not what I meant about nobody doing what he did. It's the middle part of the story that worries me. Nobody volunteers for no reason to turn himself in like that and confess to a zillion serious crimes, especially not the likes of Romo Malbonum."

"I thought you have it attested seven ways to Sunday it was Malbonum," TR said.

Mallory didn't respond immediately. She studied the crowded sidewalk as they weaved through the disorderly flow of pedestrians, TR momentarily alongside her and then narrowly behind as he dodged four young women standing shoulder to shoulder, chattering, determined to give oncoming foot traffic no quarter. Without breaking stride she lifted her arm and waved across the street at a younger man in a dark suit carrying a thin briefcase and walking briskly in the opposite direction. He didn't notice her and she turned back to TR. When the sidewalk thinned out after they had crossed Broadway, she leaned in and said, "I need you to get to the bottom of it."

"Of what? What is 'it'?"

"Wait for lunch," she said grimly. Then, barely pausing for breath, she softened and said, "Hungry?"

Perplexed, TR merely nodded and walked along silently, following as she turned them north on West Broadway and across Leonard Street to a diner on the northwest corner of the oblique intersection with Varick. The eatery, the Square Diner, was shaped like a train car, ringed by stainless steel and gray siding, and mashed against a nondescript building looming dingily above. Half-height windows overlooked the sidewalk. Inside, old-fashioned ceiling globes bounced their light off the highly buffed honey-colored wood erratically covered by a hodgepodge of testimonials and framed celebrity pictures. A Formica counter and nine old bar stools topped in red vinyl were near the door. Farther inside were booths so tightly compressed that patrons sitting across from each other played footsy or murmured an embarrassed "excuse me" several times a meal.

Near the geographic center of trendy Tribeca, the diner was on no one's list of distinguished cuisine but had been there for nearly seventy years, a favorite of generations of back-office employees, secretaries, students from a nearby law school, and middle-class denizens of the neighborhood. Years before, it had garnered a few seconds of airtime when characters on NBC's *Law and Order* would walk in. But prosecutors who worked east of the courthouses were impervious to its charms, so Mallory and TR could eat unobserved.

The counterman bade them sit where they wished; it was still before noon. Mallory scanned the interior, then settled into a half-booth on the inside wall at the back away from the windows. No one was sitting nearby. Hanging carelessly on the wall was a signed photograph of Jesse L. Martin. A blowsy waitress plopped menus and glasses of ice water on the small table and said "Coffee?" in a broad Queens accent.

"Later," Mallory murmured, examining the menu out of habit. But her selection remained constant.

"Tuna and whiskey down light," the waitress cried out, followed by "drown a thin one and sour it four" —a tuna salad sandwich on lightly toasted rye bread and a diet coke suffused with lemons.

"Two chicks on double logs and wreck 'em, burn the British, and a cold spot dry," the waitress continued, calling in TR's scrambled eggs, extra sausage, toasted English muffin, and an unsweetened iced tea.

Mallory arched an eyebrow in mock horror.

"When in a diner . . . " TR said. "Besides, I haven't had breakfast. Double besides, I'll run it off. Talk to me."

"I don't want you to think I'm paranoid," she began.

"Okay, not entirely," he interrupted.

"No, listen, I'm being serious. We can discuss ground rules if you agree to my proposition after I tell you what I'm worried about. I don't think anyone's out to get me or anything."

"Or me."

"Or you, no. Not yet anyway. But it's better to have this particular talk away from anyone who knows me."

Focusing on the condiments and the black and silver oblong napkin dispenser at the side of the table, she gathered her thoughts for a long minute, until TR thought she had fallen into a trance. But then she plunged into a series of interrogatories to forestall his.

"How closely did you follow the Malbonum story?"

"Just what was in the papers."

"Then you may not know that he made contact with our office through an FBI agent."

"That's unusual?"

"Exceedingly," Mallory replied. Ordinarily, we get a call from a perp's lawyer, asking to meet. That's followed up, a quiet discussion with vague intimations, encouraging nods, friendly suggestions, and then a lengthy negotiation. It doesn't happen in two days. And it isn't the feds who initiate it. It's always the other way around."

"So what? You already said this was the real deal. Malbonum did it. What is it you're worried about?"

She was somber, her face still. "I fear that I, the office, all of us, may have been abetting a felony or two."

"What felonies?"

"How this all got going. The ball may have got rolling from the other side of the law; you know, those extra-legal steps that drop from the narrative when the prosecutors get to court. I won't be a party to that."

"But—"

"It's a hunch," she continued. "All I can say is, something doesn't feel right. I want you to investigate."

"Investigate what?"

"The middle part. Why would he confess? That's what I want to know. Secret pressure? What?"

"You don't buy repentance?"

"Contrition, as someone briefly important once said, is bullshit. Got to be something else."

"Okay," he said quietly. "Not sure what that means, but if you give me some room, I can walk around. It would help if you had something more than a vague feeling as a compass point. Where are we starting?"

"Dewey Sisal."

"Who or what is that?"

"The FBI agent who came to see me. He's who started it, at least for me, for the office. He said they had a bad guy, had all that anyone needed to know to nail him and dozens of his associates; Sisal was right. They did have the goods on our perp and all the rest of them. But how did they get the goods?"

"He didn't say?

"The story we got is that Malbonum turned himself in. It never came up in court. Malbonum now denies he initiated, says they invaded, with a 'big flash bang.' We've pooh-poohed everything he's claimed. Still, before he recanted, we went out of our way to get him to publicly ratify everything that happened before the FBI showed up at his house. Which is why there's been no squabbling over search and seizure issues."

"You're saying you believe the FBI ignored the legal niceties to begin with."

"At least side-stepped them. Why ratify if it's all on the up and up?"

"Good lawyering? Always nail it down."

"Maybe that's it," she conceded. "But still."

TR sat back as the overloaded waitress slid the dishes down her forearms onto the table and left. TR stabbed his fork into the eggs and said, "Okay, start over. Tell me the whole thing through your eyes, from the moment you first got involved."

Mallory told the story, complete with headings, bullet points, and rhetorical summaries: meeting Sisal, talking to Carverman, sitting with her team at Malbonum's and hearing his story so they could draft the bill of particulars to which he would plead guilty, highlights of Malbonum's confession in court, the videotaping and other fail-safe procedures put in place, her sense of Malbonum's character and demeanor, a second-hand account of his recantation, the unavailing appeals, the sentencing, the pleas and recantations of the other crime bosses, Sisal's absence throughout, and the unexplained oddity of it all.

TR ate and listened. When she finished the story, her food untouched, TR popped the last bite of biscuit into his mouth and said, "You obviously think Sisal's got more to do with this than you've said. Let's start with him. Where do we find him?"

A rare instance of resignation washed across Mallory's face. "That's why I called you. I don't know where he is. He doesn't answer his mobile; the last time I tried it was disconnected. I can't find him through any FBI switchboard; neither can our investigator. The New York office says he was there on temporary assignment. He's a ghost. I didn't want to make a fuss, so the only person I know to ask is you."

TR watched Mallory pick up her sandwich. "Who am I working for? You?"

"No, not me personally," Mallory said, half of her sandwich paused in mid-arc to her mouth. "You'll be working for our office."

"But then why our lovely clandestine meeting at this boffo establishment?"

"In case you turn me down."

"Mallory!"

She flushed. "Okay. Sorry. I wasn't entirely sure. I didn't want my suspicions out and about, clouding the wrong minds. In case I'm mistaken—about Sisal."

"Then—"

"Look, we're still anticipating appeals and inquiries from our sister offices in Los Angeles, Chicago, Tulsa, and San Francisco, and—this part is confidential—two cases no one yet knows about popped up in Boston and Cleveland this morning; looks like more of same, open-court confession, plea, and recantation two days later. It would make sense to have an independent investigator helping out. That's you." She took a bite and chewed. "But I can't pay you. I mean, not without permission and a lot of paperwork that I'm hoping to avoid."

"I don't work for pay."

"How can that be?" she asked, lowering the partially eaten sandwich to her plate.

"That's always been the idea," he said. "That's why we call it Pro Bono services. We take cases that interest us, and cases don't usually interest us unless some public issue is at stake. Like some problem with the criminal justice system. Sounds like what's happening here. Plus, it's a most mysterious story. I like mysterious stories."

"You're sure? You're not saying that because it's me?"

"Never taken a fee. Well, not since high school. And once, more or less in kind, in college."

"How can you afford that?"

"The software company foots the bill."

"Really? That much revenue from your computer systems? Your salary, office supplies, shoe polish?"

"Everything—six employees, rent, electronics. Lots of part-timers. One of these days, I may get rich." Waving a piece of sausage, he added, "Of course, to get to financial heaven, we do bill for expenses. Travel, expensive lunches like this one, you know, things like that."

"I can do that. The miscellaneous expense budget even covers dessert."

"Without permission?"

She flushed. "You caught that."

He waited.

"Forgiveness later is cheaper than permission before. But mainly—I don't trust anyone."

"Not even the boss?"

"Yeah, not him too."

He stuck out his hand. "Then it's a deal."

She smiled, ignoring his hand, and leaned across the table and kissed him on the cheek.

"Okay, good, I'm relieved," she said, wolfing down the rest of her sandwich.

"I want to start with the files. When can I read them?" he asked.

"As soon as we're back at the office."

Waiting for the check, Mallory picked up a newspaper tucked into the pleat of the bench.

"Did you see this story about the president's take on immigration?"

"Headline, yeah, didn't read it. Why?"

"There's this bit from an NBC interview last night. Listen to this." Mallory folded the paper into a book-sized configuration, and read an excerpt:

Q: We all know you as a fierce antagonist of immigration. Do you feel you are? If so, can you explain why?

A: These people have come to take our homeland, steal us blind. Welfare. Jobs. They are ruining us.

Q: But surely not everyone. I mean, after all, one way or the other we are almost all immigrants.

A: No sir, not me, I am not. I am as American as they come.

Q: But if you go back far enough, your grandfather, wasn't it—

A: Not true. Not a word of it.

Q: Your grandfather did not emigrate to America from Germany?

A: Germany? Oh, for gosh sakes, Lester, we're Irish.

Q: Well, how can you be Irish and not have emigrated?

A: Just because I'm Irish doesn't mean we came here.

Q: Mr. President, that's exactly what it means.

A: Your book learning is getting the better of you. Think about it. We're non-immigrant Irish.

Q: What, the sort who is indigenous to America?

A: Exactly, and don't you forget it. We're Irish from here.

Q: But then you can't be Irish. The Irish came from Ireland.

A: Yes, the foreign ones.

"My man," TR said.

"What? You think he makes sense?"

"Of course not, but you have to hand it to him. He is humongously amusing. It's hard to believe."

"TR!" She put money on the table and stood up. "Let's go back."

He caught her arm. "Listen, one thing. We don't know if the FBI is listening or what your boy Sisal might hear. On the job, don't talk about him except as a regular part of the case. No meta-narrative."

"Meta?"

"You know, singling him out, like 'what do you know about Sisal? What's he up to? Where is he?'"

She nodded. "You think—"

"I don't know what to think, but he does work for the non-immigrant Irishman. Prudence, Mallory."

Back at her office, Mallory brought TR into a conference room laid out with large piles of paper: original trial binders, memos to the file written before and after Malbonum's plea, and transcripts of the discussions at his home. While the assistant set up a computer, Mallory handed TR a piece of paper and said, "Sign this."

"What is it?"

"Our formal arrangement. You're our ad hoc investigator, aiding in furtherance of appeals and related matters in the Malbonum case. Pledges of confidentiality. No fee; expenses only."

TR signed without reading. Mallory handed him an ID badge with a jacket clip. He put it on his suit pocket.

"You're official," she said, and left the room.

Four and a half hours later, shortly after six o'clock, Mallory walked back in. She found TR hunched over open binders, a half dozen yellow legal pads with pages askew, a fourteen-inch flat screen monitor adorned with several yellow Post-it notes, and an array of memory sticks (as they were called then). His jacket was draped over the aluminum back of the chair in which he slouched, his tie was loose, and some dozen colored pens were strewn across the papers.

"You okay?" she said brightly. "Ready for dinner?"

"Yeah, and no," he said, his voice low in his throat.

She put a bottle of Poland Springs next to him. He guzzled half of it down.

"Give me two more hours. Can you wait?"

"Sure," she said, "always plenty to do." And walked out. And came back in again at eight. Now the yellow pads were stacked in a corner, his notes placed neatly in a file folder, while several printed pages sat in another. The monitor was dark, one of the memory sticks was in his pocket, and the binders were propped up next to the CPU tower. TR leaned on a table near the door.

"Ready for dinner? My treat."

"Of course," he said, "by written agreement."

"We leave now, we can get to the Grill Room at the Yale Club by 8:30."

"Where I happen to be staying. But you knew that."

She touched the side of her head. "Yep, I know things."

"You mean because you had Lydia check when she made the reservation."

"That too," she said. "Come."

Inside the Yale Club, they ordered quickly, oblivious to the choices except for the Manhattan chowder, which TR could never find in Washington restaurants. He looked high up at the beamed ceiling and fastened on the brightly lit candelabra nearly overhead. The room was hushed and offered privacy; most diners had already left.

"What did you learn?" she asked, playing with the spoon in front of her.

"From the transcripts? Surprisingly little. It's all straightforward. I mean, almost everything written down in all those pages has already been in the papers. Almost."

"What's missing?"

"We'll get to that," TR said. "But first, let me lay out what we know before we learn anything more. We begin with your question:

did the Recanters themselves confess? Forget for the moment how it could be possible that they didn't, since, regardless of the confessions, the persons who committed the crimes to which they pleaded guilty are the ones serving the sentences. You following me?"

"Duh," Mallory grunted.

"Okay, good. Actually, it's two questions you've got. One is, was it really those guys doing the confessing? The other is whether they were forced. Start with the second question. Here's what we can deduce from what we know so far. The obvious kinds of duress can't be what prompted them to confess. You can't bribe or extort such people. What guilty secret or danger would make Malbonum throw away the rest of his life, forfeit everything, and rat out his associates? Was his family approached? Not according to any report. And who would be foolhardy enough to try to hurt his wife or children? I can't imagine. I don't think you can either. Ergo, he wasn't forced."

She nodded.

He continued, "If he didn't succumb to pressure, then it's not a question of money, either. He couldn't have been paid enough to go to jail. And it's even more unlikely that he 'repented because he meant it.' These weren't cases of contrition. They couldn't be."

"Why not?"

TR sighed. "Because, Your Chief of Unit-ness, they recanted. No one, no sane person, does what these people did for the sake of repentance, and then recants the next day."

"Two days later."

"Whatever. It contradicts the very premise. They're not that stupid. They had nothing to gain. I conclude they didn't act involuntarily, or, if you're persnickety, voluntarily under pressure, nor did they voluntarily confess from some newfound moral twitch."

"Okay, go on."

"Well, if I'm right about all that, then a wholly different possibility follows from the recanting—namely, that exactly like they said, they didn't confess."

"Unless they are crazy," she noted.

"It's unlikely any one became crazy that way, much less all of them. Why? What would have triggered them? It's more unlikely they were temporarily insane. They didn't even argue after the fact that they were."

"Kreutscher claimed temporary insanity."

"The Alibi King?"

"His lawyer did, yeah."

TR paused to digest that information, new to him.

"But the courts didn't buy it, I assume."

"No," she said, "they didn't." Mallory blinked. "Some psychologists have a paper on a new mental illness they're calling CCRS. That's for 'Career Criminal Repentance Syndrome.' It's supposed to explain why they acted against self-interest."

"What's the theory?" TR wondered idly, his skeptical mind dismissing it as useless as soon as she named it.

"Well, that's just it. I mean, I haven't read the paper, but I talked to one of the authors, and it seems to be nothing more than a different form of temporary insanity, prompted by self-loathing and horror induced by looking too sharply into the meaning of their lives."

"And the recanting?"

"That seems to be the moment they recover their sanity."

"In other words, when they confess they're insane, no matter how articulate the confession. When they recant, they're sane again, no matter how confused the recantation. That's armchair Ph.D. bullshit. The kind Khaki always warns me against, using a label to account for a cause."

"Khaki! I should have asked. How is she?"

TR put down his fork, took a breath. "It's an odd thing. She sent me a note six weeks ago, said she was going silent. Asked me not to track her."

"That's not like her?"

"Never happened before. For thirty years, I've talked to her once a week or more. Then, after her note, she stopped answering her phone. She hasn't been at her place. I've checked."

"She on a secret mission?"

"Khaki? She's a neurologist, neuroscientist, both. She's at home in labs. Where would she go?"

"You worried about it?"

He nodded. After all, he had promised her on prom night if she ever went missing, he would find her.

"What are you going to do?"

"I'm trying to track her. The team is on it."

"What did the university say?"

"Said she took leave for field work."

"Field work? You think she's in trouble?"

"I don't see how, or why," he said. "Nothing obvious." TR pushed his fork against the food remaining on his plate.

Mallory sat unmoving and when TR said nothing more, she took another bite and pointed her fork at him. "Back to our recanters, then. You don't think they're crazy?"

TR shook his head but acknowledged he might have leaped to an unjustified conclusion.

"Which was?" she asked.

"That Malbonum wasn't forced. There is another type of involuntariness, you know—drugs or chemicals. Could he have been drugged?"

"No," she said emphatically.

"Because you ran all sorts of tests, before, during and after."

"That's right."

"Okay, I accept that. And more to the point, what kind of drug would last for four or five days, against all known tests, and have such an effect? What would it be? Some sort of truth serum, like what he claimed they blotted on his face? I've never encountered such a thing."

"Doesn't mean there isn't such a thing." Mallory offered.

"That's true, but it's highly improbable—not impossible that someone's developed it, but from what your forensic tests tell us, impossible that it could have been administered—no chemicals in his system, no injection sites, nothing. But that leads us to a related matter." He paused.

"Which is?" she asked.

"Something else that could take over his mind."

"Mind control?"

"Listen," he said, "this is your query: whether it's possible these recanters didn't confess. We've ruled out being pressured or tricked or drugged into confessing. If they weren't in fact the ones confessing, then it can only be because they weren't in control of themselves. The only remaining possibility is that someone or something somehow overpowered their will. In other words, yes, like mind control."

"You mean, like the Manchurian Candidate, that sort of thing?"

"Conceivably."

"But how would that work? In the story, if I'm remembering it right, some soldiers were brainwashed by the communists. The Chinese implanted trigger words to activate the soldiers as communist sleeper agents and then suppress memories of what they were ordered to do."

"Yep, more or less, that's it," TR agreed.

"Do you think these guys could have been brainwashed like that?" she asked.

"It would be hard to get at people like your defendants. Brainwashing doesn't happen instantly. You can't brainwash someone into becoming an unconscious agent through smelling salts or pills. If you could show that one of them had been absent for a time, maybe. But they'd all have to have been taken and held by a malign power. That didn't happen. Brainwashing is in the DSM as a phenomenon, but most psychiatrists and psychologists doubt it exists as a technique of mind control. Even if it does, like the thing that cults do, it's a drawn-out process."

"How do you know all that?" she asked, eyebrows raised.

"You don't? We were both students at Yale."

"Ah, your medical courses."

"Yes, and that's about all I know. But it's irrelevant anyway, because there isn't any evidence that anyone had hold of your friends for the time it would take to implant these triggers. Or to pull them."

"Well, what about hypnotic suggestion?"

"That's less plausible. There's evidence hypnosis can change long-term mood but nothing that can explain the multi-day acts of confession and contrition involved in these cases. And even if there were an explanation, there's one thing about all this that makes it extremely implausible."

"Which is?"

"Which is the same as the earlier problem. If someone takes the trouble to plant a hypnotic suggestion to confess, and in the detail that's required, why would the hypnotized subject recant a day or two later? If you wanted to get these bastards off the street, why wouldn't you let them or make them continue to believe they are penitents who have suddenly seen the light?"

"I guess that's right," Mallory said.

"I think we can rule out all those sorts of explanations."

"Then what's left?"

TR burst into an infectious grin.

"What?" she said, smiling despite herself.

"What's left is something so preposterous that if it weren't you sitting in front of me, and if you weren't paying for my night in town, and if I weren't so happy spending quality time with you, I wouldn't dare say it."

"But you'll tell me right now, because I am slathering you with my quality time."

"After the coffee comes." He signaled the waiter.

It was close to ten, closing time, so the waiter had their cups full of decaf within the minute. Mallory sipped at hers. "So?" she said. "Where are we? What's left?"

"We've concluded that the confessions weren't the result of coercion, at least not in the usual manner. We reject the claim of some moral awakening. We've also almost certainly excluded any hypothesis of disease, like temporary insanity. In other words, you are right."

"I am? Right about what?"

"That these guys didn't confess. We've exhausted all other rational explanations. In other words, we've eliminated the Impossible. That leaves, as the Great Doyle taught, the more limited realm of the Improbable. See?"

"See what?"

"We started out thinking the explanation lies with the recanters— that Malbonum himself confessed. It's impossible that the confession wasn't his, right? That's what we've been assuming. But suppose we're wrong; suppose the desire to confess didn't come from him. Suppose, in other words, the 'impossible' is in fact possible."

"I don't quite—"

"If Malbonum didn't confess, nor did the other defendants, then, don't you see, someone else did."

"Someone else? Who?"

"I don't know yet. Let's call him—or them—an impersonator," TR said, draining his cup.

"Who? And where was this impersonator? It was Malbonum in that courtroom."

"His body was. At least it was when you drew the blood and made your measurements."

"You think somebody got him out of the courtroom before he started talking? Or that wasn't him to begin with, and an impersonator spoke his lines—"

"Well—"

"And the real him was smuggled back in again for blood samples and fingerprints? Smuggled in when? He was never out of the courtroom."

"I—"

"And if the real Malbonum was somehow back in the courtroom for the forensic tests, why didn't he squawk then?"

TR shook his head. "It remains murky. Even to a trained detective such as myself."

"Sorry," she said, "but that isn't just a confusing theory; it's a crazy one!" Her cup was shaking and she landed it with a clatter on the saucer.

"Well, I'm not omniscient, contrary to my press agent."

She stuck out her tongue. "That's not what I meant, and you know it. This impersonator thing—"

"Not impossible. It's merely highly improbable," he conceded.

"But how could it—"

"Look, I don't know yet. But the only way all of the facts, taken together, make any sense is if Malbonum was not in control of his mind; if his will was overpowered. I call the agent who *was* in control an impersonator. Who or what that agency is, how it works, I can't tell you. Not yet. But that's my working theory."

"And your theory is based on—"

He tapped his forehead. "Impeccable inference from facts on the ground and heightened common sense in cloudy corners, elementary medical know-how, and fanciful speculation in the absence of relevant evidence. In other words, it's what the 'little gray cells' tell me."

"Oh," she said. "Well, that cinches it."

"You and I," he replied, "are going to the lounge for a nightcap, where we will plan our strategy for moving our answer from the realm of the ridiculously improbable to the merely majorly improbable."

"I," she announced, "will detour slightly, by way of the you know what, and shall meet you there, along with a Remy Martin XO straight, in case you've forgotten."

"Madam Unit Chief," he said, pulling back her chair as she stood. TR was on the phone in the lounge at a table near the bar when Mallory returned.

"Canceling your date, I hope," she said, sliding into the chair across from TR.

He winked and, seeking forbearance, pointed his index finger at her, murmured his goodbyes, and put the phone next to his glass of Macallan triple cask single malt whiskey.

"Anything I should know about?" she asked, sipping her cognac.

"That was orJean," he said.

"OrJean?" she repeated. "What?"

"I thought I told you about orJean. She's the Catalogue Master and Chief of Connections."

"One of your people."

"The very first. OrJean McLenahan. Well, actually, now it's Tomkins, though she divorced the guy years ago. She's been working for me"—he stared across the room—"since, well, thirty years."

"No. How is that possible?"

"A few years shy of thirty, I guess. She was our first hire, right when PBDS started. More than a quarter-century, anyway. Paid her two and a half bucks an hour. Of course, I was only twelve."

"The more I find out about you, TR," she said, reaching out and grazing the top of his hand. "Amazing. But her name? How do you spell it?"

"M - a - r - y—"

"What?" She smacked her glass on the table. Mallory could take teasing only up to a point.

"No, truly. Story is the day after she was born, a nurse asked for the baby's name. Parents hadn't decided. Her father blurted out 'Mary—or Jean.' And that's what the nurse wrote down. That's her real name."

"Mary or Jean?" Mallory repeated. "That sounds—unusual."

"Hey, you're talking to a guy who doesn't have a first name," he responded. "Balances out. She's got two. Anyway, she always disliked 'Mary.' Her parents called her that until she was six, when she absorbed the naming story and decided she preferred the second half. After that she insisted, and her parents approved: she became orJean, spelled as one word, lower case 'o,' emphasis on the last syllable. It's orJEAN, not ORjean."

"Well, okay, you were talking to her?"

"Yep, wanted to put her on alert. Depending on the second part of this debriefing, we may need to make some calls, send some agents out, do our stuff, starting tomorrow."

"Huh? On the basis of what I'm going to tell you, sitting in this comfortable chair, getting buzzed?" she said, her cadence betraying a growing confusion. "*But I don't know anything.* It's all a fog."

"You know a lot of things though you may not know you know them. A mystery is mostly a tangle of events. Something that's happened—or hasn't—that you can't explain. Often, they're events you don't know about or can't properly connect. Solving a mystery means looking around for dots to connect. When you start, you're in a gloomy darkness—or it's a dim blur or a muffled rumble. You see no more than an inch ahead, you hear indistinctly. If fortune smiles, you stumble across something that leads you on. You hope these early clues stick together, reassemble. The new shape helps you construct a theory, a searchlight that illuminates what's hidden."

"This your introductory lecture?" Mallory wondered, taking a long swallow of her cognac.

"No, I usually keep my sleuthing to myself. I'm trying to make you see why you can still help."

"Let's get to it," she said, draining her glass and holding it aloft until the bartender noticed.

"Our working theory—mine, anyway—is that the confessions came from an impersonator," TR continued.

Mallory supplied the footnote, "Who or what, nature of beast—unknown."

"Correct. But you said you wanted to begin with Agent Dewey Sisal. Let's do that. Talk to me: everything you know about him."

"I already told you. I don't know anything about him."

He smiled at her and reached for her hand. "That's interference from the buzz. You'll have to think over it. Okay if I lead the witness?"

"Sure. You can lead me anywhere."

"In your entire life, how many minutes have you ever seen Sisal?"

"Maybe thirty."

"At the bar near your office."

"The Undersludge."

"And you're sure you've haven't seen him before or since."

"Certainly not since."

"Before?"

Mallory was quiet, replaying the scene in her mind, watching Sisal walk over to the table where she had been waiting. Sticking out his hand, she then shaking it, and saying something. The first thing she had said was, "Do I know you?" Saying it aloud right now, as she recollected the moment, Sisal seemed familiar.

"'Do you know me?'" TR echoed, puzzled.

"No," she said excitedly, talking high above the background noise that sounded in her remembered conversation at the Undersludge that night six weeks before. "That's what I said to him, when I first saw him."

The bartender turned in her direction. She put a hand over her mouth, then lowered her voice. "I said he seemed familiar somehow."

"Do you know how? Did you figure it out?"

"He said we'd met at a conference of assistant U.S. attorneys. He was on a panel or something."

"That's it?"

"That's it."

"You don't remember meeting him at the conference?"

"No."

"He didn't tell you which panel or what was being discussed or when or where?"

"No."

"Okay, what else? He wasn't there during your time at Malbonum's house?"

"No."

"Did he say where he'd be?"

"He was in charge of rounding up all Malbonum associates. They needed to scoop them up before the news broke. I don't know where he was when he was doing that."

"And you haven't talked to him again."

"Only the call yesterday."

"When he didn't say anything useful."

"Right."

"Okay. Tell me about Malbonum."

"You saw the video."

"I mean what you saw of him when you were with him, not on video. Tell me about your time with him before he pleaded."

"I spent at most two full days, with my team, in his house."

"How did he behave?"

"Relaxed. Gregarious. Welcoming, in a way. Sometimes funny."

"Not like a guy who was cornered and knows he's going down for life."

"No, but remember, he told me this was what he wanted."

"Nothing out of the ordinary, beyond the facts of the case in the record?"

"Well . . . " she began.

He waggled his fingers at her, beckoning her to spill whatever had come to mind.

"There was the cat incident."

TR sat up straight. "A cat? Talk to me."

"It was around five o'clock. We'd been going for nearly eight hours, with a short time off for lunch. We were sitting on a sofa. Wait, *he* was sitting on a sofa. My guys and I were in chairs opposite him. We were talking, taking notes. All of a sudden, this cat comes out of nowhere, makes a beeline for the sofa where Malbonum is sitting, and jumps up next to his lap. Cat totally surprised him. Malbonum jumps, I mean, straight up off the cushion and moves sideways to the other end. Then he realizes we're watching. He's embarrassed and says, 'She startled me.' At that point, the cat walks over to him, puts its paws on his wrist and plops its face onto his hand, and starts purring. Malbonum's looking at the cat as if he wants to be anywhere else. Then he shakes himself and reaches across with his other hand and timidly pats her on the head, but like he's not used to it. The cat is somewhere blissed out on his hand, still purring loudly."

TR was transfixed. "Then what?"

"Then we went back to our discussion."

"And the cat just sat there?"

"For a while. After a few minutes when Malbonum shifted position, the cat got up and moved over to the other side of the sofa, curled up, and fell asleep."

TR smacked the table. "Progress," he said.

Mallory squinted at him.

"Don't you see? This curious incident of the cat?" he said.

"What curious incident? The cat didn't seem to mind. She purred."

"That's the curious incident."

Mallory stifled a yawn. "I'm not understanding."

"Did you interrogate the cat?"

"It was a cat, TR. Nobody interrogates a cat. What are you talking about?"

"Whose cat was it?" he continued.

"I don't know. His. Malbonum's, I assume."

"Are you sure? Could it have been his wife's or his kids'?"

"I don't know. Maybe. It knew its way around the house."

"You saw it afterward."

"After and before. It wandered in and out, along with the dog."

"But didn't go near Malbonum?"

"No, well, I don't know. If he's cat phobic, his family could have kept it away from him. When they go out of town maybe they lock the kitty up, but the FBI let it out. He freaked when it wandered to where we were."

"But you say it came and went. He didn't pay it any attention otherwise, hence it wasn't locked up."

"I guess." Mallory looked down, and then, wandering along a different lane, asked, "She attractive?"

"Wait, what? Who?"

"Your orJean." Mallory was fading.

"Well, yeah, in a grandmotherly way."

"Grandmother? She's—orJean's a grandmother?"

"She married young."

Mallory nodded, her head falling forward. "Just wond'ring."

"Listen, Mallory, before you conk, was this little cat interlude by any chance recorded?"

"Audio. You wanna hear it?"

"Definitely. Tomorrow, if at all possible," he said.

She nodded.

"You hear anything else that was not recorded?"

"No. Taped everything, even lunch and dinner."

"What about what the lady said in court?"

"What lady?"

"The lady drawing blood. The video showed she said something, and he responded. But it wasn't audible."

"Tomorrow, everything to . . . mor . . . row." Mallory answered, stumbling over the last word.

She put her elbows on the table and let her head fall forward into her palms. "A five-minute nap."

"I think we're done for the night," TR said, signaling for the check. "Can't sleep here, old girl."

"Toooo late," she sighed, eyelids shut.

"You're shit-hammered."

TR put his arms around her, raised her from the table, drunk-walked her to the elevator, and was happy to find it empty when the door opened. A minute later he managed to walk her down the hall while fumbling for his key card. Once inside his room, he led her, fully dressed, to the bed and tucked her in. For several seconds in the nightlight's dim glow, he let himself admire her blond mane splayed out on the pillow. Hearing her even breathing, he flung his jacket over the upholstered desk chair and wrapped himself in an extra blanket, tossed two pillows on the floor next to the bed, and hit the deck. This was, of course, strictly against the rules. Only one person per studio. He closed his eyes and began working through what he had learned in the lounge; he got as far as realizing he could not name the cat before his mind quit for the night.

CHAPTER 11

MORE CURIOUS INCIDENTS

A TOE POKING HIS STERNUM PRODDED TR awake. He opened his eyes to see Mallory standing over him barefoot in a terrycloth robe.

"What are you doing down there?" she said mildly.

"I didn't want to risk your barfing on my exciting gray pants."

"You could have removed them," she said, "I mean, for the sake of the pants."

"No place to put them in this cheap room you've got me holed up in."

She sighed. "I'll get you a suite for tonight. You'll have plenty of space to hang everything up." She let the thought settle in on him. "Was I too too awful last night?"

"You don't remember?"

"Not much past the first drink," she conceded.

"You had a second one."

"From which you can deduce . . . "

"That it's time for breakfast."

She shook her head. "I need clean clothes. Got to go home."

"It's eight in the morning," he said. "It's a Saturday. At least permit me to let you buy us breakfast."

He followed her gaze to her crumpled clothes at the edge of the bed.

"You can shower first," he offered.

"How dare you!" she said, in mock indignation. "I've already showered. You can't tell? Some detective you are. Why do you think I'm in this robe other than my clothes are smelly? You don't seem to have much experience in these things."

He gave her a goofy look. "Sorry; ready in twenty minutes."

"I already used the toothbrush," she said, as he walked into the bathroom.

"This trip I remembered to bring my own," he said, and shut the door.

She knocked on it seconds later. He opened it a crack and stuck his head out. "You've come to watch?"

"No, not this time, she said wistfully," she said, not especially wistfully. "You can meet me at the buffet breakfast. I'll be the uncomfortable one in yesterday's clothes."

TR joined her twenty-two minutes later, blazered but tieless, his customary casual Saturday travel uniform. Mallory sat with one hand curled around a cup of coffee, the other on her mobile phone. She looked up as he pulled out his chair.

"You're now in Suite 911," she told him. "They'll move your bag. One night—but we can extend it."

"A day at a time, Mal."

"It's the nights I'm thinking about."

"Lola can't always get what she wants."

"Holy Moley," she said, "he quotes from musicals."

TR looked over at the buffet tables.

"You're thinking about the game, the game, the game. That's it, isn't it?"

"I'm thinking about breakfast," he said, getting up. "Let's."

Mallory ate quickly and went home to change. When they met at her office two hours later, the audio "cat tape" was queued on a portable cassette recorder. TR slumped into a chair; Mallory pushed a Styrofoam cup of coffee at him and hit Play. She thought the audio revealed nothing additional, but understood that TR was chasing a hunch. The segment ran for less than ninety seconds: the first ten were scratchy static sounds, punctuated by a single loud "eeuww!," followed by a male voice asking, "What happened?" and then another voice, "What's the matter, afraid of your own cat?" The next voice was Malbonum's. "She startled me." His reaction, TR thought, sounded much more of disgust and fear than the startle and surprise of cousin Sterling around the Christmas tree how many years ago.

Mallory followed up with a recording of the brief courtroom encounter between Malbonum and the dark-haired woman about to draw his blood. The video showed the woman removing a needle and tubing from her small bag and Malbonum pushing up his sleeve. The woman looked away from what she was doing for a few seconds and said something to Malbonum that came out in a low mumble.

"Damn it," TR said, "I wanted to hear what they said."

"She said, 'Not a lot of time to watch tennis, I suppose.'"

"You can hear that?" he said, surprised.

"I heard it. Not from the tape. I was sitting right there, only a table away."

"That's what she said—exactly?"

"Yes, or pretty close."

"And you remember what he said?"

"Of course. That's the interesting part. He said, 'I only watch if Roger's playing Rafa.'"

Mallory paused the tape player and froze the video.

"Is that useful?"

"Extremely. Fantastic work, Mallory."

"Why, what does it mean?"

"I haven't the slightest idea, but it's curious."

"Another curious incident?"

"Precisely. Why would a woman taking his blood ask about tennis?"

Mallory shook her head.

"I think it's a code," he said. "Or the start of a code."

"Code for what?"

"Our job to find out. I've a few loose ends to track down," TR replied. He stood up. "This is lousy coffee. Can we get something better in the neighborhood? I feel like taking a walk."

"Sure," she said, understanding his request. "Down the block, a Dunkin' Donuts. Better'n we can make."

They left the building without talking and when they emerged into the sunlight, she said, "You're on to something. What?"

"Nagging feeling. Maybe something, maybe not. Let's review right now; we can go to work on all of it back upstairs."

She pointed to a storefront down the block. "The coffee's that way."

"When you were in Malbonum's home, were you with him the whole time?"

"The whole time? Mostly, but no, not the whole time."

"Why not?"

"The guy had to use the bathroom several times—older guy, you know. And the team and I took a brief walk outside after lunch; he stayed inside. Then a couple of times one of the agents took him somewhere for a few minutes."

"Where?"

"I don't know. I didn't think about it. I guess I thought he was using the bathroom."

"Did an agent always escort him to the bathroom?"

Mallory squinted. "No, I don't think so."

"So why would an agent only sometimes need to take him to the bathroom? How long were they gone?"

"I don't know. Maybe twenty minutes each time."

"But you don't know for sure where they went."

"No."

"They didn't say where they were going or what it was about?"

"Nope."

TR stopped talking when they entered the crowded shop.

"Allow me," Mallory said, pulling a ten-dollar bill from her wallet. She ordered a latte and a regular blend, grabbed a handful of napkins, and handed the blend to TR as they exited. He leaned against a parking meter and sipped from his cup.

"Anything else we can't talk about when we get back to the office?" she asked.

"Depends," he said. "I'm going to need to talk to a lawyer for one of the other recanters. And to Malbonum himself. Can you arrange that?"

"Yeah, if I can say I'm the one calling. He signed an agreement to talk to us whenever the need arises, with or without his lawyer. Any reason I can't be in on the call?"

"No, that's fine. They should be short."

"Which recanter's lawyer do you want?"

"Is there a lawyer who wasn't called in solely for the plea? Someone who was a recanter's lawyer before and remains his lawyer now?"

Mallory stood still, mentally thumbing through her index of the defense lawyers' names, most of whom she had talked to after their clients' appeals were rejected.

"One," she recollected. "He represents Kreutscher, the so-called alibi king, in San Francisco. Kreutscher's used this one guy strictly for defense work for the last ten years and he hasn't been implicated in any of the crimes; believe me, they checked."

"He'll talk to you?"

"Kreutscher waived client confidentiality; his lawyer is free to talk to anyone."

"All right, one other thing, if you've got someone knowledgeable. I'm thinking there may have been a test of this thing."

"What thing?"

"The central thing. The impersonation if that's what it is. Stands to reason. You don't let loose an unproven weapon on the world. The army didn't drop an atomic bomb on Hiroshima without testing whether it would work. They detonated one in New Mexico first. If what's going on with these recanters is close to what I'm coming to think it is, it's like adding a nuclear weapon to a criminal prosecution. I'm betting the FBI or whoever it is tried out their system before visiting your guy."

"Tried it out how?"

"Same as what they did with all these guys. But not as a spectacle. Probably some low-level crook, in and out and under the radar. But look for the same thing. Guy who confesses to some crime—probably a single event, not a major incident—and then recants."

"But TR, that happens all the time. Lots of people confess and then think better of it, or their lawyers find a hole in the charges or claim the confession was coerced or point to some procedural error, and the defendant takes it back."

"Yes, but probably not some guy who stands up in court and confesses details of his evil doing and agrees never to appeal and then hours later claims he doesn't know anything about the confession that everyone heard him make."

"No, I'll give you that; that doesn't happen."

"Can you find out if it ever did?"

"It's a big country, TR."

"Limit it to one of the recant cases in the news. See if some grunt working for one of the recanters fits the profile."

They had stopped outside the entrance to the U.S. Attorney's office building. "It's Saturday, you know."

TR shrugged. "Nevertheless."

"Yeah, okay, I know an AUSA I can call. Pretty good with databases and records."

"Then let's make some calls," he said.

"I repeat, it's Saturday," she said, back in her office and dialing the number. "Might not be home—Sam!" Mallory exclaimed, surprised the phone was answered. "Listen, we've got a bit of a puzzle to—yep, yep, right now, at the office, for a few hours—you're a sweetheart."

She hung up. TR was examining the photographs hanging on the wall.

"I didn't know you know a president," he said, peering at a group photo of six people in evening dress, Mallory in a ball gown standing next to Bill Clinton.

"I don't. It was a fundraiser. Went with the guy on the left of the picture."

TR looked closer.

"Oh? You dated—"

"That was more than ten years ago. Haven't seen him since," she said. Then added, "Like a lot of people."

TR felt a sharp pang. He tried to sound casual. "Are you dating—"

"No," she said, "I'm not. Short supply of essential candidates. You?"

"Mallory, you know me. Perpetual work."

"That's what we say, isn't it? Not to change the subject, but help is on the way. Well, for one problem, anyway. Sam is terrific. If Sam can't find what we're looking for, I doubt anyone can."

"Don't be too sure," TR responded earnestly. "I've got a guy—"

"Other than your people, of course. Anyway, let's get on with it. I can call Kreutscher's lawyer right now."

"Let's."

"Konrad, it's Mallory Greenstock," she said when the lawyer answered. "Hope it's not too early. I recall you get up early, or you never sleep, whatever. Listen, I'm here with a consultant to the office; we're still working on the Malbonum matter. I know, endless. Anyway, we have a quick question or two for you, and I want to put it on speaker; is that all right?"

She put the handset on the desk and pressed a console button.

"Konrad, I want to introduce you to our consultant, T.R. Softly. TR, this is Konrad Ruhig." She pronounced the last syllable as if it were born and bred in Oxbridge.

"Mr. Ruhig," TR said.

"Mr. Softly," the San Francisco lawyer replied without a trace of accent. "Your name is Tiara?"

TR gave his practiced chuckle, then his initials. "My parents, Mr. Ruhig. They wanted to name me after a president without being ostentatious."

"Ah, lucky you," said the voice from the console. "My parents could not restrain themselves. They named me after Chancellor Adenauer, without asking me. Well, how can I help?"

"I've been asked to assist with an appeal in the Malbonum case," TR said.

"Another appeal?"

"It's the twelfth," Mallory said.

Ruhig whistled. "Lucky you. Keeps us lawyers going."

"Yes, well, I've been listening to various bits and pieces of recordings that weren't part of the main hearing," TR said. "And I also heard about one curious exchange between the woman who drew the blood sample toward the end of Malbonum's plea."

"Yes?" Ruhig said, as if he knew what was coming.

"She passed the time by commenting, in a whisper, that she supposed he didn't have a lot of time to watch tennis."

"Ah," said Ruhig, "and I bet Mr. Malbonum said, 'I only watch if Roger's playing rougher.'"

"Are you sure?" TR asked.

"Of course I'm sure. I heard her whisper it too, to Kreutscher. I was sitting right there."

"You'd probably lose that bet. Is it possible your man said, 'if Roger's playing Rafa,' not 'rougher'?"

Ruhig said nothing.

"Are you there?" Mallory said.

"Goddammit!" Ruhig broke his silence. "Rafa? *That's* what he said? I've been puzzling over it for weeks. Especially because Genzman Kreutscher doesn't pay any attention to tennis. Fact is, I don't either; I had to ask around to find out who Roger is and how he plays. No one could tell me how to play tennis rougher."

"Rafael Nadal," TR said. "Young sensation."

"Didn't make sense. Now I get it."

"Really? Now it makes sense?"

"No, not really. Because as I said Mr. Kreutscher doesn't watch tennis."

"You're certain he doesn't—" TR began.

"Absolutely. I asked him about this the first time we talked after he recanted. I couldn't understand what he was doing when he said he was turning himself in. As mystifying as his confession was, I wasn't a bit surprised when he recanted. It's like he was coming down from being hypnotized or something."

"Did he seem off-kilter the day he pleaded guilty?" TR asked.

"No, that's the curious thing. Seemed himself. Seemed himself the days before, too."

"What did he say when you asked him about the tennis conversation?" Mallory said, joining the thread.

"Nothing printable. Thought I had gone bonkers. Wouldn't believe I heard him say it in the courtroom. But I know what I heard—well, as corrected." He paused. "I was sitting right there when she asked him."

"In a normal tone of voice?"

"Well, no, more like a whisper, but as I said, I could hear them."

"I want to thank you, Mr. Ruhig. You have been very helpful." TR said.

"That's all you want to discuss?" Ruhig said, his puzzlement audible.

"It is, at least for now. Mallory?"

"Nothing from me, Konrad," she said.

"But what does it mean?" Ruhig asked.

"I'm not sure," TR said. "If we find out, I'll let you know. Until then, thanks."

TR picked up the handset and put it back in its cradle, killing the call.

"And now, Malbonum?" he said.

At that moment, a figure appeared in the doorway. TR looked up to see a slight young woman in jeans and a baggy blue sweatshirt with a cartoon of a brown bear on which was superimposed the letters "Cal." Horn-rimmed glasses shielded blue eyes. Her face was topped by a mop of light-brown hair that covered her ears.

"You rang?" she said, knocking on the open door.

"Come in, Sam," Mallory said, "and meet my friend T. R. Softly, consulting for us on Malbonum. This is Samantha Pepperdie. She's the most down-to-earth super-intelligent assistant United States attorney I've ever had the pleasure to know or to work with."

"That's impressive," TR said, walking over to her.

A pink tint spread across Sam's cheeks. She shook his hand.

Mallory rose from her desk and sank into a chair by the sofa. "Sit," she said, "and let us tell you what we need." She blinked from a sudden thought. "You know, it takes a bit of doing to call into Lewisburg Penitentiary, and he arrived there only last night; let me get that moving. You two sit, and TR, start your brief."

Mallory returned to her desk and picked up the phone. Speaking quietly, TR sketched the assignment for Sam: locate any low-level employee connected to the recanters who had confessed to a crime and who then, despite the plea, denied the crime, the confession, and the government's right to cart him off to jail.

"Yes, I can do that," Sam said.

"Great," said TR.

"Yes, his name is Diego Carslip, a driver for one of Kreutscher's associates."

TR was taken aback. "I admit it; that's faster than my guy could get it."

"Sam, how on earth—" Mallory said from behind her desk, eavesdropping while she waited for her call to go through.

Samantha Pepperdie burbled at the pleasure of confounding the boss, whom she idolized. She was afraid of explaining—the surprise of an immediate answer was surely worth more than its verification. But a unit chief's question deserves an answer.

"Don't you remember, I did up that All Known Associates chart tracking relationships among everyone who ever worked for any of the recanters or their people? Carslip was one of the first I found, probably because his name was in the police blotter a month before Malbonum's big day in court. I can get you the specific date—"

"Or better, a memo with everything you have on his arrest, confession, and recanting," TR interrupted.

"Okay, I can do that. Strictly local news. Nothing made the papers back here. Most of it will be from FBI and police records."

"What did he plead to?" Mallory asked.

"Trivial. He ran a red light, clipped a car in the intersection, mildly injured the driver. No real damage. But when the prosecutors found out who he was they figured it was a way to get someone to flip on Kreutscher, so they threw the book at him. He confessed to all of it, got eighteen months in a state correctional facility. He recanted the day after the plea. But since he'd agreed to forfeit all rights and forgo all appeals, they denied any further proceedings and that was that. I figure he was probably pretty lucky."

"Oh, why was that?" TR asked.

"If he hadn't been locked up, he'd more than likely have wound up in the San Francisco dragnet when the feds picked up all the rest of Kreutscher's troops and he'd be facing a much longer jail term now. They more or less forgot about him. I'm figuring he did himself a favor."

The phone rang. Mallory picked up.

"Greenstock," she said, then fell silent. Then: "I can talk to him now." She covered the receiver and whispered to Sam to write the memo. "Succinct. Whatever you can do in an hour."

Sam jumped up and left. Mallory put the phone on speaker. A man's voice said to hold, that Malbonum would be on the phone in less than a minute.

The well-known nasal voice said, "You got me. What for?"

"Mr. Malbonum," she said cheerily, "it's Mallory Greenstock, U.S. Attorney's Office in New York. I hope you remember me. We spent a couple of nice days together in your home, and then back and forth in court the past few weeks."

"Not the way I see it," Malbonum grunted. "Not the house part. The rest, sure, you're the cutie in the—"

"Well, that's neither here nor there, luckily," she said, talking over him. "I've got you on speaker with T. R. Softly, an investigator for our office. He's got a couple of questions for you."

"Couldn't it have waited? I was in the middle of reading this fascinating book *The Common Good*."

"I congratulate you, Mr. Malbonum," TR said, "on retaining your sense of humor."

"Yeah, I'm a funny fellow. What's the question?"

"Two questions, actually," TR said.

"The first one."

"Your cat."

"Valachi? Is he okay?" He breathed heavily. "Goddammit, no one tells me anything."

"Relax, Mr. Malbonum. As far as I know, the cat's fine. I want to learn about your *relationship* to the cat."

"My relationship? I love that cat. It's almost as hard to be apart from Valachi as it is from my family. But don't tell them that."

"You've had the cat a long time?"

"We got him as a kitten. He was a stray. Found him at our doorstep one morning. Very affectionate. And *loyal*. He'd come up to me in the evening and sleep on my hand or wrist when I watched TV."

"How old is she now?"

"He. Valachi's a he. Must be, lemme see, probably, yeah, he's ten. Why all this interest in Valachi?"

"Just checking. My job to run down every lead."

"Lead? You going to get me out of here?"

"Not my job, sir," TR said.

"Well, it sure isn't hers. No offense," Malbonum said.

"None ever taken," Mallory said.

"I'm only a Princeton graduate," he said, "but even Tigers know how to count higher than two. That's a lot of questions, Mr. Softly. Is that it?"

"My apologies," TR cut in. "I should have said two sets of questions. My other set is about your relationship to tennis."

"Tennis?" His puzzlement was clear. "I don't have a relationship. Don't play. Never have."

"I was thinking more about watching. You watch any tennis?"

"Oh sure, on my giant flat-screen TV in the palatial solitary cell I've relocated to."

"I meant, *did* you ever watch tennis? Are you interested in the game?"

"I doubt I've ever watched a match all the way through," Malbonum said.

"Any player in particular?"

"McEnroe, I guess. Always liked John. Irascible son of a bitch. Good show."

"How about Roger Federer?"

"He the rising star?"

"I'm asking you."

"Don't think I've ever seen him play. What's this all about?"

TR drew his hand across his neck and nodded at Mallory.

"Thanks, Mr. Malbonum," she said. "You may not realize it, but you've been mighty helpful."

"To whom?" he demanded, as she hung up.

"Strange," TR said, "after all these years to be involved with a Malbonum again."

"Again? When were you ever—"

He held up his hand. "Strictly in my mind. Came across his grandfather's name when I started reading true crime books in high school. I thought it was a funny name. Never supposed I'd actually talk to one."

She drummed her fingers on the arm of her chair. "That one seemed to contradict himself."

"You noticed that, huh?"

"Hard not to," Mallory replied. "The Malbonum at the hearing only watches tennis when Roger plays Rafa. The Malbonum in prison has never seen Roger and has only ever watched John McEnroe. Curious."

Nodding, TR said, "It was already curious when we first heard it; I thought it might be a code. It is beyond curious when you also consider that the Kreutscher in court likewise was glued to Roger and Rafa but Ruhig's Kreutscher, supposedly the same man, never watched tennis at all."

"What do you make of it?" she asked.

"That someone went to a great deal of trouble to construct a narrative that appears to show no one taking any trouble to get it right."

"What does that mean?"

TR stood up. "I'm going back to my suite," he said.

"Just like that. Not answering my question? Leaving me to shrivel up and pine?"

"You should wait for Sam's report, and email it to me when you get it. Then come join me uptown."

"Oh goody!"

"To work, Mal. And I know you're not that kind of woman, so don't get your hopes up."

"Dashed," she said.

"But before I leave," he said, surprising her, "tell me if you're a theater goer."

"Theater? You mean Broadway? Practically never. Off-Broadway now and then. Generally can't afford it. Why do you ask?"

"You said something about musicals earlier. Did you ever go regularly?"

"No, not . . . " She closed her eyes. "Hold on. When I was in law school, I used to go to Yale Dramat productions. It was good theater, and cheap in those days. Nice way to relax."

"Any shows in particular?"

"One or two years I had season tickets, saw them all."

"Interesting."

"Why? What's the Yale Dramat got to do with any of this?"

"Maybe by this evening we'll know," he said, already walking out the door.

CHAPTER 12

FINGERED

BY THE TIME TR EMERGED FROM the subway and into Grand Central Terminal, Sam Pepperdie's report had landed in his inbox. He eyeballed it on his phone as he walked past the iconic clock and rode the escalator up to the exit opposite the Yale Club. The report looked favorable: Carslip's plea had been taken in a suburban courthouse, twenty or thirty miles down the peninsula from San Francisco, where it would be much easier to track the government players.

TR went directly to his suite in the Club, flung his blazer on an armchair, and set up his laptop on the desk. Then he phoned orJean.

"TR," she said, "how ya doin'?"

"Getting closer," he said.

"Where are you?"

"New York. I meant, closer to solving this thing."

"Zeroing-in stage?"

"I'm a detective, not an oracle. Closer to the end of the beginning. Did you reach Call-In?"

"He's standing by. Figured you'd call direct."

"Will do."

"Nothing from Khaki?"

"Like always: straight to voice mail."

"Anything else you need from me?" she asked.

"Hate to do this to you on a Saturday night," he said, "but I may need some of your time."

"That's okay, TR. Not like I've got a heavy date. Last heavy date I had—"

"The 230-pound blind date last November?"

"You stole my line."

"Okay, I'll make it up to you."

She rang off before TR could say more. He dialed the PBDS resident New Haven agent, Colin Mardsworth, dubbed Call-In and famous during his college years at Ohio State as the first caller on sports talk radio programs. He would attempt to impress the hosts and his girlfriend *du jour* with the depth of the *Jeopardy*-like trivia he could spout. He was renowned for hyperactively waving his hand whenever a professor asked a question, often without having the answer. He wanted to command and be the first to step up to any open mic. A literature major then, he now spent much of his time running a sophisticated statistical database for major league baseball, NFL football, and NBA basketball. The balance of his time he ferreted out facts for PBDS, mostly by calling around, shaming informants into disgorging pertinent information, and scoping out unlikely connections.

TR sketched two lines of inquiry. First, FBI connections to Diego Carslip in his down-peninsula trial, particularly whether Call-In could find evidence that an agent was staying in a hotel near the courthouse. Second, locate an actor named Dewey Sisal, in Yale Drama School productions in the early nineties. If not Sisal, then the top three male actors measured by the sheer diversity of roles each played.

"Diversity of roles?" Call-In said. "What's that mean?"

"You know, markedly different. Serious drama, light musicals, bedroom farces."

"You mean, like *Hamlet* and *Noises Off*?"

"You'll figure it out. And Call-In, flank speed."

A single knock at the door signaled Mallory's arrival. She handed him a sealed, oversized envelope containing Sam's report on Diego Carslip that he had already skimmed. He tossed it atop his blazer.

She said, "Where are we?"

"We're in Suite 911, your wildest fantasy."

"You have no idea about my wildest fantasy," she snapped. "Where are we on the case? What have you figured out?"

A chastened TR motioned her to the sofa. He fell back into the other armchair and weighed his approach to the summary he was about to deliver. Then he got up again, retrieved two diet Cokes from the half-height refrigerator, and brought them to the table in front of the sofa.

"We're closing in," he began. "The mystery scene is materializing hour by hour."

"And what's glittering at this hour?"

"The recanters were almost certainly manipulated. My working theory is it's some sort of electronic telepathy."

"You mean like psychic mind reading?"

"I have no idea what it could be; I call it 'telepathy' for convenience. Some kind of brain manipulation. Probably remote, possibly implanted. Maybe a super-sophisticated version of the gadgets that telephone hackers used in the seventies to make free calls. Or a version of the trick in *Roxanne:* an airhead repeats romantic words heard in earphones to woo fair damsel. It doesn't matter how it's done. What matters is *who* is doing it."

"How can you be sure anyone is doing it?"

"Because of the curious incident of the purring cat and the tennis code."

"The Roger code?"

"Yep, what Malbonum said to the woman drawing blood in the courtroom. 'Roger plays Rafa.' Once in New York—your case—and once in San Francisco—Kreutscher's case, as his lawyer told us. And maybe, if we checked further, in the other cases too. It's code for something, because neither of those guys watches tennis, and they certainly don't dote on the two young players. It's like in the movies. A spy comes up to a guy on the bridge who's smoking a cigarette and says, 'How lovely the moon.' The smoker says, 'Only when it's blue,' and the spy knows this is his man. I think Roger–Rafa is an identity check, not of the defendant's body but of whoever's running the telepathy machine. It's a signal that the impersonator is in charge."

"And that the technician who drew the blood is in on it."

"Yes. That's an important point. A significant point, because it means this isn't some rogue telepath doing this. It's a coordinated effort. But it's sloppy."

"Sloppy how?"

"Sloppy in two ways. Smart agents don't re-use signals. One-time only. This code reads like a signal to an investigator. As if whoever's in charge wants anyone going to the trouble to listen to realize it was someone else voicing the confessions. And the second piece of sloppiness—well, you pointed it out this morning: there seem to be two different Malbonums giving two different answers: one in court, one after recanting. Kreutscher, the same. Someone didn't think it all the way through. Or *really* thought it all the way through. It's either extremely sloppy or extremely sophisticated signaling."

"Come to think of it," Mallory said, "that's not the only reason for thinking it's sloppy planning, or a signal intended for someone else."

"What's another reason?" TR said, leaning forward.

"Why should the woman care at all? She's got a guy there whose blood she's supposed to take. It's plainly Malbonum. Why bother exchanging pleasantries? Why should she want to know at that point whether someone's running him or controlling him?"

"Why indeed? That, my dear Mallory, is why you're chief of unit. A subtle unraveling of the signal's bona fides. Excellent." TR's eyes glistened for a second, as they sometimes did when he reflected that he was in the presence of real intelligence.

"You're such a gentleman," Mallory said. "Why, that flattery will get you to where you apparently don't want to go. But let's move on. The cat?"

"Ah, the cat. That's also subtle, but it's also more convincing—and it's consistent with our analysis of the Roger code. It's possible that these people are sloppy though I doubt it; what they've done is pretty amazing. But the curious incident of the cat is not a sloppy signal. It's an elucidating moment. You know cats?"

"No."

"Well, contrary to some opinion, cats are amazingly social creatures, most of them anyway, if they're treated right. They may not answer to their name, but they crave attention. My cat wouldn't—"

"TR Softly! You have a cat?" Mallory interrupted with a whoop.

"Sure. Grew up with a cat. Except for college and my Navy time, cats have been my housemates."

"What's his name?"

"Her name is TK."

Mallory smiled. "Of course, what else?"

"Not what you think—I think. I wanted to give her an appropriate name. I'm pretty sensitive to how things are named, in case you don't know. I wasn't sure what to call her, and a journalist friend came by a few days after I got her and when he asked, I admitted I hadn't settled on anything. I figured you'd be insulted if I called her Mallory."

"You think I'm catty?"

"See," TR said, "exactly the point. My friend said to call the cat 'TK' until I came up with a name—"

"Because in journalism speak, 'tk' means 'to come.'"

"Yeah. And the name hasn't come yet, and by now it's probably too late for her to be called anything else. It's certainly too late for her to change her ways. She wouldn't dream of avoiding me on the sofa. She's forever jumping up and purring and trying to climb onto my lap or sit on my hand. She knows me, and she expects that I'll welcome her attention. It's obvious that's what Malbonum's cat expected." TR paused in admiration before continuing. "Valachi, what a splendidly ironic name—doubly so, when you think about it, because unlike the real Valachi, a cat can't testify. But Valachi" (and here TR got to his point) "genuinely *did* testify though not in so many words. Anyway, it's obvious what Valachi was doing the evening you were there. And you saw how Malbonum reacted. I don't say "eeuww!" when TK jumps up on my sofa. I know it's TK. But Malbonum wasn't expecting a cat. Or more precisely, Malbonum's 'controller,' or whatever you want to call the impersonator, wasn't expecting a cat. *That* person is ailurophobic—afraid of cats. He freaked out when Valachi landed though the Malbonum whisperer wasn't physically there in the house. Primal instinct: he wasn't ready for a cat. Wasn't properly briefed, I guess. Because if he had been, he would have tried his damnedest not to show fear in front of all of you just as he did a minute later when he feigned petting the cat.

"But how do you know this impersonator, this telepathy person, wasn't there?"

"Because Malbonum the person *was* there. You saw him."

Mallory pressed. "For the sake of argument, the person who was physically there couldn't have been Tom Cruise in a Mission Impossible mask?"

"But Valachi was purring. The cat expected Malbonum, even if Malbonum's controller didn't expect the cat. And Valachi found what he was looking for—Malbonum's body, his shape, his sound, his smell, his surroundings. Valachi doesn't know about telepathy; he just wanted to be petted. But for that one instant, the telepath, the guy in charge, lost control. How else can you explain it? Malbonum wouldn't lose control like that over his own cat, a cat he told us he loves. And one more thing. *Your* Malbonum called the cat a 'she.' The Malbonum now in prison called Valachi 'he.' You heard him say so this morning. That's no small thing. In fact, it's a conclusive thing. The telepath screwed up."

"That's it?" she said when he finished.

"Yep, that's what we know," TR concluded, "or what's likely to be the case when we get all the facts—even as improbable as—" He paused in mid-sentence. "Come to think of it, there is another thing."

"Which is?"

"Whatever they're doing, they don't have total control of it. Think about how fast all these hearings played out. In each case, our recanters cooperate for what, five days? Then they revert to badass. Like the impersonator's power sort of wears out."

"A criminal defendant who becomes inhabited or a zombie who's run by a remotely connected telepathic impersonator who wears out." Mallory shook her head. "Any minute I may become sorry I invited you."

"Can't be a zombie. A zombie—"

"TR, enough. You can enlighten me on zombies on your own time. What about real facts? Got any?"

"You know, there is one more. It just hit me. You know it too."

"What am I buying you lunches for? Spill it."

"Well, think about it. Malbonum the recanter claimed he was trapped in a room and heard a voice asking questions. He was real insistent on that. The other recanters made no such claim. Malbonum told his whole life story. The others, after Malbonum, didn't."

"Meaning?"

"It's like the impersonator is learning, adjusting his game. Stripping it down to essentials."

She shook her head. "I meant real facts. Like, who this impersonator is. And how does he impersonate."

"If you can hang on a bit, we may get an important real fact or two soon."

"Well, that's good, because it strikes me that everything you're saying that we know rests on the thinnest of inferences," she said.

"You don't trust my chain of reasoning?"

"It's not based on any solid evidence."

"Well, it is, in a way. Not your kind of courtroom evidence, true. It's based on detectives' evidence. The lawyer in court is like a scientist in a lab. They both have to demonstrate an empirical reality, not rely on 'I think therefore it is.' They are obliged to persuade by perceived fact: 'I show therefore it is.' The detective, on the other hand, may often rely on his practical knowledge of human behavior. Suppose I ask whether you have ever possessed a stolen car and all you say is that you do not now have a stolen car in your possession. What other conclusion can we draw but that you once did? These are the forms of the questions the detective learns to ask. It's not enough to take to a jury, but it's enough to take the matter to be true. Anyway, you're not paying me to prove the case, just to state it."

"I'm not paying you anything," Mallory reminded him.

"Nevertheless," he said.

Mallory shook her shoulders and straightened her legs from the sofa where she'd been curled up since she arrived.

"So what shall we do while we wait?" she said brightly. "You know, when you're in a hotel room with a handsome man on a Saturday at"—she looked at her watch—"two-thirty in the afternoon, there're only two things a woman can want."

TR stood up. "I agree. Let's get lunch."

"Thank goodness," she said, exhaling audibly. "I don't really need a new hat."

The call came three hours later. The ever-excitable Call-In was excited. Back in the suite, TR put the phone on speaker and introduced Mallory.

"Two good newses. I looked around, I called around. Then I walked around. You're going to like it," Call-In exclaimed. The first was verification of TR's hunch about the trial of Diego Carslip.

"You're not going to believe it, but that name you gave me as a possible actor, Dewey Sisal, well, I couldn't find him as an actor, but he was in town for the Carslip trial. Not just in town. He had a three-room suite at the poshest hotel, two blocks from the court. And here's what's odd. The hearing was held on a Wednesday. Sisal checks in on Tuesday afternoon with two colleagues—that's what the assistant concierge I talked to called them—and none of 'em leave until the following night. Hours after the court hearing. They're in that room for what, thirty straight hours? No one sees 'em enter after they check in or leave until they check out. But Carslip must have. He arrives unescorted an hour after Sisal and his crew get there. He asks at the desk for the suite, says he's there to meet his lawyer. Awhile later the lawyer goes up, and then the town prosecutor joins the party. They stay for several hours, order room service dinners. The lawyer and prosecutor leave around nine. The next morning, the big day, the lawyer shows up at eight, breakfasts with Carslip, and the two of them march off to court.

"Everyone was buzzing about it because it was all over the local news that this guy not only pleaded guilty but agreed to be sentenced and signed away his right to appeal. Not only that, the DA was quoted as recommending a lighter sentence in return for Carslip's cooperation in providing information on 'other matters.' At six o'clock Carslip comes back to the suite all by his lonesome and stays there."

"Let me tell you what happened next," TR interrupted.

"Yeah?"

"At some point a police officer or two arrive and go up to the room, and a shortly thereafter Sisal comes out with colleagues."

"That's right. About a quarter to eight two policemen show up and take the elevator up. Ten minutes later Sisal comes down with two others, a man and a woman, and checks out."

"And then there's a ruckus," TR ventured.

"Why do you bother having me check it out?" Call-In said. "Apparently a real shitstorm starts blowing in the room. They have to drag the guy out of there. Carslip's yelling and cursing and demanding to know what's going on. He swears he couldn't have been in court and didn't plead to anything. They have him in cuffs and march him out the elevator straight through the lobby telling him to zip it. It was real loud."

"And Carslip goes direct to jail?" Mallory asked.

"I didn't run it down, but I can if you want me to."

"No, that's okay, Call-In," TR said. "What you found is exactly what I suspected and what we needed to know."

"Okay, you want the second good news?"

"Today, Call-In."

"Walked over to the Dramat. Found a guy was in his office. They have a collection of all the old playbills. Spent an hour, or a little more, going through productions from the early nineties. Like I said, no Sisal. What I did was, I looked in the programs for the four most dissimilar plays each year and picked the top three actors measured by how many of those divergent plays they did. In my book, the top guy is the one who was in *King Lear, Finian's Rainbow, Clarence Darrow: A One-Man Play*, and Shaw's *Don Juan in Hell*. All in a single season. I mean, he's a long-winded king, a leprechaun who sings, a lawyer who yaks on stage for two straight hours all by himself, and then, well, it's Shaw. His sentences can stitch the early afternoon of one day to the late morning of the next. But to be certain, I'm sending you two other contenders as well. Not in the same league, but runners-up. Sending photos right . . . now. Your laptop on? Can you check?"

In three seconds the photos displayed.

"Holy Moley!" Mallory was dumbstruck.

"What you wanted?" Call-In asked mildly, afraid to compete with Mallory's intensity.

"That one," she said, pointing at the screen, "the one labeled 'number one contender'? That's Dewey Sisal. Younger, but he's the guy."

"No shit?" Call-In said. "Bull's-eye."

"Thank you, Call-In," TR answered. "I owe you one."

"Wait a minute, wait a minute!" Mallory yelled.

"What?" the two men said simultaneously.

"His name. What's his real name?"

"It's in the email," Call-In pointed out.

Mallory spoke the name. "Nicholas B. Nimsey?"

"That's what it said in all the programs."

"Dewey Sisal is Nicholas Nimsey?" Mallory repeated.

"I leave it to you," Call-In said.

"Later," TR told him, and hung up.

TR and Mallory looked at each other. She leaned in and hugged him, a gesture he reciprocated.

"I don't know how you did that," she said. "No secrets, tell me."

"Elementary, my dear Mallory."

"Come off it. You found the guy in, what, thirty-six hours?"

"Well, no. Found his name. We still have to locate him. We're only at the beginning of the middle."

"Well, humor this old lady, and tell me how we got here."

"The old-fashioned way, from meager evidence to chains of inference. Someone is taking charge of defendants and making them confess. I figure they're broadcasting and the range is short. They've got to be somewhere close. With Malbonum, they had his house. For Carslip, I suggested Call-In look for nearby hotels. It was probably not a coincidence it was Sisal. How many people could have such a skill? How many agents are trained to be impersonators?"

"How do you even train for that?" she asked.

TR shrugged, shook his head.

"But there's one thing wrong with your theory."

"What?"

"Malbonum's house isn't anywhere near the courthouse where he spent all day talking. So how did they 'broadcast,' if that's what they did, all the way into Manhattan when Malbonum was in court?"

"Well, maybe they do something to their subjects before they can be FBI vessels," TR said. "I don't know."

"And the theater angle?"

"Stands to reason. If there really is an impersonator as we're imagining, who better than a trained actor? Someone who can memorize a prodigious amount of material. And then dump it and master more in short order. And can assume different personas. When you said you thought you recognized him, I figured you weren't remembering him from a single hour at a conference, but it could be because you'd seen him more than once on the stage. And then you said you didn't go to theater, except during your years in New Haven. That was easy."

"Must be why you're so well paid."

"Well, the suite is nice."

"Yes, and stay in it awhile and listen to what else is wrong with your theory so far," Mallory said.

"I'm all ears."

"Well, first, if the cat's pouncing tells us it really was Malbonum on the sofa when we were interviewing him, why would the impersonator freak out? What does he care, if he's really somewhere else running his telepathy machine? I mean, it's not as if the cat was sitting on *his* hand."

TR nodded mutely.

"And why don't any of the recanters remember being 'controlled'? When the impersonator turns off the control or it wears out, why don't they remember where they were or what they said? It's clear they don't."

"Beats me," TR shrugged.

"And then, how in the world would Dewey Sisal as an impersonator know things that only Malbonum knew, like shooting his own father?"

"Beats me thrice, but I'll be sure to ask Dewey—or Nick—when I find him."

"You'll find him?"

"Only a matter of time," he said.

"Any off-the-cuff, evidence-be-damned thoughts where he is?"

"Thoughts, yes. Confidence, no. I'm assuming he's really FBI. Hard to understand how a freelancer could be involved. If he's connected to all these cases, he's probably working out of a principal field office. Or the DC HQ. Too much effort from an out-of-the-way hamlet. We have his two names now. We'll track him down."

"Soon?" she asked.

"Hope to."

"Trying to get rid of me?"

"Mallory! You're a one true thing. Don't ever think I want you to leave."

She reached out for him, pulled him toward her, and pressed her lips into his. The kiss was firm, definitive, not subject to misinterpretation. He gave into it for as long as she was willing, then hugged her tightly and disentangled himself, almost dizzy from the close encounter. He steadied himself against the desk.

He looked at her. "Don't take this the wrong way—"

"Oh-oh," she murmured.

"I'm heading out."

"What, now?"

"Need to solve this case."

"TR Softly," she said, color rushing to her face, "the game, the game, the game. You owe me an evening in this suite."

She retrieved TR's blazer and helped him into it. While he buttoned the middle button and smoothed the pockets, she closed his laptop and handed it to him and then went to the closet and offered the strap of his overnight bag to his other hand.

"If you need me later," she said, "I'm staying here tonight. I already rented this room, and I see no reason to waste it." She turned on the TV. "No hurry," she said after a few moments, "but the movie is about to start, so scram. I may get two bags of potato chips for company. You might want to think about your timetable before I get fatter."

TR opened the door to the hallway and paused, scrutinizing the floral prints on the wallpaper. "When we find out what's going on, what are you going to do?" he asked, not turning around.

She responded soberly to his back, "That depends, as you constantly say, on what you find out."

He closed the door and returned to Penn Station. Once aboard the Acela back to Washington, he wondered what he was going to do about Mallory Greenstock, unaware that at that same moment she was wondering what he was going to do about her too.

The White House
Washington, DC 20500

June 15, 5:00 p.m.

A Treat from Your President

Enuff Already
(Statement on Spelling)

Presidents get called lots of names. The First Lady tells me it comes with the landscape and relax but it shouldn't but it does. All health officials agree I'm more openminded than anyone else who has ever had this job but even I have My superhuman limits. And the past few weeks the enemies of Our Democracy have gone too far much too. You'd think I'm being coy if I leave it at that and don't name names I'm pointing directly at you Washington Post. It's degrading and sickening and beyond human tolerance to call me "Spellchecker." The Leader of the Free World has more important things to do than to have to put up with such nonsense. Just because once (or okay twice) we've had a malfunction or what have you with the godforsaken software everyone does. It's got to stop. I'm not Spellchecker. I'm much more like that guy at the end of the old movie M*A*S*H, Spearchucker Jones. I've even played football. I don't even know how to use one. Why can't they get one to work? This country has a serious problem not getting spellcheckers to spell. What's the matter with these programmers? Not like the Russians. My job is barnstorming important policy plans and turning them over to Very Top Botch people in the Administration to carry out their marching orders whatever I say or do. But I don't need to use one because I am known ever since my youth when I first found out what spelling is as a Very Perfect Spoiler. So let's get on with the real work of getting the people of My back.

Action taken: Concern communicated (see above).

Bottom line: Don't worry about me, despite the torment I'm ubiquitously the coolest. White-hot cool.

Technical Correction to the Presidential Treat, Today's Date: Because of a speelcheck impediment in the White House Secure Treat Room, the word "Spoiler" should have been "Speller," "Botch" should have been "Knotch," and "barnstorming should have been "brainstorming." The phrase replacement feature erred in substituting "getting people of My back" for "governing Our People."

CHAPTER 13

SOFTLY SEEKING

TR SOFTLY AWOKE LATE SUNDAY MORNING. Nine o'clock. Sensing a cat's paw swatting him on the cheek to the accompaniment of mewling, he emerged from a dream of being pummeled in a boxing match. TK was sitting atop his pillow, alerting him to a hunger crisis *in situ.*

"OK, old girl," he said, chucking her under the chin until her purrs threatened the glass on his night table. He stuffed his feet into shearling moccasins and walked out of the room. TK was off the bed in a flash, zipping past him down the stairs so she could sit nonchalantly in front of her empty bowl with a tilt of her head that took him to task for making her wait. When TK finally plunged her face into salmon supreme, TR powered on his Keurig and retrieved his *New York Times* and *Washington Post* from the front steps. He skimmed both papers over a glass of juice, then went back upstairs to make himself presentable. At ten o'clock he called orJean.

"How about a second cup of coffee?" he asked, without preliminary ado.

"I'll throw this one out," she replied. "Where?"

"Here," he said.

"In thirty," she said and hung up. A Sunday morning summons meant bring her latest database changes and a clear mind. At that hour from her home in Tenleytown, near American University, it was a mere twenty-minute drive down Wisconsin Avenue to TR's townhouse on Dumbarton. A few minutes extra to find parking and by 10:40 she was sitting with TR at his kitchen counter, holding a mug of fresh-brewed dark roast coffee latte to which she had added a dollop of chocolate. She wore trim white slacks and an amply rounded gray T-shirt with a large, tan "P" embedded in a larger, obliquely pitched Navy blue "P." Her elder daughter Betsy was a proud Purdue alumna. OrJean looked more brunette than when TR had last seen her three weeks earlier.

"Sorry about putting a hold on your plans last night," he said. "Decided to run for the train."

She showed off a row of dazzling straight white teeth. "What's going on?"

TR laid it out.

"In other words," she said, the sarcasm stretched tight across her rambling sentence, "what you're saying is we need to find a guy with two names who may or may not work for the FBI in some secret location most likely but not certainly in the lower forty-eight who's involved in some super-spooky hypnotic mind control plot that's probably an official conspiracy but may be nothing at all. Within the next thirty-six hours."

"About sums it up."

"Jesus, TR, this one's worse than the case of the lecherous hedge fund manager, and you gave us forty-eight hours to close that one."

"But there it was her husband who had two names, and we didn't know anything else to start. This one's practically solved. We've got both of his names."

"And that's about all you've got."

"He's FBI."

"Probably," she amended.

"Anyone in the Nickname Club available?"

OrJean bent over her laptop and called up a spreadsheet listing PBDS Washington agents with Degree One, Two, or Three connections to the FBI. Each of the agents answered to nicknames conferred by TR and orJean in whimsical moods.

"Today?" she asked.

TR nodded.

"Three are available today. Merry Grunstone, Karol Nonce, and of course Formerly."

"Formerly's free?"

"He finished the beauty pageant thing."

"He found the stash?"

"Was in the wheel well of Miss Okra's daughter's car."

"Case all wrapped up?"

"Friday, like fish."

"Well, for gosh sakes, orJean, he's had a day off. See if he can come over."

"Why can't *you* do the job instead? Give the guy a break. You're pals with what's his name, the guy who practically runs the FBI's HR department."

"I can't use a Degree One contact, orJean. Would raise way too much suspicion if I called him direct for information like that on something they're desperate to bury. I don't want him to know we're looking for one of his ultra-secret agents. I contact my guy only when absolutely necessary, not if there's some other way to get the goods. This one's extra delicate. We need to move sideways."

OrJean speed dialed their man. He didn't answer, not surprisingly, since he routinely screened his calls.

"It's orJean," she said when the recorded message ended. "TR's asap, and call to confirm when."

Less than a minute later, her phone rang. "IT'S LANCE LEWIS." The words could be heard across the room. Formerly Mumford at his usual loud pitch.

"Formerly, hey," she replied.

"OrJean," he complained, "I just got back."

"Asap," she said. "When?"

"Ah, Christ, an hour."

"We'll have deli," she said and disconnected.

Lance Lewis, aka Formerly Mumford, arrived ten seconds behind the deliveryman from Gentlemen's Meats, the wildly successful delicatessen restaurant several blocks over on M Street. Its menu featured more than fifty sandwiches by name; others could be special ordered for take-out. To be safe, orJean called in an order for a dozen. Lance Lewis, born Mumford Lewis, stood patiently behind the driver as orJean signed the credit card slip. The deliveryman, not looking, turned to depart down the stone stairs and bumped directly into the stolid, stationary agent, who stood six feet, two inches in his socks and worked out daily.

"Shit, man," said the deliveryman, "watch where you're going."

"I wasn't moving," Lewis said, standing his ground.

The deliveryman stepped around him and Lewis walked inside.

"Hey, Formerly," orJean said.

"Hey, yourself," he said. "I wish you two wouldn't call me that."

"Oh, come on, you don't mind it. In fact, I bet you secretly like it. You're part of the Nickname Club."

Embarrassed since he was five or six by his name, Lewis legally changed it to the much more striking "Lance" when he was eighteen, a year after TR helped him out of a tight spot. He and orJean wouldn't let the name drop but did him the honor of recognizing it was no longer officially Mumford by calling him Formerly Mumford or, of course, Formerly, for short.

He picked up the large bag of sandwiches and walked into the kitchen, where TR was putting out plates and napkins.

"Formerly," TR said, nodding at his agent.

"Boss," Formerly nodded back.

TR waited until Formerly finished his epic double Reuben,

requiring five large napkins and two bottles of Plumagranate Snapple, before outlining the mission. OrJean was only halfway through her rare roast beef, raw onion, and cream cheese club. While he talked, TR watched her eat it, having overcome his gag reflex a year earlier.

"We need a Degree Three contact," TR said, after explaining the entire setup to the much mollified Formerly.

"Because?"

"Because we need to be heavily insulated. If this guy Dewey Sisal is in fact a big deal super invisible agent, they'll be watching for lurkers and spotters. That's why I personally can't do it. We've got to get in through the side door so that anyone looking will think we're there delivering milk."

"Okay, I think I've got it," orJean announced, as she peered at her laptop, which was displaying a page in her government connections database several layers deep. "Someone you've met, William Willewood, who knows a guy in FBI office administration."

"Bill Willewood, yeah, I know him," Formerly acknowledged. "Talk to him at the gym from time to time. Occasionally have a drink. What do you have in mind?"

"Nothing fancy," orJean instructed. "You're trying to locate Dewey, an FBI agent. Mislaid his phone number. You recall your pal Bill knows a guy at the FBI who could maybe check for you."

"Even better," TR weighed in, "you bumped into Dewey at dinner in San Francisco a few weeks back. He left something behind, his jacket or something. You'd return it but you don't know where he is. You thought he gave you his card, but can't find it. You just remembered that Willewood mentioned having some FBI pal. Can your pal call his pal and get the address?"

"And I ask him to leave my name out of it when he calls," Formerly said, climbing aboard.

"Exactly. Also, you're going away for a week bright and early tomorrow and trying to work your way through your overdue to-do list. You're hoping he can call his guy right now, this afternoon."

"Why not?" Formerly said, and pulled out his phone. He looked at orJean. She met his gaze and shrugged. "His number," Formerly said. "You must have his number in your database there. I don't."

"Ah, sorry," she said, "daydreaming."

Formerly dropped his phone into her outstretched hand. She entered the number and handed it back. He tapped the call button. Willewood answered on the third ring.

"Hey, Bill," Formerly said, "it's—Lance Lewis. Listen, sorry to trouble you on a Sunday," and from there he sold his buddy on his simple need to clear his desk of unwanted tasks so he could embark on his travels unburdened. Would be a big help. And in case his FBI friend doesn't have what he needs, better to not give him Lance's name—just say he's calling for a friend, real low key. Don't want to have an FBI agent trying to track down Lance, wondering what the call was all about, ha ha.

"He'll get back to us," Formerly said, pocketing the phone. "But it sounds like you have a suspicion. Where do you think he is?"

"Here in town," TR said. "Mallory said the New York mobile number was disconnected. Looks like he's running all over the country for these recanter cases. If he's really FBI, I think he's FBI in Washington. This thing smells like it's being run from headquarters. I'm willing to bet on it. In fact, let's see if we can get a jump on things. We'll go downstairs and talk about it while we wait for Formerly's guy to call."

Downstairs was not the usual furnace, laundry, or rec room with pool table and oversized television set. It was, even TR allowed, out of the ordinary. Among the extensive renovations to the four-story townhouse TR oversaw when he moved in about a decade earlier was a "downward adjustment" to the basement floor. The depth set by the original architect was seven feet. For more than eighty years it housed a run of old washing machines, boilers, and mildew. TR decreed an additional dozen feet plus one. The floor was now twenty feet below grade, far enough down to permit a loft ringing the upper walls with an open floor and ceiling in the middle. The entire basement was suitably modified otherwise as well, including an extensive air purifying and conditioning system. The upper loft space became his office and library. At the bottom, he yielded to his Yale-inspired obsession and began to install printing presses, letterpress machines that craved real lead. He retaught himself how to set type, make up and lock up the form, and ink the plate.

His maiden acquisition was a hand-operated tabletop eight by twelve Pilot Press, manufactured by Chandler & Price in the early thirties (the numbers indicating the size of the chase, the frame holding the type). A year later he added a motorized ten-by-fifteen C & P Craftsman to his collection. A good pressman, as TR became in time, could pull fifteen impressions a minute on the larger press. Some months later he managed a Vandercook proof press. The walls of the basement began to disappear behind rows of type cabinets, printers' stones, cabinets for wooden blocks (known as furniture) used in the chase, and other arcane tools of the trade (composing sticks, quoins, slugs and leading, inks, solvents, cuts, and shelves and more shelves of fine paper).

Two years after the first presses managed their precarious descent down the stairs (the Craftsman in pieces), TR was seized by a pipe dream that eventually yielded to a vision. He fancied nothing less than a press monster, capable of high-speed hands-off production. He resisted for several years before yielding. Dedicated workmen took several weeks to widen and shore up the doorway and steps, and then installed a set of ponderous tracks and pulleys to enable permanent residence to an immigrant with a proud lineage: a Heidelberg SBG cylinder press, weighing in at six and a half tons, standing six feet high, twelve feet long, and nearly seven feet wide. Locating and acquiring an appropriate model took several months; moving it to Washington, three more. Installing it from the disassembled parts in which it was shipped took another month. It would be the better part of two years before TR began to master the iron beast. Meantime it was sitting in its new home, having arrived three months before orJean and Formerly walked down the stairs on this Sunday afternoon.

"I'm gobsmacked," orJean said, using a word she later claimed not to have known.

Formerly, uncharacteristically, kept quiet but expressed his amazement with widening eyes and furrowing brow.

"You like it?" TR, proud papa, demanded to know.

"What is it?" orJean asked.

Formerly was already walking around it. "It's a Heidelberg Cylinder," he said, regaining his wits. The name was embossed on a tablet-shaped metal plate on which five of the Ten Commandments might have been written. It was affixed to a side, over which was draped a cat's paw. From her upper roost, TK eyed them all lazily.

"Formerly can read," orJean said, following him on his journey around the press.

"Why?" Formerly demanded.

"What do you mean, 'Why?'" TR asked, hoping his face displayed his anguish at the offensive question.

"I mean, why do you have it? Why is this here?" Formerly asked.

"It's his hobby," orJean said. "Though I agree it looks like it's getting out of hand."

"I'm not done," TR said, sounding vaguely petulant. He could put up with almost any manner of rebellion, but not this. Not against letterpress, a genuine craft. "Artisanal word processing," TR liked to call it.

"Give the man his hobby, Formerly," orJean said. "Every detective is entitled. Sherlock Holmes had his violin. Nero Wolfe, his orchids. Shell Scott, tropical fish. Marlowe played chess. Harry Bosch listens to jazz; Miss Marple knitted. Gibbs builds boats in his basement with old wood tools. TR Softly, printer."

TR was tickled that she remembered the examples he had given her. "And Lord Peter Wimsey?"

She stood mute.

"Collected incunabula."

"Candelabra?" Formerly said.

TR sighed. "Extremely rare printed books. Fifteenth century. Can't get any rarer."

"You got any?"

"Can't afford 'em."

"That's because we don't charge for our services."

"Do you need a raise, Formerly?" TR asked.

Lewis held up his hands. "Sorry. I get carried away."

"So did I," TR said and stuck out his hand. They shook. Formerly's phone rang.

Bill Willewood reported in, much faster than anticipated. Formerly listened, frowned, hung up.

"It's a no go," he said.

"Why, what'd he say?" orJean demanded.

"There is a guy named Dewey Sisal who works for the FBI, but they don't have any address listed for him."

"Then how do they know they have him? How is he listed?"

"Special duty. That's all it says. The whole phrase is 'Detached, special duty' with a date."

"What date?"

"About two years ago."

"Well, that's something," orJean noted.

Formerly looked alert. "We've got more. Seems Bill's friend was curious. He was unaware of 'special duty,' and asked the computer to report on anyone else in that category."

"And?"

"And there are about forty of them."

"Forty agents unlisted except for special duty?"

"That's what the FBI guy says."

Formerly's phone rang; it was Bill, with another report. Growing ever more curious, his FBI contact further interrogated the administrative database and found two minor references. A marginal note in a record that had been deleted but a copy of which had been left unintentionally elsewhere in the system said all requests for information about special detached duty were to be addressed to the FBI's general counsel. How about returning Dewey's sweater to the GC, Bill suggested to Formerly. Also, he could find only one other hint of special duty in the database—a footnote in a draft of a proposed annual budget for the FBI Washington field office, indicating approval for an expenditure of $45 million for construction of "special unit administrative headquarters (Subsection-S)." That document was more than three years old, Bill said, and the entire budget, including the $45 million, had been approved and the moneys appropriated. But Formerly's FBI friend could find nothing in the computer system called either "special unit headquarters" or "Subsection-S."

TR was beaming when Formerly thanked Bill and rang off.

"You hear something I didn't?" Formerly asked.

"Think about it," TR said, his eyes bright. "Assigning queries to the general counsel means it's not some special little unit at a particular field office. Someone high up has to have a hand on something invisible—or at least a connection to it. And then there's the budget. They've tagged the Washington field office with fiscal responsibility for it. Would they do that for an operation located somewhere else—New York, Chicago, Seattle, wherever? No, it's central, it's right here."

"And the size of it!" orJean chimed in.

TR's head bobbed up and down. "Yes. Forty agents. Forty-five million bucks. That's not an office renovation. That's office construction. They've built something. Right here in the District." He looked around at his printery.

"But where?" Formerly mumbled.

"You're going to find that out," TR said.

"But how? I mean, if it's not in the FBI system . . . "

TR squinted at him.

Formerly pursed his lips, a tell for hard thinking.

"Let me show you something," TR said. He led them to the back of the printery. About ten feet up, a few inches below the soffit supporting the balcony overhang, a framed document hung on the wall. Formerly peered but couldn't make it out, so TR reached for a nearby grabber, lifted the frame down, and gave it to Formerly to read, with orJean standing by his side.

"It's your construction permit," Formerly said.

"Yep. And what's it say?"

Formerly read the many lines of bureaucratese in silence, then wheeled around and handed it back to TR.

"It approves digging."

"Yes."

"Digging down into the ground."

"Yes. And?"

"And nothing. It's a construction permit to dig down."

"Who permitted it?"

"DC buildings department; formal name Department of Consumer and Regulatory Affairs."

"In other words," TR said, "you may be the FBI, but you are still going to have to apply for a construction permit and let them know you're tunneling down."

"Oh," Formerly said, and then, "ah," as he understood the point.

"Okay," TR said, walking to a set of stairs in the middle of the printery. "Let's go up to the loft and give this the old three-prong attack. Formerly, you chase down the permit. What's been approved in the past two or three years, underground, forty-five million worth? Get into whatever you can get into. I'm going to work on Dewey Sisal. He has to live somewhere nearby. Can't imagine him as much of a commuter."

"And me?" orJean asked.

"Organize a surveillance crew. I'd say four or five. Our best. Starts tomorrow, assuming we find Dewey, or his alias Nicholas B. Nimsey."

The loft had seven computer stations: desktops that were fully loaded (including several programs that TR didn't fully grasp) and cabled to the Internet, high-resolution monitors, latest iteration Intel chips, and color laser printers. Formerly sat down at one of the stations and began his search. Two stations away, orJean brought up the Findem program to search for an ultra-reliable surveillance team.

TR plopped down at the rightmost station, ignored his computer, and pushed speed dial number 2.

"Hi there, TR," Martin Softly said to his son when he heard the voice. "Calling a bit early."

TR usually called his parents every Sunday at six pm.

"Not a social call, not right now, Pop. I need the mailman." Code for finding someone the old-fashioned way and let's skip the family gossip.

"Okay, shoot, boy."

TR explained the problem. How to find someone living in a large city, population around six hundred thousand souls, who does not want to be found. Living off the grid, submerged. Probably gets mail, if he gets any, under a pseudonym. Phone books show no listing for either name, and neither appears on any Internet site. He's a federal worker, but the federal branch does not show him in its own directories. Nothing else known.

"And you need to find this guy, like, fast."

"As soon as humanly possible."

"Then it's a good thing you called me, and not one of your computers. We humans can do it faster."

"I know that, Pop."

"All right, what are the names."

TR gave him Sisal and Nimsey.

"How soon?" his father asked.

"I'll hang up. You call me right back?"

Martin laughed. "You want the moon soon, huh? Well, let's see if I can deliver. Call me back at the normal time, say hello to your mother, and I'll tell you what I can tell you."

TR looked around. Formerly was deep into several screens while orJean was sitting back waiting for him.

"Six possibles," she told him, "depending on when."

"Look at this," Formerly called out, pointing to the lower left of his monitor.

TR got up. OrJean wheeled around, looked toward the monitor, then bowed to the infirmities of middle-aged eyesight and joined TR by Formerly's chair. The display showed an application for a permit for 32,000 square feet of office space, with special electrical needs: a serious construction job. The requester's name meant nothing, but his title required attention: special FBI procurement officer c/o the general counsel. As did the box on the form calling for construction location: "Withheld for reasons of national security." As did the nature of construction: "Below grade."

"You're getting close," TR said after a moment.

Formerly stared at the screen, willing it to provide an answer. Then he straightened out. "I got a guy."

"Of course you do," orJean said, patting him on the back. "Shake a leg."

The power company supervisor was a bit reluctant, but when reminded of how quickly Formerly had uncovered the motivations of his teenaged daughter's would-be suitor (a wholly unsuitable twenty-seven-year-old con man posing as a college student), he shook off his Sunday lethargy and agreed that Formerly's request was neither unreasonable nor difficult to satisfy, since the information was freely open to the public though somewhat obscurely archived. In fact, if Formerly were to hold the line, he would return in a mere minute or two with the answer. Which he did: electrical work of the magnitude Formerly presented was completed three years earlier somewhere in Georgetown.

"That's us," orJean said. "Are we sitting on top of them?"

"Probably not literally," TR said. "But who knows? Anyone disagree we've found our special unit?"

"Eighty percent," said Formerly, famously downbeat.

"High confidence, coming from you," TR noted amiably. "Then that's it, unless you want to hang around for a couple of hours and hear first-hand whether we've also located Sisal."

"Are you kidding? I got nothing else going that's this exciting," orJean said in mock disgust.

"What, no hot date?" Formerly asked.

"Last week, had dinner with a guy, thought he was cute, even age appropriate. Works for Social Security, statistical branch. Took me to Ris, nicely upscale, not crowded, quiet evening for talking."

"What went wrong?"

"Left me with the check. You think a guy in the statistical branch forgot his wallet for real?"

"You need to date younger guys, orJean," Formerly said.

"They need to date me," she replied evenly.

"While we wait," TR interceded, "we can go upstairs and hear more about orJean's dates"—she stuck out her tongue—"but my vote is to hear all about Formerly's encounter with Miss Okra's daughter's diamonds—"

"Rubies," Formerly said.

"Rubies. How they got into the wheel well of her car. You up for that?"

"I can drag that story out," Formerly said.

While Formerly nursed his tale, a phone call from FBI headquarters rang on a secure line across town in an auxiliary office known to a mere handful as Subsection-S.

"You asked to be alerted to inquiries about one of your agents, Dewey Sisal," the caller said.

"Yes?"

"Thirty-eight minutes ago. Event was flagged when one of our computer specialists initiated an electronic search for the string 'special duty.'"

"What's he say?"

"Someone calling to find Special Agent Sisal on behalf of a friend who he says he left a sweater behind after dinner in San Francisco. Friend wants to return it. Call was from an acquaintance, William Willewood. He did not tell our guy the name of the sweater holder."

"Okay," came the answer. "Stop it there. No further action at your end. We'll take it."

At six o'clock, TR called his parents. While orJean puttered around his kitchen and Formerly pretended to watch a gardening show, TR told his mother about his trip to New York without mentioning Mallory Greenstock, breezily answered questions about Khaki, inquired after his mother's part-time job at the library, and asked how the old man was behaving deep into his retirement. Then she passed the phone to Martin.

"Got him," said his elated father. "I brought home the bacon, and it's already sizzling."

"For real?" TR exclaimed, loudly enough that Formerly muted the television and orJean leaned motionless against the kitchen counter. "Listen, Pop, I've got my team here. I'm going to put you on speaker. Pop, this is orJean and Form–Lance."

"OrJean," said Martin, "it's been years. How's that daughter of yours, Betsy? How old is she now?"

"Mr. Softly, my baby girl is a new mommy now. I'm a grandmother."

"What?" he cried. "You beat me?"

"Pop!" TR bayed.

"Right. And Lance, is it? Don't think I know you. Been around long?"

"A few years now, Mr. Softly. Working for PBDS for like five or six."

"Okay, next time I'm in town."

"Pop," TR wheedled.

"Here's what happened," Martin Softly said, getting down to his story. "We're looking for a fellow named Sisal and/or Nimsey. Somewhere in DC. Work site around Georgetown. Okay. I'm looking at a map and figure he's not going to live way out in Anacostia or up on the Maryland line. Probably not as far as Capitol Hill. Somewhere around his work, being super secret. You see what I'm thinking. I've avoided having to talk to most of the postal carriers. Had to, you said we need an answer today. I called a friend who's the main postal supervisor, and asked him to get the word out chop-chop to the carriers in Georgetown and the area around it. That's mostly zip code 20007. That's twenty, then oh-oh-seven. Spooky, huh? Or maybe it was meant to be. Anyway, that area has seven or eight carriers. My friend calls these fellows and finds most of them. And we got lucky. One recognizes the name Nimsey. But it isn't what you'd expect. I give this carrier real extra credit. Julius Forefather by name. Your guy isn't a delivery anywhere on Forefather's route, not by his names directly. But four or five times a month a care-of letter goes to a Nimsey. You ready? The care-of is Kate Binkerman. Name on the door is 'K. Binkerman.' There's your name. There's your door."

"You're saying this Julius Forefather now and then delivers mail to someone named Nicholas Nimsey, care of Kate Binkerman, and he remembers that?"

"Nicholas B. Nimsey. He recognizes the whole name, and the care-of."

"And this Kate Binkerman, she gets mail every day?"

"Ha!" his father exclaimed. "You thought I'd forget that point, didn't you?"

"Not for a second, Pop. Knew you wouldn't."

"Well, she does."

"And has he ever seen her?"

"Kate? You know, that's funny you should ask that. He said he found it puzzling. Never has."

TR pumped his fist in satisfaction. "Your man's got the address?"

"Of course, son. What have I taught you? Have it here. Address is 2806 Olive Street, Northwest."

"Pop, that makes Kate Binkerman practically a neighbor. Four or five blocks away."

"So go introduce yourself."

"Well, for reasons I'll tell you later, Pop, I can't do that. I have to go, but I need to know one more thing."

"What?"

"What's Julius drink?"

"What?"

"What's he like to drink? I'm sending him a bottle. Or better yet, you find out, send him a bottle, on me."

"I can do that."

"Thanks, Pop. You really came through."

"That's what fathers are for, TR. And you could find that out for yourself if—"

"Bye, Pop," TR said quietly, and disconnected. "Of all the homes in all the blocks in this whole big city—"

Ever practical, orJean ignored him. "Surveillance team. Let's nail it down."

They settled on fielding all six agents. One in position to pin the front door, beginning 6 a.m. One each a block away from any of the four corners Sisal-Nimsey could turn when walking out his front door, and a sixth two blocks west on Olive, allowing enough time to signal the others if he walked left instead of right. Formerly would float, orJean would be on switchboard in the loft alongside TR, monitoring every voice piped in. He did not want to risk being seen until he was certain of their prey's destination.

"Home, folks. Get a night's sleep. You're going to need it. And remember, coffee is for orJean and me. The rest of you—that's you, Formerly—could be a long day. Abstain. Remind the others, orJean."

"We have to do it tomorrow?" Formerly wondered.

"Why, you got somewhere else to be?"

"No, but the time is tight."

"Has to be," TR said. "We made a lot of calls today. One of them could get back to Sisal. The FBI guy could report the conversation with his friend, and as soon as they hear 'Sisal,' they'll alert him. Or our new friend Julius could ring the doorbell and tell Kate someone was asking about her friend Nick. Except I don't think there's a Kate."

"Why not?" orJean asked.

"Way I'd do it. If Sisal—that is, Nimsey—were the primary resident, people would know it; certainly any ordinary mailman would. If you're undercover, you put someone else's name on the door. That way, Sisal's identity is two steps removed."

"We found him," she said.

TR shrugged. "We need to move on this. Our best chance of catching him."

"What about the van?" orJean asked.

"Will we need it?" TR asked.

"Would be useful. Park it down Olive, east beyond the sight of his front door, use it as a changing station if needed. Go with the Verizon markings."

TR nodded. Formerly volunteered to drive it in. TR nodded again, and they were out the door.

CHAPTER 14

SOFTLY DESCENDING

A<small>T</small> 5:55 <small>A.M.</small> M<small>ONDAY, A</small> <small>THICK-SET</small> man perhaps in his forties, wearing jeans and a thin tan windbreaker, walked down a
tree-lined sidewalk on Olive Street toward No. 2806. It was a
narrow two-story, sky-blue pastel townhouse across the street
with four brick steps leading to an L-shaped path. On the wall
by the front door, a slim black mailbox bore a tiny plastic label:
"K. Binkerman." In the middle of the block the man kneeled
down three doors west of the house as if to fix a shoelace. He
palmed a tiny black device that he planted with a single swing of
his arm in the soil next to a small flower near the curb. His
practiced maneuver aimed the gadget's elfin eye at the lock side
of the door.

"Got it," said orJean, sitting at one of the computer stations in
the loft. The monitor showed a dim view of the front door; it
wouldn't be sunrise for another two minutes.

The agent stood up, idly brushed the leg of his pants, lit a
cigarette, tossed the match onto the ground, and sauntered east.
As he turned the corner, he noticed a Verizon van drive past him
on Olive Street and slow as it crossed the intersection. Looking
at nothing in particular, he continued down Twenty-Eighth
Street and began a winding course that circled the block every
six or seven minutes.

"Camera in place," TR said to the six agents with earpieces tuned to his transmission. Four agents, each a young woman wearing different designer workout shorts and running shoes, looked to be nothing more than college girls out for a morning mile. Each was posted on one corner of the rectangle that surrounded the house. Formerly sat in the van and, disobeying the anti-coffee injunction, sipped his morning's brew from a chipped mug.

"Now we wait," TR said into the microphone at his workstation.

At 8:15, he decreed a set of rotating bathroom breaks, with Formerly to stand on ground vacated by the agent seeking relief. At 8:40 they were all back in place, and the door to 2806 Olive remained closed.

"Maybe he's not in town," Formerly ventured, back at his perch in the van.

"Does seem he's starting late," orJean said.

"We wait," a terse TR repeated.

OrJean went up to the kitchen. She opened the paper, which had been folded on the counter. "Holy Christ!" she shouted, but TR didn't hear her. She walked back to the computer loft and repeated herself.

"What?" TR called out, swiveling in her direction.

"Did you see this?

"What is it? I haven't looked at the paper."

"This thing about the President."

"Christ," he said. "Not another thing. Do me a favor, orJean, look at it later. Let's not get distracted."

She threw the paper down on an empty portion of the desk. "Okay, but wow!"

At 10:10, the door opened, its red paint bright in the morning sun. Clearly visible on the monitor, the figure who emerged was wearing trim navy-blue pants, a teal polo shirt, and a tan herringbone jacket. His brown hair was cut straight, short and neat.

"Highly affirmative it's Sisal," TR broadcast to his crew. He paused, waiting to see which way the target went. "He's turning west. Everyone stand by until we're sure where he's going. Ebbie, where are you?"

The heavy-set agent stopped and said, "N Street, just west of Twenty-Ninth."

"Okay, hold it there."

A minute later, Sisal crossed Twenty-Ninth Street, still on Olive.

"He's walking straight. Ebbie, go to Thirtieth," TR ordered.

"On it," came the expected reply.

"The same for the rest of you," TR instructed the other four agents, "but not onto Thirtieth until he takes his turn." Olive dead-ends at Thirtieth Street; the figure they were following would have to go north or south.

He went south, toward M Street.

"Mia, you on M Street?"

"Yeah, boss," she said.

"Where?"

"Crossing Twenty-Ninth."

"Okay, you're jogging, but keep it slow until you see him, then pick it up. Give him ten seconds more and then stop and bend over and huff and puff another five and follow from there. If he's coming at you, window shop. Nothing obvious. If he turns west, follow half a block behind. Call it in when you see him. Formerly, can you get that van over to Thirtieth Street while he's still walking? Find a space. Pull over and watch."

Two minutes passed until Mia reported their target was west beyond Thirtieth Street.

"Formerly?"

"M and Pennsylvania. At a light."

"If you make it, pull up past him into any open space. The rest of you. I don't think you can get to M Street ahead of him. Medium pace toward Thirtieth. Hang back."

A minute later, the target appeared on the monitor. Sisal was walking along M Street, showing no particular intention to be anywhere at any particular time.

"Boss, it's Becca. It'll take me only one minute to get to Wisconsin and N. If he keeps going, I can turn down and cut him off at M."

"Okay, go. Usual rules."

Silence for another minute, until Mia and Formerly reported simultaneously. Formerly pulled in front of a fire hydrant a quarter block short of Thirty-First Street, and was looking back. Mia was a block behind. On M Street, Sisal pulled out his mobile.

"He's on the phone," Mia said.

Sisal's destination now seemed clear. "He's gone into the Georgetown Bookery," Mia and Formerly said in concert as Sisal disappeared silently behind the interior blinds covering the glass of the large front door.

"Formerly, get around the block as close to the back of the store as you can," TR directed. "Mia, park yourself across the street. Who else can get there?"

"Me," said Becca.

"I'm close," the heavy-set agent added.

"Okay, Ebbie, you're on foot behind the store, or wherever there's a back entrance. Becca, you're floating. You other two, find the van, take a load off. Now we wait again," TR said.

"What time does the bookstore open?" TR asked orJean, resting his headset on the desk near his computer.

Seconds later she answered. "Ten o'clock."

"That's why he left late," TR said, the thought occurring to orJean as well.

"Couldn't get in before," she said.

"Not if he wanted to blend in with regular book browsers."

"Unless he really is browsing."

"Not likely on his schedule."

"Yep," she agreed.

They waited an hour; Sisal did not reappear. TR told one of the agents in the van, now parked nearby, to enter the store and canvass, browsing deeply, front to back.

"He's not here," she reported twelve minutes later, her voice muffled from her position in a long aisle of books in the interior of the store.

"You're sure?"

"Been around it twice fast, once slow. Peeked in the ladies' room. Even the men's. It's quiet in here. Only a couple of others. Plus three clerks, and someone at the register in front."

"Any other rooms he could be in?"

"There's an office upstairs, off one of the wings, through the biographies. It was open; I didn't see anyone. There's also a closed door behind some computer terminals where maybe they keep stock. An older woman went in and out a couple of times. Heard a phone ring and it got picked up. Also, I'm not sure, but what sounded like an elevator."

"An elevator?"

"Like doors opening and closing."

"Maybe for freight," Ebbie said.

"Ebbie, any movement?" TR asked.

"Nothing. I'm in the alley around back. There's a door to the alley and two large, hinged metal plates on the ground near the edge of the building, like what you see behind grocery stores and things. It's gotta be stairs or a motorized platform to their lower level."

"You three with eyes on the place, stay alert. Everyone else, back to the van. I'm going to walk over. I'll be there in about seven or eight minutes. When you see me enter, stay alert for about half an hour, then you can pack it in if I'm not out."

"What are you going to do?" orJean asked as TR stood up and reached for his jacket.

"If he's not in the aisles, then we've found our FBI entrance. It's somewhere in that store. Must be. He hasn't come out any way we can see, so he's somewhere underground."

"You mean like a tunnel?"

"Not *like* a tunnel. An *actual* tunnel. This has to be where they built their special-duty space. Makes sense when you think about it. You ever spend time in the Georgetown Bookery?"

She shook her head.

"Well, I have. It's a neat bookstore. It has real books, none of those this-month-only romances and latest movie tie-ins. And it has lots of books, used and new, covering more fields than I can remember. And it goes deep. Current affairs titles take up three double aisles. Classic philosophy in addition to New Age shit. Film studies, serious art books. Gourmet cookbooks. An entire alcove of psychology. University press books. Loeb Classics."

"Your point?"

"What I'm saying is that it's too good."

"Too good for what?"

"Bookstores are going extinct. First the big chains softened them up, killing them one by one. Online selling is going to finish them off. But the Bookery keeps growing. In the last couple of years, they've opened up more alcoves and expanded to an entire upper floor. Now it's clear why. It's a front. I bet it's here because the FBI subsidizes it."

"But people shop in it."

"Yes, they do. Me too. And the Georgetown college crowd some-times. But lots of times it's empty. More staff than shoppers. Hard to see how its customers can keep a store going that's this overstuffed."

TR wriggled into his jacket and reached for his phone. "I'll have my earpiece and mic, but the order may be radio silence. If I'm not out in thirty, I've found what we're looking for."

"And then?"

"Don't know. I'll try to get a message to you."

"If not?"

"We'll play it by ear."

"I want to hear from you," she said, staring him in the eye. "No fooling around."

"Do my best," he said, patting her arm.

His three agents alert to his movement, TR strolled into the bookstore a few minutes later. The thin metal blinds clattered against the glass as the door closed. TR blinked at the abrupt dimness of the cool, musty interior and walked slowly through the front space past best sellers and the cash registers and then out into a book-lined corridor: True Crime, under the heading "Crook Books." He was alone, just an ardent reader with time to burn. The stillness of the aisles amplified the squeak of his shoes across the uneven wooden floors that were dotted with rubber-matted step stools to allow customers to reach the higher shelves.

The cloistered atmosphere evoked his childhood awe at roaming the Cropcross Book Annex, now sadly failing following the death of old Mr. Cropcross, ninety-six, a year before. When his father sent him a clipping about its straits, TR thought about buying the disheveled store and its inventory from Mrs. Cropcross but reluctantly decided he could not manage as an absentee bookseller.

But here he was again in a browser's Eden, one worth exploring a step at a time. Scores of bookcases. Thousands of books, tall and short, fat and skinny, most jammed together tightly, some angled and sprawling across gaps in the shelves. Each one the frozen voice of human thought. TR blinked and reminded himself he was here to mine the premises, not plum the contents. He—

"May I help you?" a woman who appeared to be in her fifties asked. She wore a red blouse with starched collar under an ivory-colored sweater, buttoned in the center. Her hair was in a bun. A pair of light purple framed glasses hung in front from a long necklace of paperclips. She held a clipboard and a red Bic pen, as if taking inventory could impose order on the tomes over which she exercised dominion.

"I'm just browsing," TR answered, hoping his forced smile would appear as shyness. "But now that you mention it, I'm wondering if you have a book called *The Common Good.*"

If ever the cliche "a merry peal of laughter" befit the circumstance, it was the woman's response. "Oh, gracious, I guess you didn't notice our display in the front room. Come, follow me."

She led him back to the space he had just crossed. In the center was a carousel that bore at its top a hand-lettered sign reading "Which one did Malbonum own? Try these." Arrayed on its short round shelves in duplicates of twos and threes was a large assortment of books with "common good" in the title.

"A student of the recanter cases, are you?" she asked.

"I guess so," he said, his face reddening. "I've been curious, is all."

"Don't be embarrassed, for heaven's sake," she said briskly. "Lots of people are. I've sold fifteen or twenty of these in the last month, can you believe it?"

He removed a solitary volume at random. George Anastaplo, *Human Being and Citizen: Essays on Virtue, Freedom, and the Common Good.* A University of Chicago title, 1963, jacket intact, resting comfortably in this old-age home. He slid it back on the shelf and withdrew a volume near it. Richard Rousseau, *Human Dignity and the Common Good: The Great Papal Social Encyclicals from Leo XIII to John Paul II.* Praeger, 2001. No jacket. He reshelved it and scanned the rows. At least twenty-five different titles, many of them long out of print, arrayed before him in a carousel in the Georgetown Bookery.

"Amazing, isn't it?" the woman said. "I do wonder which one of these books—if it was one of these books—that that man actually had in his library. You know, nobody has ever said. And he claims he didn't have it. Strange business, don't you think?"

TR nodded. Soulfully, he hoped.

"Well, you go right ahead and look. I'll be here all day. You're welcome to be, too."

Her shoes sounded sticky as she was walking away, like tape being pulled from the floor, when, as a studied afterthought, he called out, "I'm also interested in tennis."

"Oh?" she said without inflection, wheeling around and sliding her glasses on over her ears.

"Yes," he continued. "Do you have a section on that?"

"We do." She paused for a moment, and then asked, her voice straining gently, "Is there any particular aspect of the game that especially interests you?"

"Mainly tournaments," he said, "I only watch when Roger plays Rafa."

"I see," she said. "You know, we may have what you're looking for. Will you follow me, please."

She led him along two corridors to an area housing a large desk with computer terminals and a roll of wrapping paper. In back of the large desk was a set of swinging doors, each covered in black vinyl and inset with a small circular window.

"I'll be a second. Will you wait here?"

She walked behind the counter, and with her forearm pushed one of the doors inward. She disappeared for some three minutes, then reemerged in the company of a tall man. Not just tall, but surpassingly tall. He wore a crisp blue suit and a tailored white shirt without a tie. TR could see the outline of a holster and firearm at belt height beneath his jacket. His black cordovan shoes gleamed. He was not introduced.

"Phone," he said, holding out his hand. Seeing no reasonable way to defy him, TR took out his mobile phone and put it on the man's palm. The hand remained in place. "Mic and earpiece too," the man said, "and your watch." TR sighed and handed them over.

"Follow me," the man said, waiting for TR to join him. Inside lay rows of stacked boxes, two desks, and two bookcase tiers. Twenty feet ahead to the right lay a steel pocket door with no latch. They walked to it.

"Through here," the man said. He fished for a key on a ring chained to his belt and inserted it into a keyhole to the right side of the door. As the key turned the door slid smoothly into its slot on the left wall.

"See you again soon, Mr. Softly," the woman said.

TR turned to look. Her face was blank.

"I hope so," he said and followed the man into a small space that dead-ended in concrete walls ahead and to the right. Once they were on the other side, the door slid closed with a muffled whump. The tall man had already turned left and walked down a bare concrete staircase with a metal railing. In the dim light, TR felt a chill. The stairway turned back on itself halfway to the next floor and ended in another locked steel door. The man opened it, and they entered into a similarly small empty alcove. Immediately opposite was a set of metal doors and a button on the wall next to them. Thirty seconds later the doors opened. The two men stepped into a spartan elevator. The man turned a key next to a button on a side panel. The doors closed and the elevator lurched and descended slowly and nonstop—thirty-five seconds by TR's count. They came out onto a landing in still another small alcove, also ending in a steel door. Yet another key opened it and they stepped inside.

TR winced from the intensity of the overhead industrial lighting. The man led him down an open corridor hemmed on either side with cubicles, at which people, paying him no heed, were working at desks and monitors. They turned into a perpendicular corridor, this time bordered by vacant walls. Two more turns brought them to an office with a frosted glass door and three large windows covered by Venetian blinds. The door had no name and no number. The man knocked.

"Come," said a muffled voice within.

The man pushed inward and stood in the doorway, blocking TR's line of sight.

"Thank you, Ned," a woman said.

"You're welcome, Doctor," he responded, waving TR inside as he backed out of the room and closed the door behind him.

TR took two steps forward and stopped as if he'd slammed into an invisible wall. His eyes went wide.

Across the room from behind a walnut Queen Anne desk, a broadly beaming woman in a white lab coat said, "Willikers, Bulldog, what took you so long?"

Subsection-S

Softly discovers an ancient political truth:
some explanations astound, even when they don't explain.
Especially when they are the official version.

CHAPTER 15

GEEKS BEARING GRIFTS

"GIVE ME A BREAK, I ONLY started Friday," TR Softly said, his mouth dry, his voice cracking, as he rallied from his mute astonishment at finding the missing Dr. Khaki Blumenthrace ensconced in the secret space reserved, he had supposed, for rogue agents. "That must be a record. How many people ever found this place in three days?"

"No one has ever found us," she acknowledged, "or even suspected we exist. I guess we're not as good as we thought we were."

"Or I'm better than you supposed I could be."

"Impossible. You eternally surpass all the others."

She came out from behind the desk and threw her arms around him, nuzzling his neck. Then she pulled her head back, held his face with both hands, and looked straight into his eyes. "What's wrong?"

"Finding you here, for starters."

"How *did* you find me?"

"I didn't know I was finding you. I was looking for *this*—whatever *this* is. You work here?"

"For the time being. But answer the question, how did you find us?"

"Your agent was sloppy. Two different cases, same tennis code? C'mon."

Khaki smiled. "Same code, *all* the cases. I *told* them to use the same one. I expected *someone* to notice."

"Not sloppy, then. Like I told Mallory. Of course, I would have found this place without your damn signal. That was the least of it. The real clue was the cat."

"What?"

Khaki pulled back in surprise when TR told her about Malbonum's fearful reaction to Valachi's sudden appearance on his hand at his home all those weeks ago.. "I didn't know about that," she said. "He didn't tell us—me. That wasn't planned." She frowned. "That's not good."

"Take it up with Sisal."

"Count on it, I will."

"So it *was* Sisal," he said.

"That's beneath you, TR. You knew that, or you wouldn't be here. So kudos to you, oh mighty PBDS Agent Number One. Welcome to The Cave."

"That the official name?"

"No, but it's what stuck."

"This whole operation is yours?"

"Oh no. I oversee psychological and neurological aspects—the mind part."

"Then let me rephrase. Talk to me. What are you up to?"

"Ah," Khaki said, "now *that's* the right question."

She turned her back and went to the kitschy ice bucket sitting prominently on a credenza behind her desk. She returned with a tall glass of iced tea. She pulled TR to the sofa, handed him the glass, and pushed him down onto the cushion.

"Speak," she said.

"I rather think you should speak. What in hell is going on?"

Khaki took a deep breath, held it, thought. "How is Mallory?" she finally said.

"She's worried. She thinks she's become part of a sinister conspiracy."

"Is that what you think?"

"Certainly a conspiracy. Underground space that no one knows about? Pseudonymous agents? Mysterious confessions? Sure. Whether it's sinister, well, that depends on your purpose—"

TR suddenly sat up straight. He felt his left wrist, then remembered surrendering his watch to Ned.

"What time is it?" TR demanded.

He followed Khaki's glance up to a large round wall clock. In place of the usual numerals were colored cross sections of twelve parts of the brain.

"Half past the prefrontal cortex," she said, her eyes sparkling at his puzzled look. "Why?"

"It's—the team. I've got to get a message to orJean by twelve thirty or they'll—"

"Relax, TR. It's been sent."

"What? How?"

"Ned, the agent who brought you in? He gave my assistant your stuff. She sent a one-word text from your phone to orJean—'safe.' Will that be enough to keep Mrs. Drumgullery safe, too?"

"Who?"

"Adele Drumgullery. Our lady in the bookstore."

TR threw up his hands. "I'm not sure of anything, least of all your Mrs. Drumgullery, but it's your show."

"Then tell me what you think is going on."

"I think the FBI is staging these confessions through some kind of telepathy breakthrough. Now that I find you here, I'm convinced of it. Brain stuff. That's you."

He searched her face for confirmation.

"Telepathy," she repeated.

He raised his eyebrows, daring her. "Yep. Somehow Sisal put words into the repenters' mouths. But since it's the repenters speaking—their bodies, I mean—they get convicted. Which means the FBI can illegally wiretap with impunity or whatever they do to get the ball rolling, because who's going to know different?

Malbonum may have invited you in, but *which* Malbonum? Mallory is correct. It *is* a sinister conspiracy."

"That's pretty good, TR. It's mostly wrong, of course, but still, nicely reasoned."

"Are you going to tell me the real story, then? Or shall I go home?"

"Oh no, stay, of course stay. I can't wait to see the look on their faces. I told them you'd find us."

"Them? Who?"

"My colleagues."

"You knew I'd—since when?"

"Since you left the message from the train in New York Friday morning that you were on your way to Mallory."

"You got my message?"

"I got all your messages."

"Then why didn't you—"

"You had to find us. That was the point."

"Damn it, Khaki, what point? Stop with all the riddles. Talk to me."

"I will, but in stages. It's the best approach. Otherwise . . . " she paused. "By the way, what will you tell Mallory when you've got the real story?"

"What she asked me to. What we always do at PBDS. You know that. I'll tell her what I found out."

"Exactly. That's why you need to let me tell the story my way."

"Does that include telling me why I got invited to the party—and by whom?"

"Of course it does. In fact, that's probably the whole point."

TR sighed.

"We're an operating unit of the FBI."

"Figured," he said.

"But we're secret, so secret that nobody knows about us."

"I do."

"Not yet you don't, not much."

"Well, then, your general counsel does."

"Not anymore."

"What do you mean?" Wrinkles appeared on TR's forehead.

"The GC might have known about it when this place was started, but that was two people ago, and the first one died a few years ago and inexplicably forgot to tell his successor about our existence."

"Well, surely the director of the FBI knows."

"Perhaps. But the next one might not."

"Walling yourself off from the government itself?"

"Yep."

"Systematically?"

"As much as we can."

"But funding? You can't unplug from the government if you're part of it. Who pays the electric bills? Who buys the pencils?"

"We're self-funding."

TR was silent.

"It's explained in a brief written history we commissioned for new recruits," she said.

"A history of Subsection-S?"

Khaki coughed. "How do you know that name?"

"Are you going to say you're amazed at the prowess of your co-founding partner at PBDS?"

Khaki flashed him a lopsided smile. "I shouldn't be amazed. Not anymore, even though I usually still am. But how *did* you learn it?"

"It's referenced in construction permits."

She grimaced. "Our government! Well, keep the name to yourself. We don't use it publicly."

"Not even here in the Cave?"

"Verboten. But it's explained in the history. I'll give it to you if GOGS approves."

"Who?"

"It's Washington, TR. There's grand nomenclature for every unit and chief. Remember Barnaby Joister?"

TR looked blank.

"A politician," she said.

"Now there's a surprise. But no."

"He was a governor a few years back, maybe more than a few," Khaki said. "He won in a big upset. There was even talk about a run for the White House, but it petered out. Then a few days before Desert Storm, the president put him in the FBI—assistant director. Insiders found it strange that Joister accepted. Anyway, he became invisible and that was the point. He founded our little enterprise and he's been here ever since."

"That doesn't explain COGS."

"Not COGS, GOGS." Khaki said slowly, enunciating the initial *g*. "It's a tribute to an affectation. He likes to be called Governor. Back home he called himself 'Governor of the Great State.' Around here people call him Governor to his face, 'Governor of the Great State' behind his back, but he accepts 'GOGS' in pretty good humor. He takes it as a sign of affection. You can call him Governor Joister."

"Do I get to meet him? Is he going to tell me what I'm doing here?"

"Yes and maybe. Let's go meet him right now."

Khaki marched TR through several twists and turns, stopping before an office with several windows looking out to a bank of cubicles. Like Khaki's office, it lacked a number, but unlike Khaki's a name appeared prominently on the upper glass panel of the door: Governor Barnaby Joister, Head." The wide Venetian blinds were raised, and TR could see the governor seated at his desk. Khaki knocked.

"Enter," he said, looking up.

Governor Joister rose as the door opened. He stood behind a large butcher-block slab with L-shaped returns on either side. Along the front edge of the desk, facing visitors, sat a memento from his bygone days as Governor of the Great State—a long plaque proclaiming his motto in big bold letters: "Come in Peace or Go in

Pieces." The desktop was bare, aside from four monitors, two on either return, associated keyboards, an elaborate telephone console, a picture frame facing the governor, a notepad near the telephone, and a wide mug labeled "Great Our Grandpa's Stuff" filled with sharpened pencils.

"This must be the celebrated T. R. Softly," he said with a smile, extending his hand.

TR shook it and replied, "Governor, a pleasure to meet the head of Subsection-S."

Joister looked sharply at Khaki, who shook her head.

"I didn't tell him, Governor; he came here knowing it," she said.

"I'm all the more impressed," the governor said, motioning them to sit in the chairs fronting his desk. "And worried," he added, waiting for his visitors to comment. They sat silently.

"How may I help you?" the governor finally asked, studying the detective who unabashedly stared back.

"I rather think it's the other way 'round," TR replied resolutely. "Isn't that why I'm here?"

"You think you're here to help us?"

"Khaki hinted that you issued a challenge to be found. I turned out to be the investigator who found you. I assume for some purpose."

"Tell me why *you* think you're here."

"An hour ago I would have said because of clever sleuthing. And, I would have added, on behalf of a determined federal prosecutor with an acute nose for mischief. I'm investigating whether the FBI is involved in some unlawful conspiracy."

GOGS whistled. He scratched his chin and said, "An hour ago. What about now?"

"Now I'm guessing two agendas. One is my client's, the other is yours. I don't know what yours is."

"Fair enough," Joister responded. "I propose to tell you, if we can come to terms on confidentiality."

"I can promise to say nothing to anyone about what I learn—other than my client."

"Mallory Greenstock."

"Yes sir."

"Who reports to the United States Attorney in New York and who authorized your investigation."

"She does. I don't know about the second part."

"Can you persuade her to refrain from disclosing what you tell her?"

"That depends entirely on what you tell me."

"A judicious answer, Mr. Softly. I think when you learn what we do, you will find every reason to stay mum. I am going to trust you because Dr. Blumenthrace here has entreated me to the point of raised voices to trust you. Also because we have in place a pretty good self-inoculation program. If news of our enterprise were to get out, I'm confident it would be greeted not only with indifference but with downright ridicule."

"And Dewey beat Truman, sir," TR said genially.

GOGS snorted. "Touché, Mr. Softly. By God, the only things standing in the way of your confidence are the facts. Or as Cicero might have said, *Plura in eius capite quam in cerebro accomodari possunt.* More things are in his head than can be fit in his brain."

"A Latin-speaking governor," TR said *sotto voce.*

"My Greek is better," GOGS responded.

"Ah, Attic Greek and basement Latin."

"By God, Khaki, he *is* something."

TR held up his hands in surrender. And said nothing.

"As a sign of good faith," the governor continued, "tell me how it is you came to learn the name of our little shop, which we have thought for some time was unknown to all but the merest handful of people in the entire world."

TR told him most of it, omitting details that might implicate his informants or his methods.

"I see," the governor said, pinching the bridge of his nose. "We aim to be as invisible as a black hole, but I see our record purging has been incomplete; the inconvenient detritus of Washington paperwork has yet to cross our little black hole's event horizon. I thank you for bringing these strands of our existence and whereabouts to my attention. That's precisely why you're here."

"To tell you about your paper trail."

"That, at a minimum, yes. You're here, Mr. Softly, to conduct a stress test. Or to put it more accurately, you're here because you've *passed* a stress test. Adroitly, at that. I congratulate you."

"More like you failed it."

The governor smiled but remained silent.

"That's why I was—what did you call it?—'summoned'?"

"I didn't say summoned. Much too strong a word. Dr. Blumenthrace concluded early on that we needed to know how watertight we are. Check for leaks. She salted the legal proceedings with a muddled code as a clue. For whoever might recognize it and follow up. Turned out to be you. On Friday, as I hear it, you signed on. The good doctor briefed me after learning you were on your way to the prosecutor's office. Khaki said you could do it. I confess that I doubted it. Didn't think it could be done. You've proved me wrong. Proved we have work to do."

"If you don't mind my asking, Governor, won't there always be people beyond those working here in the Cave who will know? Isn't that how Washington works?"

"Increasingly fewer, I'd say," Governor Joister replied.

"But the President must know, and the director of the FBI, and the payroll people—at a minimum."

"The President does not know," Joister said. "The man who was president at our founding knew, and I'm sure he remembers, but he undertook not to tell his successors. Yes, the director knows, as do his predecessors, but their knowledge of what we do is strictly confined, and they are encouraged not to peer too closely. Most of what attaches us to these so-called 'recanter' cases is seen through the prism of the Washington field office. Payroll knows nothing of us, only of our dozen agents, who are listed, as you know, simply as 'special duty.' We are working hard to stay off the grid."

"A dozen agents? I thought you have forty." TR said, puzzlement in his voice.

"Forty? Good heavens, no. Give or take, we have forty trogs working here, but most are not agents."

"Trogs?"

"From the Greek," GOGS said. "Troglodytes, people who live or work in caves."

TR nodded. "And your budget?"

Governor Joister nodded back. "Our budget is ours. We can spend what we raise. What I'm about to tell you is confidential. No telling anyone, including the U.S. Attorney. Do I have your attention?"

"Yes sir, you do."

"It's best expressed in a phrase that our mutual friend here coined some time back. We are 'Geeks bearing grifts.' Someone's bound to steal that line, claim it's theirs, but remember, you heard it here first," the governor said, perhaps implying that Khaki should cede credit to Subsection-S.

"The sacrifices we make," she said.

TR nodded. "Kudos to you, Khaki. But what does it mean?"

Joister responded. "We were spun off from a Defense agency twenty-five-odd years back. It was originally called the Defense Integrated Research Projects Agency or DIRPA although in its first year some wag labeled our initiatives as Defense Impossible Research Projects, and that name stuck. To dissociate from purely military projects and the silly moniker, we were renamed Subsection-S and brought under the umbrella of the FBI. It all happened when someone slipped an opaque change to the criminal code into a technical bill cleaning up language concerning jurisdiction over federal waterways. It passed without comment. We are subject to oversight only by the president and the director and unless restrained by either may act at our own discretion."

"Why 'S'?" TR asked.

"'S' is for 'special,' and before you ask 'special what?'—all in good time, Mr. Softly. But one of the ways we're special is that we don't do what the FBI can do without us, and we don't rely on the public fisc. As I was saying, we are self-financing. You're aware of so-called Nigerian scam letters?—the unknown relative who has died leaving you a fortune, and suchlike. Now they come by email. The basic ideas are hundreds of years old—sophisticated con artists parlayed the Nigerian prince game to princely sums in the mid-nineteenth century. The modern version didn't start in Nigeria. It started right here, I mean by us, electronically. Our people pioneered the electronic con—scams, tricks, identity theft. I regret to say we were not careful in the early years, and sadly some unsuspecting Americans were taken in by our ever-inventive geeksters. Thankfully, we've fine-tuned our techniques. These days we limit our fleecing to corrupt dictators, money launderers, criminals, and, in the unlikely event they don't overlap, wealthy individuals worth north of a hundred million who dabble in dubious businesses. We remit ten percent to central FBI for overhead and keep the rest.

"Dictators fall for Nigerian widow scams?"

The governor looked pleased at the question. "No, I'm sure they wouldn't, but our grifting is far more sophisticated these days. Our grifter trogs are highly proficient in the long con. Their division stages elaborate scenarios that have never been unmasked and have led to multimillion-dollar windfalls. And we're branching out, away from pure flimflam. It probably wouldn't surprise you to learn that we are entitled to a substantial portion of the forfeitures these 'recanter' cases will bring in. We think Malbonum has upward of a billion dollars subject to forfeiture. At least several hundred million more from the other recanters. Six of our people run the financing through our Office of Material Resources."

"Sounds cozy," TR said when the governor sat back after his near monologue.

"It is," GOGS agreed.

"Well, good for you, Governor," TR said, "and it would rise to the level of fascinating if it weren't all beside the point."

"To the contrary, it's very much to the point. What I have told you is who we are."

"But not *what* you do—the projects the FBI can't handle. And the project Subsection-S can't handle—or why I'm here to help you."

"What makes you think—"

"Governor, I came here tracking your agent. Now I'm hearing I was sent for, or lured. It must be for your purposes I'm here talking to you, instead of being sent back on my way once I proved I could find you."

The governor sighed. "In the old days, my little snow job of a speech would have deflected congressional committees from further inquiry. I'm growing old, losing my touch. Why, in another decade or two I may have to turn over the reins."

"I'm a postman's son, Governor."

GOGS turned his palms up. "What?"

"Neither snow jobs nor rain nor heat nor gloom of night stays this detective from the swift completion of his appointed round of inquiry."

"Can't stop you," GOGS concluded.

"No, sir."

Governor Joister rose and said, "I trust you will enjoy the rest of your visit to our little establishment."

"Here in the Underground State," TR responded pleasantly.

"Yes, as far down as the Cave is dug," the governor retorted. "But know this, we're a force for good."

"The claim of every rake and rogue," TR said.

"But this one means it." Joister flung an arm out, pointing his index finger to the door. "Khaki," he said, "be gentle."

They sat in Khaki's office, awaiting delivery of lunch. She offered TR a choice: tuna salad on toasted rye or tuna salad on toasted rye with melted cheese. TR wondered aloud at such an abundant selection a scant three blocks from Gentlemen's Meats.

"Willikers," she upbraided him. "You're not thinking straight. An invisible agency can't direct quantities of food to an underground location. It's the downside of being down below."

A knock at the door and a young man in shirt sleeves entered carrying a tray with two sandwiches wrapped in tin foil and two small bags of rippled potato chips. Two pickles drooped over the edge of the paper plate with the food.

"Out of cheese," the delivery trog said.

"Government kitchen," Khaki added. "You'd think with all our money . . . "

TR shrugged, took the sandwich that Khaki held out for him, and carefully unwrapped it over an empty paper plate perched on the edge of the coffee table near the sofa. Khaki tossed a pickle onto it dead center.

"Perfecting your game," he said.

Khaki sighed. "All I have to do every day."

"You need to get out more."

They ate in silence. When he had swallowed the last of his chips, TR asked what she thought Joister meant when he instructed her to "be gentle."

"Who knows?" she said, looking away.

She pushed back the trash on the table, wiped the salt off her hands, grabbed TR's glass, and freshened his iced tea. She turned back to him. "Time to get to the point?"

"Yes, sweetie."

She put her hands together and said, "Identity theft."

TR's eyes narrowed.

"That's what we were talking about. One of the specialties of our work here in the Cave. You can make good money assuming other people's identities."

"Sure, that's what theft is for."

"But not all that it's for. It could get you all sorts of other things if we could learn to perfect it. Just think about it. The identity theft we read about is primitive. I steal your charge card, your driver's license. I get the key to your car or house. Even better, your social security number and your passwords and your usernames. But that takes you only so far."

"Pretty far. You could empty out a person's house, bank accounts, secrets."

"True, if they're stored on his computer or online," she agreed. "It's unpleasant but a victim can recover from it. But that's old-time identity theft, primitive compared to the new stuff. What would you say if I told you we can now steal an entire identity? Pass ourselves off as another person altogether."

"I'm not sure I—"

"Suppose you wanted to assume my identity without raising any suspicions; actually *become* me so you could walk into my bank in person and access my vault; talk to my friends and be 110 percent certain they would swear they'd been talking to me; traipse through my past to reveal memories that are mine alone—how would you do it? Not by wearing a clinging mask like they did in *Mission Impossible,* or talking into those voice changers that fool listeners only on the telephone. I'm talking one thousand percent foolproof. Provable."

"You can't guarantee that."

"But we can. I give you Romo Malbonum."

"Only one way to guarantee it."

"Yes?"

"I'd have to borrow *you*," he said. "You know, like physically. I could threaten you to go along with me or hypnotize you or implant a radio transmitter. But I thought the techs had disproved all those things. That the person speaking for sure *was* Malbonum in that courtroom."

"Are you sure? You're not thinking hard enough."

"The real Malbonum who is not Malbonum?"

"That's a good way to put it."

"All I come up with is it's some form of telepathy; I can't see how else."

"Well, no, still not good enough. You keep avoiding the obvious though it's staring you in the face."

TR bunched up to the front of the sofa and rested his hands on his knees. He was as skeptical of her certitude as he was when she had proposed to eliminate the threat of Junior Skootums by writing a ridiculous note.

"Well," he said finally, still watching her for any sign of encouragement, "if you could somehow teleport me, or I guess my mind, into your brain."

"Exactly," she said, not stirring a muscle, barely breathing. "We call it Swapping."

TR convulsed in laughter, gasping for air.

"You think that's funny?"

It took many deep breaths to recover his voice. "Khaki, what are you all smoking down here, Metro fumes? All those body swapping stories are bunkum."

A knock at the door interrupted. The young shirt-sleeved trog cleared the plates and handed them each a warm, wet towel. TR took his gratefully, dabbed at the laughter-induced tears around his eyes and wiped his whole face. He dropped the towel onto the outstretched plate the trog held in front of him, and then his vision blurred. Before he could fully sense his predicament, much less fight it, he slumped back onto the arm of the sofa. Khaki moved over and cradled his head.

The door opened and a dark-haired woman walked in, accompanied by a taller man. She swung her briefcase onto the table in front of TR's knees and opened it. "Quickly now," she said, removing a small gray canister from which two thick cables extended onto soft cloths that looked like old-fashioned heating pads. One of these she wrapped around TR's head, stretching a strap around his chin.

"Will you do the honors?" the woman said to the taller man, while Khaki and the trog looked on. "The code is zero one zero. Wait until the light is green."

"I know, Helene," he said, sitting next to TR on the sofa.

He removed the other pad connected to the second cable and strapped it around his own head, and then entered the code on a keypad in the gray case connected to the canister by a thin wire. A green light winked on.

"Sorry about this," Helene said, handing him a towel like the one TR had used to wipe his face.

"You always say that," the man said, putting it to his face.

He smiled at Helene, at Khaki, and then his chin fell forward to his chest. Helene bent over the canister and pressed "Enter" on the keypad. For thirty seconds no one moved until the green light on the canister winked again.

"Okay, everybody out," Helene commanded brusquely, "including him," pointing to the sofa.

"I'm staying," Khaki insisted.

"All right, stay. Let's go," Helene said, removing the pads from the heads of the two men and then putting pads, cables, and canister back into the case, closing it and throwing the strap over her shoulder. She reached for the arm of the still-unconscious man whom the shirt-sleeved trog had propped up, and together they dragged him out the door.

Khaki sat next to TR, waiting for his fog to lift. She knew it would be merely a minute or two but still, she was anxious. She was rarely this close to the center of an operation. As she waited, TR opened his eyes and looked around uncertainly.

"What happened?" he asked, feeling his forehead.

Khaki took his hand and looked at him with concern. "Are you all right? I think you fainted."

"Whew, something happened," he said thickly. He didn't register that the timber of his voice was off. He took the clean towel she thrust at him and wiped his face again.

Khaki pointed across the room. "There's a bathroom through that door."

Gratefully, TR stood and walked unsteadily to it. His left leg twitched, each step landing at a funny angle on the floor. He fumbled for the light switch with shaking hand. The sink was straight ahead. With the towel over his left arm, he leaned on the basin and turned on the faucet. The water running through his fingers felt cold. Waiting for it to warm, he looked up into the mirror—and recoiled in horror.

The face he had observed many times daily for nearly four decades—*his* face, the face of T. R. Softly, consulting detective, son of Luana and Martin Softly: Gone. His chin, his mouth, his cheeks, his nose, his eyes, his everything: Vanished.

Staring straight back at him was the unmistakable visage of his seventy-two-hour prey, Dewey Sisal, who was looking blank, then puzzled, then panicked. TR touched his forehead and watched in the mirror as the specter of Dewey Sisal touched the same spot at the same time. He opened his mouth—or Sisal's—and let escape a feral cry. It was not TR's voice.

The fearsome sound so unnerved him that he dropped the towel, spun around, and raced from the bathroom on an increasingly gimpy leg in time to see a man walking toward him through the open outer door of Khaki's office. TR's breathing became more shallow and his pounding heart felt as if it might burst through his chest when he saw that the man coming toward him could be no one other than himself: TR Softly wearing TR Softly's clothes and TR Softly's smile and extending TR Softly's arm while saying amiably, in TR Softly's voice, "I'd know you anywhere. Welcome to the Swap Shop."

TR's legs—or was it Dewey's?—crumpled, and everything went dark. This time he really did faint, whoever he was.

The White House
Washington, DC 20500

June 16, 10:00 a.m.

A Treat from Your President

Wither Weather?
(Statement on Climate Change)

Nothing like the weather to bring out the grumblers. Lots of ignoramuses complaining lately about how My environmental policies will destroy the world. Well I have news for them and you too if you're one of them. The world is not going to end, not that way anyway. Hamorrhoids though. That's something else. Little round things from outer space but very heavy. Suckers could ram into earth any time that's why we've got telescopes pointed up at them. But climate grouches say we human beings are mucking up the planet. It happens to be true that everyone who has ever lived lived on it. Amazing, and with fossil fuels and coal and other things that give Americans good jobs and paychecks. We're not going to risk those good things. That's why I'm pulling us out of so called "climate accords." Not necessary and cost needless dollars. What warmer? I've seen snow. #BeAssured I have very much deep knowledge about climate matters. Studied it at length with degrees much more than these scientists. There wasn't even a science of climatology or whatever much before I was born but presidents have been around for hundreds of years. I'm an acknowledged master of climate, since America runs on trucks and I've been everywhere. I've stepped out and down on the ground to sample air and the other things. The so-called climate people are saying these things because they're paid to. Never trust a person who gets a paycheck. We want neutrals, not people who always stick up for scientists. Resist!

Action taken: Saving your money by cancelling all those trips to foreign countries to talk about the weather.

Bottom line: Everything will be jake.

Technical Correction to the Presidential Treat of Today's Date: Owing to a fluctuating disturbance of electrical current brought on by today's hurricane, highly unusual in Washington, the White House spell-checker was temporarily disturbed and rendered "asteroids" as "hamorrhoids." It also unduly suggested presidential academic degrees in meteorology instead of higher body temperature as intended. A repair crew is due by 4 p.m.

CHAPTER 16

COGNITIVE DISSIDENTS

TR OPENED ONE EYE TO FIND Khaki ministering to him. A stethoscope, its buds in her ears, coiled down to his chest. He looked side to side before determining to open his other eye. When the eyelid popped up Khaki shined a bright light directly into his pupil and in a stern voice told him not to move, but she didn't forbid him from speaking.

"Mirror," he mouthed.

Khaki clucked but held up a black lacquered hand mirror that returned TR's own face to his fearful sight.

"It's you again all right," she said.

"What the hell was that?" he asked, clearing his throat and struggling to sit up on the sofa.

"*That*, my dearest TR, is what we do."

"That was gentle? Your GOGS said 'be gentle.' I heard him. Damn, girl, that was not gentle."

"It was puff pastry," she said, tittering at his attempts to appear peevish.

"I was *inside* that guy!" he yelled, his hoarseness giving way to astonishment.

"That's one way to say it."

She suppressed her amusement and settled her face into its medical mode: "I'm your doctor," it seemed to say, with a shy smile that exuded trustworthiness.

"How do *you* say it?" he squeaked, damping his desire to shout.

"We call it an LOS," she said quietly, putting her hand on his forearm.

"What the hell does that mean?"

"A Level One Swap. It means no real intrusion. You swapped into him; he swapped into you."

"That's not intruding? Khaki, you've been underground too long. You've lost your grip on common sense."

"Mostly a *motor* intrusion, not a full-scale *mental* one," she continued. "Facts are facts. He didn't have access to your mind or memories. Your secrets are safe. It's all fine stuff."

She patted him on his shoulders, bowed her head and lifted the stethoscope off her neck and up and over her short, bobbed hair, putting it on a cushion next to him. He glanced away from her freckles and fixed on a point on the wall, refusing to meet her eye. When she took his hand in hers, he looked down at their interlaced fingers.

She tapped him on the end of his nose. "Come on, don't be angry," she encouraged. "You're fine."

"Why did you do that?" he finally asked, studying their hands. "You could have warned me."

"What would you have said if I had told you we were about to put you into Dewey Sisal's body?"

"More like you swapped our minds," he corrected.

"It's pretty much the same thing, don't you think?" She squeezed his hand. "C'mon, what would you have said?"

Mulling the question over, he saw an anxious look in her eyes. "I guess I would have asked how somebody like you could tell such a tall tale." His pitch was back to its analytical normal.

"Exactly. You needed to believe before you could understand. You have to know it, feel its reality, before I or anyone could stand a chance of getting you to listen, much less learn how it works."

"Well, now that I've done it, don't do it again, okay?"

"Not until you're taller."

"Much taller," he said, his good humor mostly restored. A thought occurred. "Have you ever done it?"

"Twice," she said. "Same as you, except they told me in advance what was going to happen. I sat in the chair, in the Swapper. That's what we call the lab. They wouldn't let me move, only let me look."

"At yourself?"

She smiled. "Oh yeah, at me myself. There I was, sitting right there next to me. Knee to knee. But more about that later, all in good time."

"Have we got that? Good time? Any time at all?"

"What do you mean?" she asked, puzzled. "Of course we do. Why wouldn't we?"

"I don't know, since you haven't told me yet. But I'm not sure we do. I accomplished the mission—your mission, well, GOGS's mission. But I'm still here. There must be a reason. Something must need doing."

"TR," she sighed. "I don't see why it can't wait a day for you to be read in. The briefing won't change between now and tomorrow. Go home, feed the cat, get a good night's sleep."

"You mean I can leave the Cave?"

"You're not a prisoner."

"Felt that way, coming in."

"Coming in was security."

"Anyway, I don't think I can go home now, not without knowing more. I'm sure the team will be there—orJean, Formerly for sure. They'll feed TK. Let's press on."

Khaki patted his hand and stood up.

"Your wish commands," she said, as she riffled through a drawer under the ice bucket. "Here's what you need to see."

She handed him a two-inch-thick spiral-bound book. Near the top of its laminated cover was the title, "Project Palimpsest. History, Mission, Science, Prospects." The middle part of the cover proclaimed the contents to be working papers of the Special Weapons and Psychology Unit of Subsection-S of the Federal Bureau of Investigation. The lower part warned that the book contained Top Secret contents "not to be copied or removed from the premises. Note taking is forbidden. Readers are subject to all pertinent provisions of Title 18 of the United States Code." The copy TR held was printed twelve months earlier.

"Out of date," he observed.

"They're still working on the update."

"You mean the recant cases."

She nodded. "And related stuff. Anyway, stay here. Read."

Subsection-S had its origins, the report began, in the Decade of the Brain, a ten-year initiative designated by President George H. W. Bush in 1989, to run through the last years of the twentieth century. Mostly it was public relations—by design, a joint effort between the Library of Congress and the National Institute of Mental Health to promote public interest in brain research. Some of it was practical, particularly efforts to develop neural prostheses to aid veterans recovering from brain and neural injuries.

But what happened out of sight was more significant. Without fully understanding what it had wrought, Congress appropriated an appreciable chunk of money for research by a new unit of the FBI, the Special Weapons and Psychology Unit, created specifically to explore law enforcement and military uses of neuroscience. At the turn of the century, DIRPA began working on "augmented cognition," a means of enhancing mental capacity through a brain-computer interface. They called this "neuromorphic engineering." But Subsection-S went in a different direction, eventually developing Project Palimpsest.

TR scratched the back of his head. Frustrated by these unfamiliar terms, he skimmed the history and collided with the nearly impenetrable section explaining the science.

"Khaki," he snapped, "what is all this? 'Transcranial ultrasonography'? 'Palimpsestual circuitry.' 'Maximally augmented hyperautocatalytic neurosyntesis.' 'Gammaaminobutyric acid suppression'? 'Neural circuits.' Can't you give it to me straight?"

Khaki swiveled from her monitor to face him. "Welcome to my world. Anyway, what's wrong? Have you become the Yalie who can't read?"

"Not this stuff, not at my age, not in an hour," he sniffed. He thumbed through the section. "There're seventy-five more pages of this stuff. I haven't got the time or patience. And I don't think you do either. Just tell me what this is all about."

Khaki sighed and stood fussing at the Keurig. "Okay, but bear with me because I can't eliminate all the science if you honestly want to understand what's at stake. Think of it this way: have you ever wondered why you are a twenty-first century American You, instead of a sixteenth-century Ming dynasty You, or a twelfth-century monk in a Cistercian abbey scratching out a living from the soil, or a You belonging to a pre-agricultural tribe of nomads wandering around northern Afghanistan 11,000 years ago—"

"From time to time," he admitted.

"Thanking God you were born male?"

"Can I plead the Fifth?"

"You're not alone," she continued, "lots of people wonder why they came into existence now, why here instead of there. Usually they're grateful they weren't born before anesthesia, or in places without air conditioning, or in societies that condone slavery and foot binding. The unexpressed thought—maybe it's fair to say the unthought thought—is that they could have been intromitted, sorry, *inserted* into any body at any time, but for no reason they can fathom, they occupied the one they got into. You with me so far?"

He shrugged. But he was no longer scratching his head; his hands were now folded in his lap.

"But," Khaki went on, "the truth is that's the old Cartesian view. Descartes held that the mind is separate from and precedes the body. The mind is something that has to be put there, injected prenatally through God's Big Needle. From a little pinch a mighty punch. But that's not what happens at all. It's much the other way around. Sorry Grandma. Sorry Padre. The body is formed cell by branching cell, unbelievably, almost incomprehensibly."

"From a little squirt a mighty spurt."

"God almighty, TR," she said, "focus."

"Sorry, couldn't resist."

She sighed. "I know. It's my one failure."

He stuck out his tongue.

She resumed her lecture. "The body can grow, cell by cell, without a You. But it can't live as a sack of cells or a bundle of fibers. It needs a neural system to keep going. What we haven't appreciated until recently is that the You—your consciousness—develops in a growing brain. No consciousness or practically none when a baby first cries out its arrival song. But soon. The spreading brain monitors internal systems and begins taking in sensations. They're worked over, and eventually the brain tops off the package with a cherry of self-consciousness. The body makes us who we are. The You isn't put *into* your body; it's made *by* your body. The body makes me I, makes you You. You came into existence when you did because your body made you for its uses, like giving you intelligence and making you sociable so you can live longer."

"The Neuron hatches a You."

"Yes."

"And this has to do with neural circuits because—"

"I'm coming to that. What you need to understand first is that most popular accounts of the brain are a metaphorical mess. It's so damn complicated and mysterious that all we've got are analogies to explain it: the brain is like this; the brain is like that. Usually some genius compares it to the reigning scientific theory. In the age of hydraulic engineering, thinking was explained as humors washing around in the body. In the early days of electricity, they thought the brain was like a telegraph system. Now it's digital computers: the brain as an information processor. That's why our futurists speculate about uploading minds to computers or think that a ridiculous Star Trek beam can transmit bodies and minds at light speed. Won't work, not even barely."

"You're sure?"

"Of course. First of all, because even if the science would work the technology won't. We aren't going to have sufficient computer power in the lifetimes of our great-grandchildren's great-great-grandchildren, at least along present lines, to model a brain. Upwards of one hundred billion neurons. And it gets worse. It's the connections that count. Some neurologists ballpark the number of synapses at one *quadrillion*. Some skinflints put the synapse number at a mere hundred trillion. In any case, entirely beyond our capacity. Leave a note for your great-great-grandchildren not to hold their breath."

"What's second?"

"What?" Khaki was momentarily confused.

"You said what you just said was the *first* reason nobody can model a brain."

"Oh, right. The second reason is that the brain isn't a digital computer. It's something else."

"What?"

"A brain."

"A brain is a brain? That's your explanation?"

"The brain is unique. We should be comparing other things to a brain, not a brain to other things."

"Like what?"

"Well, that's just it. We haven't got anything yet that's like a brain."

"Except another brain."

"I knew I could count on you," Khaki said, and then continued. "Your point is spot-on if you understand your own suggestion.

Nature doesn't build transistors or work with purely electric signals. It uses wetware. The long-term project is to grow a wet brain, using materials not yet engineered. But saying that makes it seem there's a way forward. Nobody knows. Can you throw a conscious You into a box? That's conventional wisdom for some people. I don't buy it. A brain has to be embodied. It has to have an upbringing with sense perceptions from the outside world coming in as it learns. It has to have desires and needs."

"But nobody knows," he said, hoping to forestall yet another tangent.

"This is where I say, 'Yes, dear,' and move on," she exclaimed, standing up and walking around the room. "So let's do that."

"Neural circuits," he said.

"What about neural circuits?"

"You said you were coming to them. I'm waiting for you to catch up."

"Yes, neural circuits. I guess we're ready to talk about them."

Khaki bent over to use the phone console. "Helene, can you stop by for a bit?"

"Helene Barberoi?" TR asked.

"Wonders don't cease, TR. How in heaven's name do you know that?"

"Her name is on the office window next to yours, Khaki."

Seconds later a knock at the door, and then a wiry, dark-haired woman in her late forties walked directly to TR with an outstretched arm. "I'm pleased to meet the real you," she said.

"You were sitting on the sofa when I came out of the bathroom . . . or when Sisal did."

"I'm amazed I registered in your consciousness," Barberoi said. "You were down and out in seconds."

"Doing my job," he said, looking her over. "You're also the DNA woman at the Malbonum trial."

Barberoi smiled and nodded. "Yes, I was."

"TR, meet Helene Janice Barberoi," Khaki said. "She's our head Swap Operator and Chief of Training. We were about to discuss the science of swap, Helene, and I thought you should be here."

Helene settled herself and Khaki continued. "You don't need the blow by blow, TR. Suffice to say that one day about three years ago, one of our scientists discovered something amazing. Neurons connect through chemicals called neurotransmitters. Skipping details, these neurotransmitters continue in a chain, propagating signals to thousands of additional neurons. What our guy found is that certain organic molecules, acting as catalysts, rapidly speed up connections. Not just doubling. They set off an exponentially recursive reaction."

"Which in my feeble grasp of scientific language means—"

"It's when the result from the preceding calculation is used in the next one. If you're multiplying by three and start with the number two, you get six. Take that result, multiply by three again, and you get eighteen. In just twelve steps, you go over a million."

"It gets big fast."

"You better believe it. But that's slow compared to what *we* can do. Seconds after our catalysts are absorbed, our neural circuits zoom into overdrive. Since the new molecules we've devised are hyperautocatalytic, the reaction feeds on itself in a swoosh. A normal doubling goes two, four, eight, sixteen. But in ours, the *exponent* increases. The first connection involves two neurons, and you square that number to get the next set of connections—four. The third connection is the cube of four—sixty-four. Raise sixty-four to the *fourth* power and you get more than sixteen *million*. It multiplies before you can blink. Within a few seconds, you can make trillions of connections. That's what we call 'maximally augmented hyperautocatalytic neurosyntesis,' to use the full technical name, which is what you choked on reading the Palimpsest report earlier."

"Uh huh," TR said. "And why 'palimpsest'?"

"As usual, you're zeroing in on the point," Khaki acknowledged. "Palimpsest is the key. What we can now do is copy the neural circuits of one brain to the other. We don't need to store the Connectome, the entire synaptic map. The process of neurosyntesis can be encoded in neural instructions and transferred from the Inhab's brain to the target's. Because of the enhanced speed, the neural circuits of the Inhab—our agent—can ride atop the circuits of the target brain, without deleting anything. An Inhab circuit rides in the gaps of the target circuit's pulses. It's like an ancient manuscript palimpsest, where a new text is written over the old words while leaving traces of the original. We can run one mind atop another and even temporarily eliminate the chores of some sections of the native brain. The Inhab co-opts them to his own purpose. We call it 'tuning down the I.' We can also leave a significant chunk of native neural activity alone, namely the sensory and motor nerve activity of the original brain. In essence, we're overlaying that part of the agent's brain that is his 'self' onto the target brain. The Inhab learns to steer the native circuits. And that, omitting lots of pesky details, is what our labs have wrought."

"Couldn't you have done that without knocking me out?" TR demanded, when Khaki fell quiet.

"We could," Barberoi answered. "But for scenario purposes we needed you to be unaware of the swap. We needed to get those organic molecular catalysts into your blood stream, and we usually do that through that facial towel. In your case, we merely added a couple of knock-out drops."

"You can get chemicals into my brain that quickly?"

"Yes, we have catalysts for that too. They work fast and dissipate fast. We've even got drugs to inhibit nervous system functioning, which we usually use on a dark target. We didn't subject you to them, because for obvious reasons we wanted you to wake up. But how we do it depends on the story we're telling."

"That's the chemistry and neurology of it," Khaki concluded, as if to change the subject. "Got it?"

"Then it's not truth serum."

"What? Why do you say that?" Barberoi asked.

"I didn't. At his recant hearing, Malbonum claimed you doped him with truth serum."

"He's told a lot of stories," Barberoi said. "No truth serum. We don't do that. Why would we need to?"

TR shrugged. "What are you hiding?"

Khaki clapped her hands and, looking at Helene, said, "See, I told you he was smart."

Barberoi grinned. "She's hiding most of it."

"The important stuff," TR prodded.

"The important stuff is how you deal with your new landscape once you've swapped," Barberoi said. "It's like telling a traveler that all her problems are solved because we've developed airplanes to take her places. But plop her down in Croatia, and her real problems are just beginning. She doesn't know the landmarks, she can't speak the language, she doesn't know the idiom, and she doesn't know whom to ask. After the theoretical breakthroughs come the practical problems."

"Which are?" TR demanded.

Barberoi crossed her legs and looked TR more squarely in the face. "The most significant problem, I guess, is the Kryptonite Catch."

"What? You're kidding me," TR said.

"I wish I were. After the breakthroughs, we hit a big wall. We call it the Kryptonite Catch because it's a deadly weak spot in the neurochemistry. No intrusion can run longer than about six days. Then the circuits degrade and the control collapses. Like surfers riding a big wave that suddenly bottoms out. One minute you're high in the sky, touching the sun, and the next you're down in the muck with a concussion, drowning to boot."

"That's what I told Mallory," TR said.

"What?" Barberoi's hand shook at his comment. "What could you know?"

"Something was wearing off," TR said. "It seemed obvious the recanter cases had to wrap up quickly. Tuesday night to Monday morning or the equivalent in each case."

"We were cutting it close," Barberoi confirmed. "We think it's a matter of life or death, or serious injury, anyway. If the Inhabs aren't back within that time, they're scrambled beyond repair."

"How do you know this?"

"We didn't when we began," Barberoi said. "Our first tests were limited, very short-term. Two minutes, five minutes, then thirty, and an hour. But as we went along we got cocky. I got cocky, I admit. One of our agents, poor Timmy Fawlson, got the not-so-bright idea to try an extended intrusion, like astronauts logging months in orbit. We let him talk us into it and then lost him around dinner on the sixth day. Him and the swappee, who happened to be the grown son of a mobster in Memphis."

"Lost him? What do you mean?" TR asked.

"Well, technically they're still with us, but I'm pretty sure they're gone. They're physically comfortable in a secure hospital facility. But they have no conscious brain function. We're still working on it, two years later. The crisis came on quickly. One minute he's talking to us, and the next he's babbling incoherently, then words dropped out, and then he lost motor control. It was all videoed, and he was attached to neural monitors, so we have a pretty good idea of the sequence. But now we know to keep it to—tops—five-and-a-half days."

"But within that time period the Inhab, as you call it, is in control?"

"With training. You can't swap the first time and just walk off into the night. You remember how you felt when you got up?"

"I was feeling clammy."

"Besides that. You were walking funny. Your footstep was off. And then when you came back in here from the bathroom you collapsed."

"Is that what happened?" TR blinked rapidly at the memory.

"Among other things. The collapse was because you had no training in motor control. You have to learn to navigate the new body, pick up on its signals, where your body parts are, and how they move in relation to the rest of your body and the world. It's called 'proprioception.' You don't think about it in your own body, but it's a challenge in a new one. An experienced agent, like Dewey, who's had extensive training, can now propriocept within about a minute, but newbies can't. And it's not only movement. Everything can be a trifle off—which way your knees are pointing, how you hear, your eyeball characteristics."

"It's amazing," Khaki interrupted. "We now believe people see colors a bit differently. I don't mean you see red where I see green. Brains are not that inconsistent. But if what our agents report is true, the Inhab's perception of, say, a green hue, independent of saturation or tinting, might be noticeably different from how the swappee perceives it. That's revolutionary. We think we've breached what until now has been the completely secure vault of the mind. It's early days, but it might mean we can begin to verify subjective feelings as well as sensations: not just how colors look but how emotions feel, like joy, melancholy, annoyance. That would be a first, and it wouldn't be possible without swap technology."

"You can measure qualia?" TR asked, dredging up memories of long-ago discussions that began in a philosophy classroom and lasted into the wee hours of Paternosterian retreats—debates about the experiences one can have that can't be described or explained in words to someone else.

"Maybe not measure it—but explore it," Khaki said in an excited voice. "Not the objective fact that a molecule wafted into your nose from that round thing you were cutting but that when it gets there you experience the specific smell of an onion."

"You're talking about the old Thomas Nagel paper, 'What is it like to be a bat?' The problem of the interior subjective sense of things."

"Specifically, the problem of explaining what it's like to be a particular kind of conscious being," Khaki replied. "Even part of the solution would be worth a Nobel—except that we can't publish, so the King of Sweden won't get to meet us, because we'd be shot for revealing state secrets."

"Bummer," TR observed.

"Damn straight," Helene Barberoi agreed morosely.

"How long does it take?" TR asked.

"Does what take?" the two women asked simultaneously.

"Training. Until an agent gets adept."

"Six months, give or take," Barberoi answered. "There's much to do, and many ways to approach it. An important part is the psychology of being undercover in plain sight. We teach agents what life was like for Resistance fighters, who had to pretend by day to be living normal, humble, non-provocative lives. If you're in another guy's body, you have to act like it's normal. You also have to be good at the quick turnaround. That's why we teach improvisation. Dewey excelled because he had already done improv comedy. You might think it's easy, but I don't think there's anything more treacherous, or a more unwelcoming space, than another's body. Not outer space, not cyberspace—neurospace. You've got to learn to outperform the cat who hides under the chair but whose tail is sticking out. You need to know what's showing."

"Lately, it's even more complicated," Khaki said, picking up when Barberoi paused. "That's why the Malbonum case was significant. It was a real-time extended Level Two Swap. Dewey had access to Malbonum's neural traces, like memory. That's why he could tell Malbonum's story. It's completely new and we're still feeling our way, but it's workable. The cases have all been slam dunks."

"That's what Mallory sent me to investigate," TR said. "She's worried that legal safeguards can't stand up to whatever proves to be the cause of Malbonum's confession."

"I know, I said it's complicated. But it's fascinating, what we're learning.: Khaki leaned forward. "Did you know there's a difference between a memory and a memory of a memory?"

"It was Sisal who briefed us on that," Barberoi said, regaining the conversation. "When he's inhabing, he can, for lack of a better phrase, plug into the swappee's memory until it feels like Sisal's own remembrances. But when he outloads—gets back to his own body—he can at best remember a sense of the memories that were vivid to him as recollections of real events."

"And what about the swappees? Must they be comatose?" TR wondered.

"Well, not every single time—you and Sisal were both active, but that was to allow you to experience yourself as someone else. Since we're the only people who know about the Palimpsest technology, it wouldn't usually take us anywhere to co-swap two agents, though we have done that for testing and training. But in the real world, putting the swappee in a coma preserves our agent's body and prevents the target mind from having to adjust to the nightmare of being in some other body, or in some other place, seeing no one, not knowing what is happening or what to do, or even that something sinister is afoot. Imagine being awake in a body that doesn't feel like yours and not knowing how you got there."

"I don't have to imagine it," TR said.

Barberoi slapped her forehead. "Plus," she continued after a moment, "if you're comatose, nothing needs to be rebutted later, other than a feeling that you've been absent a day here or there. The swappee never knows what's happened and feels foolish trying to explain the feeling."

"You're saying that when Malbonum the body was being led by Sisal the mind, Sisal the body was—"

"Lying comatose in Malbonum's panic room," Barberoi said. "It's what he does. For the common good."

"And his body was likewise comatose in a room in a posh hotel suite down the peninsula during the Carslip trial," TR said, going through his mental checklist.

"How on earth do you know about that?" Barberoi took off her glasses, exposing a pair of wide eyes.

"It's what I do."

Barberoi tapped her phone. "I've got a six o'clock," she said.

"Go, go," Khaki said, waving her hands in a brushing motion. "Dinner is at seven."

"Staff mess?"

"GOGS's table," she said, "we're dining in style."

Barberoi's eyes widened with pleasure. "That means good wine." She waggled her fingers and left the room.

When the door closed, Khaki jumped up from her chair with unbridled enthusiasm. "C'mon, one more person to meet," she announced. "Then we'll have dinner and some serious talk."

She led TR down another endless, fluorescent-lit corridor.

"Who?" he said, hastening as in the old days to catch up to her fierce drive to be at the next place, doing the next thing, without dawdling now to point out the Autocatalysis Lab or the Materials Fabrication Center.

She halted in front of a door marked Zesto Moffin, Scripting. "Our Scenario Master," she said to TR, knocking once and turning the doorknob.

CHAPTER 17

THE SCENARIO MASTER

THE MAN INSIDE, WHO APPEARED TO be short of thirty, had a guarded look and medium-length sandy-brown hair, a thin nose, ruddy cheeks, a dimpled chin, and mischievous blue eyes. TR saw these features first until his gaze took in the man's clothing: an ivory-colored double-breasted suit, cut trim over a slim body, adorned with a bright red-beaked parrot painted on an extra-wide cerulean tie. A matching handkerchief poked out of the left jacket pocket. The shoes, TR saw when the man came out from behind the desk to shake hands, were burnished walnut cap-toe Oxfords. The cuffed hem of the pants ended a quarter inch below the first shoe-lace eyelet. A twenty-first century dandy.

Khaki introduced them with infectious enthusiasm. "This is Zesto Moffin, our Scenario Master. He's neat, isn't he," she said.

The two men appraised each other coolly.

"Those," said TR, "are impressive duds."

"Four years at Carleton." Zesto shrugged.

"They taught you to wear that suit at Carleton?"

"I taught *them*."

"How many did you teach?"

"Well, I lectured everyone but converted no one. My classmates wore sweatshirts and hoodies."

"It's cold in Minnesota."

"Not indoors," Zesto said. He scanned the figure in front of him. "Left the gray suit at home, I see."

TR burst out laughing. "You told him," he said, looking at Khaki.

"You don't think I could have deduced it?" Zesto affected a pout.

"No," TR answered. "Nothing about me suggests gray suits. Nothing you could read about me—"

"Other than reading about your fancy for awesome gray suits," Zesto suggested.

"Other than that. But you didn't. No one writes about me."

"Why not? From what I hear, they should."

"I keep a low profile," TR said. "Ground level."

"So do I," Zesto said, pointing down. "Subterranean." He turned to Khaki. "He doesn't know, does he?"

She shook her head. "I'm briefing him as we go along."

"Tell me what?" TR asked.

"Zesto is a famous writer," Khaki bragged.

"She means I use a famous pseudonym," Zesto said. He waved them into chairs.

"Are you going to tell me?"

"Ever hear of Hap P. Navidad?"

TR pursed his lips, squinted into the distance, and drummed the armchair with his right fingers for a long moment. Then he gave a knowing nod.

"The swap novel guy. Of course. Those are *your* stories? How many by now?"

"I'm working on number fifteen," Zesto said diffidently.

"That's a lot of books."

"Yeah," Zesto chuckled, "one every six months. Awesomely prolific. Prolific crapster. Master of the mediocre. Those are the more courteous reviews."

"Don't trust the critics," Khaki ventured.

"Oh, but I do," Zesto said. "They're undoubtedly right. That's what I'm proud of. My swapper books are written to be flayed, vituperated, scorned, and keelhauled. That's the whole point."

"I was under the impression that they *do* sell. Didn't I read about Hap Navidad a few months back? Am I remembering right? You sell a hundred thousand paperbacks out of the gate."

"Yeah, they sell; I have a lot of loyal readers," Zesto said.

"With time on their hands. No offense."

"None taken. I don't write them for the critical glow. It's my job to create a specific impression—that the idea of swapping is sheer nonsense."

TR looked at Khaki and snapped his fingers. "Ah, this is your self-inoculation guy. What Joister talked about. Of course: the more ridiculous it is, the more unlikely anyone will take seriously any of your actual swapping. All your novels keep people from imagining that any of this is real."

"Exactly," Khaki said. "If you want to ward off an investigative reporter or even a whistle blower, preexisting ridicule of the very idea is much more sensible than blackmail or violence as a deterrent after the fact. The public mind will be closed too tight for anyone to pry it open. Why even bother to investigate?"

"You ever read one?" Zesto seemed eager to have TR's reaction.

TR shook his head.

Zesto jumped up, moved quickly to his desk, extracted a folder from a cherrywood project box and handed the top sheets to TR. "First couple pages of the new one."

TR held them up and, with Khaki looking over his shoulder, read them without pause.

Thorpey Takes a Test
by Hap P. Navidad

Thorne Thorpey was finally feeling fairly feisty.

He'd just survived another birthday party and managed to keep his age stable, at 34, for the fourth year in a row. Not even his mother could remember, so she went along with the story.

His thirty guests, sprawled out after their fourth Dos Equis in the private room of his Club, Duffers Destiny, marveled at how youthful Thorne seemed. His undercover secret was intact though he risked exposure for the sake of a simple parlor trick, always a problem when he began drinking an hour before his guests arrived. He bet anyone who wished to play that within sixty seconds after someone gave a signal he could name the first person his patsy had ever had sex with. Ghislaine Svensson, the pert twenty-seven-year-old Swedish statistician who wore the funny hats with the koala bears in back and who arrived with Thorpey's golfing buddy, Clem Southam, volunteered.

"You couldn't possibly," she sniffed breathily, her face alight in a brilliant smile of naive affection for any novelty. "I have been in U.S. only eight moon times, and I betting you never journey to Jönköping, Sweden."

"No, I haven't," Thorne acknowledged.

"*Smaskig*, then give signal."

Clem stepped up to the mound and readied the pitch: "Okay, on the count of three. One, two, *three!*"

Thorne stared at the nubile Svensson, crossed his eyes, and blinked the Morse code letters that only he and sixty-two other agents of the hypersecret Swappers Alert knew and had mastered. D*i-di-dit, di-dah-dah, di-dah, di-dah-dah-dit* (s-w-a-p). Well, Thorpey thought, no one ever said it would be easy.

After the requisite two-second delay, to account for the transcranial crossing, the mind of Thorne Thorpey was now enmeshed in the crevices of Ghislaine's adorable fusiform gyrus, in Brodmann Area 37 of her bewitching neural matter. And, of course, she had traversed the crossing to his. A look of mighty confusion raged across "his" face. Thorne got to work, surveying his hostess's memory banks. With sex, there were usually three or more dozen ways into the labyrinth of past recall. Within thirteen seconds, he had his answer and before anyone had noticed, "her" eyes crossed and "she" blinked the code: *di-di-dit, di-dah-dah, di-dah, di-dah-dah-dit.* They were both back safe and sound, the reversal complete, though Thorne had come back across the neural divide with actionable intelligence.

The real Ghislaine Svensson blinked again, this time in clear, trying to make sense of her quarter-minute adventure. Since it made no sense, she stopped thinking about it.

The real Thorne Thorpey smiled benignly, raised his hand to the hushed onlookers to signal victory, and announced: "Karl Olof Wågström, summer camp, at the end of the dock on the lake, when you were fifteen, at five-thirty in the morning. You got a splinter in your right butt cheek."

Ghislaine fainted. After that the party sort of broke up.

When Thorpey awoke at home hours later, he swallowed four red generic Tylenol pills and contemplated the assignment he had decrypted from the depths of his mano-a-mano supercooled Alert quantum computer that could solve any problem within one-third of a nano-a-nano second. His orders were to impersonate a former U.S. Army Ranger who wished to attend the University of Southern California. To be admitted to USC the Ranger was required to sit for the all-important SAT test. Thorpey's orders were to take it for him. It was crucial he avoid a scandal, since the Ranger was the son of an important member of the U.S. House of Representatives from Ohio and head of the education subcommittee of the big committee with jurisdiction over teaching and smoking and stuff like that. But the risk was worth it. Who would know? No one would ever think of cheating their way into USC. Plus, it meant a lot of money; the lobbyists would pay up handsomely for their Congressman pal. A short-term test-taking Swap would be awesome: just what the doctor ordered after last night's saturnalia.

"This is fine stuff, isn't it, TR?" Khaki said. "It's your best yet, Zesto."

"From your lips . . . . But you know what drives me bonkers," Zesto said indignantly. "It's not that the critics hate it; it's that they misread it. They're careless, you know, sloppy. A few weeks back, when the papers were full of stories about the first recanters' cases? A lot of them had the nerve to misstate how it works, in front-page pieces no less. These lamebrains wrote that all Thorpey does is blink and, hey presto, he's run an intrusion. That's not true. Couldn't work that way at all. Ridiculous. Everybody should know that. You have to blink *in goddamn Morse code.* With your *eyes crossed.* And you have to be *looking at* the swappee when you blink. Who's going to read a book about a blinking agent who looks any old place in order to inload a mind?" He stopped abruptly, scowling at the thought of incompetent reviewers and news analysts who hadn't the courtesy of reading every comma of a Thorne Thorpey adventure and then telling it straight.

"You get to keep the royalties?" TR asked.

"Eighty-eight percent." Zesto said. "Division gets overhead. Plus not counting the agent's commission."

"Division?" TR wondered.

"That's Zesto's little joke," Khaki said. "It's what he calls Subsection-S. You know, from *La Femme Nikita.*"

"No one believes Division exists, either," Zesto said. He pounded his fist on his knee.

TR nodded sagely. "Anyone who suggests you guys are doing this for real will be taken as a paranoid nut or an overexcited fan of escapist fare. Or a moron."

"Or all three," Khaki said.

"Works for me," TR said.

"Works for everyone," Zesto concluded. "Especially when you add it all to the existing body-swapping literature—which, by the way, starts way back in the nineteenth century. Most of it's cheesy but some is venerable. Movie-wise, everyone's seen *Freaky Friday* and stuff like that. Debbie Reynolds did a good job with Tony Curtis in *Goodbye Charlie* in the Sixties. Technically that's a reincarnation flick, like *Switch* in the Nineties. Arnold himself made one—*The Sixth Day*, a mind-to-clone story. Steve Martin did a two-in-one variant, *All of Me*. That's double loading, a Level Three-B Swap. *We* haven't even done that yet. We're working on it.

"And then the books. Best one was Thorne Smith's Thirties' classic, *Turnabout*. I borrowed his name for the Thorpey stories. Husband and wife are swapped by an Egyptian statue who's been sitting on a shelf and gets fed up with their quarreling. Husband suffers through an entire pregnancy in the wife's body. *Au courant* to the max. A lot of sci-fi writers did the mind upload thing. Mostly into computers, which is silly, but it's a going concern. The classic is *The Body Snatchers*—alien pods taking over human bodies, but how it worked was never explained. The point is, add all my new stuff to the literary background and no one will ever believe any of it."

"But a few weeks back a couple of commentators speculated it might be real."

"Yeah, and got royally lampooned. Even though my series actually explains the swap. I don't ignore the how-to like most of them or rely on absurd things like Egyptian statues or carnival genies. Reincarnation movies, not a clue. I think Malbonum was proof of more than one concept. Not only can we do it, but as far as the world's concerned, whatever happened in the courts the last few weeks wasn't by swapping."

Moffin sat back in his chair and crossed his arms over his ivory jacket, his cherubic face broadcasting "I dare you." TR said nothing, waiting for further enlightenment.

Khaki broke the uncomfortable silence. "Tell him about your real work, Zesto."

Brightening, Zesto launched into the "soft science" of Project Palimpsest. "Think about it for no more than a second," he said, "and you'll realize you can't succeed with neuroscience and derring-do agents alone. You have to have a storyline and play it out. Take the simplest case, a One-Tasker. You've got ten minutes, tops, to walk into the enemy's space and grab a key that unlocks the file room. You're running a Level One-A intrusion, simple as it gets. No spoken lines. Enter, retrieve, about face, exit."

"It might be simple if you explained it in English," TR objected.

"Sorry. Let me put it this way. You're our agent. You're to be the Inhab—swap into, inhabit the body—of a guy who stands post outside your adversary's quarters. You don't need access to his memory circuits. You're not likely to have to speak to anyone. Go in, grab the key, come out, close the door. What do you do?"

"What you said."

"But first, where do you grab the guy? How do you power up the Synapticator? How do you know where to find the key? What happens if you can't find it? Is it safe to ask someone? What if he asks you who you are or demands to know why you're looking for a key that you don't have a right to or shouldn't know the location of? What would you say? Do you have a memorized cover story? What if it fails? If he says X, do you say Y or Z, or do you make up any old story? What if he asks for a passcode? What if he says stop right there and put your hands up?"

"Lots of variables," Khaki observed.

"Exactly, even in the simplest case. They all have to be scoped. There has to be a variable script that plays out against a scene we set. You have to explore the scene with your agent before he runs the intrusion."

"This one time, an early practice run," Khaki recalled, "the Inhab couldn't speak Romanian to his grandmother who unexpectedly showed up at what she thought was the home of her grandson, who was raised in Bucharest but we didn't know it."

"Like calling a cat 'she' instead of 'he,'" TR said under his breath. Zesto looked at him. "What?"

"A screwup. One of the researchers, I think. I'll tell you later," Khaki said.

"Well, exactly—it's not simply swap in, swap out," Zesto said. "You have to know what's going on. It needs research. You've got to read the story you're walking into and figure out how to mesh yours with the one that's in place."

"And that's what you do?"

"Yeah, I script as much as I can. And we stage the scripts beforehand. Moot them, as the lawyers call it, with the Inhab agent. Think about the Malbonum case. That was the most complicated intrusion we've run to date, a public Level Two-A. Guaranteed to be on all the front pages. We spent months working it through. A simple example: immediately after the swap our agent Chuck Vlastic is going to have Malbonum call a lawyer. The Inhab—"

"Sisal," Khaki said.

"Didn't know you knew," Zesto said. "Yeah, Dewey. He suggested, and we agreed, he shouldn't know in advance the lawyer's name. Increases the bona fides of the encounter to spring it on him, as they would have on the real Malbonum. No need for Dewey to anticipate talking to the lawyer. Better to make it a real conversation for both of them. There are hundreds of decisions like that to be made, setting up the capture, placing the Intrude Operator to oversee the swap procedure, selecting the code words to make sure we're talking to an actual Inhab, approaching the target, and, as in Malbonum's case, anticipating reactions from the prosecutors and the judge. You get the point."

"Not to mention the cat," TR observed.

"What?"

"We flubbed, Zesto," Khaki interceded. "Luckily it wasn't costly. Turns out Dewey has a phobia about cats."

"That's the hardest part," Zesto said. "Knowing about spatial and object phobias of Inhab and target."

Khaki changed the subject.

"Zesto's working on a classification system for swap scenarios," she said. "It's impressive."

Zesto took a breath. "Not something we thought about at the start. But it became clear there are different types of operations, and it would help to analyze the needs and moves. Take the category called 'Snatch.'"

"Snatch whom?" TR wondered.

"All sorts. It's easier to grab an outside low-level guard than a VIP, like a senator or a cabinet secretary, or an important businessman or a famous quarterback or a movie star. Some people you can snatch in broad daylight right off the street; others you have to approach gingerly or lure. It might entail several lower-level serial swaps until you snatch the one you want. And all the while, and at every turn, you have to bear in mind the Pumpkin Point."

"The what?"

Khaki explained. "You know, what I told you, the Kryptonite Catch. The Pumpkin Point is the instant the palimpsestual circuit decays and theoretically the Inhab would vanish, like Cinderella's coach reverting to a pumpkin when the spell wears off at midnight. After the disaster with our agent Timmy Fawlson and the mobster's son in Memphis, we haven't explored anywhere close to the Pumpkin Point."

"The point is," Zesto said, "the plan has to be contained within the six-day window."

"And don't forget the Moffin test," Khaki added.

TR threw up his hands. He chose to stay mum and let his companions continue their alternating disquisitions.

"That's what Khaki calls it," Zesto said, his cheeks reddening. "It's like the Turing test—you know, a way of finding out whether you're talking to a computer or a conscious person.

Except here it's a test to determine who's in charge of a particular brain—whether you're talking to the mind of the native or the interloper. A partial test is a passcode, like the code that Dewey had for Malbonum."

"Roger–Rafa," TR offered.

"Yep, that one. That's pretty simple-minded, of course. It doesn't tell you much, and it could be faked. We don't have an adequate general test yet; we're working on it. If a person you suspect has been swapped can't tell you his parents' names or can't speak his native language, you've likely found an Inhab. But with our ability these days to run Level Two and even Level Three intrusions, that's getting closer to child's play for the Inhab. A deep dark secret revealed doesn't necessarily point to native or Inhab. What we don't know is whether a well-trained Inhab can scour the neural depths for every last secret. But it's an important assignment for us because it might be the key to providing an intrusion antidote or even a way of defeating detection."

"Like fooling a polygraph test," TR suggested.

"Exactly," said Zesto. "For now, we think we're the sole power deploying Palimpsest. But if it ever gets out, we'll have the most vicious arms race in the history of the species. We'll need antidotes."

"We need to make sure the secret doesn't spill," Khaki said somberly. "And one way to ensure that is to explore its outer bounds. A bunch of us are charged with imagining anything and everything anyone could ever do, no matter how crazy. Like taking an SAT test for someone else or visiting Paris sitting on your sofa—"

A baritone buzzer stopped her in mid-sentence.

Khaki swatted her wrist. "Hate to cut this short," she said, "but in a little while we're expected at dinner."

"With GOGS?" Zesto asked.

Khaki nodded.

"I think I'm at that table."

Khaki took TR back to her office and handed him the Project Palimpsest briefing book. He drummed the closed edge, gauging its thickness, and turned it over.

"Is this going to tell me anything useful?" he asked in a subdued voice. "I'm exhausted from all this yakking. It's leading us nowhere. We've been at this for hours, and you still haven't answered me. Why am I here?"

CHAPTER 18

WHY AM I HERE?

"I CAN'T, TR, I SWEAR I can't tell you. Not because I don't want to. It's bigger than me. There are things even I don't know. The governor will tell you why." Khaki was perspiring.

"Then tell me what *you're* doing here, Khaki. What is this place all about?"

"You've just seen it, TR. Up close. Seen it and heard about it."

"No, I've heard about your capabilities, but not what you're using them for."

"We put away bad guys."

"There's got to be more to it than that or I wouldn't be here. Lots of people put away bad guys."

"We put away bad guys who couldn't otherwise be put away."

"Okay, but that still can't be all. Come on, talk to me, Khaki. What's the real point of Subsection-S?"

She took a deep breath and exhaled slowly.

"That's a deep sigh, Khaki."

"Find the paperclip," she said.

TR felt along the top edge of the three hundred bound pages. Some hundred pages in, he felt the smooth curl of a metal clip fastened to the first page of a classified list of swap technology uses chronicled by Subsection-S planners. TR read through the four-page executive summary, at first skimming, then slowing and weighing the items in his mind. He did so with growing alarm and a sense of dread.

Subsection-S

Interim Report #23a

Executive Summary

Redacted / Restricted Access

To: Internal Files

From: Task Force C (chair: ███████████)
　　　Members: █████████████ ; ████████ ;
　　　███████████ ; ███████████████)

Re: Special Weapons and Psychology Unit (SwapU)
　　Mission Types Identified to Date

Date: June 30, ████

This report is submitted, pursuant to the Director's request, on the █th anniversary of the establishment of SwapU, and provides detailed explanations of program mission and progress.

Program Objectives: █ *33 Ways of Looking at Swapping*

SwapU has identified ██████████ thirty-three mission types now operational or likely in the foreseeable future through Swap technology (chiefly, neurosyntesis), arranged below in rough order of similarity and concisely annotated; fuller explanations are set forth in the full report to which this Executive Summary is appended. Intrusion levels are indicated as known; multiples depend on operational type and complexity.

INFORMATIONAL

1. *External information gathering for internal use.*
    - obtain financial and other forms of compiled information, including but not limited to account numbers, passcodes, electronic and paper files, including medical records;

- transcribe objective information, including inventories of assets;
- preserve sight-sound events through photographic and recording memorialization;
- secure biologic signatures, such as fingerprints, DNA samples, and the like.

Most often but not always, such information can be secured through basic Level One.

2. *Neurocranial information gathering.*
   Information available only in someone's head. Level Two and/or Level Three. Level Two will likely come online within the next six months. Level Three is not antici-pated before twelve to eighteen months.

3. *Information verification.*
   Anticipates enhanced polygraph assessments through neural verification procedures. Level Three.

4. *Evidence gathering.*
   Obtaining, verifying, interpreting, and assembling tan-gible and informational evidence usable for all forensic purposes, especially conviction following criminal prose-cution. Levels One, Two, or Three.

5. *Ingress to inaccessible information repositories.*
   Providing means of obtaining access to normally inac-cessible venues, such as locked and secret rooms, offices, buildings, camps, and ships. Ordinarily Levels One or Two.

6. *Other non-evidentiary information external transmission.*
   Information gathered for purposes other than trial and for use by others outside the purview of Subsection-S or government agencies, such as passing on tips, secrets, and other confidential knowledge to outsiders for a variety of purposes. Levels One, Two, or Three.

7. *Obtain confession.*
   Level Two or Three.

8. *Turn enemy agents.*
   Level Two or Three.

9. *Commit crimes or actions generally acknowledged as such.*
   Assassination, murder, robbery, kidnapping. Level One
   or Two.

10. *Disguise motives.*
    Divert suspicion from actual agents of crime or other act
    through falsification of actors. Levels One or Two.

11. *Establish alibis.*
    Paint story variance from factual occurrence (see Item 10).
    Levels One, Two, or Three.

12. *Run false flag operations.*
    Cast suspicion on others for covert and other operations.
    Levels One or Two.

13. *Reset scenarios.*
    Planting evidence, distorting narratives, revealing
    secrets, and other actions likely to disrupt opposi-
    tion plans and operations, especially by luring
    third-party law enforcement to intervene. Levels
    One, Two, or Three.

14. *Extract hostages and kidnapping victims.*
    Quickly terminate volatile hostage situations and resolve
    kidnapping events by swapping with kidnappers. Levels
    One, Two, Three, or Four (remote swaps).

15. *Remove opposition players from field.*
    Eliminate dangers and disrupt enemy's strategy by
    removing opposition players from field of operations.
    Levels One, Two, or Three.

16. *Dislocate and remove enemy actors by opposition.*
Cast suspicion on motives and actions of enemy's own agents, forcing their removal from operations and scene of action by enemy itself. Levels One, Two, or Three.

17. *Incarcerate and civilly commit oppositional actors and agents.*
Commit enemy actors to prison or civil clinic (and see Item 12). Levels One, Two, or Three.

18. *Inactivate enemy agent in place.*
Shut down mental capacity of enemy agents or actors in place without intermediate intervention. Levels Four or Five (theoretical).

19. *Enhance empathy.*
Reform opposition actors by enhancing their empathy, reforming their moral compass, providing them with feelings for the circumstances of Swappee or others. Level Three.

20. *Change policy.*
Alter, substitute, or eliminate public, corporate, or private policies. Levels One, Two, or Three.

21. *Enhance quality and effectiveness of torture.*
Implement new forms of torture, e.g., transferring an enemy mind into the paralyzed body of a living cadaver to induce oceanic panic and willingness to comply with any demand of Subsection-S agents to produce operational results detailed above. Level Four.

22. *General disruption.*
Provide means and opportunities for all other forms of disruption to opposition aims, plans, and activities. Levels One, Two, Three, and Four.

REPUTATIONAL

23. *False flag culpability.*
Frame enemy agents and other actors for actions undertaken by U.S. forces and agents. Levels One, Two, or Three.

24. *Privacy nullification.*
Expose damaging secrets, tarnish reputation. Levels One, Two, or Three.

25. *Reputational alteration.*
Alter, damage, disrupt, or reset reputation of any given individual for strategic or tactical purposes, including falsification of life narrative either to condemn or exonerate and otherwise to promote affirmative or negative reputational adjustment. Levels One, Two, or Three.

26. *Secure pardons, sentence reduction, and prison release.*
Provide legally justified rationales to promote pardons for selected imprisoned personnel and/or reduced, suspended, and commuted sentences as circumstances require (see Item 20). Levels One, Two, or Three.

27. *Self-interest substitution.*
Prompt changes in actor's perception of self-interest, leading to proclivity toward or actions against self-interest. Levels Two or Three.

AGENT OPERATIONS ASSISTANCE

28. *Hiding while remaining active.*
Allow active agents to hide while remaining active by swapping into unknown operatives. Levels One or Two. Level Five for long-term operations.

29. *Self-funding.*
Engage in operations to obtain money, assets, equipment, and other necessary goods and services through covert and untraceable activities. Levels One, Two, Three.

MEDICAL INTERVENTION

30. *Physical enhancement.*
Restore lost or impaired senses; e.g., regain operational eyesight (blind Swapper). Level One.

31. *Mental rebalance.*

Resolve, repair, or restore equilibrium in mental functioning via psychoanalytic transfer (under premise that a visiting mind can understand what the Self cannot). Level Three.

LONG-RANGE PROSPECTS

32. *Teleportation or instant relocation.*

For official or recreational travel (e.g., instant remote sightseeing in Paris without physical relocation. Level Four or Five (not yet possible with current state of technology).

33. *Life extension and/or immortality.*

Regain younger body as necessary when physical (biological) organism fails. Permanently retain memory and cognition through immersion in and control of non-decaying physical vessel. Level Five or Six (not yet possible in current state of technology).

Technical Note on Swap Levels

Level One: Dark Swap. Swapper and Swappee are bodily exchanged but without intrusion on mental circuits of the other.

Level 1A: Target is dark (i.e., Inhab functions; Swappee body comatose and at rest).

Level 1B: Neither is dark: both awake and functional.

Level Two: Mental Intrusion.

Level 2A: Inhab capacity to penetrate memory circuits of Swappee; Swappee suppressed.

Level 2B: Both can penetrate memory circuits (theoretical; tested but not refined).

Level Three: Traces. Trace accessibility of Inhab mentality
available to Swappee and vice versa.
Level 3A: Traces only (to varying degrees)
Level 3B: Double loading: full interchange: Inhab and
Target experience each other in body.

Level Four: Remote swap. Internet or radio or other electro-
magnetic waves. Theoretical.

Level Five: Non-decaying swap. Kryptonite limit overcome.
Theoretical.

Level Six: Mind storage. Full mental transfer long-term to non-
biological neural substrate (computer, wetware). Theoretical.

TR was in ill humor when he entered the dining room with
Khaki a few minutes after seven. Neither the trip to Khaki's unexpected residential quarters in the Cave nor the surprising discovery
that she had bought him a gray suit and a bespoke Paternosterian
necktie dispelled his gloom. Khaki could read his mood; she had
seen it before and called it his "Holmesian funk" (after the fits of
irritability that sometimes afflicted the Great Detective). But despite
her efforts, she didn't lift TR's spirits.

"Why so sour?" she ventured as they walked toward the dinner
meeting. "Is it our work?"

"Your work, as you call it, is unsettling; it's enough to make anyone
anxious. We'll get to that. But it's not what's making me sour. You
ought to know, Khaki. When have I ever been happy at being deliberately kept in the dark by people who want my help? You've provided
me with a science tutorial, a history lesson, and an afternoon's enter-
tainment with your pals. None of it explains my presence now, on
the way to dinner with your boss, at a job you've been working that I
never heard about until today. This is not like you, Khaki."

"It's not me, TR, I swear. A couple of weeks ago the governor
hinted of trouble. Not the Malbonum case—something else. He

wouldn't say more. Then when I told him you were on your way he said he could use an independent investigator who had the stuff to find us. But that's all he said. That's all I know."

"And if you did know more, you couldn't tell me. Classified and all that."

Khaki didn't meet his eyes.

"You've been down here since you sent me that message?"

"Off and on about a week before the Malbonum case went live."

"Because—"

"Because we needed to be on call for any emergency. We didn't know how it would play out. We called it a dry run, and working in my office it mostly seemed like an academic exercise. Helene ran the day-to-day from New York. But once it got going, it wasn't academic. It was real. And then more cases, and more real."

TR shook his head. "I don't like it. I don't like the idea of this place, or its power. It's menacing and dangerous."

"But we're here. And something is wrong. Whatever the danger is, the governor wants to stop it. You're on the right side here, TR, trust me."

"I hope so."

"TR, it's me. Please hear the governor out. Your steely sense has to be utterly engaged."

He gave her a weak smile. She stopped, turned to him, threw her arms around his shoulders, and buried her head in his neck. He hugged her back, kissed her on the cheek.

"Okay." He took a deep breath. "I'm reserving judgment—for you. Let's see what your GOGS has to say."

They entered the executive dining room, a modest space with a large, round table centered on a green and gold Persian rug. A door on the opposite wall opened into a kitchen. A serving board sat along one wall near the table, which was set that night for six. Three of the walls were draped in murals of Washington's architectural marvels.

Governor Joister was already seated, along with Barberoi, Moffin, and Sisal, who stood and walked toward TR and extended his hand. "We've already met. Relatively intimately, if I recall. No hard feelings, I hope."

"Mr. Malbonum," TR said.

"The two and only," he replied. "That's an Inhab's inside joke. How'd you know?"

"It had to be," TR said. "Last explanation still standing that fits all the facts."

"Well, my boy," the governor boomed, "How's your day?"

"Ha!" TR exclaimed. "Exactly what I expected." He attempted an appreciative grin for the governor. "Though it has been a while since I've been swapped into the body of an agent of the FBI and then subjected to a TED Talk on maximally augmented hyperautocatalytic neurosyntesis—all in a single day."

Sisal clapped him on the shoulder and held out a chair.

"I am impressed," the governor said, passing wine to the new arrivals.

The six diners whiled away a convivial hour in amiable conversation, as a trog steward came and went to serve and clear. When he was out of hearing, the talk mostly centered on the philosophy and operational mechanics of training without advance knowledge of the body to be inhabed.

"Hard to do?" TR asked.

"Exceedingly," Sisal responded.

"You've tried it?"

"Part of the training regimen," Sisal said, pointing at Helene. "She makes us."

"Why?" TR asked, looking at Barberoi.

"General fitness," she said. "Ready for any emergency. Flexibility. Experience building. Empathy enhancer. Plus, it adds to our storehouse of knowledge."

"I have to agree with Helene," Sisal said. "If you want to be an argonaut of neurospace, you have to train for everything."

"Argonaut of neurospace?" Zesto sounded exasperated. "You stole that from me."

"That's my profession, I'm an actor and an Inhab," Dewey said. "We steal from everyone."

After the steward had departed with the last of the dishes, the meeting came to order.

"We have a crisis," Governor Joister began. "And by we, I mean us, Subsection-S. The situation is as sensitive as they come. I'm declaring this a No Report discussion under our Classified Meeting Protocol. No notes now, no notes after, no discussion outside any SCIF facilities. Your offices are certified SCIFs, as is this room, my office, and the situation room. That's all. Nowhere else, and with no one else. Is that understood?"

"Yes sir," said Moffin, accompanied by nods from the others.

"What about him?" Sisal asked, pointing to TR.

"You know SCIF?" GOGS asked, turning to him.

"Sensitive Compartmented Information Facility."

GOGS nodded. "You are well-informed, Mr. Softly."

Looking around the table, he continued, "Mr. Softly is bound by the same rules under the Consultant Guidelines. Whether he will continue in that capacity depends on a decision he must make at the conclusion of this meeting. But what you learn here tonight, Mr. Softly, is subject to federal non-disclosure requirements under the criminal code. And under worse retaliation from certain zealots in Subsection-S. Understood?"

"Perfectly," TR said. He sat up straight. The strain of the evening was evaporating as it became clear that answers would at last arrive, followed by what he presumed would be concrete plans that he would likely help shape. Why else was he there?

"Very well," the governor said.

"Then gather 'round and listen," Zesto whispered in TR's ear.

"Gather 'round and listen," the governor said. "Weeks ago, before the first 'recanter' was hauled into court, Downtown reported

picking up a snippet of telephone chatter using the phrase
'Subsection-S'—"

"Who?" Sisal barked. "One of us?"

"I don't know," the governor said. "Burner phone, disguised
voice. But please hold your outbursts until I've finished what I'm
about to say, because we'll need to confront the stark reality that
this and later discoveries present."

Sisal and the others nodded.

"That snippet was out there by itself. No one could place it or
identify the speaker. It was said only once. And for several weeks
that was all, despite continuous monitoring. Then, a couple of
weeks ago, those words were overheard twice again, and in one of
the intercepted calls the listener crew logged another phrase,
'Time to end it.' *That* call was definitively placed right here in the
District, at 10:00 p.m., a week ago last Thursday. The cell tower
puts the call origination close to us. The Director agreed with me
that under these circumstances the calls most likely constitute a
national security breach, and he committed to ramp up electronic
surveillance. The system's set to provide automatic alerts for a
variety of phrases, one of which popped up last week. The words
were 'recanter mode.'"

"We've got a mole," Zesto blurted

"A saboteur," Sisal added.

The governor held up his hand. "There's more. A few days ago,
Saturday night, we got this: 'piggyback on mission' and two hours
later, 'Thorpey style.'"

"Jesus," Zesto said into his cup and then reached into the fruit
basket for an apple.

"Yes, Mr. Moffin, I agree with you," the governor said. "But at the
moment Jesus is likely otherwise occupied. We do, however, have
the resources of Pennsylvania Avenue, our own SwapU engineering,
and the added expertise of Mr. Softly here. But that still isn't all of
it. Let me tell you the bad stuff. Yesterday, we logged something

more chilling than anything I've told you to this point. Yesterday, we heard 'Fruitcake.'"

Sisal paled.

"That means something?" Khaki asked. "I mean, other than a dessert? Couldn't that refer to—"

"'Fruitcake' is the FBI's code name for the president," Sisal interjected.

"You really call him 'Fruitcake'?" TR asked.

"I don't," the governor said. "I hold to the proprieties. It's HQ's little joke. Early on they thought about calling him 'Jellyfish,' because even if nothing's there, he can still hurt if you encounter him. But it's not 'Fruitcake' by itself that gets my attention. It's what we heard forty-nine minutes later: 'Hot Banana.'"

"Christ on a stick," Sisal yelled, thumping on the table.

"Precisely," the governor said.

"Will someone—" Khaki began.

"Another name?" TR asked.

The governor nodded.

"The First Lady?" TR ventured.

"Nail on the head, Mr. Softly," the governor said grimly.

"Willikers," Khaki muttered.

"Fruitcake and Hot Banana?" Zesto echoed and guffawed.

"Mr. Moffin!" the governor said with fury in his voice, "Put a sock in it."

"Sorry," Zesto said meekly. He pushed his chair back from the table and laid his forehead on the table, then raised it and banged it down twice.

"Fruitcake and Hot Banana. The President and the First Lady." TR enunciated slowly. "You think this is about them?"

The governor nodded. "I'm afraid I do. If what I'm hypothesizing is true, it will require the cooperation of every single one of you starting right now to avert an unthinkable catastrophe. Taking the other scattered intercepts, I fear it's possible, maybe likely, that we have stumbled on a plot, from somewhere within our sanctuary, our headquarters, our center of operations, maybe even by one of our own. You want to know why you are here, Mr. Softly? Not that I, personally, would weep for the future if it should come to pass. You're here to help avert the assassination of the President and the First Lady of the United States."

The White House
Washington, DC 20500

June 17, 9:38 a.m.

A Treat from Your President

Statement on Major Governmental Reorganization

Fantastic news this morning. Effective midnight, the federal government has been completely reorganized, slimmer and trimmer, by cutting away deadwood, merging overlapping functions, and funneling major policies through a new unit reporting directly to Me. I wanted to call it the Office of Potential Systems, but those words don't explain its function and the acrobat would be Oops, which media ninjacompoops would outrageously claim means mistake. Lying scum. Instead, meet the White House Office of Counterfactual Congruence.

For too long Americans have been kept guessing about what its government is doing. We White House patriots have implemented super effective plans to end wars, prevent crises, and lower taxes, but sour soreheads always muck around in the details and bash the brand. Believe me, I know about branding. Like when I proposed our great American corporations could pay to use their names in place of states. Would have dramatically lowered taxes. But the media called it Washington, BS. Pathetic. Thankfully, problem solved. From now on, the Known Facts, or as some prefer to call it, the Conventionally Understood Scenario, will be adjusted to the Preferred Explanation. We're working 24/7 to convert the Prevailing Story into an Acceptable Story or Modified Explanatory Story (or Extra-Nasty). Everyone wins. (If you're wondering, there's no connection between the date of this announcement and the anniversary of the water grate breaking back whenever it was.)

Action taken: A few people have been allowed to take early retirement and various budgets have been consolidated, transferred, or shrunk, in line with our national mission. Nothing serious. Saves billion$$.

Technical Correction to the Presidential Treat, Today's Date: Budget savings total $425 billion by eliminating redundant emergency services. The Office of Government Software Technology apologizes for its indolent spellchecker, which meant to say "acronym" for "acrobat," "executives" for "ninjacompoops," to delete the hyphen in "Extra-Nasty" and spell it "Explanastory," and to refer to the Nixon thing as the Watergate break-in.

Bold New Age

*Presidents set agendas but as often provoke
countervailing ones, especially in an age of scientific
marvel and derring-do. That's why presidents so
often rise and fall, as Softly surmises when events
come to a boil in the heart of the Oval Office.*

CHAPTER 19

THE MEJACIAN

MARK MALLEYCORN POHTISS, THE ODDEST OF the forty-odd
presidents of the United States, took his accustomed resting chair
in the Oval Office at 8:25 as usual but was still smarting from his
humiliation at the breakfast table. Not that he had come out badly.
The record would show that he unfailingly surmounted all difficulties strewn in his path. He plucked a plain manilla folder from the
coffee table near him. It and companion folders with identical contents lay within easy reach on each table in the office and were
refreshed daily. They compiled, in order chronological (on salmon-
colored paper) and categorical (on sky-blue paper), his hourly
successes. The top page recorded seven of his triumphs the previous
day. He made a mental note to dictate a brief account so that his
secretary, Malka Evershoot, could memorialize how he overcame
this morning's misadventure, which began when he sat down in the
family dining room. The First Lady, Innogen Krepidian Pohtiss
(known to all as Ike), folded the newspaper she had been reading
and remarked, somewhat casually, "My, you certainly are ubiquitous
this morning." The president managed to lower his coffee cup onto
its saucer while spilling only a few drops.

"*Now* what am I supposed to have done?" he asked, scowling that
Innogen would so heartlessly report his failings before he'd had a
chance to wake up.

"Lots of things. Three on page one alone. Two more on pages four and five. The speech in Omaha, the groundbreaking ceremony at the desalinization plant in Utah. You know, those things."

"Why is that bad?"

"Who said they were bad?"

"You did. I hate being called ubiquitous. It's tremendously depressing being compared to one of those Old Testament monsters who hung out in their dins of inequity. Woe to him who calls me names."

"That's iniquity, Mark. I didn't say you were iniquitous. I said you're ubiquitous—meaning everywhere."

The president regarded his wife for a long moment and then slapped the table with his palm.

"Are you saying I don't know the English language?" His face was flushed. "I have a college degree. From Micklesburgh State, as you should know since that's where we met. You *do* remember?"

"Yes dear," she sighed, as she did most days. Last week's word was defamation, which had caught his eye on a chyron of a news program playing in the background. "Can they say that?" he had asked her in some wonderment. "I didn't think they could talk about shitting in a broadcast, even if it's a station I listen to." That time he was speaking only in her hearing. It was not nearly as embarrassing as the moment at a cabinet meeting in his second month in office when the secretary of defense mentioned a Navy skipper and Mark had wanted to know how far he could skip and what they were doing to catch him; or the news conference when he confessed, standing in Red Square in Moscow, that he couldn't read acrylic, I mean, how could anyone?

Innogen's poor darling was palpably overwhelmed, and she wished she could help. But he would never talk to her about the important things: South American trade policy. Linguistic outreach to non-English speaking immigrants. Fracking. Stem cell research. Archaic patent procedures. Nuclear proliferation. The

Fed's interest rate reductions. Global warming. But Innogen reckoned he didn't talk much about those things with anyone else, either.

She had mentioned the climate issue only a month before, but he was in a foul mood and told her that what he could not understand, "not for the life of me," was why so many scientists who, after all, were Americans, would lie about the outdoor weather. "Most days," he had said, warming to his subject, "you need at least a windbreaker to walk around outside."

Now, at breakfast, Ike fixed him with her incandescent smile and wrinkled her snub nose that even now would help make her the homecoming queen she once was. She discerned, she said, a subliminal message in the ubiquity of the stories about the president in the morning paper. "It means you're on the go, Mark. Some of the papers can't come right out and say it directly, you know, because they're owned by the oppo, so they make their point in a shroud that their readers will see through. "Our president is a bundle of kinetic energy, almost in two or three places at once, working for you!"

"You think?" he asked with a tentative smile.

"No question," she said.

"But why Connecticut? Why not the whole country? I have enough energy for everyone."

"You do," she said, deciding to overlook his second verbal mistake of the young day. "Energy for all."

"That's nice to know." He looked around. "What's for breakfast?"

"They made your favorite, creamed chipped beef on toast."

He brought his napkin to the top of his tie and tucked it over and partway down into his shirt. "It's going to be a good day," he prophesied.

The steward entered with the food. Pohtiss ate in silence, rose, caught Ike's eye and pointed to a black mug with "Potus MOJ" (meaning "President of the United States Mug of Java") in silver lettering. But she saw no need to instruct the steward in his duties since they never varied. When the steward had filled the mug, Pohtiss took it and left for the West Wing, grunting toward his wife as she extended her daily wishes for success. "Deep Mind on the move," the agent said, referring to the Secret Service code name for the boss.

Pohtiss entered the holy of holies, the Oval Office, and sat in his big black chair. He thought expansively about his domain. Not merely the White House, or his personal staff, or the armed Forces, or the executive branch as a whole, but the *entire* world. "I am president of the United States," he reminded himself each morning, "and therefore, the world is my oyster," and for these same eight minutes every day, he was indeed a very self-satisfied oyster. That was the important thing—he was the *president*. (Or "Me," as he usually thought of it.)

And so his meditation sped by. The door opened. He looked up at the clock. Eight thirty-three; his private time was over. Eight quiet minutes a day, all he ever got. Short of a Nuclear Attack News Bearer, for those eight minutes no one could enter the room or disturb him, and that included Lieutenant General Mandarin Faber, the chief of staff; the First Lady; their six children; or even Soapy O'Tumley, his oldest chum and advisor. The rest of the day, and often the evenings, was for all the stupid meetings and other mind-numbing things, none of which he gave a shit about. His own fault, really. He had told Malka on the second day of his term that he needed eight minutes a day "to be alone with my brilliance." He could have asked for more, such was his brilliance.

"Ubiquitass," he now said to General Faber, who had not missed the appointed daily entrance time by more than eight seconds in several months.

"Hail to the Chief, Mr. President—what?"

"Oh never mind, Mandy, just a thought I had—about the bad guys. Let's get on with it. What's up today? Anything I get to blow up?"

It was a standing joke, though it hadn't started as one. Forty-three days after the inauguration, Pohtiss had stared out at the Rose Garden from what he called the "Offal Office," watching the bushes that were peacefully swaying in a mild March breeze, and wondering what he should do. When the general entered, Pohtiss told him, almost wistfully, that he wished he could do something all on his own, make a hard choice, reach a tough decision, without all those damn cabinet types and assistant secretaries and staff analysts and other dumb-ass experts. Because, like, since in the long run it wouldn't matter, why couldn't he put his hand down on a map that Faber could bring him to mark the town or woods that a Navy fighter could strafe, or an island they could bomb the hell out of, not to kill anyone, but for the heck of it? Because he could, because he was president of the United States, commander-in-chief of all the uniforms, leader of the entire free world. Otherwise, what was the point? Hearing this, Faber had promptly phoned the new secretary of defense to suggest the need for an immediate protocol, "as necessary and under the circumstances," to belay such orders. By then everyone already knew what that meant.

Mark Malleycorn Pohtiss portrayed himself as a "log cabin" president, a self-description on which he had launched his campaign forty months earlier. It is technically true he was born in a log cabin, a Montana log cabin, on a New Year's Day, fifty-three years and a few months before the morning Ike told him he was ubiquitous. But that's because it was skiing season and his parents were unable to flee their vacation residence ahead of a "storm of the century" that kept them shut in until January 4. Luckily for Mark and his mother (if not the American public), an obstetrician from New York, who was vacationing in a nearby luxury cabin in Big Sky country northwest of Yellowstone, took charge. Mark spent his fourth through seventh days in the maternity ward of a hospital in Butte before being airlifted to their home outside Phoenix. Still, the truth's the truth.

He spent a semi-pampered childhood in the dry heat of the Southwest, where his father ran a trucking business hauling goods to western and mid-western states. Mark was an indifferent student, uninterested in the glory of school athletics, preoccupied by no discernible hobbies, but gifted with a preternatural relish for befriending anyone he came across and abetted by a sense of gab unruffled by his ineptitude in deploying words appropriate to their meaning. He spent most days after school wandering around town talking to strangers, inquiring about their lives, their concerns. Most of them obliged, rarely resenting what in others would have been seen as impertinent probing. In high school he cultivated a wide circle, though not through any organized activities. He was not a member of any team, club, or branch of learning or inquiry. But he was a friend to jocks, eggheads, poets, dancers, and the ones in a hurry. He went to all their parties, volunteered to help his friends' parents, and chose to laugh along with his classmates when his teachers mocked him for once again missing the point. He discovered the virtues of girls when he was twelve and their vices at fourteen and was never without someone to call or meet for a milkshake or, later, to spend intimate evening hours when that was possible. He took odd jobs and didn't mind the work as long as he could wriggle out of commitments on a day's notice. In his yearbook, he was voted Most Likely to Succeed at Being the Most Popular Man in America.

His father's strings landed him at a nearby college, Micklesburg State, where he majored in General Studies, talked girlfriends into writing his papers, and came to know three-quarters of his undergraduate class of some four thousand students. Two of those with whom he shook hands over his four years at college were Innogen Krepidian and Gavin O'Tumley.

Innogen grew up in Tucson, the daughter of a local pastor who plotted out every minute of his only child's existence, so she found immense relief in the carefree, misshapen adventures that being at Mark's side promised every day. She realized that he cared deeply, but only about the moment. For his part, Mark was smitten by Innogen's looks, easy manner, and willingness to accompany him.

Gavin was something else: an intense striver majoring in public relations and thus dedicated to understanding humanity in all its vagaries. He was fascinated by his classmate Mark's obvious but elusive skill, and within weeks the fascination gave way to personal warmth that blossomed into lifelong camaraderie.

For two years Mark drifted from job to job, because his father said he would not support an idle son who had a B.A. Mark moved out of state, worked in a lumber mill, became an appliance repairman, then took a job with a landscaping company. He hung out at the local chamber of commerce, chatted up slightly older women (some single), but found himself pining for Ike. Responding to a deeper urge, one day he dressed in a fine seersucker suit, flew to Phoenix, where Ike was living with her parents and finishing a master's degree at Arizona State, and went to her home holding a bouquet of some dozens of roses. They were married a month later. His father adored Ike from the start and now cajoled his son into the trucking business to end his vagabondage. Mark made a show of learning the business, but nineteen months later, on a day when Mark was preoccupied in renewing insurance contracts, the elder Pohtiss fell flat on his face, dead of a heart attack before he hit the floor. He was fifty-seven. Mark was twenty-six.

At his mother's insistence, Mark took over the company the next day and within a week he was devoting more energy than he knew he possessed to every corner of the business. Pitching in, Ike gave him three months of her time and then insisted he hire a right-hand man; she was quitting the company to pursue a Ph.D. in public policy. When she had finished telling him her plans, Mark immediately called his oldest sidekick. Gavin O'Tumley showed up two days later and never turned back.

It was Gavin who plotted expansion of the routes, leaving Mark to organize lines of credit to finance the growing fleet; it was Gavin who suggested he ride a full route to experience the life; it was Gavin who organized a welcome party for Mark when, riding shotgun, he completed his first thousand-mile delivery. The party comprised four old friends of Gavin's, two spouses, and some young women corralled from a truckstop bar. The young women threw flowered garlands over Mark's head when he stepped, astonished, out of the truck cabin, and told him they had heard he was "new in town." It was Gavin who arranged for a photographer from the local paper to take a picture and run the small story about a "trucking magnate" who took his clients' concerns seriously, riding the goods directly to them. Mark bought them all dinner and a nightcap and they became lifelong friends. The custom of riding the route spread, and, managed by Gavin, so did newspaper and local television coverage. It was Gavin who devised the slogan that made the company famous: "Let's go trucking."

In three years, the business had expanded into twenty-seven states. Mark rode the routes to all and became adept at addressing small crowds. His Rolodex swelled with the names of the people he encountered; he attributed it all to Ike and Gavin. Ike ran a steady household as their family increased and aged. Gavin boosted the business, giving Mark the confidence he was unaware he had lacked. Mark called him his "senior ear without portfolio," a jack of all trades, and Gavin became Soapy O'Tumley from the acronym, SEW-P, a nickname and title that would eventually follow into the White House. For the first time, Mark began to think ahead.

But of these thoughts he said nothing aloud, until finally, after a quarter century in trucking, Mark confessed his fatigue to Soapy, who said he'd been waiting for that moment. Then, to Mark's utter astonishment, said, "Let's aim big. I have a plan." Mark was known in the towns and hamlets of twenty-seven states. Time to spread his blarney across a larger canvas.

"You'll have to say things you might not like," Soapy tutored.

"Who cares? I do that all the time. 'Keep 'em happy' is my motto; as long as I get what I want." And so during the twenty-five years that Pohtiss indulged his appetites for travel and hanging out, charming strangers and delighting his growing circle of friends, he held no strong views on any issue—save one. He was often swayed by what he heard from others, and it did not take much for him to adopt the view of solid American Rotarianism: God, duty, family, country, neighbors, industry, business, capitalism, and gun rights, excepting only golf, which he abhorred, cringing whenever business forced him onto the links. But he wasn't a fanatic, and he might have endorsed abortion rights and paid family leave had he met any advocates. Mostly he kept his opinions to himself, save the one.

But that one was the doozy: a topic on which even fewer Americans failed to have an opinion as the years passed. Mark's opinion was that immigration stunk, and from this he did not waver. Mark hated immigrants.

He hated immigrants because he hated himself down to the core. He hated himself because he was the son of a man he hated for suppressing a basic truth. When Mark turned eighteen he was required to register for the draft, and he and several buddies decided to "man up" and take care of it on their own. One day right after the new year, before his final semester of high school, Mark and his friends drove downtown. First stop, the Maricopa County Office of Vital Records, where for a small fee Mark found himself staring for the first time at a document recorded two days after his birth, listing him as Karl Mark von Pohtiss. He wilted into a chair. He snarled at his buddies to leave without him, the first time that clouds formed over his sunny disposition. Eventually, he picked himself up and went home. That night after dinner, he pulled out the envelope containing the document and slid it across the table to his father.

His father opened the envelope without expectation and therefore no warning. Seeing the certificate for the first time in eighteen years, he first grew dizzy and then fell off his chair. Mark's mother ran in from the kitchen and yelled at her son to help pick him up. When she stooped to take hold of her husband's arm, she saw the paper. Her face turned white.

"What have you done?" she shouted at Mark, who was struggling to prop up his father.

"That's not the question," Mark said evenly, his white-hot anger held in check by a supreme effort. "The question is what have *you* done?"

Later that evening, the story emerged. Deeply embarrassed for decades by his German roots, the elder Pohtiss brooded on the unused "von" and when Mark was one month old finally decided to change his family's name. Mark's recorded first name and the prefix of his surname were expunged. A new and fanciful middle name was inserted. The older record was supposed to have been purged and a revised certificate should have been substituted for the original in the registry for eternity. But the bureaucrats had screwed up. Mark's father, deeply humiliated, haltingly explained to his strapping son that the family's roots lay in Rostock, not Limerick. Mark's famous charm was not Gaelic but *gemütlich*.

Thus Mark hated immigrants because he hated himself for tumbling too late to what he was. Before the age of DNA kits made it fashionable to discover that your roots lay elsewhere, it was degrading suddenly to be German and not Irish. Germans were Nazis, and Nazis were loathsome. In his own mind, Mark Pohtiss stood revealed now as squalid immigrant swill and he would never afterward willingly suffer the fellowship of people who celebrated their foreign origins; he refrained from ever talking of his own, though he would playact everyone's favorite leprechaun whenever necessary. In time his anger cooled, but not the revulsion. If his father had only told the truth from the start.

Candidate Pohtiss was fond of Truth. As he often said in his stump speeches, "The truth, like your wife, had better be your friend," even as he more than occasionally stretched, bent, battered, warped, or snapped it.

Mark learned that seeking the White House was pretty much like selling routes, or, for that matter, selling anything. Tell the customer exactly what he wants to hear, and he'll recognize it as truth. This truth overtook Pohtiss at a truck stop early in his campaign for the Iowa caucus.

"What makes you think you can stop all this insane federal spending?" an irate man in a plaid shirt and stiff leather work boots asked the candidate as the cameras rolled.

For reasons Pohtiss could not later reconstruct, he stuck out his hand, looked the man bang on, smiled broadly, and said, "Friend, I'm the man who can."

"God bless you, then," said the plaid man, the cameras still rolling. The headline that afternoon: "Pohtiss: The Man Who Can."

The next day, at another truck stop forty miles away, several people were lined up outside the front door of the diner that every presidential contender visited. "Do it, do it," they chanted. A headline that day gave full play to the candidate's boast, "He Says He Can Do It." The crowds grew. Soon, the Man Who Can took a tip from his campaign strategist: Soapy O'Tumley added a word.

"Can you do it?" the breakfast cheering squad called out.

"Brothers and Sisters," Pohtiss yelled back, "I'm the *only* man who can."

Now the crowds grew bigger still. The newspapers ran a top-of-the-fold picture with the by now ubiquitous headline: "Crowds Cheer 'The Only Man Who Can.'"

Thus the rhythm was established. No matter what his interlocutors hurled at him, Pohtiss smiled and lobbed back, until he was gobbling lozenges by the handful to soothe his throat, "I'm the only man who can."

A month later, campaigning from Illinois to Oklahoma to Idaho, Pohtiss ventured into Deep Territory: the land of Ultimate Truth. An old man, ninety if a day, standing back from the crowd, leaning against a fencepost at a roadside stop near Boise, faced the platform and hollered as loudly as he could, "Make it jake, like a cake!"

Pohtiss couldn't hear him, nor could O'Tumley, who pointed to an aide planted in the crowd. The aide walked over to the old man, who was standing near an aged woman in a wheelchair and what appeared to be a brood of grandchildren, including, it turned out, a great-great-grandchild. The man was actually 102; the seated 97-year-old great-great-grandmother was his wife. The Pohtiss aide asked the old gent what he wanted to say to the candidate. The gent repeated his mantra. The aide rejoined O'Tumley and whispered in his ear. Soapy shortened the phrase when he shouted into Pohtiss's left ear, "Go up to the microphone, look straight at that man, and tell him you're going to make everything jake again."

Pohtiss did as instructed. Fixing his gaze on the old man, he boomed, "We're going to make it jake again. I'm going to make *everything* jake again!"

The elder danced a jig (cameras rolling) and the crowd went nuts. In the space of six hours, Pohtiss's numbers shot up fifteen points. The next morning he was wearing a bright green baseball cap with four bold letters: MEJA. Make Everything Jake Again.

Mark Malleycorn Pohtiss had become the Mejacian.

Now the crowds yelled "Mejacian, Mejacian," and Pohtiss, smiling from ear to ear, would jump up on the stage and wave his arms, doff his cap, turn it around to inspect the four-letter logo, and raise it up to the crowd. "Jake Again," he would bellow.

"Say it, say it," the crowd yelled in response.

"We're going to make everything jake again," he said in registers of varying pitches and decibels, sometimes screeching, sometimes rumbling, occasionally in a monotone, mostly in an excited squeal. Then his truck caravan rolled on to the next small town, where he'd wave and yell, "With your help, America will be jake again."

In the third week of the frenzy over his new campaign slogan he had an insight: it might be useful to know—specifically—what this by now familiar saying actually meant.

"I've been thinking, Soapy," Pohtiss began one Sunday morning after the ritual stop at a Bob Evans in Chillicothe, Ohio, "that I ought to expand a bit on that phrase we're using. It's paying dividends all right, but I'm not clear if everyone out there fully understands it, and it'd be a mighty shame, a crying-out-loud shame, if people thought we were being uppity or something. Can we get our guy to pen me out something suitable to enlighten the folks with? Nothing fancy, mind you."

The next day, O'Tumley handed the candidate an index card. In neatly typed out large letters, with those words to be emphasized printed in red, it read:

> *Jake is a slang term, dating back almost a century, so it has good breeding and refinement. Rhymes with "cake." It means "all right," "satisfactory," "just fine." It also can mean "copacetic," "hunky-dory," "totally excellent, dude," "cromulent," and "okay." Bonnie and Clyde, John Wayne, Madonna, and Denzel Washington are thought to have used the word, so it appeals to all sorts of Americans, and it's a better term than its synonyms because it sounds fresh and a bit alluring, sort of the way "grand" sounds better than "great" or "Greta" sounds better than "Mabel."*

"This is swell, Soapy," Pohtiss said after studying the card for a few moments. "But how does it work? I mean, I know how to finance the purchase and sale of trucks. I know what banks and insurers want. I can convince a customer he wants to lease a six-ton forklift for two weeks and that he can afford it. I know how to stall bill collectors. I know how to settle lawsuits, five cents on the dollar. I know how to deny everything. But I don't know how to make everything jake again. What do I do?"

Soapy gave his friend a mug of the best brew west of Wilmette—they were then passing through Peotone, Illinois—and said, "It's simple, Mark, and that's the beauty of it. You're what they are calling the Mejacian. Like magic, a magician. They believe in you. They'll follow you. A Mejacian—that's you—is someone who can make things better in America merely by declaring it."

"Like a magic spell?"

"Precisely, old pal. Spot on. You say it, it happens. For instance, suppose you hear grumbling about the disrepair of our highways. Or someone yells out that the bridges are falling. You say, 'Our infrastructure is being wholly redesigned according to a plan I've been fighting for, and I'll get it going with a single signature of my pen the first day I'm in office.' And if someone objects that it will cost too much, you reassure him, 'It won't cost you a penny, friend. The top bananas will foot the bill.' We hire someone with a great voice, like that actor Ving Rhames, and have him growl 'the bakers will pay for it; they have the dough.' Try it out. We'll work on it 'til we get it right. It'll drive 'em crazy, especially your honorable opponent."

"But who are the bakers?"

"Who cares?" Soapy said.

Pohtiss's honorable opponent was the incumbent president of the United States, who for several months had become paralyzed by the shifting tactics of a bumpkin who he was sure would self-destruct no later than tomorrow. No one could be elected president, the incumbent told himself, without experience, a plan, and rational support, certainly not by relying on a lunatic slogan and a silly hat.

Mistakenly, the presidential debates confirmed his view. Mark Pohtiss as much as confessed that he did not realize that United States senators were free to ignore instructions from the president and that he could not abolish abortion clinics with the stroke of a pen when he was president or confiscate guns from people "before they become criminals." He thought he could spend as he wished from the funds available in the federal treasury; believed that by adhering to NATO and other such treaties, America's allies were bound to follow the orders of the president on military and related matters; felt it safe to avoid climate issues because the courageous Senator James M. Inhofe "has proven" climate change science a "hoax"; agreed with Robert F. Kennedy Jr. ("I mean, he's a *genuine* Kennedy") that vaccines were dangerous and should be withdrawn from the American market (his own children, Pohtiss said, had been given injections, not vaccinations); and saw no reason for presidents to spend more than four hours a day on official duties, leaving plenty of time to pursue projects he was not at liberty to talk about but which would benefit the American people "tremendously." Pohtiss omitted mentioning that one of those projects was to personally corner the world market in palladium (he had looked it up).

Despite his own mastery of the issues, Pohtiss's incumbent opponent grew ever more agitated by the vastness of Pohtiss's ignorance and subsequently was thought to have "emotionally" lost the debates by a fifty-two percent majority of those who watched. To every objection voiced by the incumbent, Mark Pohtiss declared, "No one cares what you say any more. The voters know it's time to make America jake again. And I, Mark Pohtiss, am the Only Man Who Can."

Pohtiss lost the popular vote by a mere 3.85 million votes, of more than 120 million cast, but was rescued by the miracle of the Electoral College, which handed him the election victory by 271 to 267 votes. One small state, with only four electoral votes, put him into the choicest official residence in the western world.

The White House was nice when he first moved in, but to tell the truth (*de rigueur* for his Administration), he felt envy after visiting Queen Elizabeth and seeing her digs at Balmoral. Soapy explained that the castle was hers *personally*, and not the government's, and hinted that he'd look into having some of the "wealthy ones" (as he called the one-percenters) provide the president a similar dwelling, using a portion of the big moneys they would be individually saving from the president's proposed tax reduction bill. Envisioning the dwelling, the president told Soapy, "Not too ostensible. But big."

President Pohtiss came to office with few firm convictions but many pledged policies dictated by the forces that thrust him into power. He would placate the Second Amendment diehards, push for deep tax cuts (who couldn't use a tax cut?), sell off federal land, pull troops out of wherever they were, gut environmental rules, and personally see to resolving the immigration mess once and for all. He faced no serious threat of ouster in the first year of his term. After all, things were jake, and for a man who had never held elective office of any kind (he had lost the only race he had ever entered before his White House run, the vice-presidency of his fifth-grade class), he made few serious gaffes of the sort that would prompt demands for resignation or raise cries for impeachment.

But the list of minor gaffes was robust. His earliest flub came in April when he professed to have been a Navy Seal but was quickly unmasked. He shrugged it off, saying he was misquoted. When it was pointed out that everyone had heard him make the claim in a speech to the Veterans of Foreign Wars, he said it was the "television people" who misquoted him—by broadcasting his remarks. Similarly, he shrugged off the response when he declared one day on boarding Air Force One that he had learned "no such thing" (no one later could remember what the shouted thing was) when he "went to Amherst." A reporter standing next to him on the tarmac reminded the president (and several million viewers of the moment) that he had always said he was a proud Micklesburgh alumnus. Pohtiss's face was blotchy as he insisted he *had* gone to Amherst, spent an entire weekend at a conference there "recently."

The real brouhaha came in May when he abolished the color red in two American states. At a scheduled White House press conference, a reporter had asked, with some tongue in cheek, whether the president was concerned that one of the great American political parties (and not to mention a few states) was identified with red, a color long associated with communism.

Pohtiss voiced his surprise. "Which communistas are associated with that color?"

"Red Chinese, for one," the reporter replied, "not to mention the Russians. And you'll recall the great Red Scare here in America."

"Well, I don't know about that," Pohtiss replied. "I haven't been to China yet although we have a super trip being planned, and by the best people too, very excellent China people, but it's my understanding China is green this time of year. Besides, why be afraid of red? Who's heard of anyone being frightened by a color—unless they're sick in the head, you know, loonies. And anyway, what states are red?"

Caught off guard, the reporter blurted out, "Uh, Kansas and Nebraska."

"No, they're not," Pohtiss said heatedly, as if the serious business of state were a joke to this bumptious reporter. Had Pohtiss let it go then, the sudden pundit downpour might have ended in a drizzle by the end of the day. Instead, he turned his claim into a tropical storm, declaring, "They can't be red because there is no red in Kansas or Nebraska."

The television cameras were fixed on the president's face. His exasperation was manifest.

Startled, the reporter said, "I beg your pardon?"

Feeling he had the reporter on the run, the president enhanced his claim. "You heard me, there is no red there. Never has been. They can't see red in Kansas or Nebraska. All the other colors, sure. But not red. Anyone from there will tell you. I've been there myself. More than once. Never saw red. Believe me folks, it's not deniable. If you think you've seen red in Kansas, I'd get yourself to a doctor quick. Or sue your travel agent. Because it wasn't red or it wasn't Kansas. I mean, maybe sham red. But not real red. It's gotta be fake red. Everyone knows that."

Pohtiss looked at his press secretary, Carlyn Proweg, whose face was flashing high alarm. Her mouth appeared frozen in horror.

Why wasn't she outraged along with him at the stupidity of the press corps? But warned by her reaction, he ended the press conference with what had become his fail-safe tag line, "That's all, ladies and gentlemen. I've got to get back to making things jake." The reporters fired broadsides at Proweg the instant he left the briefing room.

"Is the president being medicated?"

"Too many morning cocktails?"

"Probably best to fire the comedy writers before lunch."

"Was that a secret signal to his supporters, some code that we'll need the key to?"

"Carlyn, for God's sake, tell us what he meant, there is no red?"

Drawing herself up to her full five-ten (in heels), Proweg stared fiercely at the nearly fifty assembled reporters who were now sensing a major turn in world events. "Folks, let's all calm down. Gee whiz, of course the president didn't say there isn't any red in Kansas—"

"Or in Nebraska," came a chorus of helpful reporters.

"Or Nebraska," she said.

"What do you mean he didn't say that? Carlyn, we were all sitting here not two minutes ago, including you, when he said *exactly* that." This from a peevish network reporter.

"I don't know what you heard," she replied. "I mean, I guess you think you heard 'red,' since you say so, but that isn't correct, because he didn't say it, nor would he because, of course, that's contrary to our faith in colors and would be an example of someone challenging God, I guess."

"Carlyn—"

"In all his glory."

"Carlyn, the president said, right here on this very stage, that no one saw red."

"Well, *I'm* seeing red. Saying he didn't see red isn't the same thing as saying there is no red. He never said there is no red."

"He said the red in Kansas is 'fake' red. In fact, it's in my notes: he began with 'there is no red in Kansas or Nebraska.' Play it back. You know what you'll hear."

"Fake playback," she muttered, then pointed to a reporter on the other side of the room. "Next question."

"Pohtiss Sings the Blues" ran the headline in the *New York Daily News*. Several newspapers in Kansas, rather maladroitly, offered their readers, "Seeing Red." More imaginatively, in ninety-six-point bright bold red letters, *The Topeka Capital-Journal* trumpeted "Redlined!"

The late-night comedy shows devoted prime monologue time to this and later presidential blunders. A growing number of somber commentators who usually ignored bloopers and obvious blunders in a minor key became drawn to Pohtiss's insisting on the reality of untruths. Media outlets generally were overcoming their squeamishness in labeling his untrue statements outright lies. At a news conference (minus the president) in the fall, a dour reporter from the *Deseret News* asked with a poker face why the president was violating his own solemn oath, repeatedly voiced during his campaign, to tell the truth.

Carlyn Proweg continued to deny the fabrications. "The president does not lie."

The reporter pressed. "Does he still maintain you can't see red in the Midwest?" He held up a photo of picketers waving the unvarnished, full-color American flag in front of the capitol building in Lincoln, Nebraska.

"Look," Proweg said, her clenched fists visible atop the briefing stand, "you're showing that photo outside Kansas. Of course it's red here. Anyway, it's unproductive to dwell on these tired old incidents."

"Why?"

"Because it's distracting."

"Who's creating the distraction, Carlyn? Certainly not us."

"Yes, it is you. The President calls it like he sees it. You're the ones making a big deal out of it."

"Out of his lies."

"Those aren't lies."

"Well, what are they?"

"They're invitations to belief," she said, walking out of the briefing room.

In Pohtiss's second year, the mood grew darker. The least thing could erupt into a moral morass. When he was called on it, he pressed his speech writers to deride reporters and their editors for dabbling in the "arcane arts of bespoke news—good for this day and situation only."

During that winter, a severe cold spell brought power outages to several states in the northwest. To the first governor who sought emergency funds, Pohtiss refused. "I gave him money last year," he said in an interview. "I'm getting tired of spending American's hard-earned money on states that can't figure out how to stay out of the cold during what they say is global warming." To a second governor, Pohtiss recommended tax cuts. But he added, "Let them cut their own damn taxes; I see no reason we should cut federal taxes to please them."

In response to the uproar that followed the death of a child from hypothermia, the president counseled understanding: "To accomplish great things, there may be pain. It's distressful, I know, but it's suffering for a good cause. For fiscal sanity. Besides," he noted, "they can have another child." When asked what he would say to parents who are too old to have another child, Pohtiss replied, "They can always adopt."

In May, the president expressed displeasure at having to interrupt his Memorial Day break to attend ceremonies at Arlington National Cemetery "to pay tribute to a bunch of dead soldiers." He observed that, "Dead soldiers aren't of any help. They don't vote. They don't pay taxes. They cost the government money. And you know they can't defend the country. I like soldiers who are smart enough to stay alive. They should watch what they're doing and come home in one piece. Maybe we should court-martial a few of their training instructors. Come to think of it, that could be the problem. I'm going to stay in the White House this weekend and work on that."

Proweg, asked what the president meant when he said dead soldiers weren't of any help, resented the question. Shown the video, she said, "That's *your* interpretation."

Things grew uglier in the summer. To visiting Saudi officials, the president divulged information from a highly classified American intelligence report on "Arab assets" working for the U.S. "They're hysterical alarmists," the president said in response to strong protests from several unnamed "highly placed" CIA and FBI officials. However, the fuss died down after some weeks, and the president shrugged off the matter as inconsequential. "Everyone's safe," he said, offering no evidence to back up the denial of harm done. Agents muttered to each other that they could be next. But the FBI opened a secret investigation and notified Subsection-S.

Pohtiss remained oblivious. A week before Thanksgiving, in an address to the Universal National Prayer League, carried in full on his favorite television outlet, Know News Tonight ("where opinions count for facts and facts count for nothing"), the president "waxed poetic" (his term) over the great progress that had "befallen" America, with, of course, the noble assistance of the Prayer League. "Together," he said, "we make it happen. We make things jake." Then, without transition, he slid from "us" to "I."

"Without the power of prayer, we are nothing," he called out. "Prayer makes all things possible, pretty much as I do. And that's important for Americans of all stripes and shapes and colors to recognize. Those who accomplish so much for us, like God, deserve our prayers. And I, too, have done things likewise for my people. It wouldn't hurt, and it would please me greatly if once now and a while, loyal Americans would venerate their president. That's a speech writer's word for 'look up to.' To be worshipped, not as a

God, but still, to be seen as more than a mere man. It would be nice if, say, one in every four prayers could be directed my way."

Soapy O'Tumley caught up with him later in the day.

"How'd I sound?" Pohtiss asked.

"You were great," Soapy said, as he dependably did. But he gave his friend and mentee a cockeyed glance.

"What's wrong? Something is. I can always tell."

"I had a call from Pastor Vallandingham of the Vicksburg United Congregational Baptist Church of the Blessed Savior. He expressed concern. Asked if everything was jake with the boss. I thought that was a nice touch."

"What's he concerned about?"

"Your speech today."

"He didn't like it?"

"He didn't not like it. But he was somewhat perplexed at what you were getting at by the end, the stuff about the prayers—the ones to be directed your way. He doesn't want to confuse the parishioners. Prayers are for God, and all that, he said."

Pohtiss laughed, uneasily O'Tumley thought.

"No one can take a joke, Soapy, I swear. What's the world coming to?"

Four months later, in the early spring, Pohtiss's chief of staff, Gen. Faber, broached the darkening mood. Things were getting out of hand, he respectfully noted at a morning meeting. "There are rumblings," he added.

"What rumblings?" Pohtiss, in shirt sleeves, invited the general to sit across from him on the sofa.

"Some of our friends in the media are beginning to wring their hands over recent events."

"What events?" Pohtiss wondered.

"Well, 'Saudigate,' for one."

"I hate that word."

"Yes sir, I know. But that's what it's called."

"But that was months and months ago. Who even remembers that?"

"It's what happens a couple of years in. No love lost."

"Mandy, no one will let me do anything. They won't let me take these foreign leaders to task. They won't let me say anything about almost anything until the damn diplomats at State work a speech to death. I can't comment on a criminal trial, even one right here at home. And then there are the do-gooders telling me to lay off about all the dirty immigrants. I tell you, General, I think the only thing I ought to do, because it's the only thing I *can* do, is meddle with this government of ours. Go down the roads past where the red lights are telling me to stop."

"Well, Mr. President, if I may—"

"You don't have to worry about consequences, Mandy, if that's what this is about. I've been assured by the attorney general himself that I can't be indicted, and I can pardon anyone, including myself—and you!—whenever I want. Even better, I can tell the god-damn prosecutors to lay off. Plus they don't dare impeach me because we're finding things you wouldn't believe on them. Like treason and worse. Plus the stuff they'd try to raise against me isn't German to the discussion. Executive privilege it's called. Secrets are for me, not for them. The president is the one in charge, or someone else would be commander in chief. And then you and I wouldn't be having this discussion because you'd be taking orders from that jerk over in Congress. You know who."

"Yes sir," General Faber said, his jaw jutted in his peerless "let's be tough" manner.

"But the best thing to do is do what I'm doing. Making things jake. The people like it. A lot of the doubters are warming to it. Hell, you say there are rumblings? Well, maybe so. But that's all it is. Fact of the matter is I can beat every one of the rumblers at their own game."

"Thanks for the pep talk, Mr. President. Deeply comforting," Faber said.

Real trouble arose a year later and from a wholly unexpected quarter. The very morning that T. R. Softly burrowed into the subterranean offices of Subsection-S, a closely guarded secret White House plan was spread across the entire front page of the *Washington Post*, leaked, it was later contended, by an anonymous staffer hoping to forestall a potential cataclysm.

The plan was as chilling as it was simple. The budgets of most federal emergency services were to be drained, both to cover revenue losses from a forthcoming tax cut for the upper three percent and to support rapidly climbing personnel expenses for a booming deportation program. An unsigned memorandum accompanying the proposed "budgetary realignment" explained that most medical and administrative personnel charged with overseeing prevention and recovery efforts in case of pandemics had already been quietly terminated "with no ill effects," there being no pandemic on the horizon. The Office of Management and Budget was likewise slicing deep into staffing at FEMA and other emergency services. Hard-won expertise in fighting forest fires, evacuating flood victims, rebuilding bridges, forecasting hurricanes and tornadoes, and containing radiation leaks would be phased out over six months. One item that had been crossed out—covering salaries of airline disaster inspectors and traffic controllers—bore the notation "restore per POTUS—he flies, wants safe skies." The bulk of the leaked document listed more than three hundred programs that would be jeopardized by budget cuts, including assistance to emergency rooms, state police and health authorities, pollution control offices, women's crisis centers, poverty relief services, evacuation assistance, home reconstruction financing, vaccine research and inoculation programs, and subsidies to walk-in clinics that treated ailments apt to strike suddenly across a wide swath of the population.

No government official would speak on the record, though one "insider close to OMB" said, "It's a plan, not a policy." Another anonymous insider commented that "this plan will allow the government to do what it should be doing, tax relief and deportation."

The reaction was immediate and explosive. Cries for impeachment rang through the capital; the president's supporters were bombarded with pleas to "contribute until you're bleeding."

From the president's perspective, the most alarming report appeared in the next day's news cycle, twenty-four hours after the proposed cuts were first exposed. "President's Unlikability Quotient Soars to 81 Percent." The respected non-partisan *Bayes Statistical Gauge of Public Sentiment* reported that 63 percent of nearly two thousand sampled Americans said they "strongly hate" the president and 18 percent said they "strongly dislike" him. Only fifteen respondents, about 1.5 percent of those polled, reported that they "love" the president, "no matter what." The *Daily Fiend* summarized it best: "If we were you, we'd watch out for those sharpshooters."

The president was seething Tuesday morning when Faber entered the Oval Office for their daily meeting.

"Tell me this is all a temper in a teapot, Mandy," the president demanded.

"Mr. President, I—"

"Because this plan isn't an official policy, is it? It's, well, someone was working on the budget and all. Doesn't mean I would actually agree to all these changes. I mean, in their present form."

"Of course not."

"But, still, it could be close to what I want. I'm the president, goddammit."

Faber smiled. Outwardly. "Yes, that's true—"

"What do you suggest?"

"How about an address to the nation, Mr. President. Tell it to the people directly. The vice president has been advocating a talk for some time. Because a storm's building out there, sir. A mighty big wind is howling, and I fear the floods could follow. If you were to lay it out, give people the real low down, reassure them—"

"Good, General, that's good. Excellent. Yes, a presidential pep talk. Buck everyone up. When?"

"Soon. Immediately. Tonight. Can you work it up? Get Soapy in on it?

"Yes, yes." Pohtiss smacked the side table. "I'll start the fellas on it this minute."

"Good deal, Mr. President."

Pohtiss jabbed at the intercom on his side table.

"Malka," he shouted when she answered. "Soapy on the double."

"Yes, Mr. President."

Faber looked to and fro, which President Pohtiss understood to mean the General was weighing options.

"Mandy, what? There's a 'but' coming, I can feel it."

"No sir, Mr. President, not at all, no ifs or buts. But I was going to change the subject and pass on a story I heard this morning about Azir el-Wahary—you know, the son of the supreme leader of the Republic of Urghististan. The fellow you met last winter on your trip to the subcontinent."

"Yeah, the el-Wahary guy, Supreme Leader Wahary. Real ugly face. What about him?"

"Not him. His son Azir. Thirty-two years old. A rising power in the country. Last year he was appointed supreme commander of the Urghististani Republican Imperial Army. Everyone's afraid of him. He's been telling people no one could touch him."

"Yeah, the old man can pardon. A real handy thing, the pardon."

"Yes sir. Trouble is, the son started naming names. Managed to let the Turks know that one of the Urghististanis, who was supposed to be chief of the agricultural mission to Turkey, was actually the top Urghististani intelligence agent in Ankara. Azir, the son, never liked the fellow. Next thing you know, this top agent is dead from a suspicious car accident. Right away there's unhappiness in the Urghististani diplomatic mission. Seems they talked to the ministry of police back home. Anyway, what I want to tell you, Azir el-Wahary is dead."

Pohtiss, eyes rounded, stared at his chief of staff. "Dead? Azir, the son?"

"Assassinated. This morning. Gunshot to the temple. Through and through. As he was getting into his car."

"Just because they didn't like him anymore?"

Pohtiss shivered. He reached for his suit coat. In the Oval Office, his refuge, it suddenly felt like winter.

CHAPTER 20

SOMETHING SORT OF ODDISH

"YOU DONATE YOUR SERVICES, MR. SOFTLY? Is that what you're saying? That's a pretty janky business model. Downright un-American."

Governor Barnaby Joister delivered his opinion with an open smile, masking his puzzlement at TR's response when asked to name his fee for undertaking the assignment the governor had just laid out. The two were alone in GOGS's office, after leaving the dining room Monday night.

"No one has ever complained, Governor," TR said. "I'm offering to spare the taxpayers an extra burden. A refusal might *also* be considered downright un-American."

The governor scoffed. "I hardly think so. Not the way your representatives spend public money. Anyway, as I thought I'd already made clear, we don't cost the taxpayers—we raise the money we spend."

"Well, I can charge you a dollar a year."

"Doesn't solve my problem, I'm afraid."

"What problem is that?"

"You're here not only to get to the bottom of this assassination plot, but so I can show my bosses and the American public, if it comes to that, how we didn't ignore the threat or try to cover it up. We went outside, found ourselves the best. That's what Khaki says about you, and I trust her. But I can't show that's what we've done if we don't sign the usual retainer agreement. It won't seem on the up-and-up to the conspiracy theorists in Congress if the worst happens and there are hearings."

TR gave the governor a long look, rubbed his right eye, uncrossed his legs, tilted his head.

"All right," he said, "I'll tell you what, I do charge expenses. I'll be putting my whole team on it. They like to eat well, take taxis. They might even need equipment."

"Suppose we say per diem expenses of $5,000. For as long as it takes. Receipts unnecessary."

TR breathed deeply, then let a faint smile emerge. He looked straight at the boss of Subsection-S and said, "I can do that."

"Excellent," the governor boomed. He opened a folder on his desk and extracted a single sheet of paper. "Sign and initial," he said, handing it to TR. When the sheet came back, GOGS said, "One more thing. Your team could pose a problem. What we can't afford is having word get around about what we do here. I think I already made that point. Can you work with your team without telling them about Palimpsest? Or, for that matter, pretty much everything else."

"I have to tell them something, Governor. I can't run down a threat this serious all on my own."

"You can certainly tell them about the threat. But I'd greatly prefer your holding back details that led us to the conclusion that the threat exists."

"You mean the phrases that NSA tracked?"

"I do. And all mention of Subsection-S."

"I'm afraid that's already common knowledge—"

"Common—"

"Among the team. Three of us principals; not our peripheral agents. But I can give you comfort that we'll keep the name under wraps, and I will say nothing of your m.o. unless it's absolutely necessary and then only to one of my principal agents."

"What will you say instead?"

"That you're a special section of the FBI, as your name implies. That you take on supersensitive missions for the Bureau. That despite best efforts, I don't have a clear understanding of all the techniques you use. And even if I did, I'm bound by national security considerations not to talk about it."

"In our world," GOGS said, "the only outsiders who can be read in are spouses. And you don't have one."

"But in return for my silence," TR said, "I want to see the raw NSA reports you have now and later."

"What? Why? NSA material is delicate."

"Governor, you hired me to be delicate. If I'm to do my job, I need data, all of it. Either you trust me or you don't."

TR sat back and waited while the governor stared at something across the room.

"Very well," he finally said bleakly. He swiveled his monitor and tapped on his keyboard until a text file appeared on the screen. "You may read it, but no notes. No paper leaves the office."

TR hunched forward and read the page twice, the second time more slowly, absorbing the phrases and time sequence of the NSA intercepts. "Good," he said at last, "and now I'd like to go home. It's late. May I do that?"

"Mr. Softly, this is Subsection-S, not Lubyanka—or Gitmo. Besides, you've signed the papers. You're now one of us, after a fashion."

"Good," TR said, rising from his chair, "then that entitles me to return tomorrow."

"Until then," the governor said, extending his hand.

TR shook it, then stood silently.

"Something more I can do?" GOGS asked.

"A guide. I have no idea where I am."

"Forgive me, Mr. Softly, you see how quickly I have accepted you among our company." He leaned into the intercom. "Ned to Head," he said.

A minute later a knock at the door heralded the giant Subsection-S agent, his blue suit and white shirt still crisp, his face smooth, as if newly shaved. He held out TR's earpiece, watch, and phone. "It's been charged," he said.

TR, following Ned into the corridor, started to ask, "Is Khaki—" but Ned shook his head.

"She's retired for the evening." They walked briskly through twisting corridors and soon entered a passageway that narrowed and wound. After some minutes of this, TR observed, "Not the bookstore, then."

"No, closed. We don't go through the store after hours. The only exception is Mrs. Drumgullery, because she works there."

They paused by a key-accessed door at the end of the passageway. Opening it, Ned led TR into a familiar, small hallway in front of an elevator. TR stared at the white and black tiles of the elevator floor for what he assumed was the same thirty-five seconds that had brought them to the Cave some eleven hours earlier.

"Pardon the smell," Ned said when the elevator jerked to a stop. "And step lively."

The elevator door opened to another set of stairs. The scent of rotting garbage met TR as they climbed up the eight stone steps, surrounded at the top by three metal sides propped open by rusting metal rods. Ned raised his hand to warn TR to halt. He withdrew a small gadget from his pocket and held it at forehead height, his thumb pressed against a button. He rotated slowly in a complete circle.

"Thermal detector," he said. "In case anyone's in the vicinity looking. Never found anyone yet, though."

They stepped out into a dark alley lined with rancid dumpsters. "Dumbarton is a block and a half that way," Ned said, pointing. He turned to re-enter the basement steps.

"How do I get back in tomorrow?" TR asked. "Here?"

"Not during the day. Come back through the bookstore during regular hours."

Ned went back down the steps and three seconds later the metal sides, edged in black tape stretched tight, folded and closed to the sidewalk with a muffled clang.

TR pulled out his charged phone and punched in orJean's number. She answered on the second ring.

"TR!" she said loudly. "Thank God. Where are you?"

"How do you know it's me?" he razzed her. "Could have been my captors. Demanding ransom."

"Don't do that, TR," she grumbled. "You okay?"

"Fine."

"Where— What—"

"Get Formerly. I'll be there in five minutes."

"He's here. He refused to leave."

TR hung up. Walking out of the alley, he held the phone in front of his face and dictated, staccato, the phrases and their associated times he had memorized from the NSA intercepts on GOGS's screen. He spared his colleagues, who would see the transcript of the words he had recorded, from the phrase "Thorpey style" that NSA received Sunday, two and a half hours after the presidential names had been recorded on the intercept.

OrJean was standing outside on the landing when he turned the corner. "Goddammit, TR, you had us worried," she whispered harshly as he walked up the steps in the darkness. Then she hugged him tightly.

"Hey, orJean, it's okay; everything's—"

"What? Jake?"

"Jake as a cake. I think that's the expression," he said. When he pushed back from her he saw tears on her face. "Let's go in," he said, taking her hand.

Formerly patted him on the shoulder as they closed the door. "You had us going, boss."

"Thank you for staying," TR said and picked up the waiting "nightcap" they had prepared for him. "Okay," he said, sitting down in one of the high-backed chairs at the kitchen counter.

Formerly spoke first. "What are we dealing with?"

"Nothing much," TR said, blowing lightly on the surface of the hot chocolate in his mug.

"Must be something. You were there eleven hours."

"Okay, you got me. An assassination plot."

"What? Who?"

"The president."

The room went silent until orJean snorted, "Him? Who would mind?" But her eyes were wide and she was standing straight. "Because of this fuss over his crazy plan to kill federal funding for emergencies?"

"What plan? To do *what*?"

"You're kidding me, TR. You haven't heard? What do they talk about down there in your tunnel? And what assassination plot are you talking about?"

"I don't know. That's the problem. You better tell me what I've missed."

"Apparently the scoop of the century." She picked up the newspaper and spread it out, then sketched what had happened since the headlines, the ones TR said that morning he would look at later.

"They didn't say a word about it." TR was uncharacteristically terse. "I was a bit preoccupied."

"Must be they figured you already knew about the leak. But the reaction to it was unfolding while you were down there. How about you tell us what preoccupied you all day," orJean said, taking a large chocolate-chip cookie from an open bag and settling down on a stool.

TR laid it out, everything but the science and practice of Swap.

"There are two things I don't understand," orJean said, when he finished his report. "First, you show up there, like from out of the blue. I mean, you find their super-secret lair, this place they call the Cave. And just like that they invite you to sit down and help them out?"

TR nodded. "What's second?"

"Second is, what about all that spooky mind-reading stuff that sent you there in the first place?"

TR presented the story he had been rehearsing during his walk home minutes earlier. "I don't know about that," he said. "They are monstrously secretive down there. Lots of closed doors and brightly lit offices late at night. Exactly what they do or what their connection with Mallory's concern is still beyond me."

"They're stonewalling you."

"Yes, they are—politely."

"Then why are they trusting you with this other little thing—the assassination?"

"That's the part that has me worried. I have this feeling I have been—we have been—pulled in to play some role that I don't understand."

"Pulled in?"

"Sent for. That's what Khaki said."

"Khaki!" orJean exploded. "Khaki's there?"

"I guess I forgot to mention that."

"You forgot to mention it, after we've been busting our butts? Hah!"

TR managed to look crestfallen. "It's late, I'm exhausted, I'm trying to tell the important parts."

But orJean pressed on. "Sounds like that's an important part. She's been missing for weeks and all of a sudden she shows up too?"

"Well, no, she wasn't there coincidentally. That's where she went when she started ducking my calls."

"This Cave."

"She was there the whole time."

"She sent for you."

"I'm not clear. Possibly."

"You don't know much, my young friend."

"And *your* boss," Formerly pointed out.

"True, but he can't hide from me behind his bossness. This setup stinks. It's obvious you were *called* in. It can't be a coincidence that of all the places Khaki could choose to go, she'd be there, the *very* place you've been looking for. How is that remotely possible? It isn't. You said it yourself. Your presence was requested. You were cajoled, wheedled, summoned."

"Not summoned in so many words."

"Enticed. They tossed out a clue. It was catnip to you."

"To anyone trained to hear it." TR propped his elbows on the kitchen counter and rested his chin on his hands. "I'm still exhausted," he said in a slow expulsion of breath. "I need to sleep. Let's sort it out in the morning."

"Okay," Formerly said. He walked over to the sink and rinsed his cup. "Give you a lift?" he asked orJean.

"Where are you going?" TR asked.

"Home, no? You mean I'm not?"

"You're going to walk away from an assassination plot?"

"But—"

"You two can stay, or go, but not until you've cranked up the investigation. It's still early somewhere in the world. Let's get on it. Where is the president going to be in the next several days, and when will he get there? Run it down. Then you can flop. We'll reconvene at eight in the morning." TR left the room without another word.

He came downstairs at 7:50 the next morning, Tuesday, in his blue robe with the white and gold Paternosterian seal to find Formerly snoring lightly on the living room sofa. An aroma of coffee wafted from the kitchen where orJean, dressed in an extra-large Purdue sweatshirt and jeans, stood over coffee pods, cups, sugar, sweeteners, and milk cartons.

"Feeling better?" she asked, without turning around.

"Tip-top," he said.

"Good. Grab some of this swill, while I go kick the snoring man into a state of tutorial awareness."

TR's hoot awakened the sleeping agent.

"See, now you've gone and spoiled it," orJean said, pretending to be vexed. "Hoist your butt up and prepare to work," she hollered into the living room. She scanned the morning headlines that trumpeted the burgeoning scandal over the severe slashing of the federal emergency budget, until Formerly showed himself.

They turned to assassination rumors at eight-ten. TR kept his mouth shut, waiting for one of them to say something about what they had uncovered several hours earlier. Formerly obliged: "They're lying."

"Almost certainly," TR agreed.

"They're the FBI," orJean said. "That's what they do."

"It's an occupational requirement in Washington. Points are awarded for frequency, finesse, scope, and outrageousness. We can carp about it all day, but time is short. Tell me what you found last night. Any reason to believe there's a plot in the wind?"

"Not so far," orJean said. "We have the detailed itinerary. Most of it is certain. In ten days he goes to Asia with stops in Pakistan and India to keep everything jake between them. He'll be heavily guarded, and as far as Homeland Security is concerned, no one except the usual crazies is gunning for him despite this new nuttiness. The Secret Service is chill; they won't veto the trip. No whispers from the above-ground FBI. CIA is quiet. Pohtiss has an overnight to Iowa City to visit friendlies. In other words, nothing out of the ordinary."

Formerly's phone rang. He picked it up and after listening for thirty seconds said only, "Thanks." TR and orJean waited. "Strike what orJean just said. That was my person in the Secret Service. There *is* something out of the ordinary. Something sort of odd.

News is surfacing. A speech to be nationally televised tonight. It's only his second broadcast. Some big announcement, must be to do with this brouhaha from yesterday about the slashing of the emergency funds."

"Broadcast from where?" TR asked.

"White House."

"Well, shouldn't be security concerns there. When?"

"Nine o'clock," Formerly said.

TR tapped on the countertop. He shook his head. "My friends in Subsection-S are making it up," he said.

"No assassination attempt, then?" Formerly said.

"No, not an imminent threat," TR added. "The pieces don't add up. They're cut wrong. And too many are missing."

"Spell it out, boss."

"First, what am I doing there?"

"Following Sisal."

"But why?"

"Khaki dropped breadcrumbs."

"I said that she *said* she did," TR said.

"Why?"

"Why did she say it or why did she drop them?"

"Either one, both," Formerly said.

"She or her boss claims I was doing them a valuable service, a stress test of their ability to stay out of sight."

"And you found them."

"Yes, and that should have been the end of it. But then the boss said I should stick around and have dinner, where he announced he needed our help to foil this plot."

"He knows about us?"

"I told him if he wants me, he gets all of us."

"And he agreed."

"Pretty much. I mean, here we are. But I don't believe any of it. I think my showing up was a surprise, or an afterthought."

"But I thought you just said Khaki was expecting you?" orJean said, frowning.

"Khaki, maybe. But not the rest of them, at least not until I was on their doorstep."

"They invent an assassination plot to give you something to do?" orJean said. "That makes no sense. Does anything?"

"The intercepts might tell us something. Did you transcribe that note on my phone?"

OrJean opened a file folder and gave TR and Formerly copies of a single page she had printed out with the message TR had dictated into the phone ten hours earlier on his way home. TR read the text and said, "The boss's version of the intercepts and the text of the intercepts are inconsistent."

"Could he have just been mistaken?" orJean asked.

"Maybe. The boss told us his version at dinner. That was after several glasses of wine. The drinking and the dinner could have been staged to provide a clever excuse. Give me a slightly altered, faulty version and then if caught, blame it on Demon Rum."

"I thought you said he was a wino," Formerly said.

"It's an expression, my child," orJean responded. "It incorporates the wickedness of alcohol everywhere."

TR waved them silent. "At dinner," he continued, eyeing the page, "the way the boss tells it, NSA intercepted the phrase 'Subsection-S' seven weeks ago, when Malbonum entered his guilty plea in court. But the actual NSA report says it was four weeks ago—*after* the plea. The boss says the phrase repeats two weeks ago. NSA is silent about any repetition. He says ten days ago the phrase is 'time to end it.' But NSA has it as 'time to end.' They agree on 'recanter mode' but differ by a couple of days on when that phrase was uttered. He says 'piggyback on mission' was last Wednesday, but NSA says day before yesterday—Sunday. He says 'Fruitcake' and 'Hot Banana' were heard yesterday—Monday. NSA has those words spoken Sunday at six. You see the problem?"

"I see lots of problems," Formerly said, "beginning with total confusion about what any of these phrases mean or what difference it makes when they were said."

"Subtlety, Formerly, is what's called for here. According to the boss, the gist is it shows a plan to assassinate the president and the first lady."

"How do they get that it's aimed at them?"

"From their names."

OrJean shook her head. "They call them *Fruitcake* and *Hot Banana*?"

"The FBI does," TR said, in no mood to be diverted. "The point is, if you're plotting to kill the president would you talk about it, even in code, on a phone you must know is being recorded? When you plot to kill, you keep quiet. And putting that aside, the timelines don't make sense either. A stress test based on what Khaki did couldn't have concluded until *after* the plea hearings concluded, because I or some other investigator, relying on Khaki's planted clues, could not have been called in until afterward. But if you are looking to plug leaks, look for holes, and check for other weaknesses you'd want to stage a test that would show results *before* the plea hearings began."

"But you don't rely on drydock for testing if a ship leaks," orJean said. "You put it in the water. They might have thought no one would have any reason to snoop around until they fielded agents staging a plea."

"That's a point," TR conceded. "But it still doesn't explain Khaki reeling me in, if that's what she was doing, through this long, thin cord. Too many assumptions: maybe Mallory would check things out; maybe she would call me in; maybe an investigator would notice a passcode was repeated. But maybe not. If you're worried, you plan something more robust. If Khaki really did put someone in motion, it wasn't just to do a stress test."

"Unless that's just what she told the boss," Formerly said.

TR wasn't expecting the thought. He paused, chewing on it.

"That's possible. Perhaps by planting the code Khaki had some other purpose in mind than bringing me in to stress test their little shop. But she surely isn't planning to assassinate anyone. And there's more. The phrases they recorded that agitated them so much didn't happen before I came along. According to NSA, they happened after we were already in the picture."

"Sunday afternoon—" Formerly began.

TR cut him off. "We were making calls. You were on the phone with that gym buddy of yours tracking down Sisal. He was talking to someone at the FBI. We likely tipped them off that someone was actively probing into their whereabouts, or at least Sisal's. It's too much of a coincidence that at that exact moment the mystery caller blurts out assassination clues. That and the fact the boss tried to backdate their occurrence tells me it's all a ruse, conveniently timed to put us to work chasing down a phony assassination plot."

"Like a sideshow," orJean speculated.

"Yes, like a cover story for something else. I show up and all of a sudden it's a good thing we cracked their code and got inside and are available to help. Lucky them. We're their alibi for whatever Subsection-S is planning. The boss—"

"This boss have a name?" Formerly asked.

"I guess I can say. Remember the name Barnaby Joister?"

Formerly shrugged.

"Wasn't he," orJean began, then finished with "piffle, I had it, but I can't quite place it."

"I had no idea either," TR said soothingly. "Joister was a boy governor, something like that, with talk about running for president, but nothing ever came of it, and he wound up with a presidential appointment running this super-secret FBI unit. The sort of guy who dangles lots of people around a plan with multiple heads."

"What's that mean?" Formerly said, weary of allusions he didn't grasp.

"He's got a thing going. But he diverts us from it by dangling a juicy conspiracy that begs to be solved—right away, pronto! He tells us we came by the job honestly. All part of the plan. But I don't buy it. He's extemporizing like crazy."

"You don't think *he's* planning an assassination?"

"No, because I don't think that's what it is. Why would he plan an assassination, and then warn us of the threat? And why wouldn't he say anything about the new storm around the president? Wouldn't anyone? If you're worried about an assassination, wouldn't you at least mention to your new guy that there's a new reason for the crazies to assemble? But I never heard boo about it. What could that mean?"

"Sometimes a cigar . . . " orJean reminded him.

"Sometimes, but not this time. For some purpose, the wrapper's too shiny, or it's been shredded and glued back together, or the trademark's been scratched out and rewritten, and I want to find out why."

"Which is why you're going back there, right?" orJean said.

"You know me too well, oh Mistress of the Catalogue."

"Well, better go get ready. Wear the gray suit."

"And I want you two to wear out the welcome mat. Bring in a couple of people if you need them. Press everyone. What's special about this speech tonight? Who will be there? Call me every hour."

TR went to the sink and ran water into his mug. "The gray suit, you say?" he tossed back at orJean as he headed for the stairs.

"Your best one," she shouted. "You know, like any of the ones hanging in your closet."

CHAPTER 21

THE SETUP

TR ENTERED THE BOOKSTORE AT 10:15. Mrs. Drumgullery greeted him.

"Ah, our Mr. Softly," she said. This morning she wore what appeared to be a white lab coat over a pair of black dungarees and a frilly green blouse. The same purple glasses hung around her neck. Her left hand held a clipboard; her right hand dropped something into TR's palm. "Our keys. White key opens our door. You probably won't need it, unless it's an emergency. Come and go as you please but only during business hours. You'll sort out the elevator and interior door keys as necessary. You remember where to find the door down?"

"No Ned this morning?" TR asked mildly.

"You're on the roster now. You don't need Ned. Of course, if you want to talk books, you need me. I'm here every day and give professional advice every afternoon at four back there." She pointed to an open doorway where the countertop was open to view.

"Can't wait," he said and walked quickly toward the elevator that had taken him on his underground journey the day before. At the counter, a sudden thought turned him around. He called to Mrs. Drumgullery, who was still standing where she met him. "I don't know where to go once I'm there."

"I don't know either," she said. "Never gone down there. But Dr. Blumenthrace will be watching for you."

Three minutes later, the elevator door opened onto its subterranean floor and the cascade of bright white light. Standing to the side in her own white lab coat, Khaki was waiting. "Progress?" she asked.

"Your office," he said.

She eyed him curiously, wearing, when the elevator door opened, her most winsome look, the "you can always talk to me" smile he always fell for. But this time he wasn't falling for it. His tightened his jaw and looked straight ahead as if by not seeing her he wouldn't succumb. She held the door open for him when he came to it, two steps behind her.

She flopped onto the sofa. "What's wrong?" she asked quietly.

"Everything," he said. "Tell me the truth, Khaki."

"TR!" she exclaimed, apparently affronted. "I have always told you the truth. Always and ever. What is going on?"

"That's what I'd like to know."

"Then you haven't—the assassination—who's behind—"

"I don't believe there's any such threat. That much I pretty well do know."

She sat up straight. "That's good," she said brightly. Then she darkened, "But in that case—"

"Exactly. There's an awful lot of pretend going on. What do you know?"

"I know only what I heard last night. I'm not involved in operational intelligence. I oversee the psychology—but you know what I do."

"No one has said anything to you?"

She shook her head.

"You know about our Exalted Leader's latest Looney Toons proposal?"

"If you're talking about the boss's boss's boss's boss, yes, I do read the headlines, TR."

"I assume your colleagues do too. Funny that they didn't mention it yesterday. Not during the day, nor after dinner."

"What, I mean—"

"Do you trust your colleagues here?"

"Implicitly," she said.

"Let me ask you, who would gain around here if what you do became known outside the Cave?"

"No one. At least no one I can think of."

"No? What about your colleague Helene, chief of training?"

"Helene? Why Helene? This program is her life. Why would she—"

"People would do all sorts of things for a Nobel Prize."

"How would—oh!" Khaki put a hand up to her mouth in sudden understanding. "You think—"

"I don't know for sure. But suppose word leaked out about the science of neurosyntesis. Would she then feel free to publish a paper? Would she think having NSA eavesdrop on a single clandestine mention of Subsection-S on a burner phone be enough to bring your operation to someone's attention?"

"Willikers, is that what you think this is about? Why don't we call her in and ask her?" She reached for the telephone console on her side table.

"Khaki, no, wait, not yet. I'm not through. Hear me out. Suppose the governor pieced it together, like I'm trying to do. Instead of confronting her, embarrassing her directly, because he didn't want to lose her, suppose he threw up a smokescreen to divert NSA and your colleagues here into thinking that the snatches of conversation you've recorded are not about giving away the secrets of neurosyntesis but about something else entirely, like an assassination. It's a very subtle signal to her: you try to spill our secrets, we'll cover your tracks with a more serious alternative reading of the recordings. She knows which of those were not her statements and will realize someone else has jumped in to camouflage her leaks. GOGS invites her to meetings; she can see if she backs off, the boss will cover up her misconduct and refrain from coming after her."

"You think he concocted false phone calls and this assassination plot to scare her?"

"It might be a way of reminding her where her loyalty lies. Rally 'round the banner. Rah, rah team."

"She backs off."

"Not only right now but altogether. If she ceases her loose talk, she may see that nothing connected to her gets investigated, not even the tantalizing chatter she thought might be meaningful to NSA eavesdroppers. If Subsection-S can keep anyone from paying any close attention to her unauthorized chatter except in the context of an assassination plot, she will conclude she's got no other play. She backs off, returns to the fold, and all without the boss or anyone else having to say anything directly to her. Life goes on."

"It all blows over."

"That could be what's going on. The governor would like that. I don't think he wants to lose her."

Khaki looked at the ground for a long moment, unspeaking, her head slightly bobbing, as if weighing whether to divulge something else or feign ignorance. Finally she looked back up at TR. "Maybe," she said hesitantly. "But if you're wrong—if there really is some plot to kill the president?"

"The team is working on it. Up to now we've turned up nothing. Not a hint of trouble. We can put a lot of others on high alert if it's necessary. But I shouldn't have to say that catching assassins is not in my job description. Not why I'm here, is it? You couldn't have known anything about that when you sent for me, or at least some investigator, if that's what you did. It's a job for your people. That's what the FBI is for."

TR's phone rang. OrJean. He held up his hand to silence Khaki as he answered it. He listened and then hung up. "We've picked up a rumble. Formerly's reporting whispers from at least two sources that there could be trouble at the president's broadcast from the White House tonight."

"What broadcast?"

"You haven't heard?"

"Heard what?"

"Khaki," he said, "get me to GOGS right now."

They burst into the governor's office without knocking and found him on two phones at once, shouting into both, "Well, goddammit, why am I only hearing about this now?" He pointed to the chairs in front of his desk. He snarled into both phones, hung up his office line, and put his mobile on the desk.

"Do you know about this?" he barked at TR.

"Which part of it? The broadcast or the trouble?"

"Damn it." Then, calming himself, he apologized. "Don't mean to take your head off. Though I'd like to take someone's. Idiots. When did you hear about all this?"

"This morning, if you mean the broadcast."

"And you didn't think to call me?"

"With all due respect, Governor, I didn't think I had to. You're the FBI. If I learn about a sudden decision to televise a talk by the president, I'd have supposed you already knew."

"Only heard about it right this minute," GOGS groused. "What about this 'trouble'? What did you hear?"

"There are rumors troublemakers may try to crash the broadcast party. Not enough to act on though."

"I'd say that calls for more than standing around. How would you crash it?"

"Well, since I'm guessing you can't throw yourself into the White House, you'd probably have to infiltrate the staff, get yourself a broadcast pass, pretend to be part of the crew, something like that."

"That's what I'm thinking. Listen, you two, go find Zesto. Get him to work up a quick sneak-into scenario. If we can guess what could happen, we can take countermeasures. I've got calls to make. Regroup in an hour."

Zesto had a file folder full of such scenarios. Presidential helicopters taken over by terrorist pilots. Party crashers in the White House. Affable enemies at fund-raisers attended by the extremely wealthy, an assassin posing as a sommelier, the husband of a super model, a security agent for a visiting prime minister, or chefs with a passion for poisoned pastas.

"Cameraman's a pretty worn-out trope," Zesto said. "Also, trusted valet, best friend, daughter-in-law, political ally, spouse—in fact, you name it, there's a script out there waiting to be staged. Too many variations to have a script for each one."

"Concentrate on a broadcast in the White House."

"Where?"

"I just said, in the White House."

"I mean what room. Oval Office? Situation Room? Lincoln Bedroom? Formal dining room?"

"Assume the Oval Office. Isn't that where most presidents broadcast to the public?"

"Then maybe he's safe," Khaki said. The two men paused. "Think about it. The only presidents ever assassinated were shot with guns in public spaces. Take away the guns or surround the shooter's target and there's no assassination. In the White House you can take away and surround. Why is there a problem?"

"Khaki," TR said. "Have you forgotten *The Godfather*? Remember what Michael Corleone said, 'If anything in this life is certain, if history has taught us anything, it says that you can kill anyone.'"

Khaki stood her ground: "Under the right conditions."

"Yes, but you're confusing historical precedents with a radically changed present. Lots of ways to kill someone without guns, even in a well-guarded space. A suicide bomber, for instance."

"How would a suicide bomber get into the Oval Office with a bomb? Don't be dumb, TR. They'd screen out a bomb fast. Wouldn't they?" She turned to Zesto for confirmation.

"Who knows?" Zesto said. "Bombs come in lots of flavors these days. You wouldn't need a big one to take out the Oval Office. And we could probably come up with a different way to kill the man for every minute in an hour. But there's a simple solution to the Oval Office problem, at least for tonight."

"Clear the room," TR said.

"Exactly," Zesto agreed. "Kick everyone out after setting up the equipment. Bring the president in after the others have left and after they've swept for all the things they sweep the room for."

"That makes sense," Khaki said.

"It does, in fact," TR nodded. "But since it's likely against protocol, you should suggest it now. If GOGS agrees, he can get moving on convincing the president's staff and the Secret Service."

Zesto beamed. "I'll call him right now."

The governor pronounced himself impressed and said he would relay the idea to the "senior echelon presidential protection people." He called back fifteen minutes later. Moffin put him on speaker.

"Full credit to you, Zesto. They like the idea. But it's complicated—lots of minor practical changes they'll have to implement in the next few hours. TR still with you?"

"Yes sir."

"I'd like a report on what your people are finding out."

"Give me fifteen for the latest," TR said. "But Governor, if I may, another thought. It might make sense to send in a neutral to monitor the arrangements."

"A neutral?"

"I think someone who's not a regular might have a better eye, or at least a different one, for who doesn't belong, you know, behaviorally that is, among the camera or other crew. And a new security team would be less likely than regular agents, lulled by familiarity, to trust a White House staffer who turns out to be rogue."

GOGS hung up.

TR's bunched his eyebrows. "He mad at us?"

"Nah, he's efficient. We're having a good day," Zesto said.

"Well, it's early in this good day," TR said. "Give me a minute. I gotta call in."

"Dig deep as you can," TR told orJean and Formerly when they came on the line. "New visitors seeking entry to the White House, passport alerts at airports, train stations, abandoned cars. Last minute decrypting assignments, police alarms—"

"Boss—"

"Flutter the Catalogue. Someone will connect. Metro slowdowns or stoppages, gun store thefts, Interpol chatter, disappearance of known radicals, missing cultists, gathering mobs—"

"Boss!" Formerly shouted.

TR paused.

"We know the drill."

CHAPTER 22

TECHNICAL CORRECTION

AT FIVE THAT AFTERNOON, THE SUBSECTION-S chief of training, Dr. Helene Barberoi, and FBI Special Agents Dewey Sisal and Chuck Vlastic arrived at the front gate of the White House with orders to report to the lead agent already on scene. But the strain of rapidly changing procedures and protocol overwhelmed communications, and it was twenty minutes before they were brought to a command post set up in the Situation Room. It did not look at all like the staged photos in newspapers. The room was tiny; Sisal discovered he could walk around its interior perimeter in six seconds.

Here the Subsection-S agents received their assignments, to support the Secret Service in clearing the equipment crews who would be setting up in the Oval Office for the broadcast, scheduled to begin in three hours. The president would be closeted in residential quarters until half an hour before air time. The vice president would be arriving at eight from his home at the Naval Observatory. Sisal thought his presence a bad idea but could do nothing more than voice his objections to the head of the FBI's criminal investigative division, who was on site. He admonished Sisal to back off: "The VP goes where the VP wants."

Sisal, Vlastic, and a Secret Service agent went to the Cabinet Room to meet the sixteen crew members responsible for the evening's operations. They checked credentials and interviewed each of the crew, some of whom wanted to know why they were being treated as "common criminals."

"Orders," said the Secret Service agent.

At nearly seven o'clock the crew, along with the agents, were admitted to the Oval Office to set up. Sisal amused himself sitting in the president's chair to give voice levels and for camera framing. Chuck Vlastic sat in the back for a few minutes and then stood alongside the technicians, having them explain precisely what they were doing, and the workings of their equipment.

"Everything's shipshape," he told Sisal.

"Should be," the Secret Service agent said. "I recognize all these guys."

"No one you don't know?"

The agent shook his head.

"Anything odd?" Sisal asked Vlastic, whose terse "nothing" confirmed that those in the room posed no threat.

Barberoi, meanwhile, sat with the president's secretary, Malka Evershoot, in her room adjacent to the Oval Office. The briefing was polite and to the point. Evershoot described the previous broadcast the president had made, giving Barberoi the play-by-play from the time she and the president entered the Oval Office until the broadcast concluded. Once broadcasting began, no one was permitted to go into or out of the room though access was available immediately from either her office or the president's small study. Evershoot explained that her office opened directly into the Oval Office, that the president's study was connected through a closed corridor ending in an Oval Office door, and that two other doors also gave access to the Oval Office, one in another corridor of the West Wing, the other from the outside colonnade skirting the Rose Garden.

The set-up crew finished by eight o'clock. Unobtrusively affixed to the front of the desk was a wireless button that would activate the live camera feed and another button for the teleprompter from which the president would be reading. The crew were moved into the Roosevelt Room, across the main corridor from the Oval Office, for standby technical assistance.

The Secret Service agent took his leave of Sisal and Vlastic and headed to the residence to escort the president to the Oval Office, who was expected to arrive there at precisely 8:30. The two Subsection-S agents were parked in the president's own small study, where Barberoi joined them. They would be summoned, as a courtesy to them, to meet the president when he arrived. Sisal withdrew a folded sheet of paper from his coat pocket and laid it on the president's desk.

The vice president entered the West Wing and walked directly to his office, accompanied by two Secret Service agents and his chief of staff. Soapy O'Tumley sat alone in his office, expecting to meet the president before he began the broadcast. Carlyn Proweg was with members of the White House press corps on the other side of the West Wing. Secret Service agents stood outside the doors of each office occupied by staff. There were also agents standing outside the two external Oval Office doorways.

At 8:30 President Pohtiss, escorted by his Secret Service agent, entered the Oval Office from the West Wing corridor. They had met no one in the hallways. The normally fractious staff were obeying instructions from the Secret Service agents to stay inside their offices until after the broadcast.

"Well, Vernon," the president said to the agent who frequently accompanied him in the White House, "quiet tonight."

"Exceedingly, Mr. President," Vernon replied.

The president waved at the cameras, which were dark. "How do I start these things? Don't want the damn red light going on if my reader is black."

"No sir. That red button on the little box hanging on the desk there, right there next to you?"

The president looked down and prodded it gently as if it were a mousetrap set to spring.

"This?" he asked, gesturing the agent to take a look.

"Yes sir, that's the one. When you're ready, which I guess means at nine sharp, you press it, the cameras will light up, and you'll be good to go. Oh, and the black button next to it starts the teleprompter."

"Well, even I can manage that," the president said with what Soapy O'Tumley had termed his "aw shucks I'm one of you" grins.

The agent smiled. "Bravo, Mr. President. Well, I leave you to your speech. Good luck, Mr. President."

"You aren't staying? The last time I did this, you were here."

"Not allowed tonight; General Faber ordered extra security precautions. You're by yourself, sir. That's what I'm told. I'll be just outside. Oh! Almost forgot, we've been assisted by a couple of FBI agents new to the game who'd like to meet you before your speech. May I bring them in for a handshake?"

"Always happy to meet the FBI."

"I'll be right back."

The Secret Service agent went to the small study. He knocked once on the door and entered, gave the three Subsection-S agents a thumbs-up, and said if they hurried he could escort them into the Oval Office to meet the president. Vlastic demurred; he reminded Vernon that no one was to enter the Oval Office once the president was inside.

"Can you bring the president in here for a second?" Sisal asked Vernon.

A minute later Vernon reappeared with the smiling president.

Sisal, Vlastic, and Barberoi stood. "Mr. President," they said in unison.

"Relax folks, it's my honor. I love to meet people who work for me and who might vote for me next time around—if I charm you sufficiently."

"We'll be here if you need us, Mr. President," Sisal said.

"That's the spirit," the president said, reaching out to Helene and giving her a friendly pat on her forearm as they shook hands while the others stood behind the president in the crowded small room. Three minutes later the president turned to re-enter the short corridor leading to the Oval Office, then frowned as he did whenever an item on his mental to-do list tickled. He snapped his fingers, winked at Helene, turned to the top of his office desk, grabbed the folded paper, and shoved it into an inside pocket of his suit jacket. He had been absent from the Oval Office for no more than six minutes, re-entering it with a bounce to his step at 8:46. The room was otherwise empty. Fourteen minutes to broadcast.

Vernon took his position outside the Oval Office and locked the door. No one would be permitted inside.

President Pohtiss took his seat in the black swivel chair behind the famous Resolute desk, a gift from Queen Victoria to President Rutherford B. Hayes in 1880 and used by almost every president since. He stretched out his legs, then put one foot up on the desk. He stared at the cameras before shutting his eyes as if preparing to take a nap, but blinked them open two minutes later. From inside his suit pocket he extracted the folded sheet of paper, placed it on the desk parallel to its left edge, and smoothed it out. He swiveled his chair to look out the window past the colonnade and peer into the Rose Garden, which was lit by exterior lanterns. He sat still.

At 8:59 he turned toward the cameras. He tested a variety of facial expressions, until he sensed the friendly and honest look that would sell his plan. At 8:59:58 by the large clock opposite, he pushed the red button and then the black one to activate the teleprompter.

"Good evening, my fellow Americans," he began, staring earnestly into the cameras. "I speak to you tonight on a matter that to my surprise has captured the public attention in a way that few of this Administration's initiatives have. I refer of course to what some are unkindly calling Policygate. Since nothing that has been reported resembles the Truth, which as you know is my guiding light, I am here to set the record straight.

"I have learned throughout the day that vile innuendo, spread by malcontents and fakery artists, have led a growing number of decent Americans to ask if their President is a crazy. Well, I am not a crazy.

"Yesterday, or maybe earlier, an unscrupulous member of the White House staff, who will be terminated when identified, leaked to a dishonorable reporter an early draft of a policy document written by a low-level member of our Visionary Plans Committee who, frankly, was not up to standards. I'm looking into that. This draft has never been presented to me, your President. And the *Washington Post*, or as I like to call it, the *Washington Compost*, published it. I am seeing red. This is not Kansas or Nebraska, so why shouldn't I see red? You may laugh if you like. That was a small presidential joke, to show that I can tell one, even on myself."

Pohtiss took a breath and shivered. He let his visage relax and his audience saw his face take on a hollow aspect, his mouth diminish into a fake, frozen smile. Soapy O'Tumley, watching in his office, turned clammy.

"But back to business," the president intoned, making an effort to regain his poise, to project a quiet assurance to the citizenry that he was in control.

"I will now outline our mature plans for this great nation. The United States of America will always be prepared. We stand ever ready for any emergency. And to show you that I mean business, I am announcing a new cabinet-level Office of National Emergency Readiness. To lead the Office, I am appointing Margaret Tangiers, who has devoted many brilliant years in service to the United States with quality qualifications to consolidate and lead our emergency response teams wherever the crisis is and of whatever sort. And not because she might be the First Lady's sister-in-law's niece."

Soapy turned pale. This announcement was not in the script. Margaret Tangiers? After being publicly fired by the same president in an embarrassing Treat to the entire American public? With the family connection nakedly paraded? O'Tumley's eyes narrowed. The old boy was up to something Soapy couldn't yet fathom.

"And that's not all, no, my fellow citizens, not by a sniper shot. In fact and truth, there's more. I'm accused of putting America at risk. I will never do that. But I do mean to save our blessed nation from wasting money. Not like in that silly not-my plan that the *Washington Compost* was tricked into publishing. *My* plan is super-intelligent, efficient, brilliantly conceived by the best policy people in town. Very good people. We're finding things in the emergency plan I inherited you wouldn't believe. Some offices can only fight fires. Others spring into action to plug up radiation leaks. I ask you how many radiation leaks do you honestly think we have? Then there are all the units devoted to diseases. Epidemics. Contagion. Blight. Plague. All different words for the same thing. The sort of thing that practically never happens anyway. What plague? I don't know what that means. I've studied these matters. If there's a problem, we'll send doctors. Doctors are doctors. Just like truckers are truckers. When I want to go somewhere, I don't demand a certificate from the Society of Left-Hand Drivers if there's going to be a left-hand turn. I look around for the nearest trucker. We jump in and haul ass. We don't suffer from duplicitous skills. We have one good one and we use it. If something's wrong, get a medic for whatever ails you. And that's not remarkable. I don't even know why they say that, I mean, who marked it in the first place? Someone pointed it out, anyway, what they're pointing to. Can you see it? Which is why we're all here."

The president took a long breath.

"The point is," he continued, "we're not going to fund people to sit around twiddling their thumbs, waiting for something to happen that will rarely come to pass. We'll activate them when it does. No emergency will be permitted to last more than thirty days. We'll save the budget for things that need doing right now."

Soapy jumped up, retching. His usual appreciation for his boss's masterly cornpone was overwhelmed by nausea that the president was disintegrating before a national television audience. Espousing positions that made no sense, not even to the paranoid, and without running them by his political counselor. Pohtiss's hardcore base would go up in smoke. This was that lily-livered General Faber's handiwork; he couldn't stand the heat. The least Soapy felt he could do was sock the old soldier in the jaw. He set out for Faber's office.

"They say some people could die," Pohtiss was saying to the TV cameras. "Well, that's right, they could. People die all the time. They die in accidents, and we don't make up lies and leak it to the papers. People die in wars. We don't point that out to young recruits when they enlist in the U.S. Coastal Guardians. *Semper paratus*. Well, like the Coasties, we'll always be prepared. Except we won't patrol the waters unless there's an actual emergency. Some say plan ahead. I say planning is socialism. Plus, didn't I say I would save Christianity. And it's still here, isn't it? No one takes a tree from our good Christian tree huggers on my watch.

"Now I don't want people to die. It's bad to have people dying on us. Shrinks the tax base and then who would pay for real emergencies? Plus it costs money if people die, like providing death certificates and autopsies. Also, you know, you can't cut taxes on dead people, so it would cost more to solve problems."

Soapy burst into Faber's office. The chief of staff bolted to his feet. "Fuck you," each hurled at the other.

"You didn't write this?"

"I thought you did," Faber snapped back.

They sank into chairs near Faber's television monitor. The president was saying, "Stay with me. There's much more to come. How am I doing, Ike? For those watching who have not heard my previous presidential address, you should know that the First Lady watches my talks from the official residence after the live presentation, and I wish to publicly acknowledge her courtesy. That's one of the reasons I like Ike."

President Pohtiss took an audible breath, then paused the tele-prompter while he peered genially into the cameras. A few seconds later, he restarted the slow roll though it didn't much matter; he was entirely ad-libbing.

The president leaned back to take a smiling pause at having laid these sensational thoughts before the voters. A midterm course adjustment. For every supporter lost, he'd make it back twice over in the admiration of the nay-sayers who thought he was hidebound to a creed. You *could* make everything jake again, he thought. Did he also hear a voice? Was he talking? The people would greet his growing greatness in groves—or is it droves?

He had another plan. The big one. The surprise plan not in the speechwriters' draft. The one even Soapy could not anticipate. The plan was daring because he was intrepidicious and audacious. It would take grit and gumption, but the American people are gri-tious and gumptious—are those words? Ike would know.

Pohtiss looked at the red light. Yes, it was still lit. He switched off the teleprompter. It was old school and distracting. What he was now saying was from the heart. His mind embraced his audience, visualized the hundreds of millions of faces. He put on his best mournful, hangdog expression, stared intently at the cameras, and began anew.

"As I look out at you, my fellow citizens, I am reminded of the burdens of office. All a president ever does is things for other people. After a time, a president waxes weary. I have arrived at that time. I've suffered more than probably anyone in this country, in fact, in the whole history of the country. More and more I wonder when is someone going to do something for me? When will the people ask not what the president can do for them but what can they do for their president?

"I have a simple suggestion. All I could wish for . . . "

He stared at the camera. No time to waver. What he truly wanted was recorded deeply and indelibly in neural circuits and was readily stated: to be acknowledged as a God. The more he thought about it, reflecting on an intense, interior desire to be made whole, the more Pohtiss declared he required revering, if that was a word. Even if it wasn't. He wanted to be revered. He *needed* the adulation. He wanted people to be dazzled by his essence, his expressiveness, his ability to wield and magnify and knit and unite. The United States motto must change: no longer *e pluribus unum*, but *he pluribus unum*. Does that make sense? Does it matter? He wasn't talking, was he? Can you hear this?

He was more than their elected one, their leader, their chosen overseer, their boss, their champion, *their ruler*. More than that. He was, when you get right down to it, their—your—shepherd. Indeed, might as well use the term—their—your—*divine* shepherd. In the end, wasn't that the essence of it? What else could he be but what he was? The National Dude. Leviathan. Unmoving mover. End all and be all. Alpha and omega.

He was free at last to acknowledge to the whole American public— and the world—what he had long known, this need to be recognized, admired, celebrated—and worshipped. *He needed to be worshipped.*

Homage must be paid. His family would agree. His friends grokked his inner shining essence, his incandescent necessity; maybe, after all, it *was* his ubiquity. He *was* there for all of them. Shouldn't they submit, surrender, subordinate themselves to him? All Americans must see the luminescence that shines within, that would ignite the fire of their souls, if they had souls, not like his surely, but that would make their hearts melt at the very contemplation, the sheer, central heart-rending awareness of that joy.

Their *love*. *That* was it. That *was* it. They—you—must finally, now, inescapably express more than admiration and appreciation—you must *love*. Him, Me, Mark Malleycorn Pohtiss. You must melt your hearts and souls into a gooey mass and pour its smooth and luscious never-ending viscous liquid love upon him, *Me*, basting, enveloping, and sustaining him, I, as he sustains all.

And it was then, those thoughts still echoing as words in the ears of the numberless millions of viewers around the world who were seeing him unravel in digital color on their screens of choice, who had been seeing him unravel since he assured his loyal subjects minutes earlier that he was not crazy—it was in that moment that Mark Pohtiss seized on the sole material solution to the problems faced by all gods at all times in all places: he began to disrobe.

He undressed in the measured, deliberate, and regal manner befitting the dignity of the deity who was mortifying himself for all humanity. He unfolded each garment and placed it neatly on the corner of his desk.

Faber lunged for a box of tissues. He pulled several out at once and blotted his perspiring forehead and then tossed the box to O'Tumley.

Mesmerized, indeed paralyzed, by what they were witnessing, the network producers maintained the broadcast of their president disintegrating before the world. They dared not call time on this unscripted, unrehearsed, unhurried, sad, gruesome, and glorious unwinding. They offered the world the drama as it unspooled in the Oval Office, the president of the United States of America, ablaze in the harsh glare of television lights, disrobing button by button, piece by piece, pockets emptied, belt removed, until at last, standing now, Mark Malleycorn Pohtiss flung his arms out wide and stood naked before the live cameras of global media, his erection profoundly centered on the viewing screens of humanity.

He began to sing: "My country tis of Me, sweet land of Fibber McGee—and Molly too." Then he brought his arm down (magisterially, as he thought about it) to the single sheet of paper and pen he had laid on the desk before his performance. With a hand that needed no practice, he signed the letter, properly typed on White House stationery:

Dear Mr. Secretary:

I hereby resign the Office of President of the United States, effective immediately.

Sincerely,

/s/ MARK MALLEYCORN POHTISS

The Secretary of State
Washington, DC 20520

Then he pushed the button on his desk. The cameras went dark. Lingering a few seconds longer, he heard a sound atop the buzzing in his head, until it refined itself into human language—the ear-splitting howl of Malka Evershoot in an unrivaled bravura of horror.

"Mr. President," she screeched as she burst into the Oval Office through the door that directly connected her secretarial office, "whatever are you doing?"

She stood in front of him, her eyeballs bulging. She did not hear the door open from the president's study, or see Helene Janice Barberoi walk up behind her and clap an unscented cloth over her nose and mouth. Almost immediately, Malka slumped to the floor.

Barberoi looked at the naked body of arguably the most famous man on the planet and asked, "Is that a Dewey-eyed president I see before me?" The Roger-Rafa code had finally been changed.

The naked man—now the only president ever to resign in the nude—smiled like an altar boy being praised by the bishop. "Right," he said.

Helene stood at attention in front of the naked president and clapped her hands. "Your finest performance. Impossible to equal." Then she smirked and pointed at him, "You no longer glad to see me?"

Sisal, inhabiting the form of Mark Pohtiss, scowled, too preoccupied to engage with her banter. "Helene, we've got at most forty-five seconds before Pohtiss's minders get here. Let's move, snippety-snap, zippety-zap."

Just then, Vernon, the president's Secret Service agent, inhabited by Chuck Vlastic, burst through the door from the main corridor, a muffled commotion swelling and diminishing as he opened and then closed and locked the door behind him.

"This way," Helene said.

The three, Barberoi, Vlastic-Vernon, and Sisal-Pohtiss, sprinted the few paces along the interior corridor and into the presidential study. There the comatose bodies of the organic Sisal and Vlastic lay stretched out on the floor. Vlastic-Vernon locked the door while a bare-armed Helene Barberoi clapped the neurosyntesis shields over the heads of Sisal-Pohtiss and the organic Sisal. They could hear the thumping of agents running in the main exterior corridor and guessed that a sharp popping noise was the bursting open of the exterior door to the Oval Office that Vlastic-Vernon had been guarding. Dewey Sisal, now outloaded to his own body, sat up and shook his head. He pressed his temples with both hands and groaned softly.

"You okay?" Helene asked.

"Okay enough," he said. "Get on with Chuck."

Helene was already plastering the connected shields onto Vlastic-Vernon and the organic Vlastic. The chemical timers were set to awaken Vlastic instantly but to keep both Vernon and Pohtiss knocked out for ten more minutes. Organic Vernon was stretched out on the floor. Organic Pohtiss was sprawled in a fetal position in the padded office chair. A rough pounding threatened to crack open the door to the short interior corridor.

"Halt," Vlastic shouted, getting to his feet. "I'm opening it."

Vlastic undid the lock and pulled the door open. Two Secret Service agents, guns drawn, pushed their way in and stopped instantly when they saw a body on the floor and the doubled-over man in the chair whom they would still view as president of the United States for another few minutes.

"What in God's name?" yelled one of them.

Sisal stepped forward. In a low but commanding voice he said, "Keep it down and hold the others out. It's a royal fuckup. A minute ago, the president, all wild-eyed, comes running in here buck naked with your guy, Vernon, I think, never did get his full name, in hot pursuit. The president dropped into the chair without saying anything. When he fell, the chair rolled out, tripped Vernon on the way in. They had us blocked."

"Why was the door locked?"

"Christ, I didn't even know it was shut."

"You're Special Agent Sisal?" the agent in front said.

"I am."

"And you two are the other FBI guys—pardon ma'am—the Bureau sent over."

"That's right," Helene answered for them.

"That's what you saw?"

"I saw the president come through," Vlastic replied. "As Special Agent Sisal said, he looked crazed. Didn't say a fucking word. Wasn't looking at us. Flopped down onto his butt."

"And the door?"

"*I* locked it," Helene said.

The agent stared hard. "Why?"

"You think it would be good for someone to barge in and find the president like this?"

A ruckus swelled behind them. The Secret Service agent still standing in the doorway turned around to face a growing crowd, by now backed up in the corridor, trying to push their way in.

"Stop!" he barked, holding up his hand, halting pedestrian traffic.

"Christ, what in hell is going on?" The voice of General Mandarin Faber, unmistakable within the walls of the White House. Soapy was right behind him.

"General, sir," the Secret Service agent by the door said. "The president is obviously ill, and he's naked as shit. Someone needs to bring clothing before anyone sees him."

"You," Faber pointed to someone several feet back. "Find his clothes. Get them here *now*."

"What *happened* to me?" a woman moaned, from somewhere down the corridor, her voice carrying through the open door.

"It's Malka," someone shouted. "She's on the rug in the Oval Office. She must have fainted."

An agent ran toward the study door with Pohtiss's pants, shirt, and jacket and handed the clothing to Faber, still in the doorway, who barked, "Dress him," as he threw the clothes inside.

"Dear God," another person said as he pushed his way forward: the vice president of the United States. He stared incomprehensibly at the naked man crumpled in the chair.

"Mr. Vice President," Soapy pleaded, "we've got to get him cleaned up."

"Yes, you do," the vice president said. "I have something else to do."

"What?"

"I have just come from the Oval Office, where I found this sitting smack dab on the middle of the desk." He thrust Pohtiss's resignation letter over an agent's shoulder and into Soapy's face. Soapy read it and turned white.

"I don't know, Mr. O'Tumley," the vice president said, his voice now quite formal, "but it looks authentic to me, and whatever this is about, we've all got responsibilities." He looked around and spotted his own chief of staff at the outer edge of the crowd blocking the study doorway. "Herb," he called out.

"Yes sir," said the assistant, trying to edge past the agents and two cabinet officers standing next to him.

"Get the chief justice here, right now, immediately—*five minutes ago*! No excuses. Wake him up, break up the card game, I don't give a damn. And the attorney general and the secretary of state. And my wife. If need be, send the president's helicopter. And someone who can operate the damn cameras. This is not a drill."

"For what?" the chief of staff yelled back to his boss.

"A swearing in. Do it, man. Every second you delay is a potential disaster. *Go, go, go.*"

It was the most forceful display that any of the people standing, jostling, shoving, yelling in the West Wing had ever seen from the man whom few people could even name. He was generally called "the other one" or "hack number two," depending on political persuasion, or, on formal occasions, "the vice president."

"Goddammit, let me through!" a high-pitched voice squealed. The president's personal physician pushed to the front. He peered into the study and saw his sole patient inert and bent at an oblique angle on the chair. Helene was trying to stuff the president's torso into his suit jacket.

"What by the blessed trumpet of Israfil is happening?" he shouted.

"I—he—" Helene sputtered, for once at a loss.

"Out of the way," the doctor said. "There's a stretcher coming. Let's save the man and not spindle or mutilate him further."

In two steps he stood at the edge of the chair and looked down at the crumpled figure of his illustrious patient. A gurney, its wheels rattling along the floor, came in alongside. As medics hoisted Pohtiss onto the gurney, but before they covered him with a sheet and blanket, the doctor put a stethoscope to his chest.

"Heart rate and rhythm are normal," he said, more to himself than to the agents. He withdrew a syringe. "A sedative," he said to Sisal's look. "Keep him calm if he wakes up, and until I can examine him thoroughly."

A groan from the floor turned their attention to Vernon, the Secret Service agent. "What happened?" he asked, forcing himself into a sitting position and rubbing his head.

"You all right, man?" Vlastic asked, kneeling down. "You tripped when you ran in here—don't you remember?"

Vernon looked around and saw the medics strapping Pohtiss onto the gurney.

"Is that—"

"Don't you worry. He'll be fine."

Vernon shivered and groaned anew. The medics ministered to him while the doctor pushed the gurney out of the small office. People lined the main hallway, silent, as the ashen-faced president was wheeled past.

"And the truth shall set you free," Sisal whispered to his *doppelgänger* as the cortege passed from sight. He turned back to Vernon. "What do you remember?" he asked the Secret Service agent.

Vernon stared at him, the legs of the chairs and of the jumble of people standing by staring back.

"Nothing," he said. "I mean, last thing I remember I was on my way to the Oval Office. It's all a blank. "What's the matter with the president? What happened?"

"Some sort of breakdown, I'm afraid," Sisal said, bending down and taking Vernon's hands to help him up into a side chair. "Not your fault. Nothing you could have done. He freaked out on his own."

"Where?"

"In his office, the Oval Office, not here. He just lost it. Gave a rambling speech. No one could understand it, and then he stripped well past his skivvies for all the world to see."

Vernon buried his face in his hands. Several phones rang. Sisal, Vlastic, and Barberoi reached for their pockets. Each of them picked up on the second ring, listened for a few seconds, looked at each other, nodded.

"Yes sir, from all of us," Sisal said into his mobile, and disconnected. "Home," he said to the others.

They shook hands with Vernon and told him they'd been recalled immediately.

"Glad for your help," Vernon said.

"Not sure what we accomplished," Sisal said.

"Well, at least he wasn't *shot* on our watch."

Sisal shrugged. "Might have been kinder."

CHAPTER 23

THE TALE ACCORDING TO SOFTLY

SISAL, VLASTIC, AND BARBEROI WALKED INTO the darkened Subsection-S media room an hour later to find GOGS, Zesto, Khaki, and TR lounging in club chairs. Three large flat monitors were tuned to different news programs.

Sisal strode to the front of the room and faced his seated colleagues, who were silent and expectant. He said nothing for several seconds, then bowed, raised his arms as if to pull his audience forward, and declaimed:

> *Our revels now are ended. These our actors,*
> *As I foretold you, were all spirits and*
> *Are melted into air, into thin air:*
> *And, like the baseless fabric of this vision,*
> *The cloud-capp'd towers, the gorgeous palaces,*
> *The solemn temples, the great globe itself,*

Sisal paused and pointed to Vlastic, who rose and continued:

> *Yea, all which it inherit, shall dissolve*
> *And, like this insubstantial pageant faded,*
> *Leave not a rack behind. We are such stuff*
> *As dreams are made on, and our little life*
> *Is rounded with a sleep.*

Governor Joister stood, bowed gravely to the three returnees, and beckoned the others to join him as he applauded their performance. The three choked up, relief yielding to pride. The governor raised a glass: "Hail, varlet, think not to atone: Your sins so scarlet yet your deeds unknown."

"Mission accomplished?" TR called out.

The governor looked at him in mock indignation. "Are you suggesting this evening's tempest was our colleagues' handiwork? Do tell us what you think, Mr. Softly."

"I meant, no assassination," TR said. "That was the mission, to avoid an attempt on the president's life?"

"Yes and no. Yes, it was the official mission. No, you don't think that was our mission, and you know we don't either. In this room we can be frank without fear."

"It was neatly done, I will hand you that."

"Would you care to share your theory with us, Mr. Softly? Come up here and expound. Poirot us. I know we would all profit from your wisdom."

Softly walked to the front, standing between the television screens and the chairs. His gray suit jacket was unbuttoned and slightly rumpled, but his necktie was knotted around his still-starched white shirt. He opened his mouth to talk, then closed it again.

"Struggling for the story?" the governor teased.

"Struggling for the storyline. I'm looking for the best way to tell it. But I don't suppose it matters. If I'm off base, you'll tell me."

"Oh, we most certainly will," said Zesto, his head nodding up and down.

"The plan all along was not about averting an assassination," TR ventured, his hand in his jacket pocket. "There never was any such threat. That became clear to me yesterday as soon as it was broached. Your plan, and I admit that you've accomplished it with panache, kudos"—he bowed toward Sisal, Barberoi, and Vlastic—"your plan was to do what you did tonight—banish Mark Pohtiss from the Oval Office. You staged an unforgettable spectacle. This generation will always remember where they were during the presidential meltdown.

"What do I think happened? I think you have been planning for a year or more to rid the country of a democratic mistake. You staged the Malbonum plea and the others as a proof of concept. If you could walk a seasoned and stable criminal into a confession, you could walk an unseasoned and unstable politician out of office. You waited for an opportune moment, snatched the Deckled Don from wherever he was, in his garden, out walking his dog, and invited yourselves to his home."

"Nice try, Softly," Sisal said, "but how would we snatch a guy like that, surrounded by his guards? If we did that, we'd have to take them too. No reports of that, were there?"

TR closed his eyes and focused on the scene. In his mind he reversed the sequence, seeing Malbonum walk backwards into his home, FBI agents standing nearby. He snapped a finger.

"Of course! You broke in. He *said* you did. Our bad was that we didn't believe him. The guards have a night out. You go in. No need for a warrant when you can have whatever you do ratified. Ratification was the clue—and the key. You took him, swapped him, and the Inhab played the gracious host. Everyone would assume it was on the up and up. No one was likely to ask how it started. And you knew so much because you'd been stalking him for weeks or months or, who knows, years before."

"Sounds like a plan," Zesto said.

"But first you tested, tried it out with Carslip. That was you, as well, Dewey, wasn't it?"

Sisal sat unmoving. Zesto spoke for him. "He found you, Dewey. How did you do that, TR?"

"It's easier to find something when you know what you're looking for," TR said. "Carslip was less troublesome because there was little to talk about. Holed up in a hotel room. Much quicker. Didn't have to worry about his past life. It's a simple Level One-A Swap. Isn't that what you call it? Whatever you don't learn from him, you easily get from the records. For an actor like you, Sisal, memorizing that stuff was easy.

"Carslip was preliminary. Malbonum was the full-scale trial run and a lot harder, but you proved it could be done. A Level Two Swap during the two days in Malbonum's home before the plea hearing. But even though you were inhabiting his body you couldn't penetrate his brain completely, so you had to go into the panic room from time to time and rouse your own comatose body to get his mind to talk. But that was risky because he might recall his capture. In fact, when he recanted he ranted about being trapped in the room. Of course, no one believed him because his story was too disjointed and, obviously, *un*believable, but still it could have raised alarms. It raised my suspicions. That's why the recitals in the succeeding cases were much more spartan. You dispensed with their life stories when the other recanters offered their guilty pleas. And your practice with Malbonum must have paid off. You knew how to extract everything you needed in the later cases.

"In the beginning, I thought the plea hearings were your ultimate objective. But they were all only dress rehearsals. Still, they were real cases. And you were happy to put the bums away. But you were curious. What would anyone make of a set of closely bunched cases of confess and recant? At first I wondered, why not avoid the risk that sophisticated observers would detect a pattern that might give away your game? You could have avoided multiple recantings by changing targets. Like a simple Level One intrusion to siphon off a dictator's Swiss bank account. No one would connect a foreign financial flap to a mobster's confession in America."

"Who says we didn't?" the governor interrupted. "Dictators don't generally give interviews after they've lost a billion dollars, but they might dispatch their guards for dereliction."

TR shrugged. These were not cases he knew anything about.

"Azir el-Wahary?"

TR did not recognize the name.

"Son of the ruler of Urghististan. Killed yesterday. Talk is he was done in by friends of a rival he ratted out."

"That wasn't what happened?" TR asked.

"Well, we're not investigating so we can only speculate. I *can* tell you the son was one of only three other persons with codes to his old man's Swiss accounts. They were cleaned out five weeks ago. The other two code holders fell off a mountaintop or something two weeks back. We have that from highly-placed intelligence sources abroad."

"You're saying his father had him whacked because—"

"*That* would be speculation, Mr. Softly," the governor said. "Do continue."

"Well, maybe that confirms the point."

"Which point?"

"Why you didn't go elsewhere to test your stuff. Because you did. But you also didn't take care to minimize it here. It finally struck me. You wanted to know what people would think if recanting became an epidemic instead of a bizarre, isolated incident. And you got the answer you wanted. People thought, well, this is weird, but not much more weird than the first case, and after that they grew bored. Burned itself out. You got Malbonum and the others off the street. No one's the wiser. You're free to move on."

"Keep going," Barberoi said. "I want to know how it comes out."

"At some point early in the proof of concept," TR continued, "someone here decided to drag in an outsider. But you weren't open to just anyone. It was me—you wanted me from the outset. The governor told me he got to arguing with Khaki about my impending arrival, and she raised her voice to persuade him to trust me. Khaki seldom raises her voice. Why would anyone care whether the governor would trust me, unless it was me specifically you wanted here? Plus, by letting me in, you guarantee my silence."

He looked at Khaki. She did not meet his eye. Silently, she walked to the refreshment table, picked up a can of soda, and handed it to him. He took a long swallow.

"Why would we care who, among the many possible investigators, could find us?" Zesto asked.

"I don't know," TR shrugged. "That still puzzles me. But I do know the Roger–Rafa signal wasn't sent to help you run down any plot. Even if the public mention of the word 'Subsection-S' you heard on those NSA recordings was a breach of operational security, still, that and those other brief phrases didn't herald assassination. At most, whoever said them meant to stir things up, rattle a cage, bring this entire project to public scrutiny. Someone might gain from that."

TR looked at the other people in the room but avoided any body language suggesting he suspected Helene. She, in turn, studied the wall behind him.

"But the later NSA intercepts, the ones that came in after I was on the scent, are bogus," he said, fixing his gaze on GOGS.

"Mr. Softly," the governor frowned, "everything in those intercepts happened exactly as reported."

"No, I don't mean that. I'm sure those words really were spoken on a mobile phone, and I'm sure NSA really did record them just as you heard them. But I don't think they meant anything *real*. They were meant to convince your superiors of trouble. The words certainly weren't connected to me, didn't justify reeling me in, and didn't point to any likely assassination attempt. They were all recorded after it became apparent I had located your shop and was going to breach your tunnels. They were spoken to rope me into your operation, to convince me some dangerous plot was brewing for which you needed my help. But that's not what you actually needed me for."

"What, then?"

"You needed me as cover. The ostensible reason was for me to investigate a presumed assassination plot. But once my team began, you could plant a rumor, obscurely down the line, of looming trouble. That would get reported to me, and I would report it back to you. That way, you could relay with a straight face the rumors you started and pass them along to the White House. In case anyone asked about your involvement, your story would be that you were following up what someone else uncovered."

"Assume all that's true. How would we guarantee the big man would go on TV?" Zesto called out.

"A lucky break. The *Post* scoop forced the president's hand."

"Are you sure?" Zesto said, unable to entirely mask his smirk.

"Of course!" TR exclaimed again, slapping his forehead. "*You* arranged for the leak. That's it, isn't it? The leak jeopardized the president's approval ratings and impelled him to go on the air. His broadcast was an ideal setting for your drama. In fact, not a set-ting—it *was* the drama. It was a wonderful vehicle to stage a midsummer night's dream you've probably had since the dear boy was elected. It was a masterstroke by a master scenarist, and we all know who that is. The goal was not to avert a threat or stop the speech. It was to rid us of the president.

"But you didn't want anyone thinking you marched FBI agents into the White House for your own ends. You needed some other reason to be there. And I'm the one who gave you that reason. I was the one—your man from the outside—who urged you to send a neutral team to the White House to ensure the president's safety. You couldn't ignore a good suggestion, one that spoke to the danger that the president and the country faced. Especially given the extremely short notice. That's also why you needed me, and not another PI. *I* was summoned because Khaki would ensure I'd stay on the job."

TR looked over at her. Khaki's face reddened.

"The three of you went up to the White House, fully accredited, justifiably there for a significant reason—playing a role in ensuring the president's safety. But then something funny happened, because you have powers: abilities that no one else imagines.

"The key to it all was clearing the room. Everyone had to think the president was and had been in the Oval Office alone the whole time. But you had to get him out, briefly and unseen, to stage your swap op.

"I'm guessing it went like this, or something close to it. The three of you"—TR pointed to Sisal, Vlastic, and Barberoi—"had to do the swapping out of sight. You also needed a place where Helene could watch over your comatose bodies while the drama played out. The only place where you could sneak the president out unseen and where you three could be waiting for him was a room that connects directly to the Oval Office, like the president's small study. The last person in the Oval Office with Pohtiss was the real Vernon. He escorts the president out to meet you—maybe to shake hands. You can't go into the Oval Office to meet him because no one is allowed in after the camera crew departs. As soon as Vernon and Pohtiss enter the study where you three are waiting, you use the knockout drops and do the swaps. Now it's Chuck who is Vernon and Dewey who is president. Helene is watching over two comatose bodies—Chuck and Dewey. The president, inhabed by Dewey, goes back into the Oval Office. Chuck as Inhab takes his post outside the main door of the Oval Office. He's not there to guard the president. He's there to keep others out. As far as the outside world is concerned, the president had been in the Oval Office the whole time.

"So there's Dewey, planted in the president's body. He's sitting in the Oval Office, playing the biggest role of his life. The performance is riveting. I'd love to hear more about it. How much was rehearsed, how much ad-libbed. When it's over, Dewey-Pohtiss runs out of the Oval Office and back to the study where Helene is guarding your bodies. Chuck-Vernon gets back there too, and you both outload—return to your own bodies. You two are awake but the real president and the real Secret Service agent are still down for the count. All that Chuck and Dewey and Helene have to do is walk out. They don't have to sneak out or explain themselves, because they had been properly admitted to the White House and no one saw them do anything untoward. It was assuredly the president who spoke on camera. Everyone saw him do it. No one saw the physical Dewey or the physical Chuck anywhere near Pohtiss. When they were seen after, they were right where they were supposed to be seen.

"The real Secret Service agent and the real president are strung out on the floor or desk or wherever, which is where the other agents find them. Out cold, no explanation. The agent can't remember. The president can't either. But no one needs to explain how the president got there, because it's his office and he's visibly had a complete breakdown. The Secret Service agent followed the president; that's why he's there. He tripped or fainted. Who knows? Who cares? He's an afterthought. No one will look too closely.

"It's devilish, when you think about how it all connects. The script called for the president to self-destruct. That called for Swap. To do that you needed to position him where you could get to him, like in a broadcast prompted by a leak. To run the op, you needed to clear the Oval Office where he'd be sitting so no one would see what was going on. To do that you needed a verified threat. To make the threat believable, you needed a security breach and an outsider independently looking into a plausible plot. To do that you released phony signals to lure him in. I was the outsider. That was your game. That's why I'm here. The question is, in whose interest was it to carry out this spectacular stunt?"

"Please," the governor said, "if I were writing an essay about all this a hundred, or hell, five years from now, I'd bet I'd say it was the inevitable outcome to the story of a terribly troubled man. Call it a 'technical correction.' No one will seek a fanciful conspiracy. We're overstocked with those. Too many to pay attention to."

TR threw back his arms, surrendering the point. "Whatever," he said, " it was a damn smooth takedown. Your fingerprints aren't on the operation. The president did it all himself. Can't blame conspirators. No coup. The cabinet didn't depose him. No impeach-ment effort in Congress. It's all on him. My hat's off to you all."

No one said anything, until Helene piped up, "We're basking in the glow."

"Two things I don't get, though," TR said.

"Speak," said the governor.

"The Synapticator gadget. To run the swap, you have to use that thing. You'd have to bring it into the White House. They'd be checking anything anyone walked in with, especially something that strange."

"Haven't you ever read *The Day of the Jackal?*" Zesto asked. "Thought that'd be assigned reading for every aspiring Sherlock. Helene, will you do the honors?"

She stood up, jabbed at the button on the cuff of her left sleeve, and then raised her arm. The sleeve detached at the top of her shirt from five small studs that wrapped around her shoulder. She grabbed it with her other hand before it hit the floor. A thin flat metallic band ending in a small plug was wound around the wrist end of the cloth, part of the design. The Synapticator pad. She picked up the sleeve, snapped it back onto the shoulder studs, and was whole again.

"My pants legs come off too, but let's skip that part of the demon-stration," she said. "To save time."

To cover his embarrassment, TR nodded sagely.

"And your second question?" Zesto said.

"The speech itself. Who was really talking, Dewey? You or the president?"

Sisal was silent for several long seconds as he rearranged his stern features and offered his impression of appearing thoughtful while eager to please.

"Well, assuming you are correct in suggesting I'd have the effron-tery to play the president—"

"We're beyond that, Dewey," TR said, his mood darkening at the game his new companions were playing.

"Sorry," Sisal said in a conciliatory tone. "I don't mean to aggravate you. I'm following the playbook here; you can understand that. Still, hypothetically, let me say that we were both speaking. I wasn't extemporizing. I had full access to memory circuits. It was a blend. It's hard to explain. When you gain experience as an Inhab, you learn to draw simultaneously on the existing neural structure. Mind stuff comes in faster than an audience can detect. You absorb the target's essence—memory, experiences, feelings. What his audience heard was not just me but the actual positions and beliefs of Mark M. Pohtiss, though I'd agree, for the sake of argument, that some of the phrases were mine. But if you're wondering did I put words in his mouth, words for everyone to hear, I didn't—or wouldn't, again, speaking hypothetically. That was Pohtiss's speech at its core, not mine."

Sisal stopped abruptly. Softly sighed deeply but thought better of replying.

"What about it?" the governor asked. "Has our tale been told?"

"Well, even if our Poirot here is off by a few details, it's certainly not a tale told by an idiot," said Zesto. He lifted his wine glass in tribute.

"An interesting hypothesis, Mr. Softly, imaginatively laid out," Vlastic began. "We should—"

"Look!" Zesto interrupted, pointing at the screens on the wall.

The cameras were once again broadcasting inside the Oval Office, where several people were filing into the room that less than two hours earlier was solely for Mark Pohtiss's use. The cameras focused on each person who strode through the doorway from the main corridor: the vice president holding his wife's hand, the robed chief justice, the secretary of state, the attorney general, the vice president's chief of staff, then a half dozen other staffers, and agents wearing gray suits and earpieces.

"Someone turn up the sound," Khaki demanded.

" . . . news that President Pohtiss has resigned his office, effective an hour ago . . . "

The CNN anchor was reporting in a sober but dramatic "affairs of state" tone.

" . . . perhaps unsurprising, after tonight's breathtaking, mysterious, and unique speech from the president, who suffered a wrenching meltdown before an audience estimated at nearly one billion viewers worldwide. We'll have continuing coverage following what clearly is about to happen, the swearing in of the vice president as the new president of the United States."

Looking grim, the vice president raised his right hand and placed his left hand on a Bible held firmly by his wife, and repeated the ancient oath of office that the chief justice parceled out in chunks. The proceeding lasted less than three minutes. The new president kissed the new first lady; the chief justice shook his hand. The new president's chief of staff was smiling broadly and appeared to be the only one enjoying himself. The other faces were impassive, devoid of expression.

"Pohtiss is out?" Khaki asked, her voice rising. "That's—"

"Let's listen," the governor stopped her in mid-sentence. The newly sworn president stepped up to a lectern hastily placed in front of the Resolute desk.

"My fellow Americans," the New Guy, still nameless to most, began in the time-honored way, "tonight is a moment of profound sadness but also a moment of eternal new beginnings—"

"Oh my God," Zesto groaned. "Spare us."

"Mr. Moffin, please!"

"Sorry, Governor."

" . . . our thoughts and prayers go out to President and Mrs. Pohtiss, and I offer what I am confident is the heartfelt hope of all Americans that, with the burdens of office lifted, he will shake off his travails in short order. But now we must move on, and my first order of business is to ensure the safety and security of the nation through the orderly transition of government. To that end, I view it as imperative that the important office of vice president be filled as quickly as our constitutional process permits. I therefore am pleased to announce that, tomorrow morning, I will submit to Congress, pursuant to the Twenty-fifth Amendment to the Constitution, the name of one whom I hold in the highest repute, wisdom, and acumen to take on the functions of that office and to be an active participant in a new administration, Governor Barnaby Joister."

Helene fell off her chair. Khaki spilled her wine. Dewey pumped his fists.

"Awesome," said Zesto. He stamped his feet and fished a handful of small cigars from his suit pocket. "I'm handing these around," he called out, "but remember, there's no smoking in here."

The governor sat preternaturally still, the slightest upturn of his lip indicating his satisfaction that the script had been followed to the letter.

TR leaned back in his chair, his legs extended.

"Oh," he said, "so that's what it was."

Felix vir qui potest rerum omnium cognoscere causas. Happy is he who understands the cause of all things. If, in fact, he did.

The White House
Washington, DC 20500

June 18, 7:30 a.m.

A Treat from Your President

The Gig Was Rigged: Everything is Fake

Whatever you think you saw, you better believe it wasn't Me. Why would I do that I didn't. I never said or did those things. Not Me. I'm being set up. Who are you going to believe: your treacherous eyes or Me?

Something evil and vile has come ashore. Like the aliens they've been warning Me about might actually have landed and done something I don't know and you don't either but medical experiments. For a long time they told Me it could happen and promised a tour of the area but I kept putting it off. Always things to do. But I will get to the bottom of this. Because I'm a rock-solid bottom-line manager with very estimable earned credentials.

I've only had a short briefing from General Faber on the general picture. Blacked out, they don't know why. What do the doctors think I pay them for? After breakfast I will screen last night's events and you know heads will roll. You better believe without Me here supervising, our trouble will be completely ubiquitous.

I've been defrauded, massive, massive fraud, you better believe the most massive in history, but we'll take it to the people. Let's go trucking! I will truck from town to town from village to village from house to house listening to you. And I'll have a lot to say. Right now I'm still here in the White House. I don't know what will happen when I leave the bedroom. Sad. It's quiet here, not like the crowds out there in America when we're barnstorming the heck out of the countryside. Anyway, always remember, it's all fake. Everything is fake. You're fake. They're fake. I'm real.

Action taken: Margaret Tangiers, you're fired. Also the damn doctors. And I pardon the First Lady. No one touches her. Also oh this phone is running out of juice Soapy damn it lmcp

---

Technical Correction to the Presidential Treat, Today's Date: This account is scheduled for Dark Mode (no access to White House infrastructure) at 8 a.m. by direction of the President. The newly installed spellchecker detects no obvious errors. The content checker will be released from permanent Pause Mode at that time.

Hearts and Minds

*What mystery is more profound than the longings
of the heart? What knowledge is more obscure than
the thought of another? What trust is more sacred than
words whispered in confidence? What duty is more venerable
than seeing the task through? What answer is more welcome
than uncovering a cause? What consummation is more
satisfying than resolving the conflict between heart and head?
And what is it that continues to elude T. R. Softly?
Our detective accepts the challenge to probe each query
for a practical conclusion—and nearly succeeds.*

CHAPTER 24

UPPEN ATOM

MARK MALLEYCORN POHTISS RECANTED AT 7:30 the next morning, when the effects of the sedatives finally wore off. Not that it mattered to him or anyone else. Most people who mattered were inured to recanting. On that mad day, what counted were not the facts but the afternoon headlines: "PRESIDENT RESIGNS, THEN RECANTS" and, more colorfully, "HELL TO THE CHIEF."

This oddest of the forty-odd men who have occupied the White House was out, and his supporters melted away faster than ice cream on a pancake griddle. By the end of the day, most of his backers took umbrage when reminded that they had voted for him. An Iowa congressman, expressing sympathy for "this champion of freedom," saw his poll numbers sink by fourteen points in six hours. The theme on the nightly news was that "you can't recant what everyone saw." Someone reminded Pohtiss that only a few weeks earlier he himself had lectured a bunch of aging crime lords on just this point: "Man up; only a wuss recants."

"Our job is done," TR told a disbelieving orJean and a skeptical Formerly an hour after the swearing-in when he shut his door to his house behind him, some ten minutes after leaving the Cave through the back alley. His associates were toggling between channels, trying to find a commentator who could make sense of the news.

Many pundits were ruminating on the decided queerness of this new cycle of public guilt. In the old days, a public lowlife would steadfastly deny his wrongdoing right up to the minute before he pleaded guilty and resigned. But that was then. In this bold new age—which, commentators reminded their listeners, had only begun with Malbonum—it was the other way around: now a miscreant will concede guilt and then, when already publicly drawn and quartered, defiantly deny all and blame their ill-fortune on opportunistic prosecutors, turncoats, and enemies of the people. But no one suggested swapping as the cause of recanting—Thorne Thorpey could remain in the vasty deep: self-inoculation worked.

"Pohtiss lives, huh?" Formerly ventured. "But not as Potus."

"*Pohtiss non Potus.* Good guys triumphant," TR said.

"Someday you'll tell us," orJean said, retrieving her purse from the kitchen floor where it had sat all day.

"Nothing to tell, I swear."

"Cut the crap," she said, "begging your pardon."

"Late at night she's inelegant but precise," Formerly teased.

"My hero," orJean said, bestowing TR a peck on the cheek. Then from the doorway she paused. "Mama's telling you not to forget to put all your new friends in the Catalogue. You never know when an underground agent and a new vice president will come in handy."

"In my first spare moment," TR said.

"Get some sleep, now the case is over," she called from the front hall and slammed the door.

"Tomorrow I'm sleeping in," Formerly announced as he reopened it.

"Take two days, you earned it." TR waved airily in Formerly's direction.

TR did not need to cross his fingers, he thought, as he climbed the stairs and fell into bed. He had not lied—at least not technically. *Their* work, PBDS's work, was finished on the Case of, well, whatever it was the case of, but *his* work was not over. The basic mystery remained, he reminded himself as he gave in to sleep, and its meaning was still shrouded. Why *had* he been called from the vasty deep . . . it had been Khaki . . . Khaki's call. TR's phone was ringing . . . Khaki was calling . . .

"Uppen atom," Khaki said, in a voice that seemed too bright, when he picked up after four rings on the morning of the first post-Pohtiss day.

"What?!" He kicked the covers off as he roused himself upright on the edge of the bed, phone to his ear.

"Come on, dear heart, don't be grumpy. It's past ten. You supply the body, I'll supply the coffee."

He arrived forty minutes later—after showering, putting on an acceptable gray suit, feeding the cat, walking to the Bookery, exchanging pleasantries with Mrs. Drumgullery, descending to the Cave, and—this time from memory—finding Khaki's office. The blinds were still closed. He rapped on the door and went right in.

"Must be an unusual day," he said to the woman sitting against the armrest on the sofa, nursing a mug of coffee.

"What, you mean these old things?" Khaki said. "You don't like them?"

"I don't think I've seen you wear your Harvard sweatpants since the days when we ran on the Mall. We haven't done that lately. Are you running somewhere today?"

She looked at him mutely.

"Not before we have a chat, I hope. Isn't that why you invited me?"

"You should be the psychologist." She walked to the Keurig, which splashed its coffee-infused water into a waiting mug. She lifted it off the staging plate and handed it to him. Settling into her habitual cushion, she toasted him with her mug. As she did so, several drops of the hot dark liquid sloshed over the edge, depositing brown stains on her sweatpants. Her legs motionless, she idly brushed the wetness with a bare hand.

"Get on with it," TR said without expression, holding his own mug over the table while he sipped.

"Get on with what?" she said, patting the back of her head.

"With whatever's agitating you. You're as nervous as a cat in a bucket of ice water. This is about our unfinished business, isn't it?"

"What business is that?"

"Come on, Khaki. Do you think that in thirty years I can't tell when something's on your mind?"

"I don't think—"

"Khaki, *why am I here*? And don't feed me all that bosh and tosh and drivel and drool about I'm here to stress test this buttoned-down underground ultimate weapon you're fashioning or to ferret out a traitor or even to save a president from having his head blown off. I'm not here for any of that. That's obvious. It's been obvious almost from the beginning. You sent for me weeks ago, but you set it all up far too early for any of Joister's claims to be the reason. You wanted me here for some other reason. Talk to me, damn it."

She answered in a whisper, looking at his hands encircling his mug. "I couldn't invite you here directly."

"Because to do that would have been a security problem," he said.

"Yes, security. Secrecy. Need to know."

"From the beginning."

"Yes."

"You had to invite me discreetly."

"They couldn't know that you were being sent for. I couldn't *invite* you at all."

"And yet, here I am."

"It had to be happenstance, your little journey," she said, "just how things worked out, not connected to me. It couldn't look like you in particular were summoned here. My team had to believe you were snooping around for your client's reasons, not mine—and that Mallory could have asked anyone."

TR raised his index finger. "Three games have been playing out. One, the newest, is your colleagues' game. Subsection-S decided I'd be useful or at least not harmful, since once I'm inside, they could shut me up through the nondisclosure agreement. That's why Joister didn't resist my little expedition, which you aided by feeding morsels to your people about how my search for this place would provide a useful stress test and all that. But those claims about leaked information were malarkey, weren't they? Those words NSA intercepted weren't leaked; they were planted. To explain to someone else, if they needed to, why they were accepting my arrival."

He paused, waiting for Khaki to speak, but she looked at him, impassive and silent.

TR extended a second finger. "But the governor's game wasn't my game. *My* reason to get inside was to learn what was going on, because I promised Mallory I would. I thought Mallory was the one who was asking."

Khaki maintained her pose, her hands propped on her knees, watching him watch her.

"The governor's game wasn't your game either, was it?" TR asked.

She shook her head. "I didn't know anything about that. Not until yesterday when you did."

He held up a third finger. "Exactly. The governor had a game, and I had a game. But you had—you have—a third game. My coming here was your game, not the governor's and not Mallory's, at least not initially. You were the one who set the ball rolling, my part of it anyway. Your deft little tennis signal was planted long before any of the supposed leaks. I'm guessing you scripted it when you first learned Malbonum would be the lead case. So you had something else in mind. You still do."

"How do you know that, TR?"

"You mean other than that your hand is shaking? I know it because you raised your voice with Governor Joister. It was imperative to you that I be admitted to your Cave. You weren't taking no for an answer. You needed to make sure he would let me in. And because it was obvious last night you knew nothing of his plan and you couldn't look at me when I asked why you were adamant I be here. You've got your own agenda. It hasn't played out yet. I can see that plainly. You're about to use me for your own purpose. Say it ain't so."

He leaned back and waited. Khaki's lips quivered. "I'm afraid I can't. Because it *is* so. Oh, TR, I should have known you'd eventually figure the whole thing out."

"I don't think I have. There's still a big mystery I haven't solved. But I've run out of energy and patience. Pretend I'm nine years old again. Spell it out for me."

"It's not for me," she said, "it's for—you." She pushed against her knees and stood. "Oh God, this is hard." She reached for the desk telephone, pressed a button, and raised the receiver to her ear. Her teeth were clenched, her face rigid.

"Come," she said when it was answered. She let the phone fall onto the console, but it missed and skidded onto the desk. She righted the instrument, pushing it hard into its cradle and holding it there, as if it might pop back out given the chance. She remained still, not looking in TR's direction.

"Khaki—"

The door opened and in walked Helene Barberoi, carrying a cranial cloth and protruding wires in either hand. Her outstretched arms supported the instrument pouch. She dumped it all on the sofa.

"Did you tell him?" she asked Khaki.

"Tell me what? What's going on? You're doing a swap? What is—"

"Not exactly," Khaki said.

"Not exactly? But that's what those things are for," TR pointed out to two of the founders of neurosyntesis.

"Not technically a swap," Helene said. "It's, well—"

"We're doing a Level Three-B double load," Khaki said, sounding now like an instructor who had taken charge.

"What? Who—you two? Why am I—"

"Not her. You and me," Khaki said. "I needed to get you into the Cave for this moment. *That's* why I sent for you. *That's* why you're here."

"Oh no, not me," TR said, backing away from Helene and the equipment. "I told you, once was twice too many. I've firmly sworn off crawling around inside the cobwebs of someone else's neural cavity. It violates my religion, and I've taken holy orders in the Church of Orthodox Agnostics, so that's saying something."

"You don't have to crawl around anywhere," Khaki said. "You get to stay put. *I'm* the one joining you. Have you forgotten what a Level Three-B is? I'm transferring to you. You remain entirely intact. Your mind in your body. But I'll be there too—my mind, that is. We'll both be there in your head. There won't be anyone left inside me, well, except autonomous functions, little things like heartbeat. Better be, or I'm a goner, and you'll have to give me a long lease on a corner of your forebrain."

"Khaki!" Helene said sharply. "You're babbling."

"Sorry. I guess I'm still a little nervous."

"You've done this before?" TR asked, momentarily distracted from an incipient panic attack by the novelty and sheer audacity of Khaki's proposed safari through his cranium.

"Not entirely, well sort of, I mean, in a way—"

"We sampled the Level Three B state a week ago," Helene said.

"You two?"

"Yes."

"And?"

"And you'll be fine if you keep it to an hour. We agreed on that, Khaki, right? No more than sixty minutes. Not enough time to get into big trouble. Try to stay out of sensitive areas."

"Yes, Dr. Barberoi," Khaki said, appearing to relax somewhat.

"Wait a minute," TR protested. "Are you saying you'll be—I'll be open to—Khaki's *inspection?*"

"All your passwords will be on display, TR," Helene said. "No secrets, though with a little practice you can learn to keep some of the shades down."

"Practice? I don't even know what game we're playing. How can I—"

"Try your best," Khaki said. "You're doing this for me because, as you'll see, I'm doing it for you. It can't be done out in the field. It has to be here. And it's not authorized. Helene is taking a risk helping me out. Let's get on with it, shall we?" To Helene, she asked, "Where do you want me positioned?"

"Sit on the end of the sofa—there," Helene said. "I'll be alongside the whole time." She wired Khaki to monitors, an EKG, a finger thermometer, a blood pressure cuff, and to other gizmos that TR did not recognize.

"Is this safe?" TR asked.

"Perfectly," the two women said in unison.

"How long will I be out? I really don't like that part of it—"

"I thought you didn't like any part of it?" Helene teased.

"I don't." His voice turned cold. "And I don't think any of this is funny."

"I'm sorry," Helene said, taking his hands into hers and stroking them. "You won't be out at all. No knock-out drops. You're not outloading and there's no need for secrecy among us. We all know what we're doing."

"I don't," he said. "What *are* we doing? Tell me."

"TR," Khaki said, her voice rising. "Have I ever led you astray? I need you to trust me one more time—please! I promise, you'll see."

TR leaned back and sighed, yielding.

"I'm going to ask you to be quiet now," Helene said. She lifted one of the cranial pads and put it on TR's skull, fastening it and wiring it to the Synapticator.

"It will juice up in about two minutes, after I finish setting up Khaki. Now remember, one hour. Absolute maximum. No kidding around. And stay in the chair."

"He—we—can't get up?" Khaki asked.

"If you need to, but not for at least the first fifteen minutes. Get your bearings."

"But you're going to be here?" TR said. "Khaki, aside from how outrageously uncomfortable about this I already am, I'm even more uncomfortable if we're talking about something that—"

"You won't have to talk," Helene said. "Think about it."

TR considered the point. "Oh. I see, it's—we'll read each other's minds."

Helene's eyes narrowed for an instant. "Let's get on with it," she said.

"Okay," Khaki said, patting the cushion next to her where she wanted TR to sit.

"No," Helene said abruptly.

"What's wrong?" Khaki said, her voice straining.

"Changed my mind. I want you lying down during the time you're out."

Helene unplugged TR and helped Khaki swivel her legs onto the sofa. TR dragged a chair to sit next to Khaki's head, which she now rested against the sofa arm.

"This office needs a cleaning," Khaki said, staring at dingy patches on the ceiling.

"Hush," Helene said. "I'm powering up in thirty seconds."

They were silent as Helene adjusted a dial and watched the timer count down.

"You aren't going to knock her out?" TR asked. "For when—"

"You hush too," Helene said. "We don't need to. Have you forgotten that her body won't be conscious when the double load is complete?" She reached into a pouch next to the machine and withdrew two moist cloths. "You will need to wipe your faces with these though."

TR scowled.

"Not knockout, I promise. It's for the autocatalysis. The swap will be maximally augmented."

TR wiped his face, watching Khaki do the same.

A light glowed on the Synapticator. TR clenched his fists. He was nervous but felt nothing. At about fifteen seconds, he felt a slight tickle on the back of his head. He brought his right arm up and rested his hand on the back of his neck. The tickling sensation intensified. At twenty-five seconds he felt something else, a fluid perhaps, coursing through him; it rushed but was somehow not wet. He thought of it as a kind of frictionless liquid that was being pumped into him and which then spread out, forming a lake in his mind. Something dense—like a thick sauce—arrived from overhead but again he sensed no physical movement. At thirty-five seconds, after the Synapticator lights went out, that sensation was replaced by a feeling of "non-dimensional pressure"—though it suffused through his skull, his head felt no heavier. It seemed to fill space everywhere but did not clog anything. His head was as empty—or as full—as it ever was.

At sixty seconds, the fluid sensation evaporated like water draining from a sink when the stopper is removed.

At seventy seconds a lean, firm stalk sent a mental tendril to explore the surrounding space. Airy vegetation wrapped itself around his thoughts. He saw a green shoot encircle his consciousness. It was hallucinatory, and it was also manifestly real. To contain and diminish his internal verbalizing, he pictured the numerals of pi—3.1459—and saw leafy green sprigs dust their stems; florets brushed against his thoughts about what he was seeing. An infinite array of opposing mirrors blossomed with the greenery. He blinked.

"TR, are you all right?" Helene took his wrist, felt for a pulse. He stared vacuously at the wall in front of him without answering. Another voice intruded, but somehow it was soundless. The red hand on the clock passed one hundred seconds.

"Don't move," the intruding voice said. It had modulation and pitch, but it was noiseless. TR looked straight ahead at Helene, who was on her knees in front of him anxiously studying his face. She seemed not to notice the words he knew he had experienced.

"TR?" Helene repeated.

"He's fine"—rendered in a squeak—escaped TR's lips.

"Khaki!" Helene said. She let go of TR's wrist and fanned Khaki's face.

"The dove has landed," TR said, his voice near normal.

"Thank God!" Helene said. "You had me going there." Her eyes swept to the Synapticator clock. "Two minutes, twelve seconds. TR, tell me you are okay. Then you two can work it out."

"I'm—okay," he said tonelessly. Then he pressed his hand against his lips, surprised at the words that came out of his mouth: "I'm gonna speak Italian to Mike."

Helene, relieved, leaned back.

He "heard" Khaki's amusement, but Helene did not, nor did she see the riotously colored flowers open and flutter in a botanical garden, a virtual Fantasia bursting in the playhouse of his mind.

"Jesus—"

"I thought you were orthodox agnostic?"

"—figure of speech—"

"–pretty good, huh?–"

"Khaki, this is—"

"I know, one at . . . "

"—confusing—"

" . . . a time. Okay, big boy, then–"

"Go, you go. I'm a—"

"gentleman. Thanks. Give me sixty seconds, I need to—"

Her soundless voice fell silent. In its place he heard music, a cello rhythmically thrumming on a stage in front of him. A large clock appeared on a curtain behind, the second hand counting down from fifty-two seconds. At zero the clock dissolved, the opaque curtain turned transparent and faded away; the stage vanished. He was suddenly sitting on the chair in Khaki's office, looking at Helene attending to Khaki's immobile body.

"Needed to find out," Khaki said soundlessly.

She paused.

"What?"

They were talking in harmonics, though in what key and what chords TR couldn't fathom.

"You."

"You needed to find out what about me?"

"All about you. What you're—"

"—a lot of decades of—"

"Willikers, not everything, silly—"

"Just—"

"Let me go first."

"Sorry."

"I have known you long years. And in all that time, your intentions—"

"I love you, Khaki."

Professing his default commitment as he looked at her inert shape stretched out on the sofa, for an instant he could not breathe.

"I know, and I love you back. You are my little brother, my one-and-only, my treasure, my non-negotiable soul mate. But—let me be straight as this arrow."

He saw a cupid aiming for his heart.

"How come you don't have a girlfriend, TR?"

"There's work to be done, too much important work. Besides, I have one. You're *my* one and only."

"Oh, TR, you know what I mean."

It did not occur to him to turn the question around.

"No, I don't think I do know—"

"You would if you'd follow your instincts, or follow me—"

He pushed through a translucent window. It popped from its hinge, swung open, wrapped around and lifted him into the light. It became a book, a large volume, a folio. The word "Khaki" came into view, centered itself on the page, growing until it filled the line from left to right, and leading off from the word he could see highways, boulevards, roads, streets, lanes, paths that vanished into the perspective. In the center of each were glittering white-striped letters that spelled out associated terms: Khaki's mode of dress, Khaki's clothing inventory, Khaki's likes and dislikes, Khaki's medical conditions ("allergies: peaches" read one byway branching off from the medical conditions road), Khaki's ambition, Khaki's remembered notes from Psych 101, Khaki's loves, with a "TR" superhighway that ran far off into the depths. He turned to that roadway and raced down it until it rolled itself up. He stood still. He had arrived—

He synapsed.

"*This* is why you summoned me? You brought me here to find out why I don't have a girlfriend? The rest was a ruse?"

He saw his beating heart opened to her public inspection.

"But why *now*?"

"I've been worried about you. For all this time I left you alone thinking you'd come to your senses. But you haven't."

"Khaki, you're not answering . . . wait! You're not worried. You're feeling guilty!"

"Remember in high school I said I wished I could get inside your head to see what makes you tick? This is me now, inside. I needed you here in the Cave to see what's in your heart–and what went wrong. We never could talk about this, could we? My fault. I didn't grasp how you were suffocating, how I turned our friendship into a lasso or how tight it was. It muffled your ears. It blocked your amygdala. It's the swap today that has let me get through to you. You know you can't marry your big sister, and I'm glad to know you don't want to. But it's you who's been feeling guilty, afraid of hurting me. But how would it hurt me if you took a bride? It couldn't. It won't. I'm not distressed, TR. I'm *liberated*–because you are. I'm not troubled for you to have someone else in your life. So why should you be? Back in high school, when I talked you into taking me to the prom? I was a teenager. How could I realize the effect of my little selfish desire? I wanted to spend that one prom evening with you. I'm sorry, TR. I wish I could take it back. This is me, now, taking it back. Now get over it. Accept this little intervention and go to her with my blessings. Don't fuck this up."

"Khaki!"

"Why is it so terrible for you to be happy?"

"I've never heard you be vulgar!"

"Yeah, here's a little secret, my foul-mouthed Navy lieutenant: you're not *hearing* me. I *think* that way all the time, you fucking moron."

"You mean I should—"

"Jesus, you *are* a fucking moron. Why do you think she's never married?"

The fog evaporated. His gloom dispersed. He was skating down a funhouse slide, zipping along a shiny arc to an acre of beach balls that waited for him as he sailed into the cloudless sky.

"TR, come back!"

But she was "laughing" too. At his relief and at her own. Hers was satisfaction at having finally prompted TR to overcome his apprehension about committing to someone other than her. His was a sense of oceanic release at accepting his feelings and conquering his indecision. Khaki painted it in bright pastels: giddy gobs of gladness that gushed into buckets and overflowed onto open fields labeled "happy breakthrough."

"Relief buckets in happy breakthrough fields? Is that a Nancy Drew reference?"

His left arm suddenly sprung up, clamped down on his right arm, and squeezed it.

"Ouch!" he said. He realized he had actually heard the word when Helene jumped.

"Are you two fighting?"

"Sorry," TR's voice said, but it was Khaki's word.

"We're going for a walk," they both said in the single voice available to them.

Helene pointed to the clock. "Fifteen minutes."

TR rose, with one last glance at the sofa-tethered comatose Khaki, and walked into the corridor.

"Where are we going?"

"Up."

"Oh, the bookstore. You're going to buy me a book?"

Khaki was poking into odd corners of his mind, lifting flaps marked "repressed" as they rode the elevator up. When they entered the store, Mrs. Drumgullery awaited.

"Mr. Softly," she said, "how nice to see you again at such an early hour. Your labors are completed?"

"Almost, Mrs. Drumgullery, almost. Before I leave, I need a book. The best book ever written on intimate platonic friendship."

"Really, Mr. Softly. You surprise me. The best book, you say. Well, I'm sorry, but I'm not sure I have any such book in stock. I can order one. Will that be satisfactory?"

"Perfectly."

"Very good. Will we be shipping it?"

"Oh no, I'll drop by. Whenever it arrives."

"You're local?" She put a hand to the edge of her eyeglasses and pushed them down her nose to stare at him up close. Her briefing had been less than complete.

"As local as it gets."

"I had no idea. Isn't that splendid? I hope to see you in here more often, in that case."

"As you will, I'm sure."

Without willing it, TR felt an eyelid shut for an instant. Had Khaki made him wink at the manager?

"My goodness!" Mrs. Drumgullery said, cheeks pink as she went to the counter to retrieve her order book.

"Khaki, you stop that!"

TR's rebuke came in his newfound double-mind, single-brain language.

Tittering mentally, Khaki shot right back.

"A little willpower there, dear boy, you local devil, you. You're so local, I should move in with you."

"You already have, Khaki. The urgent objective is to move you out. We've got to get you back into a body, preferably yours."

When Mrs. Drumgullery returned, TR took out his credit card, paid, and then took out his elevator key. Khaki no longer needed to guide him to her office. But as they turned a corridor that housed a set of restrooms, she thought a sudden request.

"Will you do me one teensy, weensy favor, my chummy chum, my fortress, my–"

He thought-replied, though with happy balloons that surrounded his interjection.

"Get to it."

"Well, I was wondering: would you mind stopping in at the men's room? I've always been curious."

TR maintained his equanimity, wrapping his refusal to comply in a frothy exuberance.

"Ask me when you're my properly outloaded big sister. Then I can properly say no."

TR opened Khaki's office door to find Helene standing by her prone body.

"We're ready to uncouple," TR told Helene in a steady voice.

Helene connected the Synapticator, and as she threw the switch Khaki transmitted one final, crucial mental command.

"Call her, TR. You've wasted too much time. Call her and don't let her slip away."

A minute later, TR shook himself, faint from lightheadedness. He sat where he was and watched Helene help Khaki sit upright. Now back "home," Khaki blinked, looked at TR and after several seconds her face lit up.

"Thank you, Helene," she said.

"Did you two sort it out, whatever it was?" Helene asked, "because I've got work to do."

"We're nicely adjusted," TR said.

Helene let go of Khaki's arms, offered TR a faint smile, then turned and left.

"You're leaving now, I know," Khaki said. "Hug me, and soon we'll have a grand dinner. It's time for me to go topside, isn't that what you sailors say, to feel the outside breeze. And TR?"

"Yes?"

"I think we've invented a new form of psychiatry. Instant analysis. Works much, much better than the other kinds. The insurers will love it. One session and you're cured."

"Because it pierces the amygdala?"

Khaki honored him with her patented hemidemisemigiggle. "Neurology talk; get used to it."

TR walked home, taking in the sights, his wooziness gone. He was intensely aware of his surroundings, seeing details unnoticed on his thousands of walks along these blocks—birds in a nest in an old oak branch, a peeling shutter of a ground floor window on the pale-green house down the block, the small hole under the broken stone step up his own walk. Inside, he loosened his tie and sensed a blur of motion. TK landed neatly on top of his hand on the kitchen counter, pushing her head against his knuckles. Absently, he scratched under her chin until the loud purrs brought him back to his surroundings. The clock read 12:30. He was hungry but resisted the urge to open the refrigerator, partly to avoid discovering that Formerly and orJean had emptied it, partly because the Level Three-B Double Load still nagged. Why had all this happened now? Despite Khaki's explanation, the mystery remained. But her command echoed, outweighing his concern. Call her, Khaki said. Call her.

CHAPTER 25

A WORKAROUND

"TR!" Mallory exclaimed, when she answered his ring. "I'm on my way to lunch—"

"Can you stall it for five minutes?"

"Hang on, I'm out in the hallway."

He heard clacking on bare floors as she retraced her steps, and then the shutting of her door.

"Well, my goodness, I'm on pins and needles here. Four whole days. I'm assuming you watched the show of the year last night."

"Yep."

"Terribly forthcoming you are," she said.

"I'm still your consultant."

"Oh," she said, remembering TR's admonition in the diner in New York not to mention Sisal's name or other details in her office. "Well, around here no one's been talking about anything else except this one interesting thing."

"That he recanted this morning?"

"Yep."

"Now who's being terse?"

"Come on, TR. I'm on my mobile. Tell me. I assume that this is the handiwork of—"

"Listen, Mallory, I've got good news and bad news, but not on the phone. I'm coming up there."

"Here? New York?"

"Today, if you're free."

"For you, always."

He drew in a deep breath. "Yale Club, five thirty."

"Okay, I'll be there. Nothing on the phone, right?" Then, casually, "Should I pack a bag?"

"If you want to be on the safe side."

"Oooh," she purred before ending the call. "I'll cancel dinner with Roger and Rafa."

TR opened the refrigerator. Praise be, the two big eaters on the PBDS staff had spared enough for a sandwich. Twenty-five minutes to make it, eat it, and skim the morning's papers, seven minutes to change his shirt and pack, with still plenty of time to meet the two o'clock Acela to New York; cabs all the way. Mallory was, after all, paying expenses.

She gave him the once-over when he opened the door to his Yale Club suite. "Like that gray suit," she said, theatrically dropping an overnight bag on the bureau in front of a large wall mirror. She snuck a glance at herself, for what reason TR was unsure. Nothing ever spoiled the fresh and appealing look of Mallory Greenstock: her winsome face, her willowy frame. This time he told her.

"My heavens," she said, "the man is being sweet. Must be bad memories of this room."

"Is that how you remember it?"

"How can a gal forget the night she ruined her waistline and sobbed watching *A Few Good Men*?"

"It made you cry?"

"It made me wince, anyway. Its central premise is all wrong. But perfect for chips. Two whole bags and a liter of Coke. Well, my conscientious consultant, what have you got? Good news and bad news, you say?"

"Yes, I do say," he responded cheerily. "Good news and bad. Which do you want first?"

"The bad news first, that's my rule. Deal with the bad stuff, fix it and get past it. My father taught me that."

She sat down in the club chair.

"Okay, the bad news . . . " TR began, leaning against the dresser with his back to the mirror, but paused when she held up her hand.

"But just this once, since I'm in such a good mood knowing that you're going to permit me to let you treat me to another expensed dinner, I'll take the good news first."

He beamed. "The good news, Madam Prosecutor, is that I have completed the assignment. I have found your Dewey Sisal, and I know exactly what happened and why it is that these arch criminals you worry about have recanted."

"I thought we resolved that. Some type of telepathy, wasn't it?"

"Not exactly."

"Does it matter?"

"Yes."

"Well then, I'm all ears."

"Luckily for both of us, you're not."

"Not what?"

"Not all ears. Not that you don't have nice ears. And other nice parts too."

Her face and neck turned red, offsetting her white silk blouse.

"TR, was that an off-color reference? What's gotten into you? You know that's no longer tolerated in New York City. No talking body parts."

"Except in the Yale Club?"

"Or the morgue."

"Well, anyway, to get back to it," he said, "here's the problem: I can't tell you what I learned."

"What? Why ever not?"

"That's the bad news."

"You're saying I have to hear the bad news first after all? What if I don't want to?"

"Well, there's a workaround."

"Okay, then let's have that."

"I'm now an official consultant to the FBI at a special super-secret facility in your nation's capital."

"So?"

"You remember how when I became *your* consultant I had to sign papers?"

"Yes."

"Well, I had to sign papers down there too. And what those papers say is I can't tell anyone anything, not even in a whisper. In fact, I've probably already told you more than I should have. Forget I said anything."

Wordlessly, she kicked her shoes off, looked down at her wriggling toes, and then tilted her head up to see if TR was sticking to that story. He shook his head.

"What's the workaround?" she asked.

He walked across the room, stood before her, and took a deep breath. "There's an exception for spouses."

Her face impassive, she stood up. Then, melodramatically, she drew her arm back and punched him in the shoulder, hard, on the same spot Khaki had squeezed several hours earlier.

"Hey!" he said, rubbing his arm. "That hurt. What—"

"I wanted to make sure it was you, and not some hallucination, before I ask for a clarification."

"Shouldn't you have punched yourself, then?"

She ignored him. "Are you saying to me, T. R. Softly, that if we were married you'd tell me what gives?"

"For you, I'd even stretch the rules. If we agreed on it, for example, if you happened to be my fiancé—"

"TR, are you kidding me?" Her hand flew up over her mouth. "Is this a marriage proposal?"

He lifted both his hands and laced his fingers with hers. Though he thought of a brilliant riposte, he said, simply, "Yes."

She looked straight at his goofy, hopeful face.

"TR, that's the lamest proposal I've ever heard. And I've had a few, I can tell you." Here she took a studied pause. "But a woman's got to take them as she gets them, when they come from the man she loves."

She withdrew her hands from his to press them against the sides of his face. She kissed him—squarely, firmly, extravagantly. She slid her hands down and around his back, pulled him to her, and hugged him fiercely. Then she pushed away and with a seeming flash of fury said, "Damn it, TR, what took you so long?"

"I—"

"Yes," she said.

"Yes?"

"Yes, I'll marry you, you tardy, absent, workaholic, weird, adorable knuckleheaded vacant genius."

"Okay, well, there is this one other thing I need to know," he said.

She searched his face. "What?"

"Have you finished paying off your law school loans?"

She punched him, hard, on the other shoulder.

He burst out crying.

"Omigod," she said in alarm, "I didn't mean—"

"I'm so happy," he sobbed.

"Do you mind if I don't cry?" she asked. "I may have told you that I cried the last time I was here."

They stood looking at each other. He dried his eyes. She kissed him again.

"You're sure? Sherlock Holmes remained a bachelor. And Herculé Poirot, Travis McGee, and—"

He grinned. "Lord Peter Wimsey married. Maigret did. Even Harry Bosch. Kinsey Millhone tied the knot twice."

"Yeah, and recanted each time."

"Well, I'm not recanting."

"Damn straight you're not. I'd sue you—"

"For what?"

"For—for lack of originality. And wasting my time."

"Does this mean you now want the good news?"

"In good time," she said, unfastening the top button of her blouse. "But first, a request. Do you honor requests?"

"If I can."

"Last night, when I was watching the greatest public speech of my lifetime, my TV went wonky, especially toward the end there, when it looked to me like the president of the United States was getting undressed. And then he showed off, at least it looked like he did. That's when my picture fuzzed out. I'm hoping you can reenact the scene."

"Now?"

"Doesn't have to be now." She looked off into space, tapped her foot twice, and pursed her lips. "Two minutes from now will work. Even three." She undid a second button.

"Not enough time to rehearse," he said.

"I'm sure you can extemporize."

She pulled her blouse out from her skirt and released a third button.

"Okay, have it your way," he said, duplicating her motions on his own shirt, "improv it is."

Some time later, Mallory raised her head up from the pillow. She pushed the hair out of her eyes and said, "Holy Moley, TR, you're positively palindromic."

He rested his hand against her naked hip and raised his head next to hers. "What?"

"It's the same backward and forward. Softly's hard, and it's hardly soft."

He caressed her back. "That's not a palindrome, which depends on the order of the letters, not—"

"TR," she hissed, putting a finger to his lips and pushing his hand downward from her hip, "you've got to learn when to shut up."

Golgotha
Washington, DC

June 18, 3:45 p.m.

A Treat from Your President

The Greatest Crime of All Time

The enemies of the people are conspiring to rob you of your president: Me. Maybe you're one of them, people who think I willingly resigned. False. You know that. What I've been saying. An hour ago Lindsay Moe, the outstanding Congresswoman from [Soapy: add state] courageously issued a statement confirming the Truth.

Quote: Our valiant President and savior, Mark M. Pohtiss, has every right to ask the courts for relief from false accusations he disrobed on camera and then signed a resignation letter. I urge him to seek immediate injunctive relief from the nearest court. Let them prove that he resigned. Why should he have to prove otherwise? And what makes disrobing illegal? People taking showers disrobe all the time. End Quote.

That's exactly truly right, Fearless Lindsay Moe, and what's more, I have every right to take back my resignation. I gave it. Where does it say I can't take it back? I stand with the Indians. No offense. Plus, I will press every court in Washington, our nation's capital, which most people don't know goes all the way back to the 18th century, to allow Me to skip the next election so I can keep working for you. If those courts phayle me, I will ask the Supreme Court, which owes Me big time, because I pay their bills. Do they thing they can sit around twiddling their thumps on a full salary without doing anythink? If the justices turn Me down, I'll sue them. Courts can't tell presidents what to do. Plus I'll fire them. We'll see what voters will say to the faithless cowards who are running away from Me today I'm talking about you know who you are. Mrs. Pohtiss, by the way, is fine and at my side. She will forever be Homecoming Queen and keep her respectable cloth sash. Remember, others may cheat you, but when you cheat back, you're a cheater too, and that's unfair.

Technical Correction to Supposed Treat from the President, today's date: The above-referenced Treat was found unsent in the Presidential Treat System spool and is being transferred to the National Archives for retention. It has not been read for spelling, factual, legal, or other errors.

CHAPTER 26

THE CAUSE OF IT ALL

THE COUPLE WALKED INTO THE YALE Club Grill Room at 7:30, after Mallory enrolled TR into her wildest fantasy and then cooled down with him in the shower to throw off the head waiter. She avoided the main topic until their orders were taken. Then she leaned over the table. "All right, my heart's dearest, let's have it, the good news."

"I'm not sure you'll think it's good. It might be that what we have here is two sets of bad news. Plus, whatever you learn, you can't talk about it."

"Oh, you cruel man," she said, feigning a frown, "was this bait and switch, to get me into bed?"

"Do you want me to take it back?"

"That might be worth trying, but later, after dinner. Right now I'll settle for finally hearing the story."

He told her all of it, speaking for forty-two minutes and disposing of twenty-four interruptions, most minor, one of them a request by the waiter to clarify Mallory's choice of salad dressing. TR hadn't touched his plate.

"But TR, this is terrible!" Mallory said when he stopped talking and sat back.

"What? The story—or the fact that you can't breathe a word of it?"

"What they're doing, this gang of . . . I don't know what they are. This . . . place. The Cave, you say?"

"Listen, Mallory, it is what it is."

"I hate that phrase. It doesn't mean anything. Why not say 'It is, only because we don't change it'?"

"Usually that would be better, I agree. But in this case what it is, *is* what it's going to be. It has to be kept secret."

"Are we having our first quarrel?" Mallory asked, caressing his forearm.

"Yes, and it will be our only one, dearest Mallory."

She leaned back and looked him in the eye without blinking. "I'm waiting for your explanation."

"I grant you," he said, speaking slowly, carefully. "It *is* terrible. It's the ultimate form of identity theft. If it remains unknown, it can be catastrophic for targets with a bull's eye on them. Like Malbonum or Pohtiss. But so far, the targets deserved it. They did what they admitted to. They are horrible people. So are the others."

"But that's not how it's supposed to work," she said through thin lips. "We have constitutional rights for a reason. If the police unlawfully force you to confess to some crime, and the courts uphold the confession because the judge heard your alter ego say in your voice, 'I ratify what the cops did,' then we're no longer living in the land of the free, no matter how brave you are."

"You're the lawyer, Mallory, but I see a distinction between how a confession is obtained and where it comes from. If they hold you at gunpoint, it's coercion. If they make your mind give up its secrets, it's something else."

"How are those different? I'm not just clutching pearls here, TR. Your FBI gang may not point a gun, but it still uses force. No one consents to having their brains hijacked. The sole difference is the timing."

"All right, I'll grant you that too," TR said. "But think about the difference between using neurosyntesis while it's still a secret and using it after it's been revealed. Secret swapping violates constitutional rights. It could put someone away or cost a bundle to fight the charges. If it's used maliciously, it's unjust and wrongful—to the few people who are targeted. Mostly, it won't stick even to them if the person is being rail-roaded. The case still has to be proved. Or it can be *un*proved."

"TR, you can't really—"

He ignored her interruption. "But imagine a world in which we know that people with these tools can assume someone else's identity. Our entire social structure would buckle. Our identities are a cornerstone of trust. If we can't trust people we do business with, if we don't know who is saying what for what purposes, society will collapse. And it isn't only doubting a person's identity; people would doubt anything *anyone* says."

He stared at the table, took a deep breath, and continued, unsure that he himself fully believed what he was saying. "If everyone knew about swapping, would you fly on an airplane because some federal bureaucrat says the plane is safe? He could be an Inhab sent to reduce panic and keep profits up. All over the world we'd be driven away from the hope that the next fellow is there to help. It's the ultimate libertarian fantasy—with the ultimate libertarian cata-clysm to follow. Everyone out for himself, trust no one, cooperate with no one, make agreements with no one, go back to the land, grow your own peas."

"Then we need to go in there and rip out this Subsection-S before it destroys us," Mallory said.

"And just how are you going to do that?"

"We subpoena the FBI. We lead a group of photojournalists right down into the Cave and put them on full-color display. We tell what we know."

TR scratched his cheek. "And you think they wouldn't know you're coming? You think anyone would believe your story, a bunch of scientists and agents *intromitting* themselves into people's minds? Our friends in the Cave have taken all that into account. First, you'd be royally jeered at because everyone knows swap stories are silly fantasies. Second, they'd be long gone before you got anywhere near close. All you'd do is drive them further underground into some other space in some other city. And then they'd be watching you. The technology exists now, and it's been loosed into the world where people have been trained to use it. Unless you can figure out how to go in there and kill all those people and burn their reports and manuals and smash their machines, it will persist deeper underground. The secret agents will regroup. No, Mallory, we're stuck with it. The question is how to manage it."

"Manage it?"

"Keep it in bounds. Keep it on our side. But it has to be done from the outside."

"Is that even remotely possible, TR? The world is about to be fucked up beyond all recognition."

"When has it ever not been? We try our best. We've avoided nuclear war for more than sixty years. Saber rattling doesn't have to lead to sword fights."

TR's phone rang. He looked at the caller's name. "I've got to take this, Mallory, just for a second. It's Khaki's father. He wouldn't call unless something's—"

TR punched the button and held the phone up for Mallory to listen.

"How are you, my boy," came the booming voice of Angus Blumenthrace.

"I'm fine, sir, and you?"

"Hunky and dory, but I only have a minute. Violet and I are going off on another one of her cruises. Khaki won't talk about it, but I figured you'd help me out, one detective to another, eh?"

"Whatever I can do."

"I mean our nutty, I guess I should say former, president. There's a lot more to this cock and bull story than we've been hearing, isn't there?"

"Yes sir, off the record, that's true."

"And you know about it because you're on top of it. Getting to be the top banana, I hear from our mutual friend in her elliptical, 'this is top secret so I'm not saying it' way."

"Well, I don't know about that, sir."

"Thought so. No need to tell me more. Remember what I once told you about the virtues of silence. Anyway, good job, son. Keep at it." He ended the call.

"You heard that?" TR asked.

"Most of it. How did he find out—never mind. I guess I know how. He must trust you, to take you at your word."

"He trained me. I trust him. I'm asking you to trust me."

"You think we can manage this, whatever it is, these Cave people?"

"I don't know, but we have to try. You know, a long time ago, Detective Angus Blumenthrace sat me down and told me how the world works. It isn't simple to deal with bad guys, he said. You can't always fight injustice straight on. Bad things aren't necessarily illegal. Good things sometimes violate the law. The world is ambiguous. But it's the world we live in. Sometimes a rogue is a better leader than a straight arrow because he's not afraid to short-change his own side. Sometimes you stick with imperfect rules because in perfecting one rule you weaken another. And sometimes silence is better than the truth, even if it points toward a falsehood. Truth disturbs. Truth unsettles. Some omissions are more stable than the truth. Rarely, but sometimes. All we can do is try to manage."

Mallory reached out for both his hands. "I'm not sure it's enough," she said.

He wrapped his fingers around hers and leaned in. "Mallory, you're right to oppose swapping. It's dangerous as hell. But guys like Malbonum and Pohtiss are identity thieves too. They're liars, Pohtiss most of all. His name should be added to the old chestnut about lies, suitably revised. *There are four kinds of lies: falsehoods, omissions, predictions, and anything said by Mark Pohtiss.* Persistent lying is a form of swapping. A liar like Pohtiss constantly pretended he was something other than what he was; he'd say one thing, and do something else. A guy who denies reality, a guy who leads people to believe he supports one thing but promotes policies that make that thing impossible, a guy who yells 'fake, fake, fake,' who claims the papers are spreading lies when he's the liar and knows it—that guy is as complicit as our swappers. He's a fakester. He says he's for transparency, but he cloaks himself in lies that block our view of who he really is. He's the real swapster."

"But a power like swapping—they could make lies and their consequences that much worse."

"Yes, but this time they didn't. You saw that in the last twenty-four hours. They made Pohtiss tell the truth—"

"Not his truth."

"They let the truth be told. Sisal dug up Pohtiss's own words and own manner. The fake Pohtiss 'turned' the real one, as the spy-catchers say. Except in this case, they didn't make their target assume a false identity; they made him put his real identity on display—and broadcast it to the world with all his warts in view."

"And the God thing?"

"That was true, too. He has this dangerous mania, and it was already oozing out. He floated it months back, remember? Anyway, I'll be with you on ratting out Subsection-S if they abandon their true mission—"

"And that true mission is?"

"Using identity fraud as a weapon against itself. Borrowing a liar's identity and opening the blinds to let others see in. That's the only justification for this thing that Khaki and her friends have wrought—to bring the facts to view. They can do a lot of other things with swap technology. We have to make sure that the right play is the only play."

"You're pledging that we won't forget your friends in the Cave? We'll keep them honest?" Her normal pallor was returning.

"Me to you, it's our life's work—unless worse arrives." He pulled her hands to his face and kissed them.

"And if we don't succeed?" she demanded.

"Failure isn't having the wrong solution. It's forgetting the problem."

"I won't ever forget it," she murmured as the waiter came toward their table.

"Good," TR said, motioning to the waiter and pointing to his coffee cup.

"If you drink that, you'll be up all night."

"I intend to be up all night."

She leaned forward and kissed him lightly on the lips as the waiter appeared with a carafe of coffee.

Smiling at him, Mallory said, "We just got engaged."

The waiter looked to one and then the other and set the carafe on the table. "Right here in the Club? My heartiest congratulations," he said, extending his hand to shake theirs. "And when is the wedding?"

Mallory turned to TR. "Yes, when is the wedding?"

"Soon. The earliest possible date we can round up our parents. I've got four—five, counting Khaki; well, make it six, if you add in orJean."

The waiter's eyes widened.

Mallory held up two fingers. "Only one of each for me," she said.

"And the vice president. The new one," TR said.

"*He's* coming?"

"I'm sure he wouldn't miss it. We're both important to him. I have four or five friends. You must have some too. Let's do it right."

"Okay, we'll figure it out tomorrow."

The waiter poured the coffee and returned five minutes later with two large slices of rich chocolate cake. "From the Club," he said.

When the waiter departed, Mallory speared the cake and asked, "When did you first know you loved me?"

"Since we shook hands at 10:55 that morning on January 21, when you were in your last year of law school."

"What? Wasn't that the first day of spring term? That was the first time we met! You couldn't have—"

"I just couldn't say it."

"You were waiting until you got taller?"

"Taller than you," he said.

"Why didn't you just say that? I would have taken off my shoes."

Later that night, after TR had fallen asleep, Mallory carried a glass down the hall to get some ice. She paused at the machine to make a call.

"Thank you," she said in a low voice when it was picked up.

"He called you?"

"He came here."

"He's in New York now?"

"He's asleep. We're in the Yale Club. I just slipped out for ice. He told me everything—Sisal and the rest."

"Willikers," said her friend. "He's not supposed to do that, unless—don't tell me—did you—?"

"He popped the question, in his own unique TR way, at 5:52 this afternoon."

"Oh, thank God. It worked! I'm so happy, Mallory. For you, for him. For me too."

"I'm beyond happy," Mallory whispered. "I'm besotted. I don't want to sleep. I want to feel this way all night and tomorrow. Thank you, Khaki, from the bottom of my soul, thank you forever for working it out."

"All I did was bring him to his senses. Facts are facts."

"Whatever you did, however you did it. Though I do wonder why you didn't tell me what you had in mind."

"I couldn't have told you. Against the rules. Besides, it worked only because you didn't know. Knowledge disrupts the future."

"He talks about you so much," Mallory confided. "If you hadn't told me you were like a sister to him when we first met—you remember that weekend you came to town when I was in law school?—I would never have asked for your help in getting us together. Whatever the last few weeks have all been about, I'm grateful to have been a part of it."

"A part of it?" Khaki exclaimed. "Mallory, heart of my heart's heart, you are the *cause* of it. *All* of it. You are the purpose of my little hustle. But most of all, you are the lodestar of my motto: *Felix femina quae est rerum omnium causa.* 'Happy is the woman who is the cause of all things.'"

"Me?"

"Of course *you*. Yours is the Ur game, the genesis. My FBI guys think they are the cause, launching a new technology to bring down a felon and the president. TR first thought it began with him, responding to your desire to know what led Malbonum to confess. Now he thinks it began with me and my desire to assuage my guilt for scrambling his emotions while he was growing up. Those are the three games that TR knows about.

"But there's a fourth game that he still doesn't suspect. It's the game that began it all—when you called out of the clear blue—a year ago now or more?—and asked the simple question: How can we bring TR to his senses?

"At first it was mission impossible. I needed to bring TR inside. How could I get him into a super-restricted facility that's off limits to everyone? No one is let in just to take a tour. Even supposing he could drop by for tea, what could I do by myself without arousing suspicion? I didn't have the means nor the opportunity. Subsection-S wasn't operational. They'd been dithering for at least two years.

"Your call stirred me to action. I wheedled GOGS into going live. Enough theorizing, I said. Unless we test the tech in the real world, how will we know what we can do? I assuaged their fears: go slow, no need to rush ahead. I kept nagging until I convinced them. Truth is so much better than silence, don't you think? I could have kept quiet. But you got me to talk up—and it changed everything.

"I proposed we start with a proof of concept. A straightforward case in federal court. If it went wrong we could shut down, stay underground. The boss gave the go-ahead. After that, it was all just a practical problem."

"Then it was certainly a lucky break the Malbonum case was first in line," Mallory continued in a rush, giddy with delight. "Otherwise, I never would have hired TR, and he never would have got inside your cavern."

Khaki howled in her ear. "Luck? Luck had nothing to do with it. You're thinking like a man. You should know better than that, dear Mallory. It was the other way around. Before there was Malbonum there was *me*. I assigned myself the task of picking the first case. It could have been any of dozens. The trick was to find one that would get assigned to *you*. I ran the list of potential cases and out popped Romo. Lucky *him*.

"It was you? You plotted—"

"Don't you get it? A few days after you called, I finally saw it all at once. TR would come to us if he were tracking one of our own agents back to the Cave. Why would he do that? Who would ask him to? *You* would, Mallory. When the recant came, which it had to—the Kryptonite Catch meant the real Malbonum would regain his brain and squawk—I knew for sure you'd smell a rat somewhere, which meant you'd need to go outside your office for help. Only one plausible candidate you could call on. Our revered TR. And I seeded the operation plan with a tell-tale flaw—"

"Roger–Rafa."

"Yes, and it turned out, not unexpectedly, that our detective found other clues I was oblivious to. Any one of them would have been enough to send him on his way to us. I convinced the boss to accept the challenge as a stress test. I thought TR might need three weeks to find us; I never imagined he'd barge in three days later. You know the rest. It turns out my boss was working on his own plans, neither of which I knew about: getting rid of Pohtiss, and then installing himself as vice president. I'm still trying to digest that part of it. But when Subsection-S's official operation concluded, my original game plan could move on to its conclusion.

"By then I had the tools. A colleague of mine had committed an indiscretion a while back, never mind what. I saved her from its consequences and I swore to her that I'd stay mum. But now she owed me, and I enlisted her help to get me deep into the source of TR's blockage about you. And that turned out to be namely *me*. And discovering that, I could then help TR understand where his real feelings lay and show him the way to his own happiness. I have to admit, it worked better than any lab experiment I've ever done. Let me be the first to say, Congratulations, *Mrs. Softly*."

"Ha!" Mallory said. "She's my future mother-in-law. I'm keeping my name."

"I don't blame you. Will TR keep his?"

Mallory covered her mouth to suppress her mirth. Piercing the quiet rooms of the Yale Club's ninth floor at that time of night would not be endearing.

"The real laugh," Khaki said, "is that the boys still think this was *their* game. Ha! There might never have been a swap op and Malbonum might never have been in court if I hadn't needed TR front and center to pull off this Cupid act. Thank God for your persistence and never giving up on our boy."

"How could I? He's—"

"And thank God you reached out and trusted me. If you hadn't, I'd probably still be coasting along, indulging him in his timidity and missing out on the chance to connect him to you."

"Well, of course I trust you—"

"And even more, thank God you called when you did. If you had waited any longer, who knows whether all the ducks could have been aligned, or is it planets?"

"You would have thought of something," Mallory murmured, silently thanking her own lucky stars. She remembered that right at the start of it all, she had told Sisal she doubted his investigation could bring her rapture. She was ecstatic to be wrong. Eyes heavenward, she pressed both hands across her heart and listened to her inner voice exclaim: "Everything is jake."

AUTHOR'S DISCLAIMER

IT'S CUSTOMARY IN A WORK OF fiction to disclaim reality. I bow to the tradition. The players in our story exist solely in the world inside these covers. Their resemblance to anyone living or dead—by character, description, office, inference, or name—is unintended and purely coincidental. (None of the non-historical characters' names returned a single hit in a Google search at the time of writing.) For verisimilitude, our characters do engage with a few real places, locales, businesses, and institutions, including courts, schools, law enforcement, restaurants, and political offices and positions (alas, not the Georgetown Bookery), but readers should not suppose that the characterization of these institutions (or their office holders or room numbers) is necessarily accurate or that the people or events chronicled here lived or happened anywhere outside the author's imagination. Thrill seekers and adventurers, hearken: there is no structure bearing the number 2806 Olive Street, NW. Don't bother the neighbors trying to find it. Dewey wouldn't let me use his real address. And yes, to all you fussy realists, it's called DIRPA here so the author wouldn't be called to answer to DARPA. Some of the science and technology are real, but there is no Special Weapons and Psychology Unit, or Project Palimpsest, or science of neurosyntesis, and no bona fide experiments of the sort described in these pages have ever been reported. The time sequences of some scientific discoveries have been scrambled; the occasional anachronism saves on research and detailed explanations that readers would find boring.

And of course it ought to go without saying that no president of the United States has ever remotely resembled the figure presented in the fable recounted in these pages—no one so unselfconscious, so narcissistic, so mentally impeded and cognitively limited, so arrogant and uneducated, so dark and nasty and malign, or so profoundly un-American.

The author acknowledges that this book has not been vetted by the FBI, the CIA, NSA, the U.S. Attorney for the Southern District of New York, or any other federal agency, bureau, division, department, office, unit, committee, task force, or even the District of Columbia Department of Consumer and Regulatory Affairs.

ACKNOWLEDGMENTS

MANY PEOPLE HELPED IN TRANSFORMING AN idea and a first draft into a form and narrative worthy of the printed page, and I gratefully acknowledge their assistance, while adhering to the author's traditional and sensible obligation to accept responsibility for errors and infelicities that remain: they're my fault, no one else's.

Earliest readers were the late Elaine P. Mills, who subjected the first five chapters to an exacting scrutiny that put my prose on the right path; Sandor Frankel, Tom Goldstein, and David R. Johnson, who each read the earliest whole draft and pointed to various sins, high and low: Sandy, in particular, for explaining the way it actually happens in the courtrooms of the Southern District of New York; Tom, in particular, for verisimilitude, including TR's Macallan, and several other acute points; and David, in particular, for helping focus psychological insight on the crux of the matter and for keeping me from bloopers that littered my version of the Internet.

To my pals in our Bethesda-Chevy Chase-Silver Spring book club who agreed to break the rules and read an unpublished book and critique it to the author's face: warm thanks to Ellen and David

Belkin, Nancy and Harry Benner, Judy Tyson-Kopolow and Ari Kopolow, Kathleen and Peter Montague, Nancy Ordway, Susan and George Schwelling, and Richard Wiener for insisting that kinks in the narrative be smoothed out, and with a special shout-out to Ellen Belkin and Nancy Benner for working editorial pens over the entire second draft.

Third draft thanks to Erika S. Fine, who spotted many subtle errors, nibbled at nuance, dug deep into the hidden chronology to untangle the timeline, and helped reframe phrasing throughout; Michelle Zierler for questioning motivations and descriptions; and thanks too to Richard G. Patterson and Andrew Jason Cohen for complete reads and critiques of still later drafts.

Hats off to New York State Supreme Court Justice Diane Kiesel for explaining how prosecutorial deals are negotiated; Jerry Kelly, one of letterpress's most distinguished champions, for vetting descriptions and operations of TR's presses and printery; Alice K. Lanckton, my go-to Latinist; Nancy Guida, my go-to Italianist; Michael Roffer, for his uncanny ability to pull the factual rabbit out of the repository hat on demand; David M. Brodsky for federal courthouse authenticity; Art Lieberman for pointers on computer history; and Jake Tanner, assistant general manager of the Yale Club of New York City, for filling in details. These many decades later, my gratitude to and in fond memory of my Navy buddy, the late Coleman S. Hicks, for including me in a private tour of the West Wing, with a stop in the Situation Room, when he was serving as an aide to the National Security Advisor. If I have failed to acknowledge other significant assistance, it's merely memory lapse, which I attribute to too many practice swaps.

Sustained applause to my agent, Joe Spieler; this was our first book together. My gratitude is not just for his performance of agently duties but for his time and heroic effort, digging deep down in the weeds and scrubbing every page of the penultimate draft, as only a skilled, careful, and caring editor can and will do.

Special thanks to the folks at Three Rooms Press including co-directors Kat Georges and Peter Carlaftes, as well as editor Mary Manspeaker.

Finally, and that word appears only because she gets pride of ultimate place in this compendium, my appreciation and gratitude and love are unbounded for all the time and attention my wife, Jo Shifrin, devoted to the story as a whole and to every line on every page, through more than fifteen drafts. In addition to her many readings, Jo never frowned at the incessant interruptions when I would put before her a later version of a paragraph in the third revision of the eighth draft and ask whether what she had just read and corrected ten minutes earlier might not be a tad sharper or crisper or more intelligible in this fourteenth iteration, and so on for all of my requests on many nights of most weeks for more than a year. Many people have claimed it so of their own writing and of their heart's own dearest, but I say it truly: this book would not be but for her.

Jethro K. Lieberman
Bethesda, Maryland
January 31, 2021

JETHRO K. LIEBERMAN

ABOUT THE AUTHOR

JETHRO K. LIEBERMAN IS THE AUTHOR, co-author, or editor of more than 30 books and has had a long and varied career in law, journalism, and legal education. He practiced law for six years, including three years on active duty as a Lieutenant in the Navy's Judge Advocate General's Corps from 1968 to 1971; during the 1970s was founding editor of *Business Week Magazine*'s Legal Affairs department; and since 1982 taught in law schools, first at Fordham University and from 1985 at New York Law School, where he taught constitutional law and served as associate dean for academic affairs. He retired in 2015 as the Martin Professor of Law Emeritus. For several years he was also adjunct professor of political science at Columbia University, where he taught the undergraduate course in constitutional law. His many books include *The Litigious Society* and *The Enduring Constitution*, both awarded the Silver Gavel, the American Bar Association's top literary prize. Among his varied other titles are the best-selling *Complete CB Handbook*, a college-level business law textbook, and a pseudonymously co-authored thriller, *The Aleph Solution*. He holds a B.A. from Yale, a J.D. from Harvard Law School, and a Ph.D. in political science from Columbia. He lives with his wife Jo Shifrin in Bethesda, Maryland. This is his solo fiction debut.

RECENT AND FORTHCOMING BOOKS FROM THREE ROOMS PRESS

Three Rooms Press | New York, NY | Current Catalog: www.threeroomspress.com
Three Rooms Press books are distributed by PGW/Ingram: www.pgw.com

CPSIA information can be obtained
at www.ICGtesting.com
Printed in the USA
JSHW040350090921
18540JS00007B/8

9 781953 103116